Critical Acclaim for Alfred Coppel's
The Eighth Day Of The Week

"A superior thriller by a master of his craft."
—*Publishers Weekly*

"A champion storyteller!"
—John Jakes

"Mr. Coppel paints a chilling picture of how close
the modern world can come to destruction in the
nuclear age."
—*Associated Press Special Features*

With the help of an 80-megaton nuclear warhead planted
in the Hudson Bay, a Russian cabal, *Soyuz,* would decimate
North America. Attempting to stop the hard-liners'
conspiracy of moving back into total power, the Americans
called upon Colonel John Morgan to halt the right-wing
takeover. And in the international game of kill or be killed,
Morgan knew that global freedom is at stake. But would
Morgan's wits and cunning be quick enough to prevent
doomsday's onslaught?

THE
EIGHTH DAY OF THE WEEK
ALFRED COPPEL

LEISURE BOOKS **NEW YORK CITY**

With love for Liz—
Thanks for the good stuff.

A LEISURE BOOK®

May 1996

Published by

Dorchester Publishing Co., Inc.
276 Fifth Avenue
New York, NY 10001

For further information, contact: Donald I. Fine, Inc., 19 West 21st Street, New York, NY 10010

The name "Leisure Books" and the stylized "L" with design are trademarks of Dorchester Publishing Co., Inc.

Printed in the United States of America.

THE EIGHTH DAY OF THE WEEK

Doomsday is the eighth day of the week.
—Stanley Kunitz in *Foreign Affairs*

DECEMBER

Chapter One

*Jacob and Anna Neville, noted Canadian-American
team of nature photographers, are at work in the Canadian Northwest Territories gathering material for a
series of articles and a possible television documentary
on the effects of nuclear waste disposal on northern
wildlife. The television project will be funded by the Canadian Committee for Nuclear Disinvestment.*

—THE GREENSHIELD NEWSLETTER

THE DEVICE, *a much modified SSN-18, rises from its launcher.
The six divers attach tethers and guidelines and hover in the
icy water as the Device floats clear of the* Pravda.

*The launcher utters a hydraulic hiss and emits a stream of
air bubbles. To Arkady Karmann, overseer of the diving crew,
the submarine, an old Hotel III-class SSBN, resembles a monster of the deep sea giving birth.*

The Device, with its zero buoyancy, is guided clear of the

11

Alfred Coppel

sail, muscled into a horizontal position, and allowed to settle in the black water. It sinks into the bottom mud of the bay until only half its girth can be seen in the dim light at sixty feet.

A deep-sea researcher by profession, Karmann finds the shallow, barren waters of Hudson Bay unappealing. He floats in the frigid water, head haloed by the helmet-mounted halogen lamp through whose beam the disturbed silt roils like thunderclouds. The navy divers are careless with their tethers. Karmann, a GKNT scientist well aware of how dangerous the shabbily designed Device really is, has tried to warn them that the attachments to the Device were all powered by a plutonium reactor.

Not once, but many times since the Pravda *entered this Canadian inland sea he has told the deployment crew: "Plutonium kills people." But fascists seem oblivious to danger.*

Krasny calls the Device Soyuz—"Union." Vainglorious bastard that he is. Vainglorious and safe. Krasny is aboard the Pravda.

Chilled despite the centimeter-thick wet suit he wears, Karmann swims slowly down toward the Device. The engineering must have been done by Orgonev or one of his students. No one else in Russia is still working on high-yield nuclear weapons design.

There is no point in such thoughts, Karmann reminds himself. I no longer matter. It is Soyuz that matters to Russia— or so they tell us. Soyuz transcends all our little problems.

Actually, it is a remarkable piece of work. The old fascist, Karmann thinks, has taken an obsolete warhead and turned it into a political world-shaker. If the numbers he crunched while Pravda *crept from Kola, slipped under the polar ice, emerged into the Davis Strait, and finally crept into Hudson Bay are correct (and they are—a physicist of Orgonev's stature did not make mistakes), then the Device's yield is eighty megatons.*

The United States has stopped hardening its weapons and

12

communications systems. This monster, detonated in space above the American heartland, will create an electronic pulse that can destroy every microchip there.

What price all that *"one superpower"* talk then?

KARMANN'S HELMET LIGHT illuminates the Device. It lies in the ooze at a potentially troublesome angle, but the onboard computer and gyroscopes, when activated, would correct that. For now the internal systems are powered down for a long subarctic wait.

The water is bitterly cold. There is ice on the surface of the bay overhead. Karmann watches the huge, shadowy shape of the Pravda back away, out of the dangerous shallows. The submarine has a draft of almost eight meters on the surface. These are dangerously constricted waters for a Hotel III-class boat. Karmann does not find it ironic that he uses the NATO code name for the Pravda. He has known and worked with Westerners all over the world.

This does not endear him to Captain Third Rank Kolodin, who is overage in grade and in command of a thirty-nine-year-old boat ready for the scrap heap. The Pravda was first named the Andrei Vishinsky when it was launched in the 1960s. It was renamed the Yuri Andropov when that former head of the KGB and general secretary of the party died of a case of the sniffles lasting six months. The dissolution of the USSR after the November 1991 coup brought the last name change: Pravda—*"Truth."*

Kolodin once loved his boat, but Kolodin, like many senior officers of the armed forces, is now an irrelevant man. His imminent retirement at very low pay makes him a typical Soyuz. The whole boat crew is Soyuz. A royalist flag hangs on the wall of the wardroom. Under other circumstances, Karmann would have laughed at an organization so out of step with the times as Soyuz. But he now knows better.

Karmann read in popular novels about *"an icy hand closing over one's heart."* His weeks on this submarine have revealed how apt the cliche really is. Ex-Zampolit Captain Lieutenant Krasny has shown him that for some Russians, at least, times have not really changed so very much.

Karmann kicks, driving himself deeper. The sound his regulator makes is like the rushing noise of blood pumping out of a great heart. The compressed air in his tanks reeks of sweat and oil. They have been changed from the tanks of the Pravda and are laden with the smells of a long-endurance underwater voyage. Karmann is concerned that the air in the tanks might be contaminated with plutonium. He is certain that much aboard the Pravda is.

He glides down until he hovers centimeters from the curving flank of the Device. He sees that the fall to the sea floor has warped a seam on the missile housing. That disquiets him. Kolodin has supplied the divers with a single radiation counter. Arkady Karmann, three weeks and five thousand kilometers deep into this Soyuz conspiracy, has learned to be extremely suspicious. He has not been allowed to speak privately with the medical petty officer, but it seems that too many of the men, particularly those who have worked in the Device bay, are ill. Influenza, Kolodin and Krasny say.

Two of the unloading crew are working on the other side of the Device. From the colored patches on their wet suits, Karmann identifies them as Grushenko and Palatin, two very young ratings only recently qualified for underwater work. Palatin, an engaging young Georgian, has been ill and has only recently returned to duty. He is involved in placing the locator anchors that are needed, so Captain Kolodin says, for the time when Soyuz has done its work of intimidating the Americans and must be located and disarmed. Karmann doubts this. Before being assigned as an oceanic biologist to the GKNT, the State Scientific and Research Establishment, he had done a tour as a diving officer. To him, the mechanisms Palatin is deploying at this moment look suspiciously like antipersonnel mines.

On the sonar phone, he calls Grushenko. "Seaman Palatin is having trouble. Help him."

"At once, Academician Karmann." The reply is blurry and indistinct. The receivers in Karmann's helmet are not what they should be. Everything is falling apart, he thinks.

He busies himself with securing an inspection hatch on the Soyuz that seems to have sprung slightly when the Device deployed. Because of this he has his head down and is not struck by the shock wave of the explosion. But he hears it and is buffeted by the water surging around him. The Device rolls and settles.

Karmann fin-kicks himself away from the bottom and looks frantically for the others in the suddenly turbid water. What he sees brings him close to vomiting into his breathing gear. The two divers float in broken, angular positions. One is headless and spewing blood—black in this light—into the surrounding water. The other is rising to the surface, his weights stripped away. He has no arms, only stumps spouting blood.

Instantly Karmann begins to call to the remainder of the team. One by one they answer.

Because sound carries powerfully through water, Karmann hears the sudden roar of air and bubbles as the invisible Pravda *blows its tanks in a panic surface. The watch has heard the explosion. Karmann would have liked to believe that the submarine was surfacing—extremely risky in these waters—to render assistance to the divers. But this is not so. Captain Kolodin knows that if there has been an explosion, there are probably bodies. Russian bodies. They must be retrieved at all costs.*

Karmann and the three surviving members of the deployment team break the surface of the bay under a sky the color of lead. The color, Karmann thinks bitterly, of sudden, senseless death.

THE DECEMBER SUN was small and hidden behind a sky the shade of new silver coins. Three thousand feet below, the

Cessna's shadow fled across the silent frozen tundra. It leaped from marshlands to dirty snowdrifts and across the rafts of floating ice that nudged the desolate shoreline of the bay.

Sean McCarthy, the pilot, reached down to a valve between the forward seats to change fuel tanks. He worked the hand pump gently until the pressure steadied. He glanced over his shoulder at Anna, his expression reflecting the amusement he felt under the circumstances.

Anna Neville was watching her husband search the shore of the bay. His dour, narrow face was intent as he held the Maxxum 7000, ready to shoot. She held the Hasselblad with their longest lens because her eyes were better than Jake's and she could quickly frame a telescopic shot. Many things were wrong with their marriage, but a lack of professional skills was not part of the trouble. They were a husband-and-wife team of photographers, one of the best. The fact that they had not slept in the same bed for two years was irrelevant.

They were searching for a caribou herd, a big one. Sean said he had seen one near Eskimo Point. Jake was sure that this herd would prove his contention about the Keewatin coast being contaminated with waste from American nuclear power plants.

The Nevilles had flown the Northwest Territories with McCarthy before. Sean was the best bush pilot they had ever worked with. He also had been Anna Neville's lover.

Jake knew, Anna thought. Almost certainly he knew.

But he had insisted on hiring Sean again. Sean was professional. If Sean said there was a herd on the move down the south shore of the bay, they would find it. To Jake, first in importance was the work. The correct political view followed close after that. It didn't matter to Jake about Sean and Anna. That could wait to be settled, until it was over. Jake always outwaited—and outwitted—Anna's lovers.

Immediately below the flight path lay a stretch of ice-free tundra; to the east, hard daylight burned through a thickening over-cast. A silver sky reflected on the water of open polynyas dividing great fields of bay ice. All day they had seen softly undulating vees of snow geese flying south. Soon the snow would cover everything, and only the snow hare and the arctic fox would move. Spring, and its blaze of bright wildflowers, lay months away, beyond winter. Another world, Anna thought. It was the spring assignments she really loved, when the air was growing warmer and the animals were astir.

They had spent a week at the Chesterfield Inlet with a team of seismologists and petroleum geologists working the region by sled, Sno-Cat, and floatplane. One of the younger men, a fellow Canadian about Anna's age, had been attentive. Nothing had come of it, but Jake reacted badly, lashing out at her whenever the chance presented itself. She had listened silently, accepting punishment for past sins. Something below caught her eye. "Sean," she said. "To the right. Are there ever whales in Hudson Bay?"

"I don't see anything," Jake said. "What is it?"

The onshore wind was driving the new ice hard onto the lee shore, building jagged pressure ridges where the floes grounded on the rocky shingle. Short, steep waves broke over the jumbled ice. They were still more than two hours' flying time from Chesterfield.

"I've never seen whales here," Sean said, squinting at the scene below. "They feed on krill and there's no krill in the bay to speak of."

"But look over there, on the right." Anna had her camera up and was snapping pictures.

The two men studied the patchwork of ice and narrow open leads below. A mile or so offshore, a shape was moving through the water. Sean craned across Jake to see out the right-hand window.

"Orca?" Jake asked.

"Maybe." Sean studied the distant object through field glasses.

Anna looked through the telephoto lens. Something dark was traveling through the field of broken ice. But it was no orca. To her it looked like the top few feet of the sail of a submarine. She handed Jake the camera so that he could look through the lens.

He looked and said, "Now, what the hell is a sub doing here, of all places?"

Sean flew with one hand, held the glasses with the other. "I've seen your goddamned navy stooging around up in the Parry Channel and Davis Strait, but never down here. Let's have a closer look." Sean was Canadian and he thought Americans held Canada lightly. He remembered the diplomatic quarrels about violations of Canada's territory in the far north. American naval vessels had made several trips through the Northwest Passage without obtaining permission. The Americans contended that the passage was international waters. The Canadians denied it.

Could the government possibly have given permission for this kind of intrusion, Anna wondered. The Prime Minister and the President were friendly, but any show of American imperialism would make a great deal of trouble in Ottawa.

Sean banked the Cessna steeply and started down. Jake continued to watch the slowly moving sail. A hatch opened and a figure appeared, a man looking up through binoculars at the descending bush plane.

"They've spotted us," he said uneasily. "Don't crowd them."

Anna retrieved the Hasselblad and resumed taking pictures. As she worked the shutter, four heads broke the surface of the water near the submarine. A second man joined the first on the sail.

Sean banked away sharply, reaching for the radio microphone. At the same instant, Anna saw a white flare and a trail of fire.

"My God, they've fired a missile—" Jake shouted in a strangled voice.

Sean threw down the microphone and racked the floatplane into a steep dive, away from the rising pencil of hot light. The smoke trail twisted and curled, foreshortened as its acquisition radar locked on.

A brilliant light illuminated the interior of the aircraft. Anna Neville saw the windshield vanish. Her face was pierced by hundreds of tiny shards of Plexiglas. A cold hurricane laden with debris stormed through the cabin, blowing away the doors. Anna saw one float break away and spin into space. Something struck her forehead, her right arm. She thought: We are going to crash and die. She was too stunned to feel panic. The Cessna fell with shocking speed. Fire flashed over Anna like the breath of a furnace. The fuselage parted from the thick wings and tumbled. Then came darkness.

JANUARY

Chapter Two

The Rosario Bank/
18.03 N 83.01 W/
January 6

President Cherny has many well-wishers in the United States and Europe. He has succeeded in attracting large infusions of Western capital into his struggling Russian economy. But one must realize that the old Soviet regime was never destroyed; it just ground to a halt, leaving in place the people and framework of a planned society.

—PROCEEDINGS OF THE INSTITUTE
FOR THE STUDY OF RUSSIAN
ECONOMICS

IT HAD DISTRESSED ARKADY KARMANN to ask permission to go on deck five hours after the submarine had cleared the Yucatan Passage, but the petty officer of the deck had been too ill to protest. Though both Krasny and Captain Kolodin still denied it, plutonium poisoning raged aboard the *Pravda*. Since clearing the Davis Strait, six sailors and an officer had died. Their bodies were frozen in the food locker. Kolodin had

promised that they would be properly buried when the boat
reached Cienfuegos. Karmann had been ill himself. Diarrhea,
fever, general weakness. Kolodin claimed it was only influenza. Karmann knew it was the early toll taken by the Device.
The submarine had stayed on the surface since entering Cuban
waters. The crew was incapable of handling the boat submerged.

The petty officer had allowed Karmann out without noti-
fying the captain—a violation of standing orders typical of the
state of affairs on board the *Pravda*. Discipline was poor. The
crew was surly. As they had a right to be, thought Karmann.
Matters had grown worse since deployment of the Soyuz. The
death of the divers was particularly resented. The captain had
kept a semblance of order with promises of shore leave in
Cuba. And Viktor Krasny had taken to referring to Karmann's
"Jewishness." To show Kolodin what a faithful Soyuz he
was? Anything was possible with Krasny.

Karmann sat at the base of the sail on the narrow deck,
between the sail and the stubby vertical fin at the stern. The
air was hot and humid, but the boat's speed created a breeze
that made the heat bearable. The wake stretched out behind
the *Pravda* almost to the northern horizon; the foredeck was
buried under a thick film of water caused by the manner of
the boat's way in the sea. The wake was as white as a road
of snow. It had to be visible from hundreds of miles in space.

The deaths had decided it. Karmann intended to defect. He
should have done it long ago. But the Device the *Pravda* had
left in Hudson Bay had been the last straw. No one in his right
mind could live with that kind of madness.

The Soyuz party laid claim to the old Russian traditions:
empire, military virtue, patriotism, anti-Semitism. What they
could not bear was any rapprochement between Russia and
the West. The Western fascination with democracy was a
plague to Soyuz. The device in Hudson Bay was the modern
equivalent of Jew-burning to inveigh against the infection, a
kind of witchcraft.

He leaned against the steel of the low conning tower and tried to quiet his stomach. I may have my death in me already, he thought. Nobody really knew how much plutonium contamination one could stand.

There have been too many deaths already. The divers in the water in Canada. The unknown pilot of the floatplane. The seven sailors on the voyage south. And how many more before this nightmare cruise ends?

Captain Lieutenant Krasny appeared atop the sail and began searching the horizon to the southeast with large binoculars. Karmann remained hidden against the black steel tower. He resented the very idea of having to explain to Krasny that he had permission to be on deck. Krasny would order him below for no reason other than sheer bloody-minded beastliness.

Krasny could see Karmann only if he should look directly down over the aft spray shield on the submarine's sail. His attention, however, was elsewhere.

Karmann rested his head against the humming steel of the sail and studied the wake. Though the *Pravda* had come from the northeast, the wake curved to the west. There was a strong current in that direction, running through the Windward Passage between the southeast tip of Cuba and Hispaniola. Karmann, whose mathematically oriented academician's mind took note of such things, estimated that the boat was now close to latitude 18 north. The winter sun was very near the zenith. To the southeast lay the islands of the Spanish Main.

Behind the *Pravda* lay the Yucatan Channel; to the southwest at a distance of over four hundred kilometers of winter sea was the bent hock of Central America: Nicaragua and the Mosquito Coast of Honduras.

Krasny's open contempt of Karmann had led to continuing harassment. Krasny, of course, had heard the whispers. The Karmann family was descended from one of Peter the Great's Prussian mercenary officers, the illegitimate son of a Jewish mother, forced by his racial "taint" to take service with a foreign monarch.

The Karmanns had never denied their ancestry. Each generation they produced their quota of atheists, soldiers, and academics to serve the motherland. Arkady's own father had been decorated posthumously with the Order of Lenin at Stalingrad.

Karmann wondered why Krasny despised him. Because of the Jewish ancestral grandmother who had died in 1740, or because of his German descent, or simply because he was an intellectual? The Soyuz loathed intellectuals. They said such persons weakened the fiber of Russia.

The captain posed another problem. Each time Kolodin heard Karmann speak in a foreign language—and he was conversant in five—his pale eyes narrowed and his croaking voice grew more harsh. The voice, a result of a submarine accident in a battery-powered boat, suited Kolodin, low, harsh, and ugly.

How strange it was, Karmann thought. Glasnost had encouraged the Soyuz to grow, and now Soyuz was the force most likely to strangle the fledgling Russian democracy. Politics was rife with such ironies.

Above and behind him, Karmann heard the sudden clacking of a signal lamp. Careful not to be seen, he worked his way around the sail. Viktor Krasny was resting the lamp on the spray shield as he worked the shutter. Karmann looked to the east and saw a small, fast-moving boat with a bone of white water in its teeth. The launch flew a Cuban flag. Someone aboard was replying to Krasny's signals.

It was very strange, thought Karmann, that the political officer of a Russian submarine should be signaling to a Cuban gunboat. In recent years Cuba had been sullen and disenchanted with the Russian inability to continue the massive subsidy begun by Nikita Khrushchev, and maintained—though in diminishing amounts—by every Russian ruler since. Only Aleksandr Cherny had had the courage to inform the old and ailing Fidel that the subvention was at an end.

Krasny, distracted by some passing thing, looked down and saw Karmann watching him. Instantly, Krasny produced a revolver and fired two shots at him. Both missed, and Karmann threw himself onto the closed hatch, pounding for it to be opened.

Suddenly, there was a booming, muffled sound from below, as though an immense drum had been struck. A shock went through the submarine. It slewed, lost weigh, went dead in the water, but with a listing to port. The high stern wave smashed up and over the afterdeck, dislodging Karmann from his perch and washing him overboard.

There were more explosions inside. The deck bulged, the pressure hull opened.

A raft was thrown into the sea from the sail. Krasny followed it into the water.

A final, violent explosion broke open the hull and the sea surged into the vessel. It rolled and expelled great breaths of air, like some strange creature from the depths. For a long moment, the submarine was vertical, screws still rotating high in the air. Karmann heard screams as pistons of seawater drove through the plunging hull. Then the submarine was gone in a bubbling eructation of air and debris. Arkady Karmann was pulled down into the blood-warm sea.

THE FLOTATION VEST the petty officer had insisted he wear on deck sustained Karmann. All around him the sea roiled with farts of air and debris from the submarine. Pieces of wood and plastic erupted from the water into the air. Great bubbles of oil surfaced and spread over the refuse from the plunging hull. Karmann was struck from below by a thick piece of the sound-proofing material that had once formed part of the wardroom overhead. It was large and buoyant and he held onto it desperately.

At some distance—it was difficult to see clearly because his eyes were only inches from the surface of the water—he could spot the boat that had signaled to the *Pravda*. It was either stopped or moving very slowly through the littered waves. Were the Cubans searching for survivors? Some atavistic sense warned him against signaling or even disclosing himself. He knew—absolutely knew—that Krasny had blown up the boat.

Suddenly, quite near, a seaman broke the surface and bobbed his head at Karmann.

Karmann said hoarsely, "Be still. Don't show yourself."

The sailor stared at Karmann with bulging, water-filled eyes. The man's mouth was open, blue-lipped. A drowned sailor, brought into the air and light too late. The turbulence still rising from the *Pravda* churned the sea, and the dead sailor bobbed his head in agreement. Karmann, frightened by the empty eyes and open mouth, tried to kick his bit of floating insulation away from the compliant corpse.

The Cuban boat idled in the water, ensign hanging limply at the fantail. The crew was pulling Viktor Krasny from the sea. Karmann heard gunfire. At what could those fools be shooting? The boat's engine began to rumble, and it moved deliberately through the field of debris. Karmann, his eyes barely above water, could see that the Cuban crew were firing AK-57s all about them. He could hear them shouting to one another in Spanish. They were laughing, skylarking.

"*Allí, allí, 'sta otro!*"

There, there is another . . .

Another what, in God's name?

The gunboat moved slowly through the water and the Cuban sailors fired into the sea. Krasny stood on the foredeck, pointing out targets. Oh, my God, they are killing the survivors, Karmann realized.

It was planned this way from the beginning. It had to be. Plant the Soyuz Device, then bury the secret in the sea.

The Cubans discovered the floating sailor and loosed a fusillade. The head exploded in a shower of salt water, bone, brains, and blood. Karmann heard the Cubans shriek with pleasure. Then one of them shouted, "*Mira! Tiburónes!*"

Karmann voided his bowels into the sea. The Cubans pointed to the gathering sharks.

"*Alto! Dejan disparando!*" An order to cease fire came

from the bridge, and the boat turned eastward. Karmann stared after it, his chest congealed with terror and rage. When he could no longer hear the gunboat's diesel engines, he came up out of the water and heaved himself onto his piece of plastic flotsam. He floated in a sea strewn with wreckage and bodies. The *Pravda* was releasing her crew. Here and there were pieces of men. The Cubans and their assault rifles had been savage.

Even as he watched, more sharks gathered. Three. Five. Ten. Too many to count. They thrashed themselves into a feeding frenzy. They attacked the corpses and one another. Karmann spewed up his last meal from the *Pravda*'s galley and closed his eyes. But he could still hear the splashes the sharks made as they fed.

He lost his grip on time. The sun was low when he caught sight of the raft Krasny had put over the side from the *Pravda*'s sail. It had been hit by gunfire, but it floated and could be repaired if the patching kit were still aboard.

He hauled himself onto the raft and found the repair packet. Ignoring the noises made by the feeding sharks, he set about repairing the slender grip on survival willed him by the *Pravda*.

THE SURFACE OF THE SEA was like a mirror—a glassy brilliance reflecting a high, pitiless white overcast through which the January sun burned down on Arkady Karmann, who lay half-conscious on the slowly deflating rubber raft.

The still intended to convert seawater to fresh was gone. It had been lost two days ago when a questing shark struck the raft and overturned it. Karmann might have welcomed death then, but his terror and his rage kept him alive. The terror remained because the shark was still with him. His rage faded in the heat of the barely visible tropic sun. The last of the emergency rations were gone, lost with the still. The repair kit and the pump were gone as well, and the raft was losing buoyancy, gradually sinking into the sea under Karmann's weight.

Alfred Coppel

Karmann's pale skin was scored by the sun and salt. Blisters filled with fluid had formed on his chest and legs. When they broke, they left raw, unhealed skin exposed to sun and sea. Karmann tried to pray, but he did not know how. He had been a lifelong, convinced atheist; his conviction was fading.

He drifted in and out of dreams. Krasny dominated all of them. Krasny, the Soyuz anti-Semite. Krasny, the killer of shipmates.

The circling shark was joined by another. Karmann watched the cruising fins with swollen eyes and failing heart. The raft was perceptibly lower in the water. There was no way to repair the bullet hole put there by the Cuban gunner.

Hatred of Krasny permeated Karmann's breath-sucking terror. After four days of sun and two days without food or water, his memories were mingled with phantasmagoric horrors that surely were not real. It wasn't possible that the Cubans on the gunboat had machine-gunned the corpses vomited up by the mortally wounded *Pravda*. Yet Karmann saw it happen.

The sharks swam lazily around the softening raft. His raw skin was agonized by the thin, cloud-filtered sunlight. The raft was drifting westward. It appeared to follow the sun, which was moving behind the overcast toward the horizon. When night returned, Karmann once again would be terribly aware of the black void below. He had never felt so alone. On the first day he had seen contrails high in the sky. It was fantastic to realize that ten thousand meters from the surface of the sea commercial airliners were carrying passengers who went about their affairs, unknowing and uncaring that a man was dying far, far below them. Today there had been no jet trails, no high blue air. The haze and the overcast contained him, imprisoned him.

And the sharks circled. With a single rush they could tear the raft to pieces if they chose. Did they choose anything? How much mind was there in the tiny brain behind those dreadful, flat, black eyes?

30

The indistinct glare of the sun moved westward, steadily westward, high above the glassy surface of the sea.

THE SHARKS STAYED with Karmann all day. The original makos were joined by hammerheads and leopards. The xenophobic distrust of one species for another had so far kept the animals more concerned with one another than with the shadow on the surface of the sea. But that was changing.

Karmann slipped easily from rationality to delirium. The open sores on his skin were agonizing. He had not realized one could feel such pain for so long.

Krasny had planned all along to kill the *Pravda* and her crew, he thought hazily. There can be no other explanation. It was better to dwell on this than on the predators prowling around and beneath him. Hate gave him courage.

He looked to the west, below the glare of the sinking sun. There was a shadow on the water. He rose to his knees, precariously near to destroying the stability of the raft.

The distant shadow was a boat. Far away, but a boat.

HE TRIED TO CALL OUT but could manage only a croaking noise. For a terrible moment it appeared that the boat was moving away. Between the ever more flaccid raft and the ghostly boat in the glaring distance, the sharks still circled. Then Karmann did a desperate, foolish thing. With a sob he threw himself into the water and began to swim. Without diver's fins, he was a poor swimmer, one who thrashed at the water. The sharks took instant note.

Aboard the fishing boat, the Honduran master saw the disturbance in the water and recognized the shape of a man in the sea. He turned his old craft to make the rescue.

And halfway between the raft and the boat Karmann felt the rough bump of a shark's file-toothed skin against his own. He managed a wail of despair.

On board the fishing boat the second crewman snatched an antique revolver from a lazaret and fired a shot at the fins surrounding the thrashing swimmer. The boat approached Karmann at its slow, laboring speed. Some of the sharks took fright. Not all.

A medium-sized hammerhead swam twitchingly between Karmann's legs, its bulging eye palps brushing the inside of his naked thighs and his testicles with a dreadful intimacy. He screamed and swallowed mouthfuls of seawater.

The crewman extended a long boat hook as the remaining sharks closed excitedly, angered by the huge shadow that threatened to deprive them of their patiently stalked quarry. Karmann seized the hook with one hand, his right, and held on. With his left he struck at his tormentors.

The great mouth closed on his arm. Shock numbed him. A shake and the fish released him. But Karmann's arm ended in ragged tatters midway between wrist and elbow. Blood spewed everywhere.

The crewman on the fisher's deck heaved Karmann aboard and shouted to the helmsman: *"Ayudame! El tiburón se llevo la mano! Oygame!"* Help me, the shark has taken his hand. Hear me!

The captain acted. He was a man who had lived with terrible accidents and injuries since boyhood. That is the way of life on the Mosquito Coast. He left the helm untended and vaulted to the deck.

"Un molinete! Pronto, chingado, pronto!" A tourniquet, quickly, quickly!

Karmann heard Spanish voices and wondered if they were Cuban. He felt a belt tighten on an arm that shock had rendered numb. He tasted mescal, a bitter, oily liquor, all that Mosquito Coast fishermen can afford. He moved his head away and asked for water.

Before he could drink his fill, the shock began to wear off and his mangled left arm was plunged into molten metal. He screamed.

The Honduran fisherman used an analgesic as old as the temples in his home forests: a sharp blow to the head that brought unconsciousness. It was the only mercy he had to offer this wreck of a man stolen from the sea.

NOVEMBER

Chapter Three

Washington, D.C./November 25

Caidin Administration insiders are silent about the sudden appearance in the United States of Anna Neville, sole survivor of a mysterious airplane accident last year in Canada. Beltway Whispers has been told that the accident and certain secret Canadian-American weapons tests are connected and that Neville's accident was no accident.

—"BELTWAY WHISPERS,"
INSIDE WASHINGTON REPORT

JOHN MORGAN STIRRED RESTLESSLY as he waited in the outer room of the National Security Adviser's suite in the White House Executive Wing. It was seven in the morning of a blustery, rainy November Sunday, but this morning's traffic into and out of Kellner's office would have been considered heavy, even for a weekday. Morgan had a slight headache, the result of a reunion the night before with some Naval Academy classmates. The ring of the telephone at five A.M. had not been a welcome sound.

At the moment, Charlotte Conroy, the ambassador to the United Nations, was with the Adviser. Morgan had arrived at six-fifteen, expecting to be briefed immediately. Camilla Varig had sounded almost excited when she called, not at all usual for Varig. It took something extraordinary to excite Vincent Kellner's longtime assistant. Charlotte Conroy's presence in Kellner's office at this hour reinforced Morgan's guess that something unusual was happening.

Vincent Kellner and Charlotte Conroy were both academics in political science from Stanford. Charlotte Conroy had taught at Stanford for eight years before being chosen by Cole Caidin to head the U.S. delegation to the United Nations. Their view of the world was of those who could still remember World War II and its aftermath, forty-five years of the cold war. The two of them were elder statesmen in that sense, although they had both been schoolchildren when the war ended. President Caidin preferred uniformity of opinion from his subordinates for foreign affairs.

Morgan wondered what the pending crisis would mean to his request to be returned to active duty in the Marine Corps. He had been ambivalent from the beginning about joining the NSC staff. Nothing else interesting was available at the time of his seconding, and Kellner had assured him he was free to leave any time he found the work irksome. It became irksome almost at once. The NSC office was populated with self-important anonymous bureaucrats doing anonymous things, most of them political, and few of them useful, in Morgan's opinion. I should have trusted my hunches, he thought. After a year and a month in Washington, his inside view of politics made him yearn for the relatively uncomplicated life in the Corps.

Camilla Varig glanced across the anteroom at Morgan from behind her desk and said with a thin smile, "I regret the delay, Colonel. But being military, you should be used to hurry up and wait."

Varig—only Vincent Kellner called her Camilla—was as

38

much a part of the Adviser's surroundings as the gray steel office furniture they both favored. Morgan often had the impression that she faded into the background, leaving only a *presence*. Sadly, not a pleasant one. She had a broad, ugly face under mouse-colored hair. Her skin was thick and pale, her lips narrow over widely spaced front teeth. Her bone structure was heavy, but her body was too thin in the gray suits she favored on duty. There was a faint Germanic harshness to her voice and speech. Like Kellner himself, Camilla was the child of naturalized Germans, strictly, even severely, raised. Kellner had found her in the ranks of the Berlin station of the CIA during his term as agency director. Varig had served in Counterintelligence, specializing in ex-Stasi agents on the run. She vetted Kellner's calls and his callers, scheduled his appointments, and took precise notes at all of his meetings. You could tell immediately who was on the short list of favorites and who was on the shit list just by watching and listening. If one wanted to do business with the Adviser (Kellner, a tall Ichabod Crane-type man, preferred that title), one dealt with Camilla Varig. It was the only way.

A bell pinged softly on the console and Varig listened attentively to a murmur issuing from it. She looked up and said, "It will be a few minutes yet, Colonel."

Morgan, slightly hungover, frowned. What were Kellner and Charlotte Conroy discussing at such length? Morgan had a Marine's ingrained suspicion of anything involving the United Nations. The Corps' experience with the UN had not been a happy one.

Dr. Conroy was a complex internationalist, puzzling to those parochial politicians who thought that if one drove beyond the Capital Beltway, one would fall off the edge of the world. She was fifty-five and formidable, a handsome, articulate silver-haired woman with degrees and honors stacked high on her desk at the United Nations. The Washington rumor was that she was in line to be the next Democratic senator from California. John Morgan hoped the rumor was true. Con-

roy knew how to make tough decisions. She was wasted in
New York.

Along the row of wall clocks showing times across the
world, minute hands snapped down to the vertical position. It
was precisely 0730 hours eastern standard time. The com-
municator pinged.

"You may go in now," Camilla Varig said.

THE OFFICE VINCENT KELLNER KEPT was spartan. Two walls
were hung with lockable map cases, and a bank of four television receivers, presently dark, stood along another wall.
Across the room from Kellner's desk the paneling was rolled
aside, displaying a CIA-generated electronic projection of
North America from the Parry Channel in latitude 74 north to
the isthmus of Panama.

Vincent Kellner was the frugal son of frugal immigrants,
and his upbringing had left its mark. The elder Kellners' only
extravagance, it was said, had been the education they had
procured for their son. Kellner could have been a success at
whatever he chose—businessman, academic, perhaps even a
soldier. He had chosen a career in public service, and said so
proudly. His adversaries described him with disdain as the
perfect faceless bureaucrat, with no particular principles or beliefs. Morgan was not sure this was true. Theoretically, Vincent Kellner was a Republican, but he served a Democratic
President. He had accepted the post of Adviser for National
Security Affairs eagerly, with every intention of becoming at
least as famous as the other former Adviser of German descent.

Morgan noted that the Adviser's desk was bare, as always.
Kellner worked with ideas, not papers. In one of the office's
three uncomfortable armchairs sat Ambassador Conroy, upright and stiff-backed. She wore a black silk suit and diamond
earrings, and her fur-lined raincoat was thrown over the arm
of the chair. At this hour of the morning she looked tired, as
though she had not slept.

It seemed to Morgan that Kellner's appearance never varied. He was unwrinkled, hair smoothly brushed, and as always carefully dressed in a three-piece suit, stiff-collared shirt, and silk tie. He had his suits tailored in London, his one extravagance, to hide a small paunch. His face was full, with prominent brow ridges, and deep-set blue eyes. At sixty-three, his hair remained dark brown, causing an occasional snide comment from Style section writers to the effect that he must have "found Ronald Reagan's hairdresser."

The Republicans had captured the Senate in the off-year elections and were determined to declare "payback time" at the Democratic Administration's expense. Cole Caidin's people tiptoed along a precarious and narrow path. In foreign affairs, George Bush's New World Order had turned out to be the Same Old Disorder, with some nasty new twists. Vincent Kellner's political skills and instincts helped Caidin deal with the Republican-run Senate Foreign Affairs Committee, but the marriage of Kellner and Caidin was one of convenience, not affection.

"Sit down, John," Kellner said. "You know the Ambassador."

Dr. Conroy inclined her head and murmured, "Good morning, Colonel Morgan."

"Sorry to keep you waiting," Kellner said. "But some rather sensitive matters have come up, and I think you are the man to handle them." He deferred to the Ambassador. "Charlotte, will you begin?"

Ambassador Conroy asked, "Does the name *Neville* mean anything to you, Colonel?"

Morgan thought a moment and then said, "Yes. They are—or were—environmental photographers. Jake Neville was killed in an air crash in Canada last year. The wife survived."

Charlotte Conroy looked questioningly at Kellner.

Kellner said, "It's your decision, Charlotte. I have faith in Morgan's discretion."

Ambassador Conroy regarded Morgan speculatively. "What

41

more do you know about the Nevilles, Colonel?''

"Very left of center politically, exceedingly Green, and never missed an opportunity to skewer those who didn't agree with them," Morgan said. "Excellent photojournalists. Thoroughly persuasive, unless you are well informed about the opposite view. If you argue, you are the enemy."

"Let me tell you more about the Nevilles," Ambassador Conroy said. "Last year they were on assignment for the National Geographic Society, following caribou migrations in the Canadian Northwest Territories, or something equally ecologically impeccable. But the aircraft they hired crashed into Hudson Bay, killing Jacob Neville and the pilot. Anna Neville survived. She was injured, on the ice, in shock, able to shelter only in a piece of the aircraft's wing, for about twelve hours. Maritime Command doctors who treated her after some Inuit trappers found her say she is fortunate to be alive. She had two broken legs, a broken collarbone, internal injuries, and frostbite. She has been in a hospital in Ottawa for nearly two hundred days."

"One hell of an accident," Morgan said.

"So it appears."

"Is there a question that it was an accident?"

"Judge for yourself. Anna Neville was released from the hospital and immediately called a press conference, claiming that an American submarine in Hudson Bay fired a missile at her plane and shot it down. She said she'd told all this to the Canadian authorities, but they'd done nothing either to prove or disprove her story."

"That's preposterous," Morgan said in annoyance. "For one thing, the water in Hudson Bay is too shallow for submarine operations and for another, only Canadian forces ships would be in the bay. The only time our ships would be there is if they were invited on a joint exercise."

"That is what the Adviser tells me. I am happy to hear you confirm it. But Anna Neville's sponsor is the Canadian Committee for Nuclear Disinvestment. They have a willing audience.''

Morgan looked from the Adviser to the Ambassador and back again. ''There's something else. What is it?''

Kellner said, ''The problem is this. We and the Canadians have been conducting Tomahawk X missile tests in the Northwest Territories. The CCND claim that one of our missiles went astray and downed the plane, or that we attacked the Nevilles to keep the tests secret.''

''The Canadians *believe* that?''

''Some do, as do some American sympathizers.''

Morgan frowned. ''Why are we testing cruises in Canada?''

Ambassador Conroy fixed Kellner with a prosecutor's look. ''Well, Vincent?''

''We signed a treaty with the Russians banning long-range cruise trials,'' Kellner said patiently. ''Canada is a signatory. But the treaty has a secret protocol. It allows both powers to test existing technology. Ever since the Gulf War, we and the Russians have kept a full quiver of cruise weapons. We have used some of ours, as you know. We think the Russians have sold some of theirs, although they deny it. That's as may be. There have been Russian observers at the Northern Alberta Test Range for each flight. The range is more than twenty-five hundred miles from where the Nevilles' aircraft went down, and none of the missiles tested have that range.''

Kellner paused thoughtfully. ''Anna Neville's story is an out-and-out fabrication, John, but it is outlandish enough to appeal to the press and to the conspiracy buffs.''

''I suppose I'm reassured about the missiles,'' Ambassador Conroy said slowly. ''But consider this. The third world countries are very angry with Europe, the United States, and Canada because of the new laws restricting immigration. The situation in the Balkans is still explosive, and Russia's financial and ethnic troubles have to be dealt with daily. One never knows what will happen next in any of the Islamic countries. Our old world, awful as it was on many occasions, has disappeared, and no one knows how the new world will develop. The United States is the world's only superpower, and we're needed everywhere to provide at least a semblance of security. We *don't* need any more gadflies like the CCND and Anna Neville with her wild accusations souring the relations between the Canadians and ourselves.

"Prime Minister Halloran is fielding nasty questions every day in their parliament. He's upset. Ian Halloran is the President's friend. So the President is upset. The CCND are spoiling for trouble with us, as usual. They want an excuse to abrogate a dozen Canadian-American agreements, possibly— or especially—the Free Trade treaty. Anna Neville and her accident may provide that excuse."

"We want you to go talk to Anna Neville," Kellner said urgently. "The FBI and CIA files on the Nevilles are available to you, John. Look at them. But they can't leave the White House. The CIA file contains material about Jacob and Anna Neville that came from other sources outside the agency. Some came from the Royal Canadian Mounted Police and more from the Ministry of Defense. The Canadian cousins will take it very poorly if we let slip that they have spied on a Canadian citizen and her American husband, and then handed the product over to us."

Ambassador Conroy said, "Nathan Abramov, the chief of the Russian UN Mission, tells me confidentially that the old Communists, together with the new imperialists in the Russian Duma, would love to see us embarrassed publicly. Too many years of 'one superpower' talk has them thinking about how marvelous for the *nomenklatura* the old system was."

"What is President Cherny doing about that?" Morgan asked.

"The President is in a dicey position, Colonel, on all sides. He has made promises to the reformers that are unfulfilled. He has made promises to high officers in the military, and there is no way he can meet their expectations. Russia still has two million men under arms because they have nothing else for them to do, no jobs, still no housing,'' the Ambassador said somberly.

"Without aid from the West, delivered quickly, he's facing possible riots and insurrections, John,'' Kellner said.

"And if there is any kind of public outcry in this country and in the UN about this Neville business," Charlotte Conroy said wearily, "if the Russians insist on our taking the blame, I can see the Senate Foreign Relations Committee turning off the spigot to get even.''

"You know, John, that it's been close to impossible to get Russian aid funded in Congress as it is,'' Kellner said, "in spite of the fact that providing aid now is a bargain, compared to the costs to us, to the world, of an all-out civil war in Russia. If that happens, it can, and will, spill over the borders. And if that happens, we will rearm, at tremendous cost, fiscally and politically. Just believe me that Anna Neville can start a chain of events that will damage American foreign policy throughout the world. We do not need a political fiasco in Canada.''

Morgan regarded them quizzically. "You're saying that a plane crash a year ago in the Northwest Territories could cause the Canadians to break diplomatic relations with us? That this woman and her friends are so persuasive that the Canadians are going to make common cause with the Russians against us? Sorry. I can't believe that.''

"Believe it, John,'' Kellner said. "The Russian nationalists have invited Mrs. Neville and her friends to come to Moscow to proclaim to the world what the dangerous Americans are doing to innocent Canadian citizens. These groups are pushing Cherny to call out the tanks every time anyone gathers in Red Square. Ambassador Abramov thinks the nationalists would use a Hudson Bay incident to show that the old capitalist-imperialists are still at work. You know the routine. And here is Mrs. Neville, complete with CCND lawyer, apparently ready to play her part.''

"Where, exactly, is 'here'?''

"San Francisco, at the moment. She's visiting public television and radio stations all over the country," Ambassador Conroy said.

"Is she finding an audience?" Morgan asked.

"I would say she is," the Ambassador said. "When the RCMP treated Mrs. Neville as a simple case of post-traumatic shock, Yank-haters in the Foreign Ministry slipped copies of her file to the CCND. They're always looking for a worthy cause, and she gives them one in spades. They have provided a minder, funds for travel and legal fees, and sent her on the road. So far the newspapers haven't shown interest, thank God, but that's only a matter of time, I suspect."

"What do you want me to do?" Morgan asked.

"Talk to her. Advise her to choose her friends more carefully," Kellner said. "Advise her not to go to Russia."

"If I were Anna Neville, a man with my background would be the last person whose advice I'd take," Morgan said. "Remember what Ollie North did for NSC credibility a few years back. Why don't you go, Ambassador Conroy? Tell her just what you've told me. It's very persuasive."

Charlotte Conroy gestured impatiently, and Kellner said, "Don't be ridiculous, John. Charlotte can't get away, and her arrival would just fan the flames. In fact, there's no one but you on staff here who has the necessary expertise and discretion to check the Neville story out, to find out if there's any truth to it."

Ambassador Conroy continued, "The CCND lawyer who's traveling with her, Pierre Grau, studied in Moscow with Nathan Abramov. They're old friends. You're to see Grau and give him a note from Ambassador Abramov. Abramov wants to meet with him—to talk to him."

"Will Grau want to see Abramov?"

"Nathan tells me that the Pierre Grau he knew in Moscow was openminded. Frankly, I think Nathan may be overly optimistic. A touch of Pollyanna has always been his greatest fault." Charlotte Conroy reached for her briefcase and stood up. To Kellner, she said, "I'm taking the Shuttle back to New York. I suggest you brief the colonel fully about the Soyuz organization and their anti-Semitic sentiments. He might find it useful in dealing with Grau."

When she had gone, Morgan said, "She doesn't seem to hold out much hope about Grau."

"She's a realist. She's dealt with Russians and the left for years."

"She's ready enough to think the worst of Neville."

Kellner showed a wintry smile. "Charlotte is straight-laced Down East stock. It shows in odd ways. The story goes that Anna Neville is everybody's girlfriend. Charlotte doesn't approve."

Morgan asked, "Has she ever met her?"

Kellner shook his head. He said, "The FBI report names at least six lovers over the last ten years. Jake Neville was a better photographer than a husband. They had 'an open marriage.' In my day it was called 'free love.' Charlotte's an old-fashioned lady."

"I see," Morgan said dryly.

"Yes, you will. You'll see in the dossiers that Anna Neville was sleeping with Sean McCarthy, the pilot. It is remotely possible that what we have here is an ordinary garden variety love triangle, possibly even an attempted murder that went awry."

When Morgan looked doubtful, Kellner shrugged and said, "I said remotely possible."

Morgan did not give a damn about Anna Neville's lovers, dead or alive. "Soyuz," he said. "Elaborate."

"Indeed. Soyuz, or 'union,' is the name of the group because that's what they are dedicated to—reuniting the Russian Empire, or at least the part contiguous to Russia itself," Kellner explained. "Soyuz as a cultural group has been around for years, but when the Soviet Union unraveled and the non-Russian republics declared their independence, the true believers came out of the shadows. They love to dress up in czarist

47

uniforms or Cossack outfits, they set great store by old Russia's imperial history. Some pretend to be royalists, which is not exactly credible in a Russia so short of real Romanovs. They loathe America and the West for being 'mongrel races' and purveyors of anarchy—for that, read democracy and human rights.''

"So far you're talking skinheads and sheet-wearers," Morgan said. "We've got them in all colors right here."

"Perhaps if Marsh Gray over at CI were a skinhead, and if Charlie Fisk at the FBI were the same, and if Levining at Defense liked to make like a Grand Dragon, you might take a different view, Colonel." Vincent Kellner was unsmiling.

Morgan accepted the rebuke. From time to time the Russian extremists became "fashionable." A glossy woman's magazine had run a spread on one of the Soyuz leaders, Yevgeny Suvorov. Eight pages of text and color photographs of Soyuz members dressed up like Cossacks and (as the magazine put it) "playacting." And yet Aleksandr Cherny was rumored to be about to name Suvorov as his choice to take over the Ministry of Defense. What sort of pressure was being applied to the mild Cherny to win that particular concession? The appointment had raised no premonitory hackles in the foreign press. The United Nations was still stumbling along, trying to define its role as a peacekeeper in an all-too-unpeaceful world, on three continents. The possibility of a general Balkan war still loomed on the horizon. The bones of the old Soviet Union were constantly being disturbed by scavengers, but many bullets had to fly and much blood flow before the American media would even notice the story, let alone cover it night after night. The problems in Russia had few answers yet, if any, and that alone meant that they were old news. And the American public had troubles enough of its own: hurricanes, floods, unemployment, local bad-ass politics, taxes, terrorist bombings, and drive-by shootings.

I am as much at fault as anyone, Morgan thought. All I've been thinking about is myself—how to get out of this town.

Kellner said, "Camilla will find you some privacy. I want you to commit most of the files to memory."

"Yes, sir," Morgan said.

"By the way, do you know a reporter named Ryerson?"

"I assume you mean the bastard who tried to pull a fast one on the new press secretary at the White House. Pretended to be an Arab terrorist, as I recall, botched it, got caught, and ended up by losing his job when the shit hit the fan. The *Post* tried to do it quietly, but when he filed suit for a couple of million against the paper and the ombudsman, everyone within earshot found out about it. That Joe Ryerson?"

"I can see you know Ryerson," Kellner said. "Somehow he has picked up on this. He has been calling Camilla, asking our reaction to Anna Neville's story. He may bother you."

"Not if he values his profile," Morgan said.

"I hope you're joking. Hands off the press."

"Understood."

"Now, come over here, John." Kellner led the way to the electronic wall map. "Ryerson and his colleagues would kill to see this," he said. With a remote decoder, Kellner superimposed a display of tracks on the geography of the hemisphere. "Care to make a guess?"

Morgan studied the trace. It began at Resolution Island in the mouth of the Hudson Strait and moved steadily, in fifty-kilometer increments, along the east coast of Canada and the United States, south to weather the Florida Keys, through the Yucatan Strait, and into the Caribbean, where the trace ended.

Morgan said, "A Russian?"

"What else?"

"Taken by a KH-13 or later."

"Right again. Actually, it's the track of a Russian Navy Hotel-class submarine. An old one. The heat signature shows it to be the *Pravda,* formerly the *Andropov,* née the *Andrei Vishinsky*—a boat we thought they had retired five years ago. It was on the first list of submarines to be sent to Murmansk, to the new facility we helped them build for fuel removal and dismantlement. It left port with the others on the list, but you can see where it turned up. We're contacting our sources for a rundown on the command personnel. What makes it interesting is two things. First, of course, the date the track begins. Unfortunately, the fixes begin last December 31 . . .''

"This is very old information."

"No one thought it was important until Mrs. Neville appeared on our doorstep." Kellner moved to another panel and exposed a safe. He unlocked it and removed a photo file. "Item two is this set of pictures. They were made by F/A-18s from the carrier *Eisenhower* at extreme slant range—in order not to violate Cuban airspace. Look at them carefully."

Morgan leafed through the stack. There were twelve prints. The first was simply a hazy, long-range shot of a Hotel III traveling on the surface. The long, rounded sail identified it as an early example of the obsolescent class. Interesting, but Morgan had seen better shots of the same thing. In the second and third shots, the submarine appeared to have slewed around into a sharp turn and gone dead in the water. A Cuban gunboat appeared in the fourth shot. The rest of the pictures were a chronicle of absolute catastrophe. Clouds of steam geysered from a ruptured casing. The sub heeled forty degrees, ninety. In the last pictures the pressure hull had ruptured and the boat was clearly on the way to the bottom.

"Then there might be some truth to Anna Neville's story," Morgan said. "She might have seen a submarine."

"Perhaps."

"If it sailed from Kola with the others, headed for Murmansk, and turned the other way—How much influence has Soyuz in Cherny's navy?"

Kellner grimaced. "He swears it has none. But we have evidence that Suvorov is not the only Soyuz member in the Russian Republic's administration. Admiral Aleyev is a member; he's close to Suvorov. Piotr Kondratiev, the police general whom Cherny passed over for promotion to marshal in the last honors list, is almost certainly Soyuz."

"How much of this have you told the President?" Morgan asked.

The ghost of a smile touched Kellner's lips. "I serve the President of the United States *what* he needs, *when* he needs it. I serve him even when he is unaware that he is being served. Do you understand me, John?"

"Yes," Morgan said. When Kellner was in this mood, it was best to agree.

"Sometimes I worry. People like me are the ones who in other countries overthrow governments when they get to thinking they know better than anyone else how to run things." He paused. "But, of course, such things don't happen in this country."

"No, sir. They don't." Sermon over, Morgan thought with relief.

Kellner handed Morgan the files. "Mrs. Neville was born in Britain, but now is a Canadian citizen. She's the daughter of the late George Mathis. That won't mean anything to you; he's ancient history. But in his day Mathis was a royal pain in the ass, known as the Red Vicar. He was prominent in the British Campaign for Nuclear Disarmament of the 1950s. His father, the senior George Mathis, was a nuclear physicist, a good friend of Klaus Fuchs—and though he was never charged, there is still one school of thought over at Langley that believes he was just as guilty as Fuchs. But the British disagreed.

"His son, the Red Vicar, never did anything really illegal, but he was a thoroughgoing 1960s troublemaker. He was divorced about the time he went tie-dyed and was awarded custody of Christiane, his only child. He emigrated to Canada a year after his divorce. He became very active during the Vietnam War, spent some months in jail, came out, dropped from sight, died in 1985. A nasty little story about him is that he procured his daughter for Jake Neville because he liked Neville's politics. I don't know. Maybe he did. It doesn't matter now. But Anna Mathis Neville's left-wing credentials go way

Alfred Coppel

back. The boys at Langley and the FBI liked to keep tab on her and her husband. Jacob Neville was still making excuses for Joe Stalin until the early eighties.''

Kellner shook his head. "At any rate, Mathis legally renamed his daughter Anna after Anna Akhmatova, the Russian poet. This is the lady who is accusing the U.S. Navy of violating Canadian sovereignty and murdering innocent citizens." His voice rose in indignation.

Morgan said, as mildly as he could manage, "I haven't looked at the material, but aren't you building a case of guilt by genetics?"

Kellner favored Morgan with a bleak smile. "If that's what I'm doing, let's find out." The smile vanished. "But if she is dirty, I want to know. Before you leave for San Francisco, talk to the RCMP liaison at Canada House and see what you can pick up. Be aware that the Canadian left is prepared to love the Neville story, anticipating that this will single-handedly deliver them from Yank imperialism, acid rain, the last of the Quebecois, and the caribou itch. Also remember when you talk to the RCMP that Anna Neville charmed them," he finished with a wry half-smile. "She seems to have that ability." The smile swiftly faded. "You have what authority you need, Colonel Morgan. So get to it."

52

Chapter Four

Leesburg, Virginia/November 25, 26

Lifestyles hears that Prime Minister Ian Halloran, President Caidin's great and good neighbor to the north, will visit Washington very soon. Insiders are speculating about the agenda of this North American mini-summit, but Lifestyles can tell its readers that this is no social call. Canadian national elections are scheduled for February 25, and the CCND-sponsored appearance in the United States of the widow of environmentalist Jacob Neville, victim of a mysterious air accident in Canada last December, has Mr. Halloran looking for answers from his friend, Cole Caidin.

—"Capitol Lifestyles"

John Morgan rented a gatehouse on the grounds of an overgrown estate in Leesburg, the upper floor of which was given over to storing ancient chattels belonging to the estate. Morgan lived in the three downstairs rooms, all of which had ill-fitting French windows opening into the garden. Heavy, dusty velvet draperies kept most of the winter chill out when drawn, which they rarely were.

53

Morgan had made arrangements with the operations officer at Anacostia to catch a ride west with a ferry pilot delivering an F/A-18 to the USS *Nimitz* at Alameda Naval Air Station. Navy transport would get him to San Francisco long before any civilian airline.

He opened the kitchen window and put a dish with three cut-up slices of boiled ham on the sill. Then he put what remained of the ham between two slices of not-so-fresh rye, poured himself a beer, and returned to his thoughtful study of the Xerox copies the Canadians had given him.

In the other room the television set flickered, the sound turned down. Morgan read and ate standing at the counter, considering what the RCMP Intelligence people had to say for American consumption, about Anna Neville. Like most intelligence evaluations, the report was full of opinions; some were favorable to the Nevilles, but most were not. Though Jake and Anna had really belonged to different generations, they had apparently shared the same leftist politics so popular in the sixties and seventies. The same organizations, the same causes. Morgan paused thoughtfully. Jake Neville was of an age to have been of the Woodstock generation. But Anna must have been a child then. Yet she had followed the same path, or as near to it as she could manage, a decade later. Her father's influence? Very probably. She had practically been a red-diaper baby.

More recently she and Jake had veered off into the Green movement, where their talents were most useful. They had slipped easily into the role of environmental activists. And from there it was no leap at all into the camp of the CCND. Morgan wondered if her CCND connections had been made before or after the crash into Hudson Bay. Difficult to know, if she chose to conceal it.

Bumper-sticker politics, Morgan thought. Hardly sinister. Except that Jake had seemed to hate his country and had used his considerable talent to show it in the worst possible light. But again, nothing sinister. Just the outraged cries of an American who was looking for human perfection in those around him, and never finding it.

On impulse, Morgan had stopped at the Library of Congress to spend two hours with the poems of Anna Neville's namesake, Anna Akhmatova.

They surprised him. He had expected hard-rock Marxism. Instead, he learned that Akhmatova had lost a husband to the Stalin purges, and that she was understandably a most melancholy woman. She had been born Anna Andreyevna Gorenko.

According to the RCMP, the Red Vicar (George Mathis actually was an ordained Episcopalian minister) had met Akhmatova in the Soviet Union in 1949—at the height of the cold war. His visit had been on behalf of the British Ban the Bomb Committee. The Stalinists had been less than pleased when he chose to associate himself with Akhmatova, who was considered "unreliable."

Score one for you, Vicar, Morgan thought.

The Canadians speculated that their relationship had been intimate, but Mathis had been in his early thirties and Akhmatova had been at least sixty in 1949, so the suggestion of a love affair was questionable.

Akhmatova had died, unrehabilitated, in 1966. She had not lived to see perestroika and glasnost, which was a pity, Morgan thought. But whatever else the Red Vicar had been, he had been no Stalinist. A quondam apologist for the old monster, yes. But there had been plenty of those in the West. Intellectuals found it difficult to let go of old illusions.

Morgan felt a certain sympathy for Mathis. He had found Akhmatova's biography moving and her poems haunting.

> *This: the song of our last meeting . . .*
> *I looked back at the dark house's frame;*
> *In the bedroom the candles were burning*
> *An indifferent, yellowed flame.*

The verse struck a painful chord. Morgan's wife, Joan, had died five years ago, after a long bout with cancer. Morgan, like Akhmatova, perhaps like the Vicar, too, knew something about loneliness.

As a sidebar to the thought, he wondered how the Canadian agents knew that the bush pilot had been one of Neville's lovers. And why did that make them seem more like snoops and less like spooks?

Tripoli, a large and scarred tomcat of uncertain age, appeared in the open kitchen window. When Morgan rented the house, the beast had adopted him in the mysterious manner of cats. The sliced ham on the sill was for Tripoli. He inspected it carefully before beginning to eat.

Mrs. James, Morgan's venerable landlady who lived in the main house, tried often to tempt Tripoli out of his wandering ways with delicacies and covered sleeping baskets. But Tripoli was, like Morgan, given to the life of a rogue male, coming and going on silent errands and duties, sometimes being absent for days. Morgan understood this. There was always an open window in Morgan's house for Tripoli.

For all his battered appearance, Tripoli was unfailingly fastidious about his ham, a favorite food. He began to eat, silently and efficiently. When he had finished, he uttered a single guttural trill of thanks, dropped to the kitchen floor with a twenty-pound thump, and walked into the living room to climb into his favorite chair in front of the television set, where he set about grooming himself.

Morgan finished his sandwich and downed the last of his beer standing at the kitchen sink. He boiled a pan of water and made a cup of instant coffee, which he drank without pleasure. When he had finished, he put pan, cup, and glass in the dishwasher and turned on the appliance.

The mail was trash and went into the round file. He followed Tripoli into the living room to watch the late television news. The President and the First Lady were partying with celebrities in one part of town, while drive-by shootings and mayhem predominated in another. As far as the viewer could guess, there was no international news worth mentioning.

Morgan turned off the television and went into the bedroom. He packed an Air Force B-4 bag with a change of clothes and put it by the door. He stood at the window for a time, listening to the night sounds. Not much happened after dark in suburban Leesburg. It was a middle-class town that suited Morgan, hardly a part of the Washington complex at all. Ordinary people lived here. The kind of people he felt comfortable with, the kind he was sworn to protect. Would Charlotte Conroy dismiss his feelings as sentimentality, or would she understand? Anna Neville and her friends would make snide remarks, surely. So American.

Sometimes in Leesburg one could hear aircraft taking off and landing at Andrews. Not tonight. The stillness was palpable. It had rained in the afternoon; the woods behind the house were wet. Through the open windows of the room—Morgan's all-purpose "other" room—came the smell of damp earth. The night was unseasonably warm for November.

Morgan was tired. Tomorrow would be a long and difficult day. He was still very skeptical of the value of his trip. There was no telling how Anna Neville would take exposure to a Marine half-colonel in the service of the NSC. He was starting at a disadvantage. The track record for such colonels, those who had gone before him in Washington, was dicey at best. He was weary of telling the casual questioner that he had never met Oliver North, and that he had neither the desire nor the power to emulate North's actions.

A FELINE GROWL AWOKE MORGAN at a quarter after three. Tripoli stood stiffly at the foot of the bed where he had been sleeping. The cloud cover had thinned, allowing pale moonlight to penetrate the room. Tripoli looked enormous and angry, fur standing, tail upright and stiff as a bottle brush, back arched, and ears flattened for combat. A jungle sound rumbled in his chest while he stared at an open French door.

Alfred Coppel

Morgan did not ignore warnings. He swung silently out of
bed and reached under the mattress for a silenced Ruger .22
semiautomatic pistol—an assassin's weapon. He stood naked
at the window, listening. Something moved among the trees
behind the overgrown garden. A dark shape broke and ran.
Morgan moved swiftly.

There was only the sound of blundering, running footsteps
ahead, and Morgan's own in pursuit. Morgan cut through the
shrubbery onto the deserted street. A car was parked half a
block from his house. The running figure emerged from the
shadows a few feet away: a man, out of breath, frightened at
being discovered and pursued.

He reached the car a step before Morgan, flung himself inside, and tried to close and lock the door. Morgan stopped him
with a fistful of shirt and the Ruger jammed under a sharp
chin.

"For Christ's sake, don't!" The voice was choked by the
grip at his throat.

Morgan pulled the man out of the car and slammed him
back against the car door. The intruder was at least half a head
shorter than Morgan's six feet. Then in the half darkness he
recognized Joe Ryerson, the defrocked reporter. Ryerson's
eyes were enormous as he contemplated Morgan. He whispered, "Are you crazy, man? You're stark naked."

Morgan put the muzzle of the Ruger in Ryerson's ear.

"You can't do this. I have rights . . ."

Morgan caught his arm in a lock and lifted, eliciting a
squeal of pain.

"That way," Morgan said.

They went back through the trees and the neglected garden
and into the dark house. Morgan pushed his prowler ahead of
him, into the bedroom. "Sit on the floor. If you move, I'll kill
you."

"Are you fucking crazy?" Ryerson's voice was thin with
fear.

Morgan turned on a light. The pistol remained aimed at

58

Ryerson all the while. Ryerson blinked at the light and complained, "I lost my glasses when you started to chase me."

Morgan said, "What are you doing here?"

"Where's Anna Neville? Is she here? I understand you're going to be her keeper."

Morgan stared. The man's chutzpah was amazing. Ryerson looked absurd, squatting on the floor and asking questions like a lawyer in a courtroom. "I could have broken your neck, or shot you for peeping in windows, Ryerson."

Ryerson said, "I'm a journalist, I have a right to investigate a story—"

"You *used* to be a journalist," Morgan said. "Tonight you're a peeping tom."

"You'd like to shoot me, wouldn't you? Maybe Kellner and the President would hang a medal around your neck for killing a reporter—" Ryerson's voice was frightened, but defiant. The pistol in Morgan's hand made him sweat. He had been chased and captured by a bloody fascist, naked as a Doukhobor, and just as crazy. It made clear thinking impossible.

Ryerson gathered up his courage and said, "My source tells me you're the designated troubleshooter with the Neville woman. You're bound to fail. She's with the CCND and they'll never let you get close to her. Besides, her whole family hated people like you and Kellner."

Morgan snapped the safety on the Ruger and slipped it back under the mattress. "Go home, Ryerson," he said wearily. "It's too late for your games."

Ryerson scrambled to his feet and glanced at the packed B-4 bag. "Where is she, Morgan? What are your orders? What will happen to her?"

Morgan regarded the reporter coldly. "Happen to whom?"

"Anna Neville, for Chrissake. You're going to hide her somewhere so she can't talk, can't tell her story to the public, right? How far will you bastards go to shut her up?"

"You're an idiot, Ryerson."

"The people have a right to know."

59

Morgan's patience ran out. He lifted Ryerson by the arms and marched him to the front door. "Out," he said. "Before I forget what an important journalist you are."

"You're *dangerous,* Morgan. A good Nazi," Ryerson, struggling, said breathlessly.

Morgan thrust him out the door onto the step. "Good night."

"Listen, Morgan. I have contacts. Help me and I'll help you."

Morgan suppressed an impulse to laugh. The man was preposterous. Even as he retreated down the steps, Ryerson was asking: "Why did you visit the Canadian embassy? What were you doing at the Library of Congress?"

Morgan closed the door firmly and bolted it. Joe Ryerson had set warning bells ringing with his clumsy effort at "investigation." Ryerson had obviously followed him from the time Morgan left the White House. "My source," he had said. "I have contacts." He probably did. God knew he belonged at the bottom of the barrel of Capitol reporters, but he was getting information from someone, and damned fast, at that. Ryerson would regard disclosure of Morgan's mission as a scoop, a ticket back into the ranks of acceptance and fame and fortune. A single setback wouldn't discourage him.

But please, God, not soon, Morgan thought wearily. Keep the bastard away from me. He went into the kitchen, found a can of beer, and drank it standing naked in the dark. When Joan was alive they often did this together, wherever they were living, touching and laughing and making love amid the ignored crockery.

In the bedroom the candles were burning . . . Tell me about it, Anna Andreyevna, he thought.

Tripoli had departed.

Morgan crushed the beer can and walked back through the empty house to bed.

Chapter Five

It is conceivable, however, that the bomb will be employed by an individual, or group, whose purpose is not to achieve some positive aim but simply to wreak havoc for its own sake.

—MARTIN VAN CREVELD, *TECHNOLOGY AND WAR*

THE DEVICE now lies at twenty fathoms under the windswept surface of the bay. At 120 feet it is very dark. Fish swim lazily around the large cylinder, almost hidden by a year's sedimentation. An eel roots in the mud that has built up against the casing.

Spreading out in a roughly fan-shaped distribution down-current from the Device, the rotting bodies of killed fish litter the bottom of the bay. Other fish have fed on them, then drifted away to die elsewhere.

The plutonium oxide that powers the small nuclear generator, which in turn runs the Device's automatic systems, has been leaking for almost a year. The ancillary systems continue to function because the power source has been made redundant, a common precaution in weapons design. But for a distance of a thousand meters around the Device the water and seabottom are contaminated.

AT ONE O'CLOCK ON THIS DARK ARCTIC AFTERNOON, a hunting party of Inuit trappers is returning home to Eskimo Point along the frozen shore. They chatter as they slog through freshly fallen snow. The hunt has been a success. Fish have been plentiful and there is caribou meat on the sledges.

At one second after one o'clock, a half dozen kilometers from where they are walking, under the mud at the bottom of the bay, an electronic clock activates the power-up sequence.

The onboard computer boots. Then the primary switches snap on, and the countdown to launch begins.

Chapter Six

When dealing with the KGB, fear nothing, expect nothing, believe nothing.

—ALEKSANDR SOLZHENITSYN

JOE RYERSON LAY in Marina Suslova's bed, gazing at his reflection in the mirrored ceiling. The scent of her was all around him—on the sheets, the down comforter, the pillows. Whenever his "self-esteem" dropped below a certain level, Ryerson made it a point to seek out the Russian woman. Joe Ryerson was a great believer in the beneficial effects of high self-esteem, and the lovely part of this whole setup, he told himself, was that Marina's associates in the Mount Alto Russian compound could always be counted on to release her from her duties of the moment and send her racing for Georgetown in her black whale-tail Porsche. They believed Ryerson to be a source, an asset. Ryerson found this inflating.

Far from being a source of "product," Joe Ryerson considered himself a prime consumer. Right now, thanks to that bastard ombudsman, he had no ability to make use of any of the

Moscow tidbits Marina always brought whenever she parked the Porsche and came striding up the walk to meet him.

He had accepted a key to the townhouse without a second thought. Marina might nominally be GKNT, bright bitch that she was, but it was obvious the bills for the car and the house were being paid for by the Intelligence Directorate office in the compound. The cold war was over, but some things did not change.

The only cloud on Joe Ryerson's horizon was the chance that the inside-the-Beltway gossip machine might report that Neanderthals of the Russian Intelligence Directorate owned a Washington newsman. No one was ever going to hang a rap like that on Joe Ryerson.

But this morning a session with Marina failed to improve his humor. The humiliating episode with Kellner's man John Morgan still gnawed at him. It had been a mistake to go snooping around the Leesburg house, but he'd needed to know what Vincent Kellner and Charlotte Conroy were up to, and how they intended to deal with Anna Neville and Pierre Grau. There was a story there, a big one; Ryerson could smell it, taste it. A story big enough, he thought, to turn the ombudsman's report around and get himself rehired by the *Post*. But that goddamned Marine had run him off before he could learn anything.

He could hear Marina moving about in the kitchenette. She might have a sheaf of Russian scientific degrees, and she might work for the Intelligence Directorate or the GRU, but she knew how to serve a meal, brew a glass of tea, and chill a bottle of vodka. She was expert in pleasing a man and knew how and when to play the whore. That was an uncommon talent today, with Washington swarming with surly feminists.

Ryerson regarded his mirrored image with regret. His hair was thinning on top—maybe it was time for a hairpiece. He self-consciously pulled the covers up to his waist. He had seldom been that successful with women, and never before with a woman like Marina Suslova. She had an incredible body, more buxom than a *Playboy* centerfold.

Who in Grass Valley, Wisconsin, could ever have guessed that Joe Ryerson would be shacking up with a woman who knew how to make fucking into such a fine art. A black S-M sort of art sometimes, true. But the nail scars on his back were badges of a success he had never had in Grass Valley, where he had been raised by a maiden aunt.

Sometimes he still dreamed of returning to his hometown and regaling the high school studs, who had hazed him so unmercifully, with tales of his glamorous sex-filled life as an international correspondent.

Marina came into the bedroom. Not naked, but nearly so, in string-bikini panties that only just covered her bush. Marina Suslova was earthy. Yes, that was the word that best expressed her appeal. There was dark hair under her arms and even a shadow on her upper lip. "That is Russian, Yosip," she said. "Real Russian." She had a fetish about things being *real Russian.* Sometimes she would dress up in Cossack costume, boots and all, breasts loose under a boat-necked bodice, the rest of her buck-ass naked under an embroidered peasant skirt. And when she stripped down to boots alone, she was a sight to behold.

She carried in a silver bucket filled with ice packed around a bottle of Stoly. She never served Ryerson American booze. She wouldn't have the swill in the house.

Marina was a woman of strong opinions, sexual and political. She hated the very mention of either Mikhail Gorbachev or Boris Yeltsin, whom she regarded as traitors.

Ryerson rarely tried to argue geopolitics with Marina. And during any discussion of European politics, he had the feeling Marina was laughing at him. Ryerson was a man accustomed to the sound-byte wisdom of the Washington press corps, but such opinions were greeted with Suslovian contempt in Georgetown. On balance it was hard to dispute Suslova's judgments about Russia. She was, after all, one of the New Russians. And she knew how to convince a man, one way or another. On her back she never lost an argument.

MARINA POURED two large glasses of Stoly and handed one to Ryerson. Liquor frightened him, always had. He disliked the feeling of being out of control. His aunt had raised him on tales of the havoc caused in the Ryerson family by drink, and he secretly suspected that he, himself, was dangerously near to being an alcoholic.

It was early in the day for knocking back straight vodka, but it seemed Marina was going into one of her "real Russian" phases. "I admire man who drinks," she would say, dropping her articles in the Russian way. Actually, Ryerson thought, no man breathing would refuse a drink—or a dozen drinks—from a five foot nine, 150 pounder with breasts like melons and with hips and a belly Rubens might have painted.

There was a peasant quality to Marina's face. It was broad, with high cheekbones and widely spaced eyes like chips of blue sky under heavy black brows. Even fully clothed, she radiated sex. Naked, with her large, dark aureolas contracted, nipples erect, smelling of an hour's copulation, she was formidable. Just the way she came to the bed started Ryerson's hormones flowing again. He had never been a sexual athlete before taking up with Marina Suslova, and he was desperately proud of his ability to perform with her now.

"*Schastye,*" she said. Luck. She knocked back the vodka as though it were tap water.

Ryerson matched her. The liquor was without flavor and icy cold. Marina poured another and they repeated the ritual. Two were Ryerson's limit.

"More?" she said.

"I have things to do today," Ryerson said.

"Then go. Go." An immediate sulk. Genuine? How could one tell with Marina? But making a guess—no. Only an act. But a good one. Ryerson's erection softened.

"I don't want to go yet," he said.

"Ah," she said. She stripped off the panties. Ryerson was sure that she had put them on only for the effect of removing them again.

And it was effective. She peeled back the silk comforter and considered his half-erect penis. Kneeling on the bed, she took him in her mouth and ran her tongue over the glans. Ryerson's knees trembled. After a time she straightened, regarded him speculatively, and then straddled him, her prodigious breasts hanging over his face. Despite this being their third copulation of the afternoon, it took very little time.

Ryerson hoped that Marina was not disappointed. But she lay down beside him and allowed him to wet her breasts with his mouth. As he rubbed his cheek against her skin, Ryerson found himself guessing about her past. Was she married? Had she ever been? How could one ever know? Women were such cheats and liars. She was probably in her late thirties, he thought, but possibly as old as forty-two or three. Born, then, after what the Russians called the Great Patriotic War, and well established as an academician by the time of the Second Russian Revolution (as Americans were now calling the Gorbachev-to-Yeltsin era of Soviet disestablishment). So her political skills had to be well developed. How many members of the Soviet nomenklatura had survived as well as she?

Sometimes, she tormented him with hints that she relished lesbian sex as much as she enjoyed men. He absolutely refused to believe it. He told himself that any woman who looked like Marina and fucked like Marina couldn't be a lesbo. Impossible. There was still much Grass Valley in Joe Ryerson.

The only time they had come near to a serious discussion of sex, Marina had laughed at him and accused him of lower-class prejudice. Despite her Soviet schooling, she had not meant it as a compliment.

"What happened to you today, Yosip?" she asked. "You were angry when I arrived."

"It was nothing," he said, not wanting to speak of Colonel Morgan.

"Not nothing," she said, and caressed his flaccid penis with her free hand. "Tell me, little one."

Ryerson's anger returned. What the hell. Why not? "That fucking Marine," he said.

"Who?"

"Morgan. Works for Kellner."

"Ah. The National Security Adviser."

He pressed his advantage, implying that he knew Kellner far better than he did. "I've told Vincent many times that Morgan is going to get him in trouble. Last night I had to calm him down."

"And *is* the Adviser in trouble?"

"He may be," Ryerson said. "I'm going to San Francisco to check it out. I'll be gone—I don't know—a few days."

"A story for your newspaper?"

"Don't pry, Marina."

"What does that mean, 'pry'?"

Ryerson sat up in bed. Marina stayed as she was, her breasts spread of their own weight, white skinned, traced with tiny blue veins. They would sag one day, Ryerson thought, but right now they were primo.

"It means to ask too many questions."

"I see." Her voice turned cold. She could do that. Drop the temperature suddenly. It shook Ryerson. The thought of not having Marina available for sex disturbed him almost as much as the idea of losing her as a source of information. One of her duties was to keep all the snooping equipment overlooking Washington in working condition. She had told him that on their first or second time together. One day he might find the information useful, but not yet.

He said, "Kellner is sending Morgan to San Francisco to meddle with Anna Neville and her lawyer. Damned risky business."

"Neville? The Canadian woman who was in the newspaper last week?"

"And her lawyer."

"I don't understand, Yosip."

"Lawyer. Attorney. I don't know the word in Russian."

"Ah. *Advakat.*"

Ryerson sighed. "Something like that."

"I saw his picture. He is a Jew, I think."

Sometimes Marina's anti-Semitism made Joe Ryerson uneasy. Some people thought that he was Jewish, and he wasn't, definitely not. Perhaps he should mention that some time. Make it clear.

"His name is Grau," Marina said. "He works for the Canadians who do not like nuclear power." Then with one of the sudden switches of approach Ryerson found so disconcerting, she asked abruptly: "Why must you go to San Francisco?"

He brightened. Did she really want him to stay with her? "It's my job."

"I do not like you to go away." She turned her back.

Pouting? Bloody woman. She had more faces than a deck of cards, Ryerson thought. "It's what I do," he said, coaxing her to understand.

"Then go," she said. "What do I care?"

He touched her shoulder, but she pulled away from him. "*Go. Go* to San Francisco."

She would not be placated. Damn her, he thought. He got up and dressed with a sinking feeling in his belly.

When he was ready to leave, Marina relented. "Come here," she said. "You may kiss my breasts." After he had done as he was told, she turned her back on him again and said, "Now, good-bye."

MARINA HEARD THE FRONT DOOR CLOSE, and shortly thereafter Ryerson's Volkswagen started up. She rose from the bed and walked naked into the living room. From a drawer in an antique desk she withdrew a small notebook. It contained the day codes in effect on Mount Alto. She dialed the number and waited for three rings before hanging up. In two minutes exactly, the GRU duty officer called her on a secure telephone.

"Nosenko here," he said.

"Marina. Call Evangeline and tell her to meet me at nine tonight."

"Location?"

"She knows."

"Very good." The line went dead.

For a moment, Marina Suslova stood like a nude statue in the safehouse living room. She knew the video cameras were filming her, as they had filmed the entire encounter in the bedroom. It was rather delicious and helped to compensate for Ryerson's uninspired performance.

She stood, pelvis tipped, breasts pendulous, posing until the cameras got all her best angles. Then, smiling, she replaced the telephone handset in its cradle and returned to the bedroom to dress.

There was work to do at the surveillance station in the compound. One could not thank Henry Kissinger enough for his approval, long ago, of the Mount Alto site. From there the electronic surveillance of Washington was almost complete. Marina had a dossier on every member of Congress. She listened to personal calls, official calls, secret calls. Information that was never used. Holy Russia had a government of fools. The idiots. The Yaneyev coup in 1991, or, for that matter, the parliamentary fiasco in 1993 would have been worse, of course. Kondratiev's revolution would be different. And it was only a matter of days, now.

After the appointment with Evangeline, she would have to arrange for manpower. Fortunately, thugs and hooligans congregated on the West Coast. There were American fascists everywhere for the hiring, but regrettably most of them were bumpkins. There weren't many of the better class of American society—academics and professionals—available any longer. They seemed to have lost interest in subverting their government. But then, one worked with what one had on hand.

Chapter Seven

Brownsville, Texas/November 26

Yevgeny Suvorov, the new Minister of Defense of Russia, is rumored to be affiliated with Soyuz, the nationalist and anti-Semitic movement headed by Piotr Kondratiev, former chief of state security, demoted last June by President Aleksandr Cherny.

If so, it is a chilling indication of how weak the Cherny government has become.

David Milstein, Minister of Industry and Finance, denies that any member of the Executive Committee is a member of Soyuz.

"Fascism has no place in the new Russia," Milstein told the Times-Dispatch.

—NEW YORK *TIMES-DISPATCH*

THE RAIN, falling in sheets through the darkness, made a rushing sound as it struck the surface of the shallow, swift-flowing river. The truck had deposited the migrants a mile from the southern bank of the river, far short of what was promised, but none of the fifty men and seven women dared complain.

The coyote was perfectly capable of disappearing into the night and leaving the lot of them stranded and lost in the downpour. So far he had not done this. To that extent, thought Arkady Karmann, the brute exhibited a kind of honor.

Three of the women were traveling with young children, four boys and a single girl. What they imagined they were going to do when they crossed to the other side was anyone's guess. Karmann could not imagine the conditions of the life they were leaving that would make an effort like this seem a reasonable alternative.

Each man had paid the coyote fifty U.S. dollars for his services, such as they were. The women had paid ten dollars less, and the children had cost their parents only twenty.

Originally there had been four coyotes, but as they approached the border, the others had fallen away, leaving only the leader, a big, paunchy man who refused to give himself a name in the mistaken conviction that anonymity would keep him safe from the Border Patrol.

The night was windy as well as wet, and cold. The wind seemed to blow out of the plains to the north, and it had steel teeth. Karmann had somehow always imagined that the lands along the southern border of the United States were warm, almost tropical. The deep cold said otherwise. He wondered how the children were managing. Not one of them seemed to have proper clothing for weather like this.

No one in the straggling mob following the coyote was dressed decently. Everyone was freezing cold, some were already footsore, and most were frightened—even those who had made this crossing before.

The United States had twice made legal the presence of what the officials called "undocumented aliens," in the naive belief that the problem of the illegal migrants seeking work could be settled once and for all with such measures. But the problem did not resolve itself. Mexico was a land of low pay and high unemployment. The United States was the reverse.

Karmann wondered if his own countrymen might not respond like these impoverished Mexicans if Russia shared a relatively unguarded frontier with the United States. Tensions with Poland had risen because of the movement of Russians across the Polish border, looking for better opportunities.

Many of these people had tried before to run the border. Most had been caught and returned to Mexico by the Border Patrol. Some had contributed literally thousands of dollars to the coffers of the coyotes, the racketeers who earned their tortillas and tequila by giving the hopeful more or less what they paid for.

Arkady Karmann's fifty dollars had been hard earned. There was very little to do in Mexico if one were dirty, ragged, spoke with an odd accent, and had a steel hook for a left hand. The adults in the party, even the coyotes, had been afraid of Karmann's strangeness and his hook, but the children had loved "El Gancho." They had been fascinated by the steel barb the fishermen of the Mosquito Coast had fashioned for him, and from which he now took his nickname.

That part of Karmann's journey had long since become dream-like, phantasmagoric. The days at sea had been a nightmare, followed by a bitter fantasy of cruelty and frustration until his rescue by his unlikely saviors.

Once healed enough to travel, he had worked his way eastward, along the Golfo de Honduras to La Cieba by fishing boat and by truck. The journey, scarcely begun, had already seemed endless.

Sometime in early June, he crossed the frontier into Guatemala, plodding along barely marked roads toward Puerto Barrios. The Guatemalan truck drivers were rough men, but willing enough to pick up a ragged, crippled stranger on the long stretches of lonely mountain passes. From the fishermen and from the drivers he learned to speak a pidgin Spanish. When he could not ride, he walked. From time to time he paused in his travels to earn a few quetzales in order to buy the barest necessities. The journey northward had become his obsession.

Summer found him in Mexico, traveling the Pan American Highway between Tuxtla Gutiérrez and Oaxaca. He had begun to lose track of time. He walked and begged rides until finally he came into the high, smoggy reaches of Mexico City.

The Americans had been a bitter disappointment. He had somehow imagined that he need only present himself at their embassy in Mexico City to be taken in, listened to, given a respectful hearing. He had envisioned succor, rest, and most of all, belief. He had found none of these things. One did not appear at an embassy, dirty and in rags, and ask first for the military attaché, and then, failing that, for money enough to travel to Washington. The only person he was allowed to see had been a lowly clerk of some kind, backed by an armed guard. The clerk, baffled by the apparition before him, had asked him to return at a later date, carefully unspecified.

But the obsession sustained him.

He had turned his hand to petty crime to earn money for his passage to the north. He had worked in turn for a garbage hauler, then a whoremistress old enough to be his mother. She had been generous—or as generous as one who sold hundred-peso girls could be. She, too, had been fascinated by his steel hook.

He left Mexico City and walked north again to Querétaro and San Luis Potosí, stopping from time to time when his money ran out and he was obliged to earn or steal more. But he never stopped for long. Arkady Karmann was a driven man. Cadging rides, crawling aboard slowly rolling freight cars in the dark nights, he made his way north and north again, like an insect on a map.

To the Texas border.

THE RAIN FELT ICY as it ran down his neck and back. It was the nearest thing he'd had to a bath in months. He had managed one haircut since Honduras, but a bath had been beyond his capabilities.

"Compadre—cuándo llegamos a la frontera?"

The question, spoken in a soft and plaintive voice, came from a woman behind Karmann. In the darkness it was not possible to see her clearly, but she was carrying a child in her rebozo, using the garment to wrap her burden against the lash of the wind and rain.

She asked again, in a thin and weary voice: "Countryman, when shall we arrive at the border?" She must not have realized that she was speaking to El Gancho, whom all but the children avoided.

"Soon now, *madrecita,*" he said as gently as he could manage. But the cold and the long months of travel on foot had roughened his voice, and his accent made it threatening.

"I can carry the young one if you are tired," he said.

"No. No. *'stoy bien. 'stoy bien.*" She had recognized him and recoiled in alarm. She made a small sign of the cross on her forehead, between the wings of wet-black hair, and dropped back, putting another woman and two men between herself and the odd foreigner, who was touched by the devil and in whose eyes an angry flame burned.

Karmann slogged on. The path ran between two fallow cotton fields. From time to time a flash of distant lightning illuminated the land. It was as flat as a steppe, fading into distant darkness as the flashes died.

Now it seemed to Karmann that he could hear the sound of swiftly running water. The Rio Grande? Was it a fast-flowing stream, then? He had imagined it a stagnant waterway running between concreted banks. But perhaps that was only in summer. Back in Matamoros, a man had said that there were flash floods in the Rio Grande at this time of year. Could it be true? Karmann had forgotten how to be afraid.

The sound of the river deepened. The Mexicans grew uneasy as they approached it. The ground underfoot was mostly sand. It drank the rain as though the earth were thirsty. A distant light penetrated the darkness, and the line buckled and coiled as those in front slowed, stopped.

Karmann heard the hoarse whisper of the coyote telling

everyone to be silent and not to move. Now he could see that the lights were from an automobile, quite far away, driving across the track the Mexicans were following. Flickering shadows betrayed the wire fence that lay between them and the slowly moving car.

"Patrulla frontera," the coyote said in a hushed voice. "Be still, damn you."

Karmann realized that the Border Patrol car was on the far side of the river, probably on a road parallel to a high, treeless bank.

The headlights vanished to the east.

Someone asked fearfully, "Is the water deep?"

"Rodillas, no más." To the knees, no more, the coyote explained irritably.

The line began to move again. Somewhere behind, a child complained and whimpered.

Another hundred meters, and the coyote stopped the group once more. They stood on the crest of the bank on the Mexican side. The distant, silent flashes of lightning seemed much nearer. They reflected briefly on the surface of the river, which swirled and rippled as it rushed to the southeast, toward the city of Brownsville and the Gulf of Mexico.

"Now listen," the coyote said. *"Escuchame."*

A circle of men formed around him. The women in the group were excluded, relegated to the outer circumference of the circle. It didn't matter, Karmann realized. If the water was deep as it appeared to be, the women had almost no chance of making it safely across the river. Those with children had none at all. They would be caught by the Americans and sent back. Some might even drown because they had chosen to make their attempt in a rainstorm.

"The river is rising," said the coyote. "We can't wait around. We have to run for it right away. *A prisa. Me entienden?"*

A murmur of agreement made the rounds.

"The water is shallow," he lied. "But there may be deep

places. So stay behind me. I will guide you. Rely on me.''

Another murmur. In the darkness a child asked, *"Que dice?"*

A woman answered, "That we must follow him carefully."

Another woman said tremulously, "But it is so dark."

The coyote heard and said, "Trust in God."

He turned and vanished down the steep bank to the water. Several men followed and splashed noisily. In a flash of light from the north Karmann saw that they were all in water to their waists and the current was swift, surging and bubbling around them. He slid down the slope and into the water at the river's edge. It felt cold, colder even than the rain.

Behind him a woman uttered a cry and protested that she could never make it, and that her son would surely drown if he tried. Karmann had no reason to doubt it. In better weather, there were apprentice coyotes who specialized in helping migrants across the river. Some would even carry the old, the young, and the helpless. For a price.

But there were no such helpers tonight. There was only the wind and the rain and the river snatching at his legs as Karmann drove himself forward.

There was increasing confusion behind him, but he did not turn. He wanted only to reach the American shore.

In midriver, the water reached to his breastbone, rising as the current grew stronger. The footing was slippery.

Suddenly, over the rush of the water, Karmann heard another sound. It was the noise of a low-flying helicopter.

The men ahead scattered, some pushing on, others turning back. A cone of blue-white light exploded the night. Rain swirled in the brilliance, driven by the commingled storm and the powerful downdraft of the aircraft's rotor. The machine hovered fifty feet over the river. A stentorian, amplified voice spoke in Spanish: *"ATENCIÓN, ATENCIÓN!* Do not attempt to go on. Do not cross the river. If you do, you will be arrested and returned to the Mexican police. *ATENCIÓN! ATENCIÓN! . . ."*

The message repeated as wind and spray battered the illegals struggling in the water. Other lights appeared on the far embankment. Karmann could see figures moving across the lights, spreading out. There was a bus with barred windows in the headlights' glare.

The coyote was gone. Migrants were splashing back through the water toward the Mexican shore. In the glare from the helicopter overhead, Karmann saw standing near him the woman with whom he had spoken earlier. The one who had made the sign of the cross at him. Her child was riding uncertainly on her shoulders and screaming with fright. She stumbled in the swift water and almost lost her footing.

"Give me the child," he called. "Let me carry her."

The woman recoiled in terror and went down. One moment she and the child stood in the muddy current, and in the next they were gone downstream.

Karmann dove into the river after them, letting the current carry him out of the cone of blue-white light from the helicopter, away from the milling lights on the bank.

But the woman had vanished, as had the child.

THIRTY MINUTES LATER, Arkady Karmann dragged himself onto the American shore a half-dozen kilometers from the few lights that could be seen to mark the outskirts of Brownsville. He lay almost until morning on the muddy shingle, letting the rain pelt down on him. But when the sky began to lighten, he struggled to his feet, stumbled to and through a fence that had been cut to a tangle of wire bits by the horde of illegals who passed this way, and began to walk north.

Chapter Eight

Flight Level 47/November 26

The Caidin Administration seems to be in disarray over what is to be done about Anna Neville, Canadian widow of noted environmental photographer Jacob Neville. Neville is traveling under the auspices of the Canadian Committee for Nuclear Disinvestment. There have been Republican calls for a Foreign Affairs Committee investigation of rumored Pentagon involvement in the death of Jacob Neville and his pilot in an air crash in Canada last December.

—WASHINGTON ROLL CALL

FROM 4,700 FEET, the American heartland was lost in the gray haze of a winter evening. To the north, far below the fighter's altitude, Morgan could make out serried banks of stratocumulus and cumulonimbus clouds concealing the flatlands of the Dakotas under a line of thunder squalls.

In the pilot seat of the F/A-18 sat a young lieutenant of Vietnamese ancestry. The defeat in the Vietnam War had produced a remarkable generation of American-born, bright, dedicated soldiers, sailors, and airmen, children of the Vietnamese who fled the Communist victory.

Lieutenant Tran was delivering the newly refurbished F/A-18 Hornet to one of the squadrons waiting at Alameda Naval Air Station to be taken aboard the venerable USS *Nimitz*.

Lieutenant Tran had been eleven years old, and attending junior high school in Monterey, California, the year Morgan had graduated from the Naval Academy. That was something to think about, Morgan mused. He had nineteen years in with the Corps. A nuclear physics instructor at the academy had warned him, "You're bright, Mister Morgan. Too bright for your own good. I see a long and rather unmilitary career ahead of you, accumulating university degrees and weird assignments. Anything to keep you out from underfoot when the decisions are made. Try the mud Marines, Mister. You might be able to hide out among the grunts." And the instructor had been right on the money.

What is certain, Morgan thought, is that now is the time to decide what I'm going to do with the rest of my life. The trouble is that I'm restless, dissatisfied, and haven't got the faintest idea what I'd like to do. This current errand, putting the fear of God into troublemakers as they appeared, did not appeal.

In his headset, Morgan heard Tran giving Air Traffic Control an estimated time of arrival at Alameda. The Hornet was outracing the winter sun, lengthening the day.

Morgan spoke into the intercom. "Lieutenant, ask Alameda to call Mr. Cantwell at the Federal Building in San Francisco. Give him our ETA and tell him I will see him around 2100." Cantwell was the San Francisco FBI regional director. He was also a shellback who thought persons like Pierre Grau needed to be kept under tight surveillance.

"Want to take it for a while, Colonel?" The pilot's bantering voice came through the borrowed headset.

Morgan said, "I'm no Zoomie, Mr. Tran." He was rewarded with a brief chuckle and "Roger that." The face and

80

figure in the front seat were Asian, but the voice was pure California Valley Boy.

Morgan leaned against the padded armor plate behind him and closed his eyes. He was thinking of a photograph of Anna Neville he had seen in the contributor's section of *The Nature Conservancy Magazine*. Hardly a femme fatale, but she had a good face, framed by windblown auburn hair, cut short. A spray of freckles across a small nose. A mouth that could be called broad or generous, depending on how one felt about the person in the photograph. Photo by Jacob Neville, no doubt. It was difficult to guess the color of her eyes, because they were narrowed against a mountain sun. The photo had been taken, the caption said, in the Rockies.

Jake Neville had devoted his talent to showing America's warts and scars to the world and won many prizes doing so. He had chronicled the plight of homeless people sleeping on the sidewalks in New York, or in the city parks of Santa Barbara, with an almost lascivious devotion. He made photographing the sins of corporate America into a fine art. There was little balance in it, no glimpses of the many good things he could have seen all around him had he been willing to recognize them. Only oil spills, mine cave-ins, nuclear accidents, the detritus on the streets: those were his obsessions. Well, Morgan thought, it took all kinds. But what kind was Anna Neville? A real chip off the old block?

For that matter, what kind am I, Morgan wondered. He was under no illusions. His task was to neutralize Anna Neville. Intimidate her, if necessary. Well, what the hell—there weren't any wars around just now. Great work for a citizen soldier, Morgan thought ironically. Semper fi, Mac.

BARELY VISIBLE AHEAD AND TO THE LEFT, the Great Salt Lake was materializing out of the haze. The speed of the aircraft was daunting. Why was it, Morgan wondered, that men built their most ingenious machines for war. The Hornet strike fighter was nuclear-capable. It could deliver as much explosive

81

power as all the bombers that attacked Germany in World War II. There was only one superpower now. But the modern Marine Corps, Morgan thought bleakly, still existed in a world in which nations, even continents, could be devastated in minutes. Since the collapse of the Soviet Union, nuclear technology seemed free to roam the world. What price Iwo Jima and the Barbary Shore? Were the Nevilles of this world and their CCND friends quite the Luddite trogs they seemed to be?

"Colonel?" Lieutenant Tran's voice interrupted his depression. "Signal from Alameda, sir. There's a civilian waiting for you at Station Operations."

"Did they give a name?"

"No, sir. Ops officer thinks he's Naval Intelligence." In the navy they would have to be sure before making such a guess. Leaks, Morgan thought, remembering Ryerson's boast about his "source." Washington was a sieve.

"Thank you, Lieutenant. Just acknowledge."

Morgan had called Kellner's office before he left Berkshire to tell the Adviser about Ryerson's unexpected visit. Kellner had scoffed, insisting that Joe Ryerson was nothing but a nuisance. Morgan wasn't so sure. Ryerson was a jackass, but he shouldn't be taken lightly.

At Anacostia, while the Hornet had been fueling, an officer from Canadian External Affairs had intercepted Morgan, anxious to enlarge upon the Neville biographies. He had voiced some rather more free associative observations than were contained in the dossiers Morgan had read.

"It's damned important that you know there's considerable difference of opinion about La Neville in Ottawa, Colonel," the Canadian said. "Maritime Command security thinks she is an agent of influence, run straight out of the Intelligence Directorate in Moscow. RCMP thinks the ID is now just a department store, kept active to earn hard currency by selling off old KGB files. My Minister is a would-be spook. He's the one who sent me, so I'll limit myself to what he ordered me to tell you. It's true Anna Neville is George Mathis's daughter, and it's also true the Red Vicar was bolshie. But my Minister quite correctly reminds you that that's ancient history. Reverend Mathis has been dead for years. It would be straining credulity to believe his daughter was still defending the old CP barricades. She's traveled; she's seen the world. By this time, she knows the only dedicated Marxists have tenure at places like Harvard, Cambridge, and McGill, not in the Kremlin. My Minister thinks that all she really cares about is finding whoever killed her husband. And her latest lover.''

"And what about the CCND?" Morgan asked.

"Colonel, if advocating unilateral nuclear disinvestment were treason, half the congressmen and MPs in North America would be in jail."

"Point taken," Morgan said.

He sat now and thoughtfully considered his mission. Like many NSC assignments, it was deliberately vague and ill defined. Charlotte Conroy and the Adviser were too politically astute to put themselves on the record. It insulated them from failure. Or from success, if the price were suddenly deemed too high. Better a Seal mission on an undersea pipeline, a rescue assault on an African beach, a secret raid on an Iraqi army camp in Kurdish territory gathering intelligence—all of which he had done and would do again if asked or ordered with less reluctance than he now felt. In California, Morgan had one or two personal assets. He hoped he would not be forced to use them.

"Colonel? Bay Area dead ahead." In the gathering winter dusk, lights outlined San Francisco Bay. Oakland, Berkeley, and Alameda sparkled bright against the dark. The bridges glistened like necklaces of amber. The time was 1750 hours and it had begun to rain.

Chapter Nine

Cyrandell Valley, Virginia/November 26

> *Thus, at peace with God and the world,*
> *the farmer of Grand-Pre*
> *Lived on his sunny farm, and Evangeline*
> *governed his household.*

> —HENRY WADSWORTH LONGFELLOW,
> *EVANGELINE*

A MILE FROM WESTCHESTER, Camilla Varig turned her BMW off the Little River Turnpike and drove north through an increasingly wooded countryside toward Cyrandell Valley.

The night was almost cold enough to snow, but instead, a steady wind-driven rain had been falling since afternoon. The BMW's headlights caught an occasional late blaze of color from the leaves, but for the most part the woods consisted of trees standing tall and bare, branches swaying in the wind.

The car was new. Her fingers caressed the leather-covered steering wheel. It had been very expensive, she thought. The odd thing was that she enjoyed paying exorbitant prices for things. It gave her a feeling of ineffable joy to say grandly to the salesperson, "I'll take *that* one." Which usually was the most expensive item available. And now she was treated with great respect, fawned over, wherever she went to buy.

I pay in other ways, she thought. I paid dearly for my indulgences by bedding Vincent, something I endured. Driving the BMW was something she relished. And there was Marina—Marina who had changed Camilla's life forever.

She had waited months before beginning a gradual change from, as Marina put it so bluntly, "crow to peacock." She prepared Vincent with cryptic references to an inheritance and to stock market successes. More time passed before she showed Vincent her new apartment. He had to know that she now had "private funds." It would be too absurd to be tripped up by the ethics laws.

Vincent chose not to be inquisitorial. Perhaps he was piqued by her new independence. But it never occurred to him to investigate the source of her affluence. With heavy-handed humor, he had teased her about the fact that so many of her possessions now had the names or initials of the makers on them, rather than hers. Giorgio Armani, Louis Vuitton, Calvin Klein, Sonia Rykiel. "I have never understood a woman's passion for advertising someone else's creations," he said, "and for free."

You've never understood that, and a great deal more besides, Camilla thought. You're so dull, Vincent, and you haven't a clue.

MARINA HAD MADE IT POSSIBLE for Camilla to live surrounded by costly things. She had taken to grooming herself accordingly. Her thin, masculine body was honed by diet and aerobics. She had the small, high breasts and narrow, boyish hips of an Olympic athlete. When naked, she always ran her hands down over her stomach, just to make sure that it was as flat as it looked in the mirror. The thought that she might suddenly return to the plump creature she had been in childhood often haunted her.

The instrument panel clock showed 8:55. Ahead lay the Forest House, an inn and roadhouse she and Marina had discovered. It was not more than a dozen miles from the Beltway, yet it might have been on the surface of Mars for all the trade it drew from Washington. Of all the meeting places she and Marina had available, the Forest House was their favorite, the rendezvous of choice.

She slowed and pulled into the sparsely filled parking lot. On Monday nights, most of the suburban locals stayed home to watch football on television, and the Forest House did not keep a set in the lounge. Camilla sat for a moment, savoring the thrill she always felt when about to meet Marina. It was part of her secret life, and from childhood, she had kept most of her life secret from others. To keep anyone else from knowing what she thought and felt and did was the most important thing, the most thrilling thing. Her aunt had called her "sly," and had punished her for not confessing when accused of stealing small sums of money and jewelry. Her teachers had regarded her with suspicion when her test grades seemed to be higher than they ought to be. But she endured the punishment and the suspicion stoically, giving no satisfaction to others. She saved it all for herself. It had always been her way.

She locked her BMW, then stepped into the Forest House lobby and walked into the bar at precisely nine o'clock. Marina was there, on a bar stool, her long legs displayed in tight designer jeans, a beautiful sable coat draped over her shoulders, her perfume, Joy, scenting the air around her. She was watched closely by the three other bar patrons, all men. The two women kissed cheeks, in the Russian manner. The men frowned and looked away. Eat your hearts out, Camilla thought.

Marina led the way to a dark booth in the far corner of the bar. When they had settled in comfortably, Marina said with a sly smile, "And how is the Farmer of Grand-Pre?" It was their private joke, a natural name for Vincent, once they had settled on "Evangeline" as a code name for Camilla.

"Worried," Camilla said.

"Has he been hitting on you often?"

Camilla never ceased to wonder at the ease with which Suslova picked up the slangy Americanisms that came into favor year after dreary year. Her Atlantic Coast accent was nearly perfect. Only when she was excited, or aroused, did she drop articles and begin to speak with a Russian cadence.

The cocktail waitress appeared, and Marina ordered a vodka martini for herself and a sherry for Camilla. They sat in expectant silence until the girl returned with the order, and then departed. "You said the Farmer is worried?" Marina said. "About Anna Neville?"

"How did you know about Anna Neville?"

"I read the papers and watch television," the Russian said. "Worried enough to send Colonel Morgan to San Francisco."

Marina was glad to hear that Camilla was feeding Yosip Ryerson the same information that she was giving to Marina. After all, they were both preparing the ground for maximum embarrassment to Vincent Kellner and the American government. She smiled sweetly and murmured, "To arrest Neville?"

"Don't be ridiculous," Camilla said reprovingly, but softened it with a little smile. "The Farmer doesn't work that way."

Marina smiled. "What a shame. Will he have her killed?"

Camilla blinked. There are times, she thought, when we are really light-years apart.

Marina smiled intimately at her. "I shock you," she said. "No."

"But yes." Marina's smile seemed feral. "I was once an assassin. I never told you that, did I?"

"I don't believe that. And it is in damned poor taste."

"But it's true. It was what I first did for the KGB when I came in. Department V. Women are very good at such work." The smile remained.

"That's an absurd story," Camilla said.

"Poor Evangeline," Marina said, laughing. "You did believe me, didn't you? Can't you visualize me with my little gun?"

"Not for a minute." Camilla laughed obligingly, but thought, why the *hell* does she say such things?

"Tell me about the Farmer's soldier man. What is he to accomplish in San Francisco if he is forbidden to kill the client?"

"Frighten her, perhaps. Or maybe to see if Russians are involved in this affair. Perhaps you would know—Are they?"

Marina laughed. "What a question. As you say, don't be ridiculous."

The bartender glanced across the room at the sound of her laughter. Camilla winced inwardly. There was a streak of coarse recklessness in Marina Suslova that was troublesome. Reckless people were dangerous. Danger was acceptable if unavoidable. But Suslova pushed the envelope. Did the Intelligence Directorate understand that despite her talents, Marina's incautious ways might bring her to grief, and others with her?

Camilla found the possibilities fascinating, though. What would happen when and if President Cherny discovered the hand of the Intelligence Directorate in the Anna Neville affair? It was common knowledge that at least some agents were unreconstructed Communists, and others were nationalists of one kind or another. There were agents in the Intelligence Directorate who had supported the 1991 Yaneyev coup against Gorbachev. Intelligence people never really changed their objectives. Only their methods.

Camilla looked around the dark bar, all polished mahogany, soft brown leather seats, and deep carpets. Does Marina bring other assets here? she wondered. If so, it was cause for caution. The FBI ferrets were slow, but dogged. Vincent called them in often, concerned about the constant leaks from inside the Administration.

There had been leaks from every Administration since the Revolution. But just having Charlie Fisk's FBI snoopers around was unsettling. She calmed herself by considering the fact that half the counterintelligence coups in history were the result of blind luck. It was fortunate for spies and traitors, she thought, that the media never stopped trying to unearth government secrets. It was possible to blame journalists for almost anything.

"Tell me about Neville's lawyer," Marina said.

Fair enough, Camilla thought. Marina and her Service were hungry and must be fed. Judiciously, but cautiously, until I am sure how much she already knows. This game is dangerous but exhilarating. "His name is Pierre Grau," Camilla said, spinning the sherry glass by the stem.

"I already know his name."

Yes, Camilla thought, now we are on the same page.

"It *is* highly classified information," she said, giving the glass one more spin.

"Have you ever doubted my generosity?" Marina asked. "What do you need? Do you want this coat?" She stroked the sleeve suggestively.

Camilla treated the offer as if it were a joke. Only a stupid woman would consider a sable coat proper payment to an informant instead of its value in money; only a fool would accept it. "Those at my salary level do not wear coats of that quality, dear one," she said.

"What a great pity. I have more coats than money," Marina said, smiling brilliantly.

She *is* beautiful, Camilla thought with a sexual chill. That black, raven's wing hair. Eyes like gemstones, just as cold. Skin smooth as velvet. And a delightful ambiguity in her sexual preferences. All this, and a brain, too. I must be careful what I say and how I say it.

She said, confidentially, "Colonel Morgan is to deliver a message to Pierre Grau from your United Nations ambassador, Nathan Abramov."

"The Zionist," Marina murmured.

Camilla regarded the Russian speculatively. The knowledge of a meeting between Morgan and Grau might be more valuable than Camilla had assumed. What should she ask for this time?

"What are you thinking?" Marina asked.

That was a question Camilla had learned at a very early age never to answer directly. She answered with a question of her own. "You want to be kept informed about Colonel Morgan's activities?"

"Yes," Marina said. "For the time being, give me daily reports. More frequent, if you can manage it."

"*That* will be expensive," Camilla said happily.

"I know. I have learned that in the United States, all good things cost a great deal of money."

"Which is another way of saying I am greedy?"

"Of course you are. It is part of your charm."

"What will you do with the information?"

"To use your own bureaucratic phrase: you have no need to know. Now, tell me everything. I have arrangements to make."

"Tonight?" In spite of herself, Camilla was disappointed, and showed it. "I hoped we might spend an hour or two upstairs."

Marina smiled. "What a fine idea. But I had to spend this afternoon fucking a pig. Tonight, business before pleasure. Or, as your own clever people may have said, *'Geschaft vorher cunnilingus.'* "

Chapter Ten

Alameda Naval Air Station/November 27

*An epidemic of what appears to be a hitherto unknown
form of immunodeficiency syndrome is reported to have
developed among the Inuit of the Northwest Territories
in the vicinity of Eskimo Point, a fishing village on the
western shore of Hudson Bay. However, authorities in
Ottawa discount it. A spokesperson for the Department
of Indian Affairs stated yesterday: "AIDS is not a problem among Canadian Native populations."*

—MANITOBA OBSERVER

As THE HORNET ROLLED to a stop outside the Operations
Building at Alameda, a gray U.S. Navy staff car advanced to
meet it under the floodlights. The rain fell steadily, forming a
curtain through which could be seen the looming shapes of
the cantilever sections of the San Francisco-Oakland Bay
Bridge, its graceful lines limned by the amber of the sodium
vapor lights illuminating the roadbed.

Morgan came down the ladder from the Hornet's rear seat
and was met by a line crewman who informed him that a Mr.

Jones was waiting for him in the car. "I'll take care of your gear, Colonel. Will you be staying at the BOQ, or do you need transport into town?"

"Leave my things in Operations," Morgan said, "and ask the OD to get me a rental. Anything will do."

"No problem, sir." The sailor produced a GI poncho to keep Morgan dry as they walked to the car.

"How's the morale here, Sailor?" Morgan asked. Alameda was still on the Pentagon's list for closure, but the California congressional delegation managed to delay the total closing. Morgan guessed that Alameda NAS would still be navy into the twenty-first century. Congress had a way of saving constituents' jobs. Votes were hard to come by these days.

"Morale never better, Colonel. Tell Washington."

Morgan smiled and nodded.

The front right-hand door of the staff car opened, and Morgan climbed in out of the rain. Inside was a lone civilian Morgan had never seen before.

"Colonel Morgan? My name is Jones. I was asked to meet you and give you some information. I'm on leave, terminal leave. After tonight you never heard of me."

"Whatever you say."

"I'm not navy, Colonel. I'm Company. Or I was. Until last Friday, I was a case officer on the staff of Mexico City Station." He had an even-featured, nondescript face that could be forgotten in ten minutes.

Morgan and everyone else in what was loosely called "the intelligence community" was aware that a massive, if silent, RIF was in progress. Cole Caidin's work, this time. Caidin didn't like intelligence work or the agents who did it.

"I called the NSC office from Los Angeles this morning, but you were already on the way here. I actually got to speak with the great man. Not often an ordinary laborer in the vineyard gets to speak with God. He said, meet Morgan at Alameda, so I took the cattle-car flight from LAX, and here I am." Jones had an abrupt way of speaking, as though he would rather not. It was a common affliction among CIA people in the field. It was only after a tour at Langley that they learned to talk too much and write unauthorized books.

"And why, Mr. Jones?"

The sound of the rain on the metal roof was loud in the silence. This meeting was ad hoc, but if Vincent Kellner approved it, not casual.

"About six weeks ago, a man came to the embassy in Mexico City, Colonel. He was dressed like a campesino, a hungry one. He spoke Spanish almost well enough to be a native, but not quite. I am told he looked as though he had been sick or injured. Bear in mind that I never actually saw him or talked to him. The Marine guard turned him over to our ONI office. I'm sorry to say so, Colonel, but the navy isn't worth a shit at the spook business."

"You'll get no argument from me about that, Mr. Jones," Morgan said.

"In fairness—though who gives a fuck about fairness, I'll never know—he did say that he was a survivor from a Russian submarine named *Pravda*, scuttled near Cuba. I guess that made him navy property, or so the Marine guard commander figured. The man gave the name Karmann. Asked ONI not to notify the Russian embassy." A shrug. "You have to keep an open mind in the spook business, Colonel. Karmann wanted to speak with the President. Or if not the President, then the National Security Adviser. Yeah, sure. Check with the ONI office poobah. But there was a problem. Naval Intelligence's particular poobah, Commander Willis Carter Hale III, a horse's ass by any reasonable criterion, was off parasailing in Acapulco for three days. So ONI put the man up in a sleaze box hotel and said, come see us next week." Jones shrugged. "He never did. That's when our station was alerted. Though what the fuck for I can't imagine. The guy was long gone."

"Go on."

"My boss went ballistic when he heard. We checked the Langley database and turned up the Hotel-class *Pravda*, once named the *Yuri Andropov,* and before that the *Andrei Vishin-sky.* It left Kola last November to dump its armament at sea and then report to the ship breakers at Murmansk to have the nuclear pile deactivated. Never happened. *Pravda*—a nice touch that, calling a Hotel-class sub 'Truth'—did not arrive on schedule. Did not arrive at all. Finally, she was reported to the Nuclear Disarmament Commission as lost at sea with all hands.'' Jones shrugged and spread his hands. "End of story, Colonel." He hesitated and then said, "How's that for competence? ONI's not worth a fart in a barrel."

Morgan looked at the rain falling on the air station. The runway lights glowed red, green, and amber. Beyond lay the bay and beyond that, the San Francisco skyline, misty and mystical in the rainy night. "Is that an Agency sentiment, Mr. Jones, or your personal view?" Of all the secret services in peacetime, the Office of Naval Intelligence had the best opinion of itself.

"It is a generally held opinion in the Company, sir."

"I share it, Jones."

"This Karmann, Colonel. He claimed to have walked all the way from Honduras. The Mosquito Coast. That's one hell of a hike."

Morgan flashed on the images he had seen only yesterday in Kellner's office in the White House. Men in the sea. How could they all have been lost? Had the Cuban gunboat refused to pick them up? Or had something uglier happened?

Jones said, "One thing more. Odd."

"Which was?"

"This man Karmann shouldn't be impossible to find if it is really necessary. The Marine guard who first saw him at the gate reported that he was missing a hand."

"He had a prosthetic?"

"Not exactly, Colonel. He had a steel hook for a left hand. There can't be many of those around in our enlightened age, can there?"

Chapter Eleven

San Francisco, California/November 27

*The resurrection of the Neville affair would seem to call
into question the future relationship between ourselves
and the United States defense establishment. We agree
that the personal friendship between Prime Minister
Halloran and President Cole Caidin is advantageous to
both governments. But if the price of that friendship is
the violation of Canadian sovereignty by an American
Air Force now in search of another target, we say it is
too dear. Canada is not Iraq.*

—OTTAWA NEWS-CHRONICLE

FROM HER TABLE in the glassed-in section of the grill at the
Stanford Court Hotel, Anna Neville could see the steep slope
of California Street and the broad flank of the Fairmont Hotel
across the street. A cable car was climbing from Stockton to
Powell at the top of Nob Hill, looking almost excessively pic-
turesque. San Francisco, Anna thought, was a professional
photographer's dream city despite its reputation for shaking
itself to nearly pieces once or twice each century.

On the steep slope of California, the automobile traffic flowed with an elegant disdain of the slippery pavement and the narrow-gauge tracks and cable slot of the cable car system occupying the center of the street. San Franciscans clung serenely to a transportation system that was a hundred years old and notoriously unsafe. They airily ignored prudence and common sense, riding the cable car running boards, regularly falling off and injuring themselves on the brick pavements. They suffered worse injuries, and even death, when primitive caliper-style braking systems or their brawny operators failed, allowing the quaint and colorful cable cars to plunge down the steep hills out of control, costing the city huge sums of settlement money, awarded by juries of its own citizens.

Jacob Neville, an unreconstructed New Yorker, had disliked San Francisco as too theatrical, too aware of its physical elegance, too smug. Those who did sleep in the streets of San Francisco had never convinced him they were not indulging in middle-class perversity. He said the Bay Area's true ghetto was across the bay in Oakland, the city of which Gertrude Stein was reputed to have said that "there was no there there."

Jake loved to puncture other people's enthusiasms, make fun of them, especially Anna's. He was half-drunk the night before he died, telling intimate tales about his life with Anna, embarrassing Sean and humiliating her. Jake always despised Anna's lovers. It had given him an odd pleasure to recognize them as such, then to accept them, all the while showing his contempt for their animal weaknesses.

I wonder what my life would have been like if my father had not hated my mother, Anna thought. The Vicar had married in haste, waited until she was born, and swiftly divorced. Her mother had let their only daughter go to her father by default. In 1970 Christiane Mathis Piacelli had died in Portofino, where she had gone to celebrate her fifth divorce. Anna did not attend the elaborate funeral staged by her mother's last ex-husband, an Italian film producer.

The Reverend Mathis had been a poor father, but a demanding teacher. Among other things, he had taught his daughter that most of the world's ills were the fault of the United States and its laissez-faire capitalist system. During most of her adolescence and early adulthood, she believed it. There were few voices around her to deny it.

But by the time Mikhail Gorbachev appeared to speak for glasnost and perestroika, her beliefs were far more skeptical than they had been under the Red Vicar's tutelage. He had seen the Russian experiment as one grand step toward solving the world's economic ills, and was sure that any failures in that experiment stemmed not from the premise, but from human weakness in carrying out that utopian dream. What would he have thought of the shattering of the Soviet Empire and the emergence of the new Russia? It was no more desirable than the old, if what she read was true.

Jake Neville and her father had been two sides of a coin in their mutual passion for the perfect social contract. Both refused to take history or culture into account. Their grand design for the oppressed people of the world wiped all slates clean. Absolute equality in all things was their mantra, and in its pursuit, friends must be richly rewarded, enemies flayed. That had been the only sticking point in their otherwise smooth relationship—they had disagreed on how to proceed. Anna's father dreamed one could reach the Grail by reason— teach, persuade, show and tell as children did. He excused the tyranny of Russian totalitarianism as only a small obstacle on the road to Paradise, to be discarded when all had learned to cast aside earthly vices for socialist virtues. Jake fully understood the uses of terror by Lenin and Stalin, and approved of it, albeit silently. The two had lived their lives in perpetual discontent, one an optimist, the other the blackest pessimist, both yearning for unachievable perfection.

The Vicar had as much as awarded Anna to Jake for his steadfast ideology, although she never understood just why Jake had accepted his prize. She was not at all sure why she, herself, had agreed to the marriage. Nowhere to go, nothing else to do at the time? Certainly Jake had never loved her, at least not in any way she could recognize.

There were as many ways of being used, she thought, as there were men and women to use one another. On this trip it had surprised and horrified her to discover that Pierre Grau had expected *his* loyalty and labor to be rewarded in bed. God, she thought, have I become so notorious as that?

Sitting over a cooling cup of coffee, Anna Neville felt drained and weary. This is my last burden, she thought. Once it is done, once I can lay it down, I will be free. Free to pick up my cameras again if I wish, go my own way.

THE BELLS OF GRACE CATHEDRAL struck one o'clock. Rain fell steadily out of a gray sky. She sipped at her coffee and stared moodily at the street. Before she went much further, she had to decide. Did she *really* believe that the American Navy killed Jake and Sean? Jake had cried out, just before the explosion, that "they've fired a missile at us." As far as Jake was concerned, "they" could only be Canadians—which was unlikely—or Americans. What other possibilities were there in Canada's great inland sea? I've done enough photojournalism in Central American insurrections and African and Middle Eastern wars to know what surface-to-air missile tracks look like, she thought.

But Pierre and the CCND are too anxious to blame the U.S. Navy. They resist any other solution. No matter how logically and cleverly Pierre Grau tried to get Anna to reconstruct the awful happenings that December day to match his own beliefs, her doubts remained.

She had few clear recollections of the crash, but many reminders, too many of them. Her legs ached when she stood too long, especially the right leg. Not that it mattered now, but she would probably have a difficult time if she ever chose to have a child. Her fractured pelvis had healed slightly askew, according to the orthopedic surgeon who worked on her. And she bore a scar, caused by a flying shard of Plexiglas, from the corner of her right eye across her cheekbone. Plastic surgery had made it less visible, but each time she looked into a mirror she was reminded. I shouldn't care, she told herself sternly. She did care. Very much. When you were scarred, people looked at you and then looked away, especially men.

There was always the old, familiar way of assuaging her inner doubts. Pierre Grau wanted to be her next lover. Expected to be. But Anna had enough of zealots.

As a lawyer, Grau's mind worked like a microtome, cutting slices of virtual reality into ever thinner and more transparent slices until they became as clear, and as invisible, as sheets of crystal. He was an artist in argument. Jake would have said Pierre Grau was "a master of dialectic." It wasn't surprising. Pierre had spent two years as an exchange student at Moscow University. He spoke of that time in his life in glowing terms.

Certainly Jake would have admired the way Grau put his case to the Public Broadcasting producer whom they had come to see at KQED. He was forceful, articulate, and impressive, even if he was preaching to the choir. Anna waited now for Pierre to return from his absolutely must do visit to the Canadian Consul General's office to arrange financing from the CBC for a joint venture with PBS.

She knew that she was being used by the CCND, and she was sorry for it. But she was using them as well. She hadn't the funds and resources to carry on her quest for the truth. She needed their money. She would have preferred to carry on independently, but she could not. Jake had always spent their fees as quickly as they came in. So there was an end to it. One made hard choices.

A cable car stopped at the corner of California and Powell streets. Anna saw Pierre step from the running board to the pavement. He waited on the steep street while the car, clanging its insouciant bell, climbed on toward the Pacific Union Club at the top of the hill.

Pierre was a tall, thin man who looked older than his forty years despite his efforts to mimic the younger members of his movement. He had probably lost most of his hair while still in law school, Anna thought. Unfortunately, he drew attention to his baldness by allowing what hair he had to grow long and then carefully combing it across his narrow head. It made him look like old pictures of General Douglas MacArthur, rather than the rakish fellow he wished to be. Since traveling with Anna, he had taken to wearing a strong cologne, the scent of which she found distasteful. His clothes were plain but expensive, disguising his thin-shouldered, long-shanked body. For all his directed brilliance, he seemed unaware that Anna found his attentions unwelcome.

Grau looked both ways—he was a cautious man—before stepping across the cable car tracks toward the Stanford Court's entrance. A muddy Ford Bronco, looking like an armored personnel carrier on its immense cleated tires, appeared from Stockton Street and rounded onto California. Its tinted glass windshield made it look driverless, blind and threatening. A light bar with four driving lamps spanned the roof. It was the sort of vehicle much favored by survivalists, out of place on Nob Hill. The huge tires screeched as they crossed the cable car tracks. Pierre Grau was ten steps from the curb and safety when the Bronco swerved deliberately into the oncoming traffic. The bumper and front fender struck him, flinging him high into the air, then back across the broad hood. Anna watched in shock. Grau hit the windshield, leaving a dark smear; then he fell to the pavement, sprawling there like a bundle of rags, legs on the cable car tracks, head toward the hotel. The driver of a Mercedes heading down California Street slammed on the brakes, but skidded on the slick pavement and could not stop until the front wheels had bumped over Pierre's body.

Anna sat, stunned at what she had witnessed. A woman sitting at the next table screamed. Customers bolted from their chairs to stare, horrified but curious, through the windows at the gathering crowd and confusion in the middle of California Street. Anna, finally able to move, reached for her purse, ran to the door, and pushed her way out to the street. A distraught and horrified middle-aged woman was standing, weeping, beside the open door of the Mercedes. She was explaining to anyone who would listen that "he was just *there*—there was nothing I could do—"

The Bronco had vanished.

JULIAN WALCOTT, the prim young man from the Canadian Consul General's office, was apologetic. "It is a terrible thing, Mrs. Neville. The lawlessness in this country—in this city— is unbelievable, but it was an accident and there is nothing our government can do except cooperate with the local people." He regarded Anna Neville's bleak expression with discomfort. They stood in the ugly, impersonal waiting room outside San Francisco General's trauma center. It was filled with weary people, awaiting news about their loved ones, good or bad. The air was cold and medicinal. The night sounds of a busy public hospital echoed against the bare walls and glass partitions.

Walcott, a junior consular officer under stress, made an effort to turn aside what he regarded as Anna Neville's silent accusation. He said almost plaintively, "Everything that could have been done for Mr. Grau has been done, Mrs. Neville. Please believe me."

The old brick hospital was located in the southern part of the city near the Lick Freeway, where it joined the approaches to the Bay Bridge. This was a vehicular battleground. The staff at San Francisco General was prodigiously experienced in treating the injuries inflicted by automobiles and by gunshots.

Pierre Grau had been alive when he arrived, though just barely. For three hours the trauma team had performed heroic feats. But thirty minutes ago, at 9:47 P.M., Grau had died without regaining consciousness.

"It was a ghastly accident, Mrs. Neville," Walcott said as firmly as he could manage. He stood first on one foot, then the other. This unfortunate affair had ruined his plans for dinner and an evening at the symphony.

"Mr. Walcott," she said in a low, weary voice, "I saw what happened. The car swerved almost all the way across the street to hit Pierre. It was murder."

The Canadian glanced uneasily across the waiting area to where a man in a police lieutenant's uniform was engaged in murmured conversation with an FBI agent named Cantwell and a tall, slender, dark-haired man Walcott did not recognize.

"A hit-and-run case to be sure, Mrs. Neville. But hardly murder," Walcott said reproachfully. He was tempted to say that she apparently had chosen a way of life that drew misfortunes, but he decided against it. It would be offensive to point out such an obvious truth.

"Have you told the CCND, Mr. Walcott?"

"They will be notified by the Ministry. Did Mr. Grau have a family? Other than yourself?"

"Mr. Grau and I are not related, Mr. Walcott."

"Of course, I did not mean to imply—" Walcott flushed in confusion. From what he had been told, he naturally assumed that Neville and the lawyer were "involved." Anna Neville was, well, not exactly a nun. She was not conventionally pretty, but now that he looked more closely, she did have something. Could you call it sex appeal? Such an old-fashioned phrase.

He said, "There's no family?"

No, Anna thought, Pierre had no one. No one but the fellow zealots of the CCND. A fanatical loyalty to what he called "The Movement" dominated his life. He had been an unattractive, arrogant, pedantic sort of man who had found a home in the CCND. Now he had found his death, never knowing at whose hand and in what service it came. She closed her eyes for a moment, overcome by a wave of lassitude before she answered. "No family," Anna said.

"That's a blessing, at least," Walcott said.

"A blessing?"

"I am dreadfully sorry. I did not mean that the way it sounded."

"Is that all, Mr. Walcott?"

"Unless there is something further I can do for you, Mrs. Neville?" He fervently hoped she would refuse, and it showed.

"Thank you, no," Anna said.

Walcott looked at his watch. He had been at the hospital since six and was anxious to leave. His position, the position of his government, would be that the death was an American problem now.

JOHN MORGAN, standing close to the door to the waiting room with FBI agent Cantwell and the San Francisco police lieutenant, overheard the last exchange between Anna Neville and the consul. Judging from the look on the woman's face, she was not familiar with the ways of junior diplomats. Many people had heard of the diplomatic distaste for facing unpleasant facts, but very few had ever dealt intimately with that distaste.

Anna Neville looked pallid with latent shock and fatigue, but she was dry-eyed. Perhaps Pierre Grau was not the sort of man for whom one wept.

Agent Cantwell said sourly, "Why the hell did he have to come to *my* town to get himself greased?"

Anna Neville would get small comfort from the locals, Morgan thought. She had a good face, he decided, prettier and thinner now than the one in the photograph, and marked with a scar from eye to cheek. Her hair fell across it in a wave that partially obscured the scar, a bow to a vanity she probably would have denied. She was tired and in some pain. It showed in every movement and gesture. How long had she been out of the hospital, Morgan wondered. Not long.

The Canadian offered Anna Neville a word or two more of empty condolence, then hurried out of the waiting area and down the long, prisonlike hall.

Morgan smoothed the lapel of his tweed jacket, hoping he

103

looked more like a sympathetic civilian than an adversarial American militarist. He said good-bye to Cantwell and the police lieutenant and walked across the room to Anna Neville.

"Mrs. Neville? My name is John Morgan. May I speak with you?"

"Do I know you, Mr. Morgan? I don't mean to be impolite, but I have been here a long time."

She looked at him blankly and swayed. Morgan took her arm and said, "I'm a federal officer, Mrs. Neville. I'll see that you get back to your hotel." She looked too exhausted to protest. "What you really need," Morgan said, "is a drink, and then some food."

FBI Agent Cantwell, ready for a turf fight, walked across the room and said, "Who's taking charge here, Colonel?"

"I just did," Morgan said, and guided Anna Neville out of the cold, ugly room.

Chapter Twelve

Jardines de Ia Reina, Cuba/November 27

Thank you—that through the years of our ordeal—You helped us hold ground until the fight was through. Though our belief in ourselves may have dimmed, Comrade Stalin, we never doubted You.

—MIKHAIL VASILYEVICH ISAKOVSKY,
A WORD TO COMRADE STALIN, 1947

Our Revolution is Forever.
—RAUL CASTRO

SOMETIME ZAMPOLIT VIKTOR KRASNY awoke in total darkness to the sound of the sea clamoring against the corrugated iron breakwater below his isolated cell. Half-naked, he was slimy with sweat. The humidity made the very air weep in this hellhole, he thought. For a man accustomed to colder climates, solitary imprisonment on Cayo de las Doce Leguas—the most isolated of the group of rocks in the sea known as "the gardens of the Queen"—was a refinement of torture even the Gulag never achieved.

Alfred Coppel

He lay for a measureless instant on his plank bed, certain he had heard something unusual—the sound of a boat approaching the single pier and the guardhouse. It was not time yet to change the guards, who must have committed some serious military transgressions to be assigned to Cayo de las Doce Leguas. They were allowed to spend one day in ten on the big island, but never, Cabo Roberto assured Krasny, any nearer civilization than Jucaro or Tunas de Zaza, two villages miles off the beaten track to Cienfuegos.

Krasny had been confined on Twelve League Key for nearly a year. He had failed to keep accurate count of the days, because he had—for the first five months, at least—been certain that Raul Castro would soon order his release. General Kondratiev had assured him that Fidel's brother was a Soyuz comrade.

But Raul Castro's messenger had never come, and now in late November, almost a year from the day the Soyuz missile was planted at the bottom of Hudson Bay, Captain Lieutenant Viktor Stepanovich Krasny, former political officer of the Soviet navy, still rotted on this miserable, piss-smelling rock between the Gulf of Ana Maria and the Caribbean Sea. The injustice of his situation was wearing his endurance thin. And lately, in the darkness he seemed to see shadowy figures stalking his cell as he tried to go to sleep, figures whose familiar faces mocked him. "Come join us," they whispered, "join us in hell—"

He swung his naked legs off the plank on which he slept and heard the alarmed scorpions and roaches scuttle back to their crevices in the concrete walls. He stood, scratched himself awake, and grasped the bars of his single, narrow window facing the pier and the barracks.

There *was* a new boat at the pier, a small launch with the running lights still on. Soldiers of the garrison stood approximately to attention on the pier. Krasny had never seen the guardians of this military shit pile behave in so soldierly a fashion. Whoever had arrived on the launch must be important.

His mind began to gallop. The soldiers had been gossiping about Fidel. With the Maximum Leader having been ill for three years, what would come after him was always on the people's minds. Krasny had been told by the ever-informative Corporal Roberto that any talk about a Cuba without Fidel was strictly forbidden among the military. That Raul Castro would become Maximum Leader in name as well as in fact was a foregone conclusion.

He rattled his tin dish against the bars. Like a prisoner in an American film, he thought.

"*Hola, Cabo Roberto! Hola!* What is happening down there?"

He was filled with a bursting certainty what had transpired. Old Fidel had finally breathed his last. That simply had to be it. Fidel was dead and Raul was ready to pay his debt to General Kondratiev, who had dispatched to Havana the entire cache of KGB files on Latin America. Kondratiev had also persuaded the Minister of Defense to start again to send Russian arms to the Cuban armed forces, and he had miraculously managed to find money to pay for the use of Cienfuegos Naval Base. It was all coming round at last, Krasny thought triumphantly.

"*Hola! Roberto! Tell me who is here!*"

When there was finally a response, Krasny almost sang for joy. When the new government is formed, I shall ask to be ambassador to Havana, he thought.

He was suddenly pierced by an almost unbearable sexual desire that had been absent since his confinement. He had a sudden vivid memory of a girl sailor he had seduced aboard a supply ship when first he became a political officer. Firm fleshed, clean, young. So long, he thought, since I have had anything like that.

A pair of soldiers in clean, well-cut uniforms were marching up the path to his hut. It was true, he thought triumphantly. All of his imaginings were finally true. The debt had come due and would be paid.

Alfred Coppel

* * *

A FULL COLONEL OF INTELLIGENCE in newly pressed uniform greeted Krasny at the quayside. He spoke to his escort in Spanish, then to Corporal Roberto. The corporal looked apprehensive. As well he should, Krasny thought. Debts of all kinds were going to be paid.

The colonel was young, in his mid-twenties. He wore a trimmed beard, black, but already streaked with gray. Did they all do that for effect, to imitate Fidel, Krasny wondered. When he was a child he remembered that Stalinesque moustaches had been very popular among apparatchiks in Sverdlosk, where he had grown up. What styles will we Soyuz popularize when we take power, he wondered.

"I am Coronelo Alberto Sanchez-Diaz," the soldier said. "You are to leave the gardens of the Queen." A wintry smile briefly touched his narrow face.

Not "Companero Coronel," Krasny noted. Yes, things were changing swiftly. But there was something chilling about this man, nonetheless. Why am I put in mind of Feliks Dzerzhinsky? What an odd idea, Krasny thought.

He could hear the launch's engines burbling in the hot, dark night. The smell of the sea was very strong.

Sanchez-Diaz said, "Fidel is dead. Raul is Maximum Leader. Do you wish more explanation?"

"Let's just get aboard and leave this forsaken place," Krasny said. *This rock where I thought I might spend all my days*—

"Of course," the colonel said. "Very sensible. Step aboard the launch, *Preso* Krasny."

Preso? Prisoner Krasny? He had been shoved aboard before he could react to the manner of address. The soldiers leaped aboard after the colonel and stood on either side of him. The man at the helm advanced the throttle and the launch put out from the pier swiftly.

The last thing Krasny saw of Cayo de las Doce Leguas was the single yellowish light on the end of the pier, with Corporal

Roberto standing there, looking out to sea and being joined, one by one, by his soldiers.

He addressed the colonel with an anxious formality. It was as well to establish perquisites and rank here and now. *"Tovarishch Polkovnik* Sanchez-Diaz, you addressed me as 'Prisoner' Krasny."

"So I did."

It *was* Dzerzhinsky he resembled. The same narrowly cut face and sharp features. The same shadowed, dead black eyes. Krasny felt a shiver of fear and sat down on the lazaret, his heart pounding, his legs weak. He found he could not speak, even to protest.

The launch headed steadily westward. The stars shone yellow through the heat haze. These were not the cool northern stars of Russia. They were the heat-distorted lights of a tropical night. Thirty minutes, not more, from Twelve League Key, the colonel gave an order. The soldier at the wheel turned off the engines and the launch slid soundlessly through the black sea.

"Why are we stopping?" Krasny asked hoarsely.

"You know," the Cuban said quietly.

Krasny's bones turned to water. "Oh God," he muttered. "Oh God, help me. Why?" His voice rose to a scream.

"Shut him up," the colonel ordered, and one of his aides sprang forward, striking Krasny across the mouth. As the scream died to a whimper, the Cuban said reasonably, "You must know that you are an embarrassment to your friends in Russia. And to our government, now that we are negotiating with the Americans for an immediate lifting of all sanctions. Why Fidel let you live so long is a mystery to all of us. But he was forgetful toward the end."

Krasny stared at him in despair, unmindful of the blood trickling from his mouth. This was the way it ended, then. After all he had done for the cause. Not senile Fidel, but sullen, silent Raul had agreed to clean up a small detail for Kondratiev, *an embarrassment,* just as Krasny had cleaned up the small detail of the *Pravda* and the eighty men of her crew. Their dead faces seemed to materialize in the mist over the deck. Their whispers grew louder. "Join us in hell—"

"Hold him at the rail," the colonel said in Spanish. The soldiers hauled him to his feet and held him bent over the rail.

Colonel Sanchez-Diaz put his pistol to the base of Krasny's skull and pulled the trigger. The explosion was mingled with a sound like a watermelon smashing.

"Over," he said.

Viktor Krasny vanished in the darkness.

"It never fails to astonish me," Colonel Sanchez-Diaz said, handing his pistol to a soldier to be cleaned, "how simply these things are done."

Chapter Thirteen

The Northwest Territories/61.07 N 89.90 W/November 27

The clock on the masthead of the Bulletin of the Atomic Scientists, which once showed a time of three minutes to midnight, has been moved back for the second time in this half-decade. The hands now stand at twenty minutes to midnight, indicating how far the threat of nuclear war has receded. For which our grateful thanks to an enlightened administration in Moscow.

—CCND NEWSLETTER

COLD, DEEP NIGHT LIES over the Northwest Territories and Hudson Bay. The air temperature stands at minus 14 degrees Celsius. White-capped waves clash in a steep chop with the offshore currents. Winds of almost hurricane force lash the surface of the bay and flatten the frozen marsh grasses along the shore. Elk and caribou shelter as best they can in the frozen taiga. Many are dying. Seals and otters swim under the ice, dreaming dreams of a spring they will not live to see.

In the cold dark, the Device's onboard computer counts the seconds, hours, days. The launch erector, product of Acade-

mician Orgonev's practical genius, prepares for deployment. And from the missile's modified casing, product of Academician Orgonev's criminal carelessness, plutonium continues to leak. It has turned the bay bottom and the nearby shore into a poisonous pit.

The nearest person capable of recognizing the fatal signs is a National Health physician at Churchill, Manitoba, six hundred miles from the Device. His name is James Clark and he will pay for his discovery with his life.

Chapter Fourteen

Sochi, Russia/November 27

A totalitarian system leaves behind it a minefield built into both the country's social structure and the individual psychology of its citizens. And mines explode each time the system faces the danger of being dismantled and the country sees the prospect of genuine renewal.

—ANATOLY SOBCHAK, MAYOR OF ST. PETERSBURG

It is given out that I have been relieved for the safety of the State. This is a lie. I have never threatened the State. It is given out that I have corrupted this organization with nationalistic agitation. This too is a lie. Love for the Holy Russian Motherland does not corrupt. Only weakness and compliance to the will of foreigners and Masons and Zionists do that. Russian comrades, remember me!

—GENERAL PIOTR KONDRATIEV IN HIS FAREWELL TO THE BLACK BERET INTERNAL SECURITY BATTALIONS

"LOOK AT HIM, MISHA; see how far we have fallen."

General Piotr Kondratiev, at his ease in czarist-style silk tunic and uniform trousers, was the Russian romantic's ideal of the pan-Slavic leader. Tall, but solid to the point of bulkiness, he was deep-chested and square-jawed as a Soviet heroic statue. His complexion was pale, his eyes deep set and blue, and his only slightly graying hair blond. He might have been thought handsome but for his mouth. It was small and thin-lipped, a torturer's mouth. A bitter, plotter's mouth.

Kondratiev had been a young officer in the KGB at the time of the attempted coups in the early nineties. He had watched Yaneyev and his followers at close range, tallied their failures. Later he had raged at the rebellious and inept parliament, their panic as they allowed Russia to slip from their grasp into Boris Yeltsin's after a few cannon shots. He had resolved even then that if he ever had such opportunities, he would not so misuse them.

On the television the colors were muted. It was three in the afternoon and raining in Moscow. Red Square glistened. Phalanxes of children waving bouquets of flowers and holding aloft soggy blue, white, and red banners with soggy blue, white, and red slogans plodded through the rainy square.

Atop the now-empty mausoleum, Aleksandr Cherny, swathed in fur coat, scarf, fur hat, boots, and gloves, returned the children's salute with a stiff wave. Behind him, banked flags of the Russian armed forces gave precedence to more blue, white, and red: the insipid striped flag of the new Russian state.

"Asshole," Kondratiev said contemptuously. "Barbarian."

"Don't underestimate the son of a bitch," Mikhail Orgonev said as he sucked asthmatically on a tube connected to a cylinder of oxygen. "He's devious as hell."

In the center of the circle of men seated in the gun room of General Kondratiev's seaside dacha, Orgonev—always "Misha" to Kondratiev—stared angrily at the spectacle on the television screen. This celebration was a pitiful substitute for

114

the spectacle of Revolution Day, once celebrated by the entire empire on November 7. This travesty was called National Day.

Piotr Kondratiev had no intention of underestimating the schoolteacher in Moscow. He stood by Orgonev with a glass of vodka in his hand and watched the unimpressive figures on the top of the mausoleum. Orgonev glared at the images on the screen. It was almost more than the old scientist could bear. Breath wheezed in and out of his rotting lungs, driven by impotent fury. Orgonev had a vast capacity for anger.

"There's Yulin, the treacherous bastard," he said. "Look at him. He hasn't even the balls to wear his uniform."

Ivan Yulin had been brought out of retirement to take over as chairman of the ID, once Kondratiev had been passed over for election to the Executive Committee of the parliament and then swiftly dismissed. Yes, Kondratiev thought, the old bastard in the Kremlin is devious enough for a dozen men.

Yulin looked stolid, cold, and uncomfortable in the lineup atop the black marble cube. Well he might. It was rumored among members of the nomenklatura that the bourgeois Cherny planned to dismantle the domestic branch of the Security Service once and for all. Everyone remembered the KGB intrigues that had alienated the Americans during the Gulf War, and the KGB had been at least peripherally involved in the failed Yaneyev coup in 1991. But Ivan Yulin was a trimmer, capable of being on several sides of any question. The consensus on Yulin was that he knew how to survive.

Intelligence assets, all formerly belonging to the First Chief Directorate of the KGB, were to be handed over to the rival GRU, the Military Intelligence Directorate of the General Staff. And—ultimate lunacy—eventually, to the civil police, the militia.

The mausoleum had housed Lenin's papery corpse as recently as last January. But at the New Year, the mayor of Moscow had ordered the body removed and buried as Lenin's wife had always wished. With proper honors, of course.

Piotr Kondratiev had never been a worshiper of Lenin, even

in the days before perestroika. But he disapproved of the desecration of the dead. Not out of any respect for the dead Lenin, but because the move was still another rejection of the nation's history. Whatever direction Cherny imagined he was leading Mother Russia, it could not be allowed.

A rattling snore made him turn his attention from the screen. He looked with distaste at Admiral Eduard Aleyev, commander of the Pacific Fleet, who lay sprawled in an armchair, heavily asleep. An empty vodka glass was in his lap. His dress-blue uniform trousers were stained with food and liquor. The admiral had once been a good officer. He was now a drunk—another loss attributable to the ruinous path first laid out by Gorbachev.

Kondratiev surveyed his guests. Some, like Aleyev, were useless but had to be included. Others had real value. Yuri Kalinin, for example, at age forty-nine the youngest general in the air force. Kondratiev studied Kalinin's handsome, narrow face. The man was bored and exasperated, not knowing why he had been asked—commanded, actually—by the Soyuz council to attend. His thoughts were transparent, for anyone to read.

Kalinin stirred in his chair. What good, he was thinking, did it do to glare at the television screen and call out insults? When were these old farts ever going to get to the point of this meeting? As far as Kalinin could tell, no actual details of how to handle the takeover of the government had been decided; certainly he had been told only the barest sketch of the overall plan.

Kalinin glanced around the room in the dacha. So, President Cherny thought he could buy General Kondratiev's goodwill by allowing him to keep his privileges at the same time Cherny took away Kondratiev's power. This house on the sea, for example, a dozen kilometers north of the Georgian border. Is Kondratiev playing games with the group, he wondered, keeping Cherny informed? It seemed unlikely, but then—

Misha Orgonev was telling anyone willing to listen how it

was that Russia had never been willing to develop all the dainty, "humane" weapons the Americans were so proud of, but which had never been tried in battle. "Wait, brothers," he called out in his papery, asthmatic voice. "Wait for the moment when *our* weapons find their proper use. No laser-stunning guns, no electric bolts to incapacitate trucks and tanks. We will leave that to the Americans." He glared at his listeners and sucked on his oxygen tube. "We will *destroy* our enemies," he finished triumphantly.

Misha had a warrior's mind, Kondratiev thought, but he had a fool's temperament. Here he was, crowing about the Device in front of one and all, and this was not the time for it. Not quite yet.

NOW THE TELEVISION SCREEN showed a musical unit of the air force marching past the mausoleum, the airmen-musicians playing Ukrainian folk tunes. General Kalinin got up and paced around the room. He had been a cosmonaut until the funds for space exploration had run out. Kalinin considered this a national humiliation, a vicious blow to the country's prestige. A lack of money was no excuse, and going begging to the Americans for joint projects was worse.

His own service's contribution to this National Day parade consisted of a very short flyover of a division of old Ilyushin swing-wings, and a very poor marching band that slogged through the rain playing folk music. How wonderful. Kalinin regarded the others in the room, still apparently spellbound by the marching figures, with ironic amusement. Why are we here, he wondered. Just to play at solidarity with Kondratiev, our powerless leader? This gathering was a cheap show. In Stalin's day, it would have taken real courage for a roomful of senior officers to meet with a cashiered general. But with Cherny in the Kremlin, this was no more than a kind of rump military parliament. Perhaps it was all useless; perhaps he should have joined with many of his fellow officers in cooperating with the Americans. Then his eyes fell on Kondratiev.

117

Kondratiev returned Kalinin's gaze steadily. There is magnetism in the man, Kalinin thought, beyond argument, but at the same time a streak of recklessness. Since "retiring" to Sochi, Kondratiev had taken to indulging many fantasies and fancies, designing a colorful new uniform for himself covered with gold braid. Ah, thought Kalinin, if playing dress-up would bring down those fools on the television screen and wipe out the memories of a near-century of rule by the dirty-fingernailed proletariat. If only . . .

Kalinin walked to a side table where a forest of liquor bottles stood and poured himself a glass of vodka, a huge one. Supplies for an expedition into the open air. The stink of old liquor and stale tobacco smoke in the room was overpowering, and he had to get out.

He stepped past the porcelain stove, fully stoked and radiating heat like a blue-and-white sun, and walked along the side of the room to the door. The orderly guarding it came to attention and asked, "You wish to go out, Excellency?"

Excellency? None of that Comrade General shit at Sochi. He nodded, and the man opened the door, bowing slightly. Kalinin glanced at the gross face as he passed. An informer? A Chernyite spy? He thought not. The man was a prime example of what the Germans used to call the *lumpenproletariat*. The orderly was an urban peasant who, without the state to house, clothe, and feed him, would be found frozen and dead some winter morning, because he had got drunk and had no comrades to lift him out of the snow. Kalinin had a strong feeling that Kondratiev understood this very well.

Once outside, he breathed in the cool, wet air, dilating his nostrils like a hunting animal. Yuri Kalinin had seen some action as a fighter pilot in Afghanistan as a junior officer, but his role there had been minimal. He had not arrived in country until after the Afghans received their American Stingers. The presence of that weapon had changed the entire nature of the war. A predator sought prey, not a contest. He had understood this well the first time he violated his commander's orders and made a low-level attack on a hillside bunker of bandits. It had almost been the end of him.

Next had come participation in the cosmonaut program. He had loved it, but it had ended abruptly with the collapsing economy. Then he had been posted to Air Transport, rushing to move all possible conventional weapons to the other side of the Urals, away from the scrutiny of any Conventional Arms treaty makers. That duty had introduced him to Kondratiev. He belonged to a group of high-ranking officers who were busy selling military materiel to the highest bidders and getting rich in the process. Those who were excluded called it criminal, the blackest of black markets. I prefer to describe myself as one of the new capitalists, Kalinin thought proudly. And a man needed the money—not rubles, but hard currencies, dollars, pounds, deutsche marks. In these parlous times, money was power.

Through his lofty connections, he had avoided service as an adviser to the Bosnian Serbs, instead devoting himself to his military advancement, and he had succeeded at that, too. And yet—He looked back at the low log house, watching the nearly invisible heat waves from the great porcelain stove waft out of the chimney into the rainy air. We are all alike here, Kalinin thought. It was a kind of epiphany. We are all disappointed men, all desperate men, dreams dissipating before our eyes, like the waves of unharnessed heat from a chimney.

It is not what we dreamed of, Kalinin thought. Not what we expected. Not what we deserve. From that single fact, the desperation flows in a bitter, angry river.

Across the narrow road and beyond a low line of dunes lay the Black Sea. He could see the horizon. It was shrouded with heavy, dark clouds. Occasionally a streak of lightning, like a thread of sunfire, snaked down from the clouds to the sea. He waited, counting the seconds, until the thunder rolled in. As the sound rumbled past, Piotr Kondratiev emerged from the house carrying a fresh bottle of vodka by the neck. He strode across the wet grass to stand beside Kalinin. ''Couldn't stand it anymore?'' Kalinin asked him.

Kondratiev shook his head. "That was quite a gathering of vultures on the mausoleum. And to see the Jew Milstein in that place of honor—it is enough to make one puke." He refilled Kalinin's glass and lifted the bottle. *"Nazdrovya."*

Kalinin raised his glass and drained it, letting the icy vodka cut the stale taste in his mouth. His spirits rose and his doubts about Kondratiev's motives vanished. Kondratiev knew how to solve problems, who to recruit. "Have you heard from the Chechen mafia? Will they be with us when the time comes?"

"Not yet," Kondratiev said, and spat on the ground to show his distaste of the gangsters and criminals who dominated black marketeering in Russia. "They're coy—they're waiting until we succeed. It's just as well. The last thing we want is for our enemies to claim that we have been party to mafia crimes. But they'll come around, the gypsies, the Lyuberts and the Baumanskaya, and all the rest. They'll have to—or else we will finish them."

"What about the other six hundred or so political parties, if they can be called that?"

"Most of them we don't want under any circumstances. They may be at the mercy of Masonic conspiracies, for all we know. Following the lead of the arch-Mason, Kellner."

"And the money—have the Iraqis sent the money? I'm told that the Iranians and the Libyans have contributed."

The ex-chairman of the KGB smiled. "We have all we need." He lifted the vodka bottle and inspected its contents. "So, you are to be appointed Air Defense commander for the Greater Moscow Area, as of the first of the month, Kalinin."

The postings of senior officers were supposed to be the highest secrets of state. But nothing was secret in Cherny's Moscow. Of course Kondratiev would have been informed. "Yes," Kalinin said.

"I don't believe you've been brought up to date on the latest developments, my son," Kondratiev said, his voice hushed. He looked around carefully, then draped his arm across Kalinin's shoulders. "We have contacted our friends among the Japanese and the Chinese to tell them they have nothing to fear from us. The date has been set. We move on the day Orgonev's Device changes the world."

Chapter Fifteen

San Francisco, California/November 28

*Fascism can never take root in the former Soviet Union.
The memory of the Nazi invasion and sixty million casualties makes "Russian fascism" an oxymoron.*

—THE CLEMMONS UNIVERSITY REVIEW

AT TWO HOURS AFTER MIDNIGHT Morgan and Anna Neville
sat in the bar of the Bella Italia restaurant at the foot of Hyde
Street. They were the last patrons. The bartender polished his
glasses slowly but thoroughly, patiently waiting for them to
leave. Through the steamed windows facing Beach Street and
the bay could be seen the fog-dimmed lights of a departing
ship moving toward the Golden Gate and the open Pacific.
The Golden Gate Bridge towers were blanketed by the mist,
glowing from within with the light of the sodium-vapor lights
on the span.

"Two o'clock," Anna Neville said in a thin, strained voice.
"A brave new day coming."

"Do you want to go back to your hotel?" Morgan asked.

"No. Do I have to?"

"Of course not."

Anna's food was untouched. Her eyes burned and her belly felt as though it contained a ball of lead. Her breathing was still punctuated by the trembling inhalations of a shattered child.

She could not lose the image of Pierre Grau smashing against the windshield of that dusty, dark car. Everything that had passed between that moment and now seemed disconnected, but too terribly real.

Morgan said quietly, "It might help to talk about it."

Anna Neville shot a suspicious glance at him, then looked away.

Who was this man? *What* was he? Why was she here with him?

"You will have to, sooner or later," Morgan said.

She looked across the table at Morgan. Both Pierre and Jacob would have been furious with her for coming with him as she had done, docile as a sheep. The FBI man had called him "Colonel Morgan," although he had introduced himself only as John Morgan. She had been raised to dislike and distrust soldiers, even those wearing civilian clothes. In fact, he was the first soldier she had ever talked to, though she'd seen enough of them with their shields and helmets, flak jackets and bayonets, shoving, beating, sometimes shooting protestors no matter what country they were "protecting." For all she knew, this man might be with the CIA, Jake's particular bête noire, and the agency he would have most surely have named as responsible for the death of Pierre Grau.

Then why am I here, Anna asked herself. When Morgan took charge of her at the hospital, she had surrendered with scarcely a murmur, without even asking to see his credentials. Was she so eager to avoid decisions that she would put herself in the hands of a stranger?

As they were in the car on the way to the restaurant, Morgan had explained to her that he was on the staff of President Caidin's National Security Adviser, Vincent Kellner. Assum-

ing that he was telling the truth, she found that just as frightening as the possibility he was from the CIA. Lieutenant
Colonel Oliver North had been from the NSC, after all. Yet
she found it difficult to keep her guard high. Morgan was a
good-looking man, with blue eyes and black hair, just like
Sean McCarthy and some of the others.

My God, she thought, have I become that promiscuous?

Anna looked away from Morgan. Outside the fog grew
thicker. It was unseasonal, she thought distractedly. It was in
summertime that the fog was said to blanket San Francisco.
She closed her eyes and thought of Canadian summer, of green
meadows and pine forests, and in the far north, the taiga brilliant with wildflowers. Summertime was not a season for
death. But winter was.

"Mrs. Neville . . ."

She emerged from her reverie with a start. How long had
Morgan been speaking to her?

"Yes, Colonel."

"Almost everyone who knows me just calls me Morgan."

He smiled at her. So far he'd not put a foot wrong. He was
trying to be kind, and now her instinct warned her that she
should not discourage him. Where there is danger, a man can
be useful.

"I have to be blunt," Morgan said. "This isn't over yet.
You must not be under any false impressions. The people who
killed Grau will almost certainly come after you, try to kill
you, too."

Suspicion flashed through her like a wind-driven fire. Pierre
had warned constantly that the Americans would try to silence
"the Anna Neville story."

"Who, Colonel? Who could 'they' be?"

"How well did you know Pierre Grau?"

"Pierre first came to see me when I was in hospital in Ottawa. He brought an offer of help at a time when I was desperate to find someone to listen to me. He had heard—" She
broke off and fell into tense silence.

124

"Please. I need to know if I'm going to be of any use."

Of any use to whom, she wondered. "I told the Maritime Command doctor on the rescue airplane what had really happened. The government tried to keep it secret, but the aircrew talked. There are lots of CCND sympathizers in Canada," she said defiantly. "Even in the military. And they can't all be Communists, Colonel."

"Did I say they were, Mrs. Neville?" Morgan brushed aside the contentious thrust and said, "So, you told the investigators you were shot down by a surface-to-air missile. An American missile. Is that the way it was?"

"Yes. More or less."

"More or less?"

"I have never claimed I knew for certain that it was an American weapon."

"Who suggested to you that it was?"

"No one *suggested* it, Colonel."

"Are you familiar with the flight profile of American surface-to-air missiles?"

Anna flushed. "My husband knew what a SAM looked like."

"Then it was Jacob Neville who identified the missile. Not the pilot."

"Sean said nothing about it. He was too busy trying to save our lives."

"McCarthy flew for Canada in the Gulf. He was familiar with such weapons," Morgan said.

"You investigated Sean?"

"Yes."

"And me."

"That, too, Mrs. Neville."

"Pierre said you would."

Morgan chose his words carefully. To his mind, many in the CCND organization were positively paranoid about the Americans. "Did Grau suggest that we might want him dead?"

Anna Neville winced at the forthright question. Her expression showed all too plainly how confused she was.

"I'm sorry, Mrs. Neville," Morgan said. "But what happened to Grau changes all the rules. Simple mistakes and pure accidents begin to be perceived as lies."

"There *was* a submarine, Colonel."

"In Hudson Bay."

Anna Neville's angry tone told him how many times she had heard that skeptical rejoinder. "Yes, Colonel, in Hudson Bay. I took photographs of it."

"But your cameras and film were lost, of course," Morgan said.

"Yes. *Yes.*"

Morgan regarded her steadily. "I believe you."

"Do you?"

"I believe you were, in fact, shot down by a surface-to-air missile. And I believe you saw a submarine in Hudson Bay last December. I can't blame you for thinking that it was an American boat. But it was not."

What exactly was he suggesting here, she wondered. "Whose, then if not American?" she asked.

"There are possibilities. Quite a few."

"Oh, no. *Not* the cold war again. Are you saying that it was a Russian submarine?" Disbelief and exasperation showed in her expression.

"It is entirely possible, Mrs. Neville."

"I thought even the U.S. military had got past that kind of thinking," she said bleakly.

"I wonder why it is," he said carefully, "that if there is blame to assign, people like yourself and your friends always choose to assign it to my country."

He paused, catching a glimpse of her haunted face, suddenly ashamed of himself, and spoke more calmly. "As it happens, Mrs. Neville, we have satellite images of a Russian submarine leaving the Atlantic approach to Hudson Strait less than one week after your aircraft was brought down. You can believe that or not, as you please. But it happens to be true." He stopped for a moment, considering how much further he could go, how much of what he had been told she would believe. But Pierre Grau was dead, and his death changed the whole focus of the mission. No minds could be changed, no charges withdrawn. Whatever Nathan Abramov had wanted to tell Pierre Grau would remain unsaid.

He said, "One of the reasons I came to San Francisco was to deliver a message to Pierre Grau from Ambassador Nathan Abramov of the Russian UN delegation. They were old friends, from Grau's time at Moscow University, years ago. Abramov urgently wanted to speak with Grau personally. I was not told what it was about. I was only to inform Grau. Have you any idea what the Russian might have wanted to say to Grau? Did you know the two were acquainted?"

"No, Colonel. I knew that Pierre had studied in Moscow. Only that."

Morgan shrugged. "Dead end, then. I'm only guessing but it must be related to your accident. I think Abramov wanted Grau to stop your publicity tour."

Anna Neville stared bitterly at Morgan. "You think that, do you, Colonel?"

Morgan's patience was waning. "Do you know how long it would take for a nuclear IRBM to fly the thirteen hundred miles between Hudson Bay and the ICBM fields in Nebraska or the Dakotas? Six minutes, Mrs. Neville. Six fucking minutes."

Anna stared at him, horrified by the picture his words brought to mind.

In a less hostile tone Morgan said, "I don't suggest that an enemy of the United States is trying to establish a base in Canada. But if you saw a submarine last December, we had better find out what connection there is between the people who sent it into Hudson Bay and the killers of Pierre Grau." He stopped suddenly. "What is it?"

Anna Neville's shoulders stiffened as her eyes focused on

127

the traffic along Beach Street. She said in a thin voice, "You believe they'll want to kill me next?"

"Yes."

"Oh, God," Anna Neville whispered. "Look there, across the street."

Morgan saw a dark-colored Bronco, menacing on its theatrical cleated tires, exhaust emerging eerily from its rear, poised for flight. He got to his feet, looking past Anna's shoulder. A man appeared in the open doorway to the restaurant, about twenty feet away. He had a shaved head and wraparound reflective dark glasses covering most of his face, what the grunts in the Corps called "fuck you shades." He was dressed in hunting camouflage, that showy imitation of military combat fatigues. The man held a concussion grenade in one hand and as Morgan moved forward, he rolled the grenade along the floor toward Anna.

Morgan changed directions in midleap. He scooped up the grenade and threw it through the window fronting Beach Street. The glass disintegrated. The bartender and the waiter, who had retreated to the back room, appeared in the archway, shouting their outraged protest.

Morgan roared, *"Get down!"*

He saw the Bronco burn rubber and start up Hyde Street, the grenade thrower clinging to an open door. Morgan wrapped his arms around Anna, pulled her out of her chair, and rolled with her to the floor.

Outside the night turned glare-white as the grenade exploded. The glassware behind the bar as well as the mirror shattered and fell like a shower of ice.

Morgan was on his feet in an instant. He pulled Anna up and dragged her after him, through the front door and out of the heavily damaged restaurant. In less than three minutes they were in his rented car, speeding around the perimeter of Fort Mason in the direction of the Pacific Coast Highway.

Chapter Sixteen

Devil's Slide/November 28

*Our allies are to be found not in the primitive societies
of the third world where we have wasted our substance,
but in the inner cities and small towns of rural America.*

—THE SOYUZ MANIFESTO

MORGAN SWUNG the rented, near-to-invisible gray Japanese
car through Golden Gate Park to the ocean frontage. The fog
was heavy, condensing on the windshield where the inadequate wipers lashed to and fro in a futile effort to clear the
glass. The digital clock on the dash showed ten after three,
and the wide road ahead and beyond seemed deserted. In the
park, great cypress trees rose, shadows in the fog. The wind-
mills, San Francisco landmarks, raised their cruciform arms in
silent threat. The wisping fog made them seem monstrous.

Morgan glanced across at Anna Neville. She was covered
with Morgan's raincoat and her head rested against the window. She had huddled there in silence ever since they had left
the side street near the restaurant. She was exhausted. Morgan
recognized the symptoms. One could reach a point where re-

lief came only from a kind of stupefied resistance to further change. Anna Neville was very close to that stage, and he could not allow it.

He had driven all the way from North Beach with half of his attention fixed on the rearview mirror. One didn't roll a grenade into a deserted restaurant to make a kill, then simply walk away when the attempt failed. Whoever they were, they knew when the grenade exploded in the street that they would have to try again. He said, "All right?"

"I'm still here, Morgan." It was the first time she had addressed him by name.

"That was brave," she said in a thin voice, then cleared her throat. "What you did at the restaurant." She sat up.

"It was goddamn stupid, but there wasn't much choice," he said. He was still worried about her. The effects of her last year—and her last twenty-four hours—showed in her face. What ill fortune had taken her and her husband to Hudson Bay last December, Morgan wondered. Who ever knew why such things happened? Morgan believed in Fate as a prime mover in human affairs. Third world people knew. They spoke of Kismet, Lot, Portion, Destiny. Warriors and beggars tended to invoke the same gods and sibyls.

"Who are they, Morgan?" Anna asked. "Do you know?"

"Not yet."

"You're not going to call the police?" she asked.

"They'll be investigating it on their own. We haven't time to get involved. It will only hold us up."

"Where are we going?"

"Half Moon Bay."

"What's at Half Moon Bay?"

"An old associate with an airplane. I need to get you back to Washington."

"I don't want to go back to Washington."

A mist-shrouded green traffic light marked the transition from a broad expanse of pavement to divided road. The park was left behind. Morgan drove at a steady speed. On their right lay a line of sand dunes covered with reedy sea grasses. Invisible beyond them lay the narrow strand of Ocean Beach and then the Pacific, past the momentarily glimpsed, rolling breakers and far, far past the fog that a sea wind was trying now to disperse.

The thought of taking Anna to Alameda NAS had crossed Morgan's mind, but the navy would be reluctant to carry a civilian to Washington on a navy aircraft and would spend hours checking authorizations. The airline terminals at SFO International were out of the question. The paramilitary games of the killers in the Bronco did impress Morgan. They were dangerous people. Not very competent, and almost certainly working for pay. But competent enough that to take their target to an air terminal might be asking for a massacre.

There were secret funds and resources available for what Morgan had to do, and he intended to use them. Avery Peters of Half Moon Bay, ex-Air America, was in for an early morning surprise.

Ave had been jettisoned from the Central Intelligence Agency after the war in Bosnia. He claimed he never regretted leaving the Company. "It's become a home for pretty admirals and ugly pencil pushers," he said. "But shit, boy, the Gulf was different. The Gulf was *fun.*"

Morgan, who had prowled Kuwaiti beaches stiff with Iraqi mines as a Seal would not have put it quite that way. But Ave Peters was a different sort of man. He had dealt with Arabs almost all of his career, and got along with them, as he put it, like a house afire. As was the case with some Agency types, Ave Peters had left Langley as a fairly wealthy man; hence his ability to start a charter service in Half Moon Bay. He was direct, discreet, and extremely capable. In the present situation, there was no one on Morgan's list of assets he would rather call upon than Peters.

Morgan looked hard at the rearview mirror at fog-dimmed headlights. He felt a bit easier when they swung off to the left. The empty road behind was dark as they moved inland along Lake Merced and joined Skyline Boulevard. He flexed his hands on the steering wheel, arched his back, then his shoulders, to relieve the tension. It had been a long night.

ANNA NEVILLE SAID QUIETLY, "Can I trust you, Morgan?" Her voice quavered a little.

Morgan was feeling the pressure himself. This woman attracted him and angered him and baffled him. He had always avoided allowing political ideology to be a factor in man-woman relationships. When he met an attractive woman—and he'd met several—who began haranguing him about his uniform and all it stood for, he tipped his hat and departed. Why bother? "Is there anyone else?" he asked, eyebrows raised.

"Who am I?" she demanded suddenly.

"What?"

"Say my name."

Morgan was nonplussed. "I don't understand you."

"My name. I have a *name*. Why don't you use it? Is it that you think I'll be dead before you get used to saying 'Mrs. Neville' or 'Anna'?" Hostility, fed by suppressed fear, overflowed in her. Suddenly she was crying, tears running down her cheeks as she shook with the effort to catch her breath.

Morgan checked the rearview mirror, then slowed, pulling the car off onto the verge. The headlights on the fog reflected ghostly patterns in the air around them. He fumbled with his seat belt, trying to free himself. Damned thing, it's so slow—just in the way, he thought in exasperation. Then he put his arms around her and held her. "It's all right. It really is all right."

She shook her head against his chest. "It isn't. I didn't want to start something like this. But they killed Jacob and Sean. Now Pierre. Somebody—"

She stopped, sucking in air in shuddering breaths.

"Anna," Morgan said quietly. "Anna Mathis Neville." He brushed a damp strand of hair from her scarred cheek. "Named for Anna Akhmatova."

"Fancy you knowing that," she said faintly.

Morgan looked back through the rear window. A bar of yellow lights appeared, still a good distance away. He stiffened, and asked, "Are you all right now?"

When she nodded, Morgan said, "Then slide over. I want you to drive."

Anna did as she was told without comment. *You know when to question and when not,* Morgan thought. Now Anna Neville had to take a hand in her own salvation.

When they had changed places, Morgan said, "Go." Then he reached into the backseat for the black plastic case there. He put it on his lap and worked the combination lock. Inside, nested in green felt, was a MAC-10 and its attachments: forty-five-round magazine loaded with nine-millimeter bullets, silencer, removable rifle stock, and six-power image-enhancing sight.

Anna glanced at the weapon. "What do you need that for?" she asked. God, Morgan thought. She's a pacifist, too.

"Just drive," he said.

Morgan assembled the MAC-10 and levered a shell into the chamber. "Now listen to me, carefully. We're being followed."

She glanced quickly into the rearview mirror. Even now she still found it difficult to believe that someone really meant to kill her. Any civilized person would feel the same, Morgan thought.

"About a mile from here we will come to a junction. Bear to the right. In about five minutes, we'll come to another junction, with a signal light. Ignore the signal and go on up the hill. We may get clear of the fog for a few miles. But at the top of the hill there's an interchange, with a sign that says Pacifica. Take that road and drive as fast as you can. Go straight through the town and head south. We'll have company by then."

Anna Neville's hands tightened on the steering wheel. "Yes," she said. "All right." Her eyes sought the rearview

133

mirror again. The lights behind them were brighter. They had resolved into brilliant headlights—probably halogens—and four lights mounted high, two yellow fog cutters and two more white halogens.

Morgan looked ahead. Skyline Boulevard was dark and empty. "Don't look back," he said.

She drove well, both hands on the wheel at the two and ten position, and she handled the import's inadequate power as well, or better, than Morgan could have done. He rolled down the window. Cold, wet air buffeted him and set Anna's hair flying.

I hope to God I remembered these roads accurately, Morgan thought. A dead end would be the finish for them. Morgan tried to guess what firepower was being carried in the Bronco. Something heavy and quick. People with a taste for assassinations liked assault weapons. So they wasted a few bullets—it was worth it, since success was almost always guaranteed.

They passed the gate to the Olympic Club where Morgan had once played a round of golf with a friend, a retired admiral, about a thousand years ago. Still to the right, but now at the base of sandstone cliffs, lay the dark surf.

The Bronco was identifiable now, but Anna was driving skillfully through the fog, at a speed that kept their pursuers from catching up. That couldn't last, of course, once they realized they had found their quarry.

She slipped through the junction without slowing. A sixteen-wheeler headed for one of the supermarkets around Pacifica was approaching the intersection as they sped through the red light. The angry howl of an air horn said what the trucker thought of compacts running stoplights.

Halfway up the long hill, bordered by what San Franciscans used to call "the White Cliffs of Doelger" for the builder of the tract houses that had been erected there in the 1950s, the lights atop the Bronco began to flash. The fog vanished momentarily as they climbed. "Faster," Morgan said.

Anna pressed down on the accelerator and the Bronco fell

back. "You're doing fine," Morgan said, and squeezed her shoulder.

At the hilltop interchange a sign read PACIFICA 9 and HALF MOON BAY 20. Anna headed the car seaward again.

The highway skirted downtown Pacifica. It was much modified and improved since the last time Morgan had passed this way. The fog grew thicker as they fled down the road. Their headlights barely penetrated the weblike wall before them. As the town fell behind, they began to climb through a wooded tunnel of ghostly eucalyptus and pines. Suddenly the woods vanished and the road cut deep through the spurs of land thrusting into the Pacific, a half mile away. The wounded mountains lay in steep pitches, striated with naked layers of ancient sediments. The road builders did little more than hold their own on this stretch of coast. Every hundred yards or so there were signs warning of rock slides and of sheer drops to the sea, and admonitions that this was an area where climbing, or even walking, was forbidden. Morgan had seen it in daylight many years ago, formidable and frightening. It was called Devil's Slide.

The slide was infamous. A year seldom went by without either the roadbed collapsing and falling hundreds of feet into the sea or some careless motorist losing control of his car and plunging off the cliff. It was also a favored place for itinerant killers to dispose of their victims.

The fog had lightened and the lights behind them were gaining again. Morgan frowned. How stupid could he be? He should have known. The damned car was bugged. While he had sat bemused by Anna Neville in the Bella Italia, their hunters had put a bug on the car.

They sped along the narrow highway as it clung precariously to the cliff. The sheer edge to the sea was protected by an occasional rock barrier, but most of the time there were only sand berms, meant to discourage passersby from plunging over the edge and into the surf.

"Stop," Morgan said.

"What?"

"You'll have to stop and let me out," Morgan said.

"Why?" She seemed suddenly terrified.

"Don't argue." They were at a turn in the road. The edge was hidden by a berm. Beyond it lay empty space and fog.

"This will do," Morgan said, more calmly than he felt. "Let me out. Drive on ahead. The road drops down to a beach. Stop there and wait for me. Five minutes. No more. If I don't show, drive on to the airport at Half Moon Bay. Find a man named Avery Peters. You can tell him anything you need to, and he'll get you out of here. Trust him."

"What are you going to do?"

"Stop," Morgan said. "Let me out."

Reflexively, she followed orders. Morgan opened the door, dropped to the road, and ran for the shelter of the steep rock cut on the landward side of the road. The car stayed where it was for what seemed like hours, until he ran back to it. Sure enough, she was fumbling with the seat belt. "Goddamn it, Anna! Go!" He slapped the top of the car with his hand, and let out a sigh of relief when he felt it begin to move.

The rental car's taillights vanished into the fog. Morgan knelt on the road verge cradling the MAC-10. The fact that their pursuers were slow in catching up showed him that the terrain was unfamiliar to them. Now the light bar on the approaching Bronco turned the fog around it amber and white. He could hear the rumble of a V-8 engine, the thump of deeply cleated tires.

He lay on the pavement and raised the MAC-10. The brilliance of the halogens blinded him momentarily. He squinted against the lights and fired a burst across the front of the oncoming Bronco. Steam spurted from the punctured radiator. It only looks like an armored personnel carrier, you rented bastards, he thought savagely, but it isn't one. The headlights shattered and went dark. He heard the squalling noise of rubber burning off against metal. His burst had exploded both of the huge front tires. He stood, ready to fire again. There was a flash from the Bronco's left-hand window. He heard heavy buckshot impacting on the sandstone behind him. Something plucked at his trouser leg, something that brushed his skin with a hot touch. In slow motion, Morgan watched the Bronco climb the sand berm. There was the screech of metal bending as the vehicle lurched sideways, then the large boxy shape simply vanished from his view. He could hear the sound of its air horn, first a loud banshee wailing, fading into a soft echo, then silence. It came from the black space on the seaward side of the highway.

Shaking with the effects of unused adrenaline, Morgan ran limping across the road. He edged past the broken side of the berm, careful not to slip on the loose dirt, and looked down. The edges of the rocks below were very faintly outlined with the white lace of the waves crashing against them. Otherwise the darkness was empty, and the only sound was that of the distant surf.

Morgan sagged down onto the sand berm between the deeply cleated tire tracks. Join Grau, you cowardly bastards, he thought. At least you won't get Anna Neville. After a moment he stood and began limping down the highway, heading south. He had walked only a little way before he saw the headlights. He did not know how he knew it, but he did. Anna Neville had disobeyed his orders and had come back for him.

Chapter Seventeen

Washington, D.C./November 28

President Caidin appears to believe that a personal friendship exists between himself and Cherny that will override any tensions in our relations with Russia. He also seems to believe that President Cherny is in complete command of his government. There is no hard evidence to support these beliefs; indeed, there is much evidence to contradict it.

—INTERNAL CIA MEMORANDUM

THE RUSSIAN AMBASSADOR ROSE from his seat and extended his hand to Vincent Kellner. His expression was one of barely concealed exasperation. He'd been politely put off again when he requested a personal meeting with President Caidin. Marko Borisovich Galitzin was the latest in the new breed of Russian ambassadors. Styles were constantly changing inside the country, Kellner thought. The Italian suits so prized by Mikhail Gorbachev had now been replaced by a military fashion. Galitzin's mien and posture said "soldier" to Kellner, and the CIA suggested a stint with the KGB may also have been on his résumé. What was Cherny thinking of, Kellner wondered. To what influences was he yielding?

President Caidin had scoffed at the idea that Aleksandr Cherny would send a KGB man to Washington, the most sensitive post in the Russian foreign service. "Aleksandr Cherny would send the Metropolitan of Moscow if he could," Caidin said, laughing at Kellner's suggestion. Cherny was widely pictured in the press and among the pundits of the Beltway as a religious, almost saintly man. Kellner remembered the Western press's earlier enthusiasm for Yuri Andropov, the music aficionado who had, according to reports, just *loved* Glenn Miller's music. Leonid Brezhnev, Americans were told, was a muscle car buff (just like any rugged American male). For a time the rat pack in the Western press had devoted much effort to "humanizing" senior Soviet leaders. Kellner wondered if the current crop of pundits were not repeating the mistakes of the past with Aleksandr Cherny. An intellectual, to be sure, and a mild-mannered man. But still the executive of the successor state to the USSR, a nation that had kept the world in turmoil for most of the twentieth century.

The current inside gossip said that Cherny had an icon of St. George in his Kremlin apartment. And young Air Force General Collingwood, chairman of the Joint Chiefs, had managed to anger many congressmen by assuring *Time* magazine that the icon was "worth two missile wings."

Kellner's mind had been preoccupied, and he had not been listening carefully until Ambassador Galitzin said smoothly, by way of farewell, "I hope the health of the Secretary of State is improving."

Kellner's face froze. Carl Jannings, the Secretary of State, was not improving; he was dying of AIDS. The Caidin Administration's foreign policy had been in limbo for weeks because of it. The President decided to take the unpleasant—and politically unappealing—step of asking for Jannings's resignation and nominating a replacement for him. Vincent Kellner was reputed to be the most likely nominee. Marko Galitzin, of course, knew all the gossip, heard all the whispers. Carl Jannings was a brilliant man, as well as a consummate diplomat, and his illness was a great loss to Cole Caidin's Administration. The President was being heavily lobbied to replace Jannings with a woman, and the elections were just a year away. The campaign for Caidin's reelection was to begin in January.

"I will pass along your statement of concern, Ambassador Galitzin," Kellner said politely, as he escorted the Russian to the door. "I am relieved to hear your assurance that the situation in Russia is calm, and I shall so inform the President. The President is sympathetic to your problems, but very concerned for Russian internal stability, and for the maintenance of your good relationships with your neighboring nuclear states."

Chew on that, Ambassador, Kellner thought. You still have not reclaimed all your old nuclear ICBMs from Belarus, nor all your missile cruisers from the Ukraine.

As always, Kellner thought, Russia's problems were the world's problems. Whether they were raising hell in the third world as a superpower or falling apart at home, the Russians made big waves just by existing. A democratic constitution and a sullen legislative assembly had not eased the pressures. Kellner was convinced that Russia again was moving rapidly toward some violent upheaval.

CIA's Moscow station was sending increasingly alarming reports of repeated violence in clashes between ethnic separatists and the Russian army in Kirghizia and Tajikistan, and of Afghans attacking the Russo-Muslim borders. The battles between Armenia and Azerbaijan continued, and bread riots broke out sporadically in Moscow. The latest intelligence summary lay in Kellner's drawer right now.

"The stories in your press of 'near civil war' are much exaggerated, Dr. Kellner," Galitzin said, his dark eyes narrowed at the perceived slight. "The policy of my government is to deal with all these matters by reasonable negotiation."

Kellner restrained an impulse to say that a good many in the Kremlin still preferred to send Black Beret internal security troops to deal with dissent. General Kondratiev was gone. But how far and for how long?

"We Russians may not yet have learned how to make a market economy work to perfection, Mr. Adviser," Galitzin said coldly, "but we have long known what to do with generals who refuse to take orders."

Galitzin bowed stiffly one last time to Kellner, then stalked past Camilla Varig's desk without giving her a glance. She made a face at his back. Kellner saw her, smiled, shook his head in tolerant reproof, and returned to his inner office. Charlton Fisk, the FBI director, had appeared from an inner alcove and was sitting in the chair vacated by Galitzin.

"Well, Charlie," Kellner asked. "You heard. What do you make of it? Do you believe him?"

"He's a damned liar," Fisk said. "Kondratiev may be out of town. But not for long."

"Snooping in Moscow, Charlie?" Kellner said drily, seating himself behind his bare desk.

Fisk was a career lawman who had risen from the ghetto of Bedford-Stuyvesant to his present position as the first black man ever to head the Federal Bureau of Investigation. It had been his mother who had given him his "elegant" name (she had admired the movie star who had played Moses) and taught him to live up to it. He was a product of a supportive family, a public school system that only the strong could survive, and Columbia and Harvard Law.

When political conservatives quoted numbers to make a case against affirmative action, liberals thrust Charlton Fisk front and center. By now, he was sick of the role. But he was intelligent, his abilities had been honed by twenty-two years in the Department of Justice, and he deserved his directorship.

He also poached on his colleagues' turf from time to time. Charlton Fisk was always willing to take a chance when he thought the risk justified. In the case of the new Russian ambassador, he considered it particularly so.

"He's Soyuz, Vincent," he said.

Kellner regarded the Director over steepled fingers. Fisk's soft brown eyes belied his steely character. His black hair, sprinkled with gray, had a surprising tinge of red, and his features were almost Caucasian. Kellner wondered what slave owner had cast his Irishness into the Fisk gene pool. Would he be proud of his black descendant's ability and achievement? The world being as it was, probably not. A pity, Kellner thought.

He asked, "You're sure of that?"

The FBI director met the Adviser's gaze with a directness that was challenging. "The last *two* Russian ambassadors were Soyuz. And so is this one. Something is happening in Russia, Vincent. What are you getting from Central Intelligence?"

Kellner chose to be evasive, as he often was. "I'm not contradicting you, nor doubting your judgment. I only wonder how you came to this conclusion."

"Marsh Gray isn't the only one with resources. We have a few assets inside the compound at Mount Alto, too," Fisk said.

"I know how you love to fish in other people's ponds, Charlie," Kellner said. "But you're an officer of the law. I should not have to remind you of that. I'd be surprised if you weren't tapping Mount Alto. But when your adventures take your people offshore, that could mean big trouble."

"Don't lecture me, Vincent, and I won't ask you what an NSC agent is doing mixing into a hit-and-run murder case in San Francisco."

Kellner pursed his lips and said, "All in good time. Let's stick to Galitzin for a while. All right, let's assume he is a member of Soyuz. Where does that lead us?"

"It sends up a warning rocket, Vincent. The barbarians are coming out from behind every tree in Moscow. I've never seen Cherny as a pillar of strength when the going gets tough. How

Cherny will handle an insurrection, I don't know, and I'll bet you don't either.''

Fisk added quietly, "Frankly, that scares the shit out of me, Vincent."

"Don't overreact. Not yet, in any case."

"Well, I hope you're right," Fisk said. He hesitated only momentarily before asking, "How secure are you here, Vincent? How often do you have the NSA ferrets in?"

"That's a damned strange question from someone with your reputation as a poacher, Charlie," Kellner said.

With the Administration perennially hungry for money to fund domestic programs, the demise of the cold war offered Cole Caidin opportunities his predecessors in office had ignored. One of them was to reduce the Central Intelligence Agency to a cadre. "I hate all that snooping around. I agree with Henry Stimson that gentlemen don't read each other's mail. It's unseemly. And look at the billions we'll save. But I suppose we should leave a nub so as to be ready to expand our intelligence in a crisis or in wartime," the new President had told Kellner. How little Caidin understood of international affairs, Kellner thought, and how difficult it would be to reestablish vital connections, once broken.

But Kellner and those who agreed with him had lost. The choice of Marshall Gray, a Wall Street banker friend of Cole Caidin's, to head CIA had been a clear message that the Agency was being "powered down." From the moment Caidin had been inaugurated, resignations from the Central Intelligence Agency had increased to a flood.

"Let me put it this way, Vincent," Fisk said. "There can be no turf battles where there is no longer any turf to defend, right?"

Kellner frowned. He was uneasy whenever he saw an internecine battle looming in the Caidin Administration, especially in those areas upon which he was so dependent. Marshall Gray might be a poor director of CI, but he was a pround man and a big contributor to Caidin's party. Gray knew the differences in the charters of the CIA and the FBI and he was not shy. Even if his task was quietly to turn Langley into a research center, he would fight to the bitter end. He said reprovingly, "Marshall is just doing the job that the President gave him to do. It is not for us to fault that."

Fisk leaned forward in his chair. "That's well and good, provided we live in the best of all possible worlds—But I came from, how shall I put it, a harsher environment than either Marsh Gray or the President—"

"Or Vincent Kellner?"

"You said it, I didn't. Bedford-Stuyvesant is a good proving ground for sons of bitches." Fisk's brown eyes were no longer soft; they were sharp and predatory. "People learned to cover their backs there." A thin smile appeared on his face. It did nothing to warm his expression. "Not unlike Washington, Vincent."

"Point taken," Kellner murmured.

"We've seen a sudden flurry of Russian agents lately, in Washington and New York, after several years of low to moderate effort. Almost as if they were just doing busy work. But now we see some new faces on the scene, and some old faces have returned, quietly. So I commissioned a report on the Russian situation," Fisk said. "I was going to keep it in-house. But with the fuss going on over there, and since Marko Galitzin is the third Soyuz, as opposed to Russian, ambassador, I think it needs wider distribution."

"The President?" Kellner asked dubiously.

"Yes. No question. The conclusion my brain trust draws from its investigation is that Cherny is in deep trouble. What the President chooses to call Cherny's flexibility, my boys see as sheer weakness. We estimate the chances of a right-wing coup in Russia are one in five between now and the new year. And there's a dissenting minority report that says the odds are shorter than that."

As he spoke, Fisk studied Kellner's face closely. He wondered how frank he should be, not only about the dangers abroad, but about the dangers close at hand. Kellner would be receptive to learning more about the way Soyuz was spreading like a virus through the Russian nomenklatura, certainly. But how would he react to news about leaks from the White House and the NSC office? There'd been no critical breaches of security yet, thank God. But what would Kellner say if Fisk revealed his suspicions about the source of these leaks? Vincent Kellner was a proud, even arrogant, man. He would be dangerous should he become an enemy. He would demand undeniable proof, and Fisk didn't have it, not yet. He returned to the facts he did have.

"When I was a boy in Bed-Stuy, I used to wonder what happened to all those Nazis who were supposed to have fought us so hard in the old war. Well, now I know, Vincent. They are reborn in Russia, with the Orthodox cross in one hand and *The Protocols of Zion* in the other." Fisk got up and began to pace the room. "The Kremlin and the ministries are stiff with them. So, God help poor old Aleksandr Cherny, who ought to be back in St. Petersburg teaching medieval European history. Because I wonder if he can cope when push comes to shove.

"This latest spasm of political restructuring has failed, Vincent, just as it has three times before," Fisk said passionately.

The cold look in Kellner's pale eyes silenced Fisk.

"You've been dancing on Marshall's turf, Charlie. It has to stop," Kellner said.

"Haven't you been listening to what I've been saying?" Fisk asked in dismay. "I'm telling you there's a disaster looming, and you're worrying about turf?"

"I have been listening."

Fisk threw up his hands. "Am I being the uppity house nigger? You know me as well as anyone in this town, Vincent. If CI isn't doing its job, for whatever reason, then someone else had damned well better do it. Didn't you just remind Galitzin that Russia and its neighbors are stiff with nukes? Nukes that can reach New York and Washington, Paris, London, Berlin? That makes them *dangerous,* Vincent."

"I know that, Charlie."

The hell with it, Fisk thought. I'd better tell him what else I've got on my mind while I have the chance. We may not be speaking tomorrow. "Security is shitty in this town, Vincent. It worries me. Even in this office."

Kellner said softly, "What is it you're trying to say, Charlie?"

Fisk's gaze was level. "We are all sworn to protect the interests of the United States. Some of us take risks, run agents, even if we have no authority to do so." There was a tight silence in the room.

"You're running Milstein," Fisk said.

When Kellner remained stiffly silent, Charlton Fisk went on. "Actually, it is a real coup to have enlisted the minister of finance of Russia as an American agent, even if only as an agent of influence. The whole pantheon of CIA directors must be salivating in their honored graves." His tone hardened. "So don't talk to me about turf. Marsh Gray would go ballistic if he knew."

Vincent Kellner regarded Charlton Fisk for a long time before speaking. "How did you find out?"

"We were lucky," Fisk said wryly. Then he added, "But others can get lucky, too. David Milstein is an innocent. An honest man, in spite of what he's doing. I think Aleksandr Cherny knows, for instance, and keeps silent. Maybe having a direct pipeline to an adviser to the President of the United States has certain advantages in a country that's falling apart. But Milstein is no professional spook, Vincent. He's going to get badly burned. And so could you, and through you, the President. Good God, man, the Soyuz people in the government won't tolerate him for ten minutes if they find out what you're doing. He's on thin ice now. They'll arrest him just for being a Jew, let alone an American spy." Fisk's frown deepened. "How did you manage it, Vincent? How did you recruit him?"

"I didn't. He came to me. At the G-7 meeting in Vienna. David Milstein thinks the United States is the wave of the future." Kellner smiled grimly. "He believes what the founders put into the Constitution. He wants the same thing for his country. If that makes him naive, so be it."

Fisk remained silent for a moment. Then he asked, "What do you feel about Milstein? Personally, I mean."

"I like the man. But does it matter? The contact is invaluable to us."

"The word is 'asset,' Vincent," Fisk said wryly. "You have a way to get him out?"

"Yes," Kellner said evenly. "And Aleksandr Cherny, too, if it comes to that."

"It *will* come to that, Vincent."

"I accept the possibility, but my timetable is probably very different from yours."

"Weeks? Months?"

"A year."

Fisk shook his head. "Sooner. Much sooner."

The Adviser again steepled his fingers. It was a gesture he used often, unconsciously showing that he felt pressured. "I want you to call your people off, Charlie," he said slowly. "It's too risky to have them there at this time. It endangers David Milstein."

"It's risky not to have *someone* there. Marsh Gray has moved all his good folks back to Washington."

"We have Milstein."

"You can't make him over into James Bond, Vincent. He's an *accountant*—"

"Don't make me go to the President, Charlton. It might lead to both our resignations, and for better or worse, we are the best Cole Caidin has for these jobs. Get your people out of Moscow. And tell them to stay the hell away from Milstein, or they'll blow him for sure."

Fisk drew a long, deep breath. It could have been worse,

147

he thought. But it was bad enough. "Okay. On one condition."

"Condition?"

"Two, actually. Pass my report on to the President. I will get it to you by this evening at the latest."

"I would have to give it a provenance."

"Say it's yours. Or say some think tank did it. Anything. Only see to it that he reads it. If he accepts any part of it, we can talk again. With Gray sitting in. And one thing more. I want to send the ferrets in here to have a look around."

"The first, I agree to reluctantly; the second is not necessary."

Fisk sighed. "Think it over, at least."

Vincent Kellner rarely showed more than displeasure, but for once, Charlton Fisk saw real anger in his face. "You are insinuating that I have a traitor in my office, and I deny that absolutely. I have a small staff that I selected with great care before they came to work for me. I have had no occasion to doubt their loyalty, either to me or to their government. I do not wish to speak of this again unless and until you have hard evidence to show me."

Fisk stood up and nodded curtly. "I'll have the report delivered before the end of business, today."

"Yes," Kellner said. "Do that."

As Fisk walked toward the door, a special FBI courier arrived in the outer office with a double-sealed message for him. Camilla Varig removed the old-fashioned dictagraph headset she liked to use and buzzed Kellner. "Sir, there's a messenger here for Director Fisk."

"Send him in."

The special agent delivered the envelope to Fisk. "By hand of Agent, sir."

Fisk signed off, read the brief message inside, then handed it to Kellner as though it were going to burst into flames. "Your man, Vincent," he said.

The telex was from the field agent in charge of the San Francisco office of the FBI. It read:

0250 EST BOMB EXPLODED OUTSIDE THE BELLA ITALIA RESTAURANT WHERE COLONEL MORGAN NSC AND ANNA NEVILLE DINING. PREMISES SEVERELY DAMAGED. MORGAN AND NEVILLE UNACCOUNTED FOR. SUGGEST APB. ADVISE. CANTWELL FBI.

Chapter Eighteen

Morskaja Pristan, St. Petersburg, Russia/November 28

Restructuring the nation has brought about a decay in the capabilities of all our military forces. But it is the navy that has suffered most. The industrial capacity needed for the building of new units for the Fleet has been preempted by less patriotic causes and Russian prestige suffers. Therefore the ships of the Fleet must be zealously guarded.

—Voyenno-Morskoy-Flot,
Russian Navy Journal

THE PROTECTED ANCHORAGE at the mouth of the Neva River was crowded with ships. Russian navy craft had been assembling in the inner harbor. Once they arrived, they did not depart. Admiral Eduard Aleyev stared angrily through the fogged window of the recreation hall at the snow falling gently on the mothballed ships that once had been his pride.

The missile cruiser *Slava,* which once had hosted President George Bush of the United States, was here, moored hard by the never-commissioned aircraft carrier *Oktyabrskaya Revo-*

lutsiya—a ship Aleyev, in other times, might have claimed for his Pacific Fleet flagship. The original *Kresta* was here and the last new cruiser built during Andropov's time, the *Molotovsk,* now called *The Rights of Man.* A dozen old Zulu-class submarines formed a black bridge across the harbor, and beyond them lay the last three Typhoon-class missile submarines in the navy. In the outer harbor Aleyev could see the upper works of a dozen Krivak-class destroyers.

The smaller ships in the anchorage, those few still in commission, all flew the white, red, and blue ensign of Russia. I yearn for the sight of the hammer and sickle on the field of red, he thought morosely. It was a symbol of Soviet supremacy, of *power.*

Aleyev had once been one of the young officers personally chosen by Admiral Grechko for future high command. But that was all in the past. Grechko was dust, as were Brezhnev and Andropov. As was the great Red Fleet. The bitterness of it made Aleyev grimace with pain.

Across twenty kilometers of sea lay the main Russian naval base on the Gulf of Finland, where dozens more of the beautiful ships the Russian people had sacrificed to build were being dismantled. Even worse was the fact that they were being stripped and readied for sale to entrepreneurs of a half-dozen eager third world countries. The admiral blinked to clear the hot tears from his eyes. Weeping at this moment would not be seemly. He must be strong, resolute—a leader.

Soyuz—he was to tell them about Soyuz. Invite them to join in the great crusade. He could explain that, for himself, the transition from loyal officer to conspirator had not been as difficult as he had imagined it would be. Should he mention some of the requirements for becoming a member of Soyuz? Not yet, he decided. When he was asked (as were all recruits to his particular branch of Soyuz) to supply the organization with the names of five Jews, he had been dismayed to realize he did not know five Jews he could denounce. But he made it his duty to find *six* names to give to the newly formed Black

Hundred Soyuz paramilitary. One of the names had been the Minister of Finance, David Davidovich Milstein's, of course, but then Milstein's name had turned up on almost everyone's list.

The men were staring at him. What had he been saying? Oh, yes. About Soyuz. He caressed the eight rows of ribbons on his chest and the gold stripes of an admiral of the Russian Fleet on his sleeves. Just see what I have done for the motherland, you layabouts, he thought. Can any of you say the same?

He began again, enunciating carefully. "You all have families—wives, children, mothers, fathers, brothers, sisters. Consider carefully, comrades. Soyuz is Russia and Russia is Soyuz." He paused, vaguely confused about what to say next. The faces before him gave him no clue. "Above all else, the Movement . . ." He paused again, then mumbled: "Loyalty, loyalty, *loyalty.* There is no greater virtue than loyalty, young Comrades. And betrayal is the greatest, most filthy crime. Filthy."

The sound of his voice echoed in his ears. For a full, horrible minute he looked from one blank face to another. Why did they send me? I am not a speech maker, I am a warrior. These spoiled young men—they belong to another generation. Again he felt hot tears in his eyes, and he turned back toward the window for a moment to regain his composure.

The young naval officers regarded one another warily, their faces reflecting various reactions, from contemptuous amusement to total incomprehension.

Suddenly Aleyev's words were tumbling out in a torrent, and he was drunkenly weeping. "All that I believe has been ground into the dust. I have spent my life in the service of the Supreme Soviet, of Great Russia, and I have been told now that it was for nothing—less than nothing. *I do not intend to let it end this way.*"

The faces before him were expressionless; some appeared embarrassed. No one spoke, no one asked a question. Kondratiev should have come to speak to these men himself. He was the one who could make it all come alive for them; the months of secret planning, the excitement ahead when they began to storm the walls of the Kremlin, the joy and the power that would follow fulfillment of their goals. *He* could make them hear the cheers of the Russian people when their new Soyuz leaders stood on the mausoleum.

And Kondratiev would have made them understand that all this would be accomplished as soon as the bolt of Holy Russia's lightning rose from an inland sea to strike down the *vragny glav*—the mortal enemy. They would be clamoring to be a part of Soyuz.

They really don't deserve to know, Aleyev thought angrily. They have not paid their dues, shed their blood. Let them stew and beg for favors when Soyuz has succeeded in recovering Mother Russia from its destroyers, when the Russian Empire is whole once more. He wheeled and strode abruptly from the room, then along a covered walk to where his Chaika limousine waited, the one last privilege he clung to as Admiral of the Pacific Fleet. His driver was holding the rear door open for him. Once in the backseat, Aleyev grabbed at the open bottle from the built-in bar, knocking his prized car phone from its seat, and poured himself a glass of vodka with trembling hands. He gulped down the vodka and refilled the glass before he called to his driver, "Back to the airport. Be quick about it."

By the time the Chaika reached the military airport at St. Petersburg, Admiral Aleyev was sodden and singing "Moscow Nights" softly to himself in the rear seat.

"WE HAVE OFFICERS from one of the shock armies on our side, clever ones, who have managed to ingratiate themselves with high members of Cherny's government," Sergei Korchilov said, his clenched fists on the top of General Piotr Kondratiev's makeshift desk. The two men faced one another angrily in the room the Soyuz organization maintained in the basement of an apartment building north of the Neva River and near the Finl'andskij Vokzal, for Kondratiev's clandestine visits to St. Petersburg. The building superintendant was a loyal member of Soyuz, and no one would think of looking for the general in such mean quarters.

"The Red Banner *shall* wave again over the Kremlin," Korchilov said haughtily. "We have chosen Nikolai Rostov to be our candidate for General Secretary of the Party when the riffraff is swept from our streets. You would do well to join us, put off your attempt until we can make a concerted attack on Cherny. That is the only way to succeed."

Kondratiev glared at Korchilov. This upstart, this discredited member of the old nomenklatura, trying to wriggle in so as to take credit, supplant Soyuz, resurrect the Communist corpse. He started to speak just as the telephone on the desk rang once. Just as well, Kondratiev thought, I was ready to insult him and his whole worm-eaten group. Better not to burn those bridges just yet. String them along, until we see if we need them. The telephone rang again, twice this time, and Kondratiev picked up the receiver. He said hello, then put his hand over the receiver and motioned with his head for Korchilov to go into the next room.

After Korchilov had marched out and closed the door after himself, Kondratiev said, "Go ahead. What happened? Was his invitation well received?"

"I don't know why you sent Aleyev, Piotr," said the disgusted voice on the other end of the telephone. "I did as you asked, babied him, drove him to Morskaya Pristan, and kept him almost sober until we got there, but the man's a fool and a sponge. He babbled. Those naval officers just sat and looked at him, not responding, wondering, I should imagine, just how such a fool could get to be an admiral of the Fleet. Then he broke and ran. I could hear laughter from those youngsters all the way to the car. They think the man is a joke."

"Never mind, Mikhail," Kondratiev said thoughtfully. "You did well. You never knew him when he was young. He was a genuine hero of the motherland. Someday I'll tell you about it." He paused thoughtfully. "Well, this means that we'll have to approach that captain in the Black Sea Fleet, the one who contacted us asking to join Soyuz.

"In the meantime, I've made considerable progress with old Yulin. He's not necessarily for us, but not against us, either. That means we have the Kremlin guard on our side. Yuri Kalinin should be bringing his three air regiments along with him; we'll know by the end of the week." Kondratiev laughed. "I'm looking forward to seeing Cherny's face when we arrest him."

"What do you want me to do?"

"Stay with Eduard, keep him out of mischief. His name still means something to the old veterans. We can dispose of him after the putsch," Kondratiev said, his confidence rising.

"All right, but it's boring duty," said the dubious voice of Admiral Aleyev's driver. "By the way, I hear you are to be approached by some of the dinosaurs. Watch out there. They still have steel teeth."

Kondratiev laughed heartily. "I have a dinosaur here right now, in the next room. Just a baby, though, hardly out of his shell. Don't worry, Mikhail. You'll see. We'll have them all eating out of our hands, teeth pulled, inside of ten days. Just ten days, Mikhail, and we'll own the world."

Chapter Nineteen

Churchill, Manitoba/November 28

For the sum of $26,000, rich Saudi, American, and South African thrill-seekers can board a former Soviet nuclear icebreaker for two weeks. These "atomic outings" are offered by the Murmansk Shipping Company, a Russian state enterprise aimed at keeping its icebreaker fleet cost effective. Passengers looking to starboard can see the islands of Novaya Zemlya, a stretch of land irradiated by the Soviet army's nuclear tests since the 1950s. Under the ship itself lies the world's largest undersea nuclear graveyard, used by Murmansk Shipping, among others. A thrill, indeed.

—WORLD PRESS INTERNATIONAL

The harmful effects of radiation are determined by the degree of exposure, which in turn depends not only on the quantity of radiation delivered to the body, but also on the type of radiation, which tissues of the body are exposed, and the duration of exposure. Four hundred to

156

six hundred rads of gamma radiation applied to the entire body at one time would probably be fatal.

—CURRENT DIAGNOSIS AND TREATMENT

**(Urgent report to the Ministry of Health, Ottawa.)
Physician: James Clark, KEEWATIN FLYING
DOCTOR SERVICE, Churchill, Manitoba.**

*1. On 25 November, in response to a radio call from John
Agikumi, a fisherman of Eskimo Point, Northwest Territories,
I departed Churchill in a KFDS Cessna 185 aircraft accompanied by my wife, Helen Clark, a registered nurse. Agikumi
reported a seriously ill infant of eight years of age (Edwin
Agikumi, his son).*

*2. Due to inclement weather I was forced to turn back to
Churchill on my first attempt to reach Eskimo Point. My second attempt, after an eighteen-hour delay, was successful.*

*3. The Agikumi family is of Inuit descent and is engaged in
fishing the western waters of Hudson Bay, as well as the rivers
and lakes in the vicinity of Eskimo Point. Family members are
Agikumi; his wife, Mary; and four children, daughter Martha,
sons Edwin, Charlie, and Warren.*

*4. The situation discovered at Eskimo Point was medically
desperate. The child Edwin Agikumi had succumbed an hour
before we arrived. Sons Charlie, 10, and Warren, 12, were
extremely ill with the following clinical symptoms: nausea, erythema, epidermolysis, epilation, and an extremely depressed
lymphocyte count. The girl Martha, 16, was terminally ill with
acute pneumonitis. The mother, Mary Agikumi, complained of
a cessation of her menses, and both she and John Agikumi
displayed symptoms of advanced pneumonitis with body temperatures of 39.1 and 39.5 degrees Centigrade.*

5. *John Agikumi was able to report that the family had become ill after eating Ling cod caught near the Tharanne and Thlewiaza river deltas. Analysis was impossible, as they discarded the fish soon after young Edwin became ill.*

6. *I treated the patients with dimenhydrinate for relief of nausea, and transfused both Mary and Martha Agikumi, with 100 cc of plasma each. It was my judgment (and my wife concurs) that both females were critically ill. I immediately radioed for an air ambulance to transport the surviving family back to Churchill. The air ambulance arrived within four hours, but by that time, despite the use of a respirator, both Mary and Martha Agikumi had succumbed to pneumonitis complicated by lymphocytic damage.*

7. *The living members of the family were flown to Churchill, where they are presently receiving supportive treatment.*

Confidential addenda:

1. *My wife and I habitually carry with us a radiation counter for use in our hobby of airborne prospecting for deposits of uranium.*

2. *Mrs. Clark was formerly employed at the Siemans Oncology Clinic of Vancouver, B.C., and is familiar with the systemic reaction to high dosages of radiation. We brought our radiation counter from the aircraft and examined the Agikumi cadavers with it. We obtained readings of 660 rads from the body of Edwin, 580 rads from Martha Agikumi, and 710 rads from Mary Agikumi.*

3. *We subsequently examined each of the 87 inhabitants of Eskimo Point, but discovered no abnormal readings or residuals. Only Agikumi and his sons fished the waters of the bay near the Thlewiaza and Tharanne delta, and only the Agikumi family became ill.*

4. Despite the persistence of most inclement weather, with rain and occasional snow flurries, I ordered the burial of the cadavers, and here at Churchill we have isolated the surviving patients. Mrs. Clark and I have thus far felt no ill effects from our exposure, though we presently have slightly lower than normal white blood cell counts and are suffering some depression of the salivary glands.

5. We have obtained residual readings from the surviving Agikumis. Willis Hanford, my associate at Keewatin Flying Doctor Service, diagnoses their illness as plutonium poisoning. I can only conjecture how an Inuit family came to eat fish contaminated with plutonium, but I believe the Ministry of Health will wish to investigate at once. Dr. Hanford states that the prognosis for all the surviving patients is not encouraging (see attached report).

6. I therefore request that the Agikumi family be removed from Churchill and located in a more suitable facility as soon as possible. KFDS maintains little more than a dispensary here, and the patients require more sophisticated care than we can provide.

"I thought you ought to see this," Dr. Amelia Cutter said to her immediate superior at the Ministry of Health. "It's so fantastic, it might even be true."

"Not just now." He barely glanced at her or the memo. "I'll look at it tomorrow, when I'm not so swamped."

Chapter Twenty

Silver Spring, Maryland/November 28

The KGB, once thirty-five thousand strong, has been disbanded and replaced with the Intelligence Directorate, a small research group, and five thousand security forces, the manageable number needed to guard the borders of the Russian republic.

—THE NATIONAL VIEW

Construction workers have unearthed human bones in central Moscow, and the newspaper Moskovsky Komsomolets said that they may be the remains of victims of Stalin's secret police. The bones were found by workers installing streetlights near the former home of Stalin's secret police chief, Lavrenti Beria.

—ASSOCIATED PRESS

MARINA SUSLOVA DROVE WEST through the noonday traffic to Falls Church, then onto the Beltway, circling halfway around the city and suburbs to Silver Spring. To any casual observer,

160

she was no more than a woman going about her business, enjoying the watery sunshine between winter storms. Today she had shed her upscale persona for that of a drab housewife. No one ever noticed her when she took on this guise. Everyone noticed when she was herself.

She and Camilla had laughed together over the FBI reports issued when Suslova first appeared among the Russians at Mount Alto. The psychologists at Langley classified her as one of the familiar breed of corrupt Russian apparatchiki who had grown rich, Brezhnev-style, on the prerogatives of her post. A minority of the evaluators believed that she was the mistress of a high-ranking official in the Cherny government, sent off to avoid some scandal. None of them seemed to expect that such a flamboyant character would be dangerous—her very visibility obviated that. "The last female spy Americans believed in was Mata Hari," Camilla told Marina.

Marina approached black operations with the eagerness of a predator and the caution of the trophy hunter. She had insisted that the Intelligence Directorate supply her with both the luxurious place in Georgetown (to maintain her image) and another, much less visible place in Silver Spring.

The Georgetown house might be empty for days at a time, but she visited Silver Spring daily, never in the Porsche, nor wearing her sable coat. Silver Spring required an old Dodge Dynasty for transport, and jeans and a denim jacket for fashion. The house stood on the bank of Sligo Creek, an ordinary sort of place, a little shabby, in a black, working-class neighborhood. The house contained a well-disguised scrambler telephone, a fax machine, and a personal computer.

Only Marina's own assets had access to the telephone number at Silver Spring. At the moment, these two assets were Evangeline and Joe Ryerson.

She drove down the narrow street and into the garage behind the house, closed the garage door, and let herself in through the kitchen. The house had a musty smell of dust and mouse droppings. A pallid sunlight leaked past the drawn blinds into the empty rooms. Marina strode through the house to the dining room, an inside room with no windows, where a large steel cabinet held her communications equipment. The only frivolous note was a large mirror, fixed to the wall, so that Marina could watch herself as she worked. Sometimes she wondered about her passion for mirrors. All she knew was that watching herself, no matter what she was doing, excited her, made her perform better.

In the fax machine's tray lay a sheet with a series of numbers. The caller had not created the coded readout, the computer had—from a program written by Marina Suslova. She set the sheet in a copy holder, sat down before the computer, and decrypted the message. She raised her eyebrows. The message was from Joe Ryerson. She had been expecting something from him, but not so soon.

A third of the message was his usual bragging nonsense. But the remainder was interesting, if exasperating. So the fascists she'd hired in San Francisco had done only part of their work. At least Pierre Grau would not be meeting with Nathan Abramov in this life, she thought sardonically. Ryerson's message confirmed what she had heard on the early newscasts, about Grau's death, but neither source said anything about the woman, Anna Neville. Perhaps Neville and Grau had not been together, and the attempt on Neville would have to await a more convenient time. The skinheads with whom she often had to work were always vicious, but not always efficient. The Intelligence Directorate was strapped for personnel. In the good days, the KGB had never had to go outside the organization for assassins. Well, it was a new world now, Marina thought. On occasion, one even had to do the job oneself, distasteful as it might be.

Ryerson's message asked that she call him at his hotel in San Francisco at ten A.M., Pacific time. It was just past noon in Silver Spring, 9:11 in San Francisco. She looked at the Rolex on her slender wrist. It offended her sense of security to make telephone calls exactly on the hour. On the off chance that NSA was monitoring her calls, the telephone ferrets would be just a trifle more alert at those well-defined intervals.

She dialed the number of the Fairmont Hotel in San Francisco, where Ryerson liked to stay. As she waited for a connection, she examined herself in the wall mirror, tossing her hair back over her shoulder. The gesture had always been one of her most successful moves when on the prowl, and she practiced it often.

Ryerson answered after four rings. Very likely he was having breakfast in his room. On Russian money, Marina thought. But he had, as the Americans said so inelegantly, a nose for news, and he was persistent.

"I need more money," Ryerson said without preamble.

"When do you not?" Marina asked coldly.

"I have a story. A great one."

"I am not interested in furthering the cause of freelance journalism." Marina had had this conversation with Ryerson before. There were times, and this was one, when her instinct warned her that Joe Ryerson knew very well the source of the funds she gave him, and the destination of the information he gave her. "But tell me, anyway," she said.

His voice on the telephone was ragged and tired. "No need to be in my face."

"I don't know that expression. It sounds very trendy," she said.

"Bitch. Maybe you don't need to know this."

"Good-bye. Call me when you get back." Marina waited, smiling to herself.

"Okay, I *said* I would tell you."

"I am listening."

"All right. Try this on for size. Vincent Kellner's man, Morgan, killed three people last night. My information is solid. I bribed a cop. Gave him my last hundred."

Marina's heartbeat quickened. Ryerson's reputation for tricks sprang to her mind immediately. Surely he wouldn't try to fool her. She had seen John Morgan at a Georgetown reception early in the year, and at one or two other diplomatic gatherings. Six feet tall, very attractive—very masculine. Craggy features. Wavy dark hair. Eyes like sea ice. Handsome in his way. A Marine colonel, the NSC chairman's man.

"Interesting."

"I thought you might think so."

"I will wire you some money."

"You heard on the news that Anna Neville's lawyer was killed?"

"Yes. A street accident, they say." That much of the plan had gone simply and smoothly. But what had happened next? Morgan reached the woman, and then?

A light on the telephone indicated another call waiting. Swiftly she said, "Hold for a moment, Yosip." She pressed the button and said, "Ten minutes."

It was her standard greeting and precaution on incoming calls. It gave her time to run the computer program that identified the caller's number.

She came back to Ryerson swiftly. "I am here. Go on."

"What happened to Pierre Grau was no accident."

Marina saw no need to discuss the killing of Grau with Ryerson. "Tell me about this Colonel Morgan," she said. Morgan was the key to a higher stakes game than Grau would ever have been. "Was one of Morgan's victims Grau?" she asked ingenuously.

"No, of course not. Morgan didn't arrive in San Francisco until after Grau was killed. Grau was run down by a Bronco. You know what that is?"

It kept him disarmed if she played the quaint foreigner from time to time. "A horse?" she asked archly.

"Jesus. No, a car. Big, rugged thing. To use off the road, or in the mountains."

"Did the police catch the people in the car?"

"No. But Morgan did."

Marina waited. Sometimes, she thought, Yosip Ryerson had the style of a writer of cheap novels, overly portentous and dramatic. But he would eventually come to the point. "Morgan met Anna Neville at the hospital where they treated Grau. He took her off to pour booze into her, and to pump her for what she knew. The cops here should never have allowed it, but if I know Morgan, he threw his weight around some. When he and Neville took off, the people who killed Grau must have been watching. They followed Morgan and the woman to a restaurant in North Beach. Someone, probably one of the guys in the Bronco, tossed a grenade through the door into the restaurant. Can you believe—Morgan threw the damn thing into the street. The police were impressed with Colonel Fucking Morgan. And even more impressed after he gunned down three hoods in full survival gear. Morgan is good at killing civilians."

A rather unreasonable judgment, Marina thought, given the circumstances. "When did this Colonel Morgan attack these men?"

"Sometime after midnight."

"Where?" she murmured.

"Down the coast from San Francisco, about twenty or so miles. Morgan and the woman headed that way after the grenade attempt, and the people in the Bronco followed them again. Morgan set up an ambush and killed them."

"Your story is all rather vague, Yosip."

"There are pieces missing, but I'll find them."

"Yes, I have no doubt of that," Marina said thoughtfully. She decided that Yosip had just grown too expensive, too risky, to keep as an asset. Time was getting short; she wouldn't be able to dispose of him properly before she left the country. She might have to pass along the assignment. At least she wouldn't have to bed him again.

"About dawn a highway cop noticed a hole in a sand berm on the ocean side of a dangerous stretch of the Coast Highway, a place the locals call Devil's Slide. When he looked over the edge, he spotted some wreckage in the surf at the base of the cliff. I was trying to collect information on the Grau case from the San Francisco cops when the report came in from the Highway Patrol. I invited myself along. I got there just in time to see a Bronco being hoisted out of the sea and up the slide. There were three dead guys in the car, local punks—together with an arsenal of weapons, shotguns, assault rifles, handguns—and grenades. The front end of the car and the windshield were shot to hell. The sheriff's people found nine-millimeter shell casings across the road." Ryerson's voice reflected his satisfaction. "They haven't put it together yet, but I have. It was Morgan's style."

Marina sighed in disgust for her hired killers. No one could say they were subtle or clever, what with their burning crosses, military fatigues, shaved heads, and Nazi flags. All that armament, and apparently this lot had failed to survive a single middle-aged Marine.

She dreaded having to inform Piotr Kondratiev that her imitation soldiers had done only half the task set for them. That would not be pleasant. She had better send the message now, so he could digest it before they met face to face. She had argued with him, saying that killing Grau and the Neville woman might draw much more attention to the Neville accident than just letting the two of them wander around the country telling their story. But Piotr had insisted, saying that whatever happened to them would just point to the Americans as the culprits. And he'd been right. Every news-cast she'd seen carried a background report on the downing of the airplane at Hudson Bay, together with the fact that Anna Neville and the CCND claimed an American missile as the cause. He had understood how this American free press worked, their pugnacity and their persistence, their adversarial stance. At least some of them would always believe the worst about Washington.

"That is a fantastic story, Yosip," she said, her voice filled with admiration. "Can you document it?"

"Not yet. But soon."

"I will send you *two* thousand dollars. Hang up now," she

said, and broke the connection abruptly, smiling. The NSA would give a fortune to have this conversation on tape, she thought. But the embassy people had checked just yesterday. No taps.

Now she turned to the computer. The telephone number of a public booth on Pennsylvania Avenue, three blocks from the White House, appeared on the screen. She looked at her watch. Marina had kept Camilla waiting for slightly more than ten minutes, and she would be angry.

Marina dialed the number, and after three rings Camilla answered, not angry, but excited.

"It's me, Evangeline," she said inelegantly. "I have something for you." Her voice was filled with satisfaction. "Something *delicious.*"

Perhaps this was a day for miracles, Marina thought. Well, something delicious might be very useful today.

"I am listening," she said.

"This is special."

"Special means expensive, as I recall."

"Yes. I've seen a house in Alexandria I want. I need two hundred and fifty thousand dollars for the down payment."

Marina Suslova sucked in her breath, taken aback. Americans often sold their country for money, but most came cheap. They seldom asked for money in quarter-million-dollar sums. Evangeline's most valuable items had heretofore been purchased for far smaller amounts.

"That is a very great deal of money," Marina said carefully. "And it will take some doing to raise it."

"What I have is worth it, twice over."

Perhaps, Marina thought. There was no way of knowing until a deal was made. American traitors in the past had acted on principle, for ideals, ideology. The spur was now money, impure and simple; a truly capitalistic motive. However, Marina suspected that Camilla would have spied for money, and only for money, long before treason for cash became the fashion. She usually knew to the dollar the value of her commodities. She was, after all, close to one of the most powerful men in Washington. If Camilla said something was worth a quarter million dollars, it probably was.

"I may have trouble finding that much," she said dubiously.

"I don't think so," Camilla said. "It's a bargain at the price. I want something else, too."

Bitch, Marina thought. She has me and she knows it. "Else? What ever else can there be?"

"One uninterrupted night. Tonight."

Marina breathed a long sigh of relief. What a wonderful thing was love, she thought sardonically. "You know I can't deny you anything, my dear," she said.

"Agreed?"

"Agreed."

"I want the money in my Cayman Islands account by the end of this week."

"Difficult," Marina said.

"But doable. I will meet you at nine. Our place."

"Is that all the information I am to have now?"

"A minister of the Russian Executive Committee is being run as an Amerian agent by Vincent Kellner. Think about it," Camilla said, and broke the connection.

Genuinely startled, Marina placed the telephone gently in its cradle. Information of this magnitude could make her the most powerful woman in the Intelligence Directorate. It is getting late, she thought, too close to the day that infernal Device is to go off. But when I return to Moscow, it will be in triumph.

As she started toward the door to leave, the computer screen changed colors and began to print out a message. She stopped abruptly and watched it with something akin to dread. This was the first time her private communications system had indicated a direct message from Russia.

The numbers were in four-digit groups, and there were

eighteen of them. It was a one-off encryption designed specifically for her machine. Marina's heart began to beat faster.

The message ended, leaving the number groups on the screen. Immediately she sat at the keyboard and completed the decryption sequence. Her mouth felt dry as she recognized the origin. Sochi.

The number groups morphed into letter groups. Marina opened her pocketbook and withdrew her checkbook. On the last page of the check register were written the global instructions, which she added to the file the computer was building.

When she had completed the instructions, she gave the computer the command to print.

The message from Piotr Kondratiev was simple and direct:

MEXICO CITY REZIDENTURA REPORTS A SURVIVOR OF THE
PRAVDA EN ROUTE UNITED STATES. TERMINATION ESSEN-
TIAL.

Marina's carefully laid plans of departure lay in ruins. For the first time since her association with Soyuz began, she was afraid.

Chapter Twenty-one

Half Moon Bay, California/November 28, 29

We take our allies wherever we find them, and we find them everywhere. Meanwhile, the despoilers of the Motherland search desperately for friends—and find only Americans.

—GENERAL PIOTR KONDRATIEV

MORGAN STOOD FOR A MOMENT LONGER, looking at the sleeping woman. The lines of pain and weariness on her face had smoothed out. The corners of her mouth were turned up. He caught himself sharply. Remember why you're here, Morgan, he thought. He closed the door.

Ave Peters asked, "Is she sleeping?"

"Yes. And a good thing, too. She's close to the edge." Morgan made his way around the clutter in the room, old newspapers and magazines, mixed indiscriminately with fishing tackle and hunting paraphernalia. He pushed some boxes off a scuffed leather sofa and sat down. He was as exhausted as Anna, but had been unable to sleep more than four hours, and that fitfully. His dreams had been filled with the sight of huge black off-road vehicles chasing him, and the sounds of gunfire echoing.

The air was heavy with the smell of Ave's stale cigars. The house, wood frame painted scaling white, shingle roofed, stood on the edge of the airport on Highway 1, with the town of El Granada and the sea a half mile away to the west. The narrow shelf between the Pacific Ocean and the Coast Range was rich and green, prime land given to truck and flower farms. Fog and rain were common here. In deep winter the sky, when it could be seen at all, was usually a cold silver color, merging with the distant horizon far out at sea.

A bank of wet fog drifted a mere fifty feet above the tarmac runways of the airport this November morning. The galvanized iron hangar of Peters Aviation was visible between half-drawn shades, fluorescent ceiling lights still glaring. Inside, Ave's Cessna 310 was undergoing an engine change. Morgan silently cursed the delay.

Ave Peters, a man in his sixties with the body of an aged linebacker, divined Morgan's thoughts and said, "It's in good hands. The best. Johnny and Don Desmond are as sharp and as quick as they come. She'll be ready to fly by ten tonight— safely. If that's not good enough for you, tough shit." He spat with unerring aim into the brass cuspidor in the corner of the room. "By the way, you'd better watch yourself with that little man trap in there. She's the sneaky kind—and that makes it all the worse for you when it ends."

Morgan regarded him evenly, ignoring his comments, refusing to acknowledge his suspicions. "Where can I leave the rental car?" he asked. Years ago he had learned that the proper way to deal with Avery Peters was to present him with a steady series of technical or tactical situations in need of resolving. Like many former case officers, Ave was a very practical man. He claimed to dislike problems, but he relished finding answers.

"Let me take care of it. I'll lose it somewhere down below Half Moon Bay, on one of the back roads. The sheriff's people won't find it until tomorrow. Not with all the to-do up the road." As if to emphasize Peters's remarks, a pair of black-and-white California Highway Patrol cars, lights flashing and sirens keening, raced north along the highway toward Devil's Slide. They were the fourth and fifth CHP units that had passed in the last hour.

"You sure as shit stirred things up," Ave said, grinning at Morgan. "There hasn't been this much excitement here since bootlegger days." To an inhabitant of this area, from Montara and Princeton-by-the-Sea on down the coast to Half Moon Bay, that meant the twenties, when the harbor at Half Moon Bay had been full of excitement, a favorite of rum runners and bootleggers. Storm and earthquake, intermittent in northern California, enhanced the golden memories of western San Mateo County as a haven for lawbreakers, and for those who could withstand hardship. Now its role in life was as the home of the annual Pumpkin Festival and a port of refuge for the local fishing fleets. The latter was very like the purpose it served for Anna Neville and himself, Morgan thought.

Devil's Slide seemed naturally situated in such a neighborhood. The long, steep fall to the sea had always appealed to the morbid and the curious. And it claimed a steady toll of lives, mostly of the despondent and the careless. It would have been better, Morgan thought, had I counterattacked on a less notorious stretch of road. But that couldn't be helped now.

"You can't leave now, anyhow," Ave observed. "The airport, this whole area, is swarming with local law enforcement with a description of the both of you. And if you have any idea of turning yourself over to the San Francisco cops," he said, "forget it. SFPD has more leaks than a Greek rowboat."

"I wasn't planning to rely on the local police to guard her," Morgan said dryly. "Kellner wouldn't like it." And SFPD is not the only leaky vessel, he thought angrily.

"That scar on her cheek," Ave said. "Where did she get it? In the Canadian crash? What the hell happened up there?"

"The floatplane broke up and went down in an ice field.

She says it was hit by a missile," Morgan said.

Ave looked thoughtful. "She's brave, for a lefty," he said.

"The two things aren't necessarily exclusive," Morgan said.

"Is there anything to her story?"

"I don't know yet," Morgan said. "It's possible. Something weird sure as hell went on up there."

Ave pulled on a shabby parka. "Give me the keys. I'll stash that car before somebody spots it. While I'm about it, I want to ask some questions about the good ole boys you greased. Meanwhile, you better get some rest. Washington's a long flight in a 310," he said. He zipped up the parka and stepped outside into the misting ocean air. "Don't bother my boys," he warned. "They'll be finished when they're finished. I'll be back, two, three hours."

"I won't disturb them," Morgan promised. "By the way, before you ditch the car, check it for a bug, will you? I'd like to think I wasn't just careless last night."

Morgan watched the gray rental car disappear behind the hangars. He closed the front door, then was drawn to look in again on Anna. She slept with brow furrowed and a hand against her cheek, like a troubled child. As he watched, she turned onto her back, tossing her head from side to side, still frowning. She murmured something unintelligible. He went over to the bed and gently drew the blanket up over her bare shoulders. Don't sentimentalize her, Morgan told himself. Remember who she is, and who you are and why you two have been thrown together. But he watched her for a moment more before retreating to the door. Suddenly Anna called out "No—no!" and came awake, sitting up, her eyes enormous, her back pressed against the headboard. She stared at Morgan as if she had never seen him before, her face taut with fear.

"You're safe, Anna," Morgan said in a firm voice. "We're in Half Moon Bay, remember? We're leaving for Washington in a few hours." When she didn't respond, he went over to

173

her and sat down on the bed. "You're safe," he repeated softly.

She plucked at the blanket, her eyes still blank. He reached over and took one of her hands. She clutched his hand with all her strength, and pulled him toward her, dropping the blanket and exposing her breasts, mouth searching for his hungrily. Her other hand was around his neck, fingernails digging into his flesh.

For one long moment, Morgan hesitated, every instinct demanding caution. But Anna threw off the blanket, rising to her knees and pressing against him, pushing him back onto the bed. Morgan said under his breath, "Oh, the hell with it," and responded, fumbling with the zipper on his pants, pulling his shirt over his head.

She was near to frenzied in her demand. It was an encounter of the senses, without tenderness. She lay back across the bed and pulled him down on her, guiding him into her, moving frantically under him until they both came to an explosive climax.

Morgan's head was pressed into the pillow as he savored the physical release. His sex life had been coarse since Joan died. Anna lay passively under him, eyes closed, as he stroked the damp hair away from her scarred forehead.

"Don't," she said, turning her head to hide the scar.

"All right," Morgan said. He rolled over onto his back.

She lay still on the bed, eyes closed—to shut him out? Okay, Morgan thought, that's the way it is. He stood and dressed as quietly as he could. Anna lay still, her breasts rising and falling in deep breaths. She was a million miles away, in some private preserve of her own.

He walked into the bathroom and splashed cold water over his head, drying his hair with one of Ave's thin, dingy towels. He looked at himself critically in the mirror and borrowed Ave's razor to shave. Her rebuff had stung him. But I was out of line, he thought, as he ran the blade over his cheeks. I'm supposed to be a caretaker, a protector, not a stud.

He went back into the cluttered office without looking at Anna in the bedroom. He turned on the television set, searching for news. He finally found it on a cable station, mostly national news, and not much of that. He could have recited it in his sleep. The President was still at Camp David. Prime Minister Ian Halloran would leave Ottawa tonight for a brief visit to Washington. A plane was down in the mountains of Utah. The stock market was up in New York.

After the commercial, which featured a singing toilet seat, the talking head announced that Russian National Day had been a great success. A series of clips showed children marching through Red Square in the freezing rain before President Cherny and the other Russian leaders. They still stood atop the mausoleum, only it was no longer called Lenin's Tomb. It was only an ambiguous monument to a failed system. How long would it be before they dismantled it? The papery corpse of Lenin had been put in the ground next to his mother long ago, as he had asked. Odd to think of Lenin as such a devoted child. The crowd in Red Square seemed listless, smaller than Morgan remembered from parades in the past. The people on the sidelines looked as cold and threadbare now as they had then.

As a sidebar to the Russian National Day story, the network ran a CNN clip of a Soyuz demonstration on Arbat Street. Here was the enthusiasm missing in the official celebration in Red Square. The screen was full of angry demonstrators shouting slogans, shaking clenched fists, waving banners with the emblem of St. George. When the militia tried to break up the ranks, the people resisted, charging the riot police with staves and rocks. According to the commentary from Moscow Television, the Soyuz people were trying to reach Red Square and disrupt the official ceremonies. Two policemen went down under the onslaught and were rescued by Internal Security Black Beret troops, So, Morgan thought, the Black Berets are back in Moscow. There was no sound from the bedroom.

Morgan checked the time carefully. It was 1322 hours in

Washington. Lunch break ought to be over for the duty staff in the NSC office. He pushed aside the mess on Ave's desk and picked up the telephone to dial the unlisted number. It was answered immediately. He recognized the voice of Hardy Miller, a GS-14 security man moved over by Kellner from Foggy Bottom. A man in his late fifties, and near retirement.

"Hardy, this is John Morgan," he said. "Scramble."

"Morgan, Jesus Christ, where have you been? What's happening out there?"

"Scramble, Hardy. Or I'm hanging up." Hardy was burdened with the State Department's oddly confused sense of what "security" meant.

"Oh, very well, Colonel." Whenever Hardy grew miffed, he tended to use titles rather than names. The shrill series of tones indicated that the White House scrambling system was now operating. It actually did little more than mask voices. As a security measure it was years out of date, but Cole Caidin would not request funds to improve the White House security technology.

"Is that better, Colonel?" Miller's voice was heavy with sarcasm.

"You know the regulations, Hardy," Morgan said. "Is Dr. Kellner there? Or Camilla Varig?"

"He's with the President at Camp David. I'm the only one here."

"Camilla? Is she with Dr. Kellner?"

"No, she's off somewhere, on her own. I told you I'm the only one on line. Now, will you please be so kind as to tell me where you are and when you plan—"

"Shut up and listen to me, Hardy. I'm returning to Washington tonight by charter. I have Anna Neville with me."

"Why by charter? The GAO will have a stroke."

Morgan tried to rein in his sudden anger. "Fuck the GAO. Listen. I don't have an ETA yet, but I'll try to notify you as soon as we're airborne. We land at National. I want transport standing by. Someone reliable, do you read me? And I mean

176

reliable. A backup car, too, with a driver and a shooter."

"Aren't you being rather melodramatic, Colonel? It's only one woman, after all, not the nuclear codes."

"I gave you an order, Hardy. Carry it out." Morgan was feeling an attack of hate-the-civilian coming on. It was wrong, of course. Hardy Miller couldn't help being a State Department ninny. He had spent his entire professional life learning his trade, which was obfuscation. Morgan said, "I want these arrangements as secure as you can make them."

"You know that it's really Camilla's job, dealing with you NSC specials, but I'll do the best I can."

"Don't log this call. Enter it as class two. That's all that's necessary."

"Colonel, don't you people ever get tired of playing at cloak-and-dagger?"

"No," Morgan said, and broke the connection. A class two entry in the day book would alert either Vincent Kellner or Camilla when they checked in. They could then retrieve the tape of the conversation from the White House mainframe. Hardy Miller had no need to know, and so was unaware of this kind of message triage, practiced daily by the NSC's black operations staff.

Morgan stared, unseeing, at the telephone under his hand. For the time being, he had done what was possible to assure Anna Neville's safety. But he was dogged by the suspicion that it was not enough.

"Calling your masters, Colonel?" Anna stood in the doorway, pushing a wavy lock of hair out of her eyes, a weary smile on her face.

Morgan jumped at the sound of her voice and turned to face her. He had no idea what to say to her. Her clothes were rumpled and untidy. He realized that whatever luggage she had was still at the Stanford Court Hotel, unless, of course, the FBI or SFPD had obtained a court order to go and collect it.

Anna tugged at her skirt. There was a run in her stockings.

Her brown shoes were scuffed at the toe, possibly from being pulled to the floor in the Bella Italia. She showed all the signs of having gone through a bad dozen hours. Yet there was that faintly mocking smile. Her version of sexual politics? Morgan wondered.

There was a moment of silence between them.

"What happens now?" she asked.

So we forget about what happened a few moments ago. Yes, Morgan thought. Perhaps that's best. "Nothing, until tonight. The place is crawling with police. Ave will fly us to Washington."

"I see. Am I arrested?"

"For what?"

"For being Anna Neville."

"That's not illegal yet," Morgan said. He went into the kitchen alcove and turned on the gas under a pot of Ave's inky coffee. Anna followed him and leaned against the door-jamb.

"I want to tell you about Pierre Grau," she said.

"All right, I'm listening."

"Pierre Grau wasn't a Communist, if that's what you think."

Morgan brought the pot to a simmer, then poured coffee into a thick mug and handed it to Anna. "I believe you—not that it matters."

"Why do you say that?"

"Because it really doesn't matter. He was trying to help himself, and the CCND. That's all right. There's no law against it. What with all the treaties being signed, the antinuke crowd's been running out of causes. You came along just at the right time. Now they've become headliners again. That doesn't make Grau a bad man. Just a dead one," he finished brutally.

She held the cup of bitter coffee without tasting it, looking at him steadily. "You don't like me very much, do you, Morgan?"

"How can you say that? After our moment of tenderness?" He poured coffee for himself.

"What a hateful man you are," she said hotly.

"No argument," Morgan said. "We'll talk about it sometime, and you can psychoanalyze me. But not now." Her eyes are such a dark blue they look almost black in this light, he thought.

Anna watched Morgan intently. She tasted the coffee, made a face, and set the mug down on the table. "I'm asking for a truce. Something terrible is going on, isn't it? I don't mean just to Pierre, and you, and me. Something bigger."

"I don't know," Morgan said. "Possibly."

"Those men in the car following us. You killed them."

"It seems that I did."

Anna shuddered, and the response made Morgan angry. *Protect me, but don't injure anyone in the process.* Christ, he thought, what was it with these people? On what planet did they live their utopian lives?

ANNA WALKED TO THE WINDOW and looked out, blinking away hot tears. I did it again, after all those firm resolutions, she thought unhappily. As if making love was going to save me from my demons. What in God's name is Morgan thinking behind that poker face? His contempt was only thinly disguised. Probably that I'm a fool, she thought. She studied the weed-lined runways of the airport, the colorful array of private airplanes tied down just inside the fence between the field and Highway 1. The sight brought a sudden and powerful memory of Sean McCarthy. She flushed with guilt. She had not given thought to Sean since leaving the hospital. Her couplings with him were meaningless. And what was she to say about the explosive encounter with this stranger? Intimate? Empty? Intimate emptiness.

Morgan watched her, trying to stay emotionally uninvolved. She seemed very far away again, in that private zone. He wanted to bring her back, to here and now, to him.

179

"Has it occurred to you that killing Grau, and trying to kill you, could suggest that someone is trying to stop what you're doing, stop your very public tour?"

"That's obvious," she said scornfully.

"Yes, it is. Someone wants the public to be sure the United States is trying to silence you," Morgan said. "Who would want to blame the U.S. Navy for what happened in Hudson Bay last year?"

She turned back to look at him, startled. Then, with long-conditioned suspicion, she raised her eyes to the ceiling in exasperated disbelief. "Oh, not *that,* Morgan. Not the Russians and the Communists and the KGB. I thought all that was over, even for Americans."

He said stubbornly, "The navy tracked a Russian boat from the Labrador Sea to Cuba—at which time it conveniently sank with all hands, just after your accident. And *someone* paid those bastards to kill you and Grau. Someone with access to lots of money. When our psychos run big risks, they collect big money . . ."

Anna shivered. "I can't think the way you do, Morgan. I believe in nonviolence. In pacifism. It's what I grew up believing. Those men in the Bronco—they're dead, and their deaths can't be excused or rationalized."

Her tone, her fear of him, stung Morgan. "Would you rather we were in pieces, splattered all over that restaurant? Or down on those rocks ourselves?"

Anna turned away.

I should have known better, he thought. We're on opposite sides. I'd better end this talk right now. It serves no purpose.

He collected the coffee cups and put them in the sink, standing with his back to her. "You'd better try to get some more rest," he said in a flat voice. "It'll be a long night."

AS NIGHT FELL, the sky cleared, and the horizon came ablaze with brilliant streaks of red and gold. Ave, dressed in his flying coveralls, threw a dozen eggs and some salsa into an old cast-iron skillet and scrambled them with a fork. He shoveled them onto plates, and Morgan, Anna, and he ate without speaking. There were spot newscasts about the mysterious doings at Devil's Slide. First reports had been sympathetic to the victims, but now that the three dead men had been identified as members of a local white supremacist underground, the tone had changed. One station hinted darkly that the group trained in camps in the Sierra foothills.

"Is that true, Mr. Peters?" Anna asked.

"Is what true, Mrs. Neville?"

"The report about the men in the Bronco who followed us and who were killed; that they were white supremacists."

"So the media people say."

Morgan sat back and regarded Anna thoughtfully. What if someone, perhaps Ave, perhaps Morgan himself, had to kill again to protect her? Couldn't she endanger herself and her protectors? Relax, he thought, willing himself not to care. It shouldn't matter to me. When I deliver her safely back to the NSC, my work will be done.

Ave finished his scrambled eggs and stood to gather the plates and pile them in the sink. "If you mean did those bozos need killing, Mrs. Neville," he drawled, simulating a southern accent, "that I can't say. I can tell you they won't be missed. There've been some pretty nasty incidents hereabouts recently. A synagogue was burned last month; the ACLU offices in San Francisco were bombed. Last May, a bunch of them ganged up on a gay in the Castro and beat him to death. I can't promise you those were our perps, but if they weren't, they sure as hell were members of the same club. The White Knights. Coalition for a Secure America. They make up names as easily as raghead terrorists do. Taking a few foot soldiers out won't solve the problem, but it never hurts to thin out the enemy."

He consulted the large aviator's chronograph on his white-haired wrist. "The boys should be done with that engine in a half hour or so. I ought to do a flight check, but the hell with it. I'll fax a flight plan to ATC now from the hangar."

He thrust his arms into an antique B-2 leather jacket. There was an Air America patch, much the worse for wear, on the jacket's left breast. Meo tribesmen, Hmong, the CIA and their illegal, immoral arming of the tribes in the mountains—Anna thought of them all instantly. She could hear her father speaking, thundering against the war in Vietnam and the innocents harmed thereby. How horrified he would be to see her here among the enemy.

"Stand by," Ave said, on his way out the door. "We'll be gone straightaway. Stay under cover."

Morgan had been mulling over their encounter of the afternoon, and he was simmering with anger. He went to a cabinet and took out a bottle of Ave's brandy. He found a chipped glass on the sink, poured brandy into it, and downed it like medicine. He said to Anna, "Forget about the casualties last night. It happens. Sometimes it happens to the good guys. You can't handle situations like that with sanctions or demonstrations."

She looked away, her face flushed. He persisted. "We're realistic. We've tried the peaceful approach and gotten clobbered for our pains, every time, everywhere. Extreme remedies are all that will do in certain circumstances." He poured another brandy. "I belong to a class of people you were raised to despise. Policemen, soldiers; garbagemen. The jobs we do disgust you and your friends. But someone has to take out the trash. Someone has to make your world safe so you can march around anywhere you please, carrying signs about the fate of the earth."

He slammed down the emptied glass, making Anna jump. "In the seventies, when I was growing up in California, I used to see your father's disciples carrying Vietcong flags, while *my* father was in Southeast Asia being shot at and crawling through minefields. At school I was told by the teachers that my father was a murderer."

"Your father was a Marine?"

She sounds as though she didn't realize I had a father, Morgan thought. "My father was a Marine who died in a Vietcong ambush, trying to save some children stuck in a minefield. He believed in his Corps and his country, and that his way was every bit as 'correct' as your way. I don't think he would have worried about those yahoos I terminated, and I sure as hell am not going to. Ah, shit, why do I waste my time?"

He strode across the kitchen to the door, stepped through it, and slammed it behind him. The damp ocean air cooled his burning cheeks.

WHAT A LOUSY, PERVERSE WORLD it really is, Morgan thought. He sat down on a wooden bench near the airport fence. The November stars were shining through the thin clouds. He could just make out the shape of Orion, the Hunter, rising above the mountains of the Coast Range. How long, Morgan wondered. Since before the glaciers came and went, Orion had guarded the sky of winter, with his red eye of Betelgeuse watching and the nursery of stars at his belt. In spite of his anger with Anna, Morgan smiled. Orion and his fellow skywalkers put life on earth in proper perspective. He wondered if those monuments to human failings, wars and cold wars, were being fought out there beyond the limitless miles, astronomical units, light-years, parsecs. Lord, he thought, I hope not.

"You think I'm a foolish woman," Anna said, startling him. She had come out of the house silently, to stand behind him as he looked at the sky.

"Not really," he said.

She sat beside him. "I thought I was doing the right thing. I'm appalled at what I've set in motion."

"This afternoon?"

"I didn't mean that."

"I know. That was a lame try at humor. Look, you can't blame yourself for what's happening," Morgan said quietly. He was acutely aware of her warmth next to him. He had to keep in mind that once she was delivered safely to Washing-

183

Alfred Coppel

ton, his part would be done. For some reason, the thought was not as cheering as he had expected.

"My social graces are a bit lacking, Anna," he said regretfully. "My mother died when I was a very adolescent sixteen, and the Naval Academy didn't help much. The emphasis these days is on *officer,* more than on *gentlemen.*"

She said, "The warrior ethic. Yes, I know. My colleagues grow very nervous when they encounter it. But as you not-so-gently pointed out, there are times when you need something more than an ombudsman."

Morgan smiled at her, willing to accept the offered cease-fire between them. He caught sight of Ave approaching from the direction of the Peters Aviation hangar. He was not alone. Ave held an unwilling captive in a firm armlock. As Morgan watched, the faces of the two men came into the light, and he recognized with a shock the stumbling figure of Joe Ryerson.

Ave said, "Do you know this scuzball, Morgan? He says he knows you."

Morgan regarded Ryerson with growing anger. The man was a plague. His presence in this place reinforced the fact that there was an enormous leak in the Executive Wing. Only the NSC staff knew about Morgan's longtime connection with Avery Peters. Morgan felt as thought he and Anna were suddenly standing in the Kuwaiti desert, well within the range of enemy guns.

Anna asked, "Who is this man, Morgan?"

"My name is Ryerson and I am a freelance journalist," Ryerson said angrily, trying to break free from Ave Peter's grasp.

Ave said to Morgan, "He was in the hangar, getting in the way of the boys. Asking questions. Isn't that right, Mr. Journalist?"

Morgan stared hard at Ryerson's frightened, angry face. You had to give the man credit; he was impossible to discourage. Only thirty-six hours before, he had been snooping around Morgan's house in Leesburg. Now this.

184

Morgan asked grimly, "Was he alone?"

"Ask me, Colonel Fucking Morgan," Ryerson said defiantly. "Yes, I'm alone. Doing my job."

"Ah, shut up." Peters twisted his arm.

Morgan said, "Let him go, Ave." To Ryerson he asked, "Who told you where we were?"

"Go to hell, Morgan."

"Who *is* he, Morgan?" Anna asked again, anxiously.

"He used to call himself a newspaperman," Morgan said coldly. "In actual fact, he's a lying son of a bitch. He lost his job on his paper when he called the President's press secretary, pretending to be a member of Hezbollah, saying he had hostages, and was ready to strike a deal. But he insisted on speaking to the President personally, capture the Head of State discussing a deal with a terrorist, with the whole conversation on tape. An absolute hoax. He'd made a deal with one of those tell-all television programs for lots of dough. Classy, Ryerson. Very classy."

"Why is he here?" Anna's anxiety was heightened.

Morgan said, "Ave, we'll have to take him with us." He turned to Ryerson. "This is either the luckiest night of your life or your last."

Avery Peters said in a low voice, "Kidnapping a member of the Washington press corps is big trouble. Your boss will go ballistic."

"That's the least of it. I've got to tell him that he has a gusher somewhere in the NSC." Or something even worse, Morgan thought. Much worse.

Chapter Twenty-two

The Northwest Territories/61.07 N 89.90 W/November 29

At the height of the cold war, the Energy Department's nuclear weapons laboratories considered building a warhead that would generate high-powered microwaves over a wide area, destroying the electronic equipment controlling the Soviets' mobile intercontinental ballistic missiles.

However, a member of the House Ways and Means Committee will say—on background only—that the High Power Microwave Weapon and other similar exotic devices will never survive the budget process. Such devices, he said, are too expensive, too unreliable, and too destabilizing to be built in peacetime.

—WASHINGTON POST

IN THE DEEP DARKNESS, the Device stirs. The cylindrical casing has sunk deep in the alluvial mud of the bay bottom since being deposited there by the Pravda.

At the programmed time on this date, electrical power has been shunted to a set of servomotors, and the missile slowly

*sprouts limbs that orient it, then erect it to a vertical position.
The hatch now lies only two meters from the surface of the
bay at low tide. Dead and rotting fish that had settled in the
mud are disturbed; they float away from the Device on the
current.*

*The Device's movement has widened the original split in
the casing. Watertight integrity has been lost. Within a radius
of twenty meters the contamination was already severe. It now
suddenly increases by orders of magnitude.*

*A hatch in the missile's flank opens and a small, torpedolike
unit is ejected. It sinks to the muddy bottom. One minute later,
the small unit's propeller whirs into action and it rises from
the bottom and speeds away to the northeast on a preset
course.*

*After thirty-seven minutes, the small unit's hydrazine fuel is
exhausted. But it does not sink to the floor of the bay. Instead,
it breaks the surface of the water, erects a spidery whip antenna, and transmits a signal.*

COSMOS 7201 FLIES *in bright sunlight at an altitude of 290
kilometers. As it overflies the Russian space base at Tyuratam,
the satellite's recording and retransmitting program positions
the transmitting antenna and begins to send.*

*The cover program is one of cosmic ray research over Cen-
tral Asia. Buried within the code is a message for General
Piotr Kondratiev, to be delivered by a dissident member of the
GKNT.*

*Two hours after receiving the message, a jubilant Piotr
Kondratiev boards an Aeroflot jet for Sheremeteyvo Airport,
Moscow.*

Chapter Twenty-three

Moscow/Washington, D.C./New York/November 29

Academician Mikhail Ivanovich Orgonev, creator of the Soviet Union's most powerful generation of nuclear weapons, died this morning of complications brought about by advanced emphysema. M. I. Orgonev was a reserve general officer of the Strategic Rocket Forces, a holder of the Order of Lenin, and twice cited as a Hero of the Soviet Union for his work on sophisticated scientific devices.

Preparations are under way for a state funeral to honor this great man, one of the last of his kind, who spent his life in honorable service to his country.

—RED STAR, JOURNAL OF THE RUSSIAN ARMY

Memorandum from Aleksandr Cherny to David Milstein, Minister of Finance

Thank you, David Davidovich, for your prompt reply to my request. It is my understanding that you will be attending a hunting party in Ukovo as a guest of Admiral Aleyev after Orgonev's funeral and before visiting the reconstruction work on the Dneiper Dam. As regards the dam, I will expect a full report from you on the terms the World Bank intends to levy on us before the Eurocon Organization agrees to assist us in completing the work.

More to the point, I want to see you the moment you return from Ukovo. I must know what those old wolves are up to and why they have chosen to invite you into their lair.

I have also notified the Foreign Ministry that I wish to see our ambassador to the United Nations, Nathan Abramov, immediately that he arrives in Moscow, rather than to wait until he briefs the Executive Council on the current status of events at the UN.

President Cherny hesitated a moment, then scrawled across the bottom in his own handwriting,

Dovi—Thank you, my friend, for doing me this favor, even if there is some danger involved. You are a clever man; see with your own eyes what they are up to, get at least a hint of what they plan to do—if anything. You see, I am still not quite convinced that Soyuz is the menace you think it is. In return, I will see Abramov, and I promise to listen carefully to whatever he tells me.

When Cherny had finished, and had read over the memorandum, he folded it carefully and put it into a plain envelope. "Deliver this by hand," he said to his most trusted aide, Ivan Gagarin, who stood by his desk. As Gagarin accepted the envelope, he added anxiously, "To no one but the Minister, himself."

"Be assured that I will do as you ask," Gagarin said.

"Thank you, Ivan," Cherny said, sinking back into his

chair. But it was some time before he roused himself to get on with the morning's business.

> **Secret memorandum from the Minister of Finance of Russia, David Davidovich Milstein, to the Ambassador to the United Nations from Russia, Nathan Abramov:**

Dear Nathan,

I am about to stick my head into the lion's mouth, and I may not be able to pull it out again. Can you imagine me, with my abhorrence of hunting and guns, shooting at innocent deer as they are driven by? I leave today, immediately after the grand state funeral for that anti-Semitic bastard, Orgonev. Aleksandr has begged me to go on this fool's errand to Aleyev's dacha, where I will be surrounded by enemies—his as well as mine—in order to get some sense of how far Soyuz has proceeded with their plot for the putsch we both know is coming. For some reason, the President clings to the belief that you and I, and all who are on the side of a legitimate government, suffer from paranoia. I do believe that he thinks I might be persuaded to his point of view if I spend several days in the company of this splendid group of Russian patriots. You are to see him immediately upon your return to Moscow, before you report to the Foreign Ministry. Aleksandr promises that he will listen to everything you have to tell him. I will still be in Ukovo; I come back to Moscow the following day. And, my beloved friend, pray to God that I arrive alive, and in one piece.

> **Personal letter from Nathan Abramov, Ambassador from Russia to the United Nations, to the United States Ambassador to the United Nations, Charlotte Conroy:**

My dearest Charlotta,

I am sending this letter to your office by a dear friend and associate, Olga Vetsayeva, whom we both can trust implicitly. Should I have any further need to get in touch with you privately, it will be through Olga, may God bless her and keep her safe.

I have been recalled to Moscow by the Ministry of Foreign Affairs, ostensibly "for consultations on pending business in the United Nations." I am to leave as soon as the General Assembly session on Sudan is adjourned. In actual fact, I suspect Soyuz wants me in Moscow for a different purpose altogether. This evening I received word from David that he has been asked to go on an extremely dangerous mission on behalf of President Cherny. Cherny is a good man, but an innocent in the world of political beasts. Will he ever learn that he is not dealing with a university faculty senate? I fear that Dovi Milstein may pay for the President's naïveté. If he does, it is possible that I, too, will not return to the United Nations.

My dearest Charlotta, how I wish that we had met earlier. I go back to Moscow with the greatest regret, but go I must. I have prepared a special letter for you to send on to your President should it be necessary. Olga Vetsayeva will bring it directly to you when word reaches her, no matter what the hour, in which case you must take the utmost care, both for her life and your own. Soyuz will be watching you around the clock.

Take care, Charlotta. Let us pray for saner times.

Handwritten memorandum to Vincent Kellner, National Security Adviser to the President of the United States, from Charlotte Conroy, United States Ambassador to the United Nations: PERSONAL AND CONFIDENTIAL.

Vincent—
    I have just received a letter from Nathan, telling me that he has been called back to Moscow on a pretext, and that he will

be leaving immediately after the General Assembly session is adjourned. He says that Cherny's presidency is in danger. I believe him. As I recall, you told me some time ago that Yevgeny Suvorov, the Minister of Defense, was continuing to add to the Russian nuclear forces, and that the legislature has funded his requests over Cherny's objections. I was doubtful. I was wrong. Peace is in danger.

Should anything happen to Nathan when he reaches Moscow, he has promised to send me word by a trustworthy aide. I am going to a Security Council breakfast at 7:30 tomorrow morning, and then will be in committee meetings all day. My secretary can get word to me at any time should you need to speak to me.

I will be in touch with you immediately should there be further developments.

Chapter Twenty-four

Spatha, North Carolina/November 29

Senator Theodore Dugan (D, Mass.), chairman of the Foreign Relations Committee, to Vincent Kellner, chairman of the National Security Council: "It is difficult for any person of good will to understand why there are so many in the Administration who resist sharing the peace dividend with our former adversaries. As the late Foreign Minister Shevardnadze once remarked: 'Perestroika has robbed you of your enemy.'"

Dr. Kellner: "What 'peace dividend,' Senator? How did you vote on the Gulf War? On the Bosnian intervention?"

Senator Dugan: "You are out of order, sir."

—TESTIMONY BEFORE THE SENATE FOREIGN
RELATIONS COMMITTEE

DEPUTY SHERIFF BOBBY LEE CALHOUN, a lanky young man in sharply creased green serge uniform and broad-brimmed campaign hat, stood in the hospital hallway with Nurse Irene Cullen and discussed the winter casualty the deputy had just brought in. The small Spatha Station Hospital was empty and still at this early hour of the morning.

A cold, wind-driven rain streaked the glass doors of the emergency room, Nurse Cullen's preserve for the night. Windows and shutters rattled, and twice in the early evening the power had failed, requiring the emergency generator to kick on with a clatter. Spatha Station Hospital had been built in the fifties, a little way outside the town of Spatha, in an area that city boosters and developers had expected to become an upscale community of homes with a small, select shopping district. But the development had fizzled out when a mall, complete with Walmart, had opened on the other side of town. The hospital had remained open and useful through good times and bad, though recently there had been another flurry of talk about closing the place and enlarging emergency facilities at Spatha General in the center of town.

Bobby Lee Calhoun was glad that no decision had been taken on the closing yet, and seemed likely not to be, until Irene Cullen retired.

Bobby Lee, like many of the other locals, had reasons to be sentimental about Nurse Cullen. She had once been an exotic and romantic character in Spatha. She had appeared, a refugee, in the early 1960s, from that mysterious land of Khrushchev and Sputnik, the Soviet Union. Still young when she arrived in the United States, and settling in Spatha, North Carolina, for no reason anyone could easily discern, she had then been known as Irene Rabinovich. Her sponsors were a family of prominent and wealthy Jews who lived in Raleigh. Irene had been a nurse in the Soviet Union, rising to be head of Nursing Services at the hospital in Odessa where she had taken her training. But her qualifications proved to be insufficient for the North Carolina Board of Medical Examiners. Her sponsors were furious, seeing prejudice in the decision, both against Russians and against Jews. But Irene was, above all, a practical woman. Undaunted by the uproar, she enrolled at the

School of Nursing in Columbia and within two years became a registered nurse.

Irene Rabinovich was short, buxom, and unfailingly good-natured. She was passionately grateful to her new country and worked tirelessly to discharge her obligation. She soon married Eustace Cullen, a general practitioner of Spatha, and for ten years she worked with him as his nurse, assistant, and receptionist. Among her extra duties was that of school and visiting nurse, and it was in this capacity that she captured the affection and regard of many of Spatha's young people, now-Deputy Bobby Lee Calhoun among them.

When Dr. Eustace died, Irene Cullen was given charge of the nursing staff of Spatha Station Hospital. And it was to her that Deputy Calhoun had brought the odd case he had picked up trudging east on Route 702, soaked, shivering, fevered, with a hook for a hand, a Russian accent, and no identification.

The transient was now bedded in the hospital's single ward, a glucose IV in his vein, a massive dose of antibiotic also trickling into his arm. He was running a temperature of 100.8 degrees, and he was sleeping the sleep of the exhausted.

"I think he's an illegal, Miz Cullen," Deputy Calhoun said earnestly. "He was standing out on the road, rain pouring down on him, like he was lost. I don't think he's been eating so regular, either. He was glad when I stopped to check him out. Happy to get into the cruiser and out of the rain, I guess.

"Seems like he's starved for talking; I don't know how else to put it. He never shut up, all the way here. Says he's coming from Brownsville in Texas, and that he needs to get to—are you ready for this?—Washington D.C. That's what he said, all right. He didn't seem to know you can't walk on freeways, and he didn't understand why people wouldn't stop for him at night. He said that there were 'too many roads,' whatever that means. He claims he was in Brownsville a month ago, and that it's taken him this long to get this far."

Deputy Calhoun obviously felt sheepish at having been touched by this strange transient's situation. "He said he got work along the way, like in Georgia at a lumber mill, but to tell you the truth, I don't know what he'd do there. 'Cause of the hook, Miz Cullen,'' he said. "I never seen a thing like that before.''

"You have lived all your life in happy land, Bobby Lee.'' Irene Cullen had all but lost her Russian accent. Only when she grew agitated did she drop articles and speak in the cadences of her native Odessa.

"The way he talked, he sounded the way you used to when you was the school nurse,'' Calhoun said. "It's crazy, but all at once I remembered the way you sounded the day I blew my knee out, remember? In the Abbeville game. I just couldn't see taking him to jail. He might be off a Russian ship, asking for asylum. I hope you don't mind my bringing him here.''

"You did the right thing, Bobby Lee.''

The deputy looked at the wall clock. It showed 1:40. "I have to get back on my rounds,'' he said doubtfully. "If he worries you, I can still take him in.''

"I can handle him. You go along.''

"I'll look in again when I go off watch. And I'll check that telephone number.''

"That will be fine, Bobby,'' Irene Cullen said, patting him on the shoulder. She was intrigued by the worn-down, exhausted man in the ward, muttering incoherencies in Russian. What fascinating story would he have to tell, she wondered. The sight of him brought back all the fears of her flight from Russia. Once a refugee, always a refugee.

There were no other patients at Spatha Station Hospital at the moment, and the night staff consisted of Tom, the janitor (called a maintenance engineer these days), and Clarissa Washington, a practical nurse acting as her assistant, presently sleeping in the small alcove behind the closed admission desk.

Nurse Cullen watched Deputy Calhoun depart into the storm. When his cruiser could no longer be seen from the hospital entrance, she walked back to the door of the ward, opened it, and looked in on Arkady Karmann. "For the time

196

being," she said softly in her native language, "I have you to myself. You are my own Russian mystery."

Irene Cullen was, at heart, a Russian romantic. As a girl at school in Odessa, she had fallen deeply in love with a medical student three years her senior. It was Vladimir Bogdanovich Gorenko who had, in effect, guided her choice of a profession. He had been handsome, gifted, privileged, as only the son of a high party official could be. Young Gorenko could never have become seriously involved with Irene Rabinovich because she was Jewish, but he had been pleasant to her in his way, unlike so many others. Irene never saw him again after the day he departed for Moscow University. Her memories of Vladi Gorenko became more selective as time went on, an echo of a happy time, one without trouble. Her memory of him was what she chose it to be.

And when Deputy Bobby Lee Calhoun appeared with the shivering and bedraggled orphan of the storm now in the empty ward, it seemed to Irene that he might almost *be* Vladi Gorenko, and she would be able to return his kindness. The stranger was a few years older than Vladi had been when Irene saw him last. He was broadfaced and blond, most likely a Great Russian, again like Vladi. But, unlike the Vladimir Gorenko of her youth, the newcomer desperately needed Irene Rabinovich Cullen.

All these thoughts had coalesced for Nurse Cullen when she heard her patient, obviously near to delirium, denouncing someone named Krasny. Who Krasny might be, she had no idea. But the name was Russian and deepened her sense of involvement.

For thirty years, Irene Rabinovich had behaved like the most practical and pedestrian of women. She had been a good nurse, a faithful wife, and a conscientious American citizen. But at heart Irene was still the girl who wept over Tchaikovsky's music and the novels of Dostoyevsky and Chekhov. She resolved to save this derelict who murmured feverishly in the language of her homeland.

He cried out in pain, and she moved over to soothe him, stroking his forehead, waking from her fancies.

In fact, Nurse Cullen realized ruefully, Arkady Karmann did not at all resemble Vladimir Gorenko. Her Vladi had been shorter, with a darker complexion marked by childhood small-pox. She stood looking down at the patient, medically alert to his situation.

The hook on his right arm had fascinated Bobby Lee Calhoun, and it fascinated her as well. What strange, dark story did that crude device validate? The broad face was bearded and none too clean. His clothes and shoes were a disgrace, worn and filthy. Nurse Cullen had had no qualms whatever about telling Clarissa Washington to dispose of them.

There had been almost nothing of value in his pockets. Two dollars and a quarter in change, and a pair of soggy work gloves. Apparently her new Vladimir sometimes disguised his grotesque prosthesis—perhaps when asking for aid, or work. A wet book of matches from a cafe in Meridian, Mississippi, the name Betty Lou Sims scrawled on it, together with a telephone number, a sandwich wrapper from a fast-food restaurant in Demopolis, Alabama, a crumpled oil company road map of Georgia: traces of the long, hard journey from Browns-ville.

And one thing more, a scrap of paper, carefully folded, taped to his chest, with a Washington, D.C., area code telephone number written on it. Bobby Lee Calhoun had promised to investigate the number before going off watch. Irene Cullen regarded her patient with a vast, gentle curiosity.

Should she investigate the number herself, she wondered. She could do it for only the small cost of a late-night telephone call. She studied the man's damp face more carefully. He was clearly ill. Earlier, while Bobby Lee was helping her get him bedded down, he had vomited. The amount of vomitus had been small, possibly because her stranger had been eating in-frequently. He was anorexic, showing signs of extreme lassi-tude. Capillaries in his eyes had ruptured, causing small local hemorrhages. He could be a drunk—as a Russian, Irene thought swiftly of this possibility—but she discarded it. She needed to do a complete work-up on him, then spend some time with the books. It had been a long while since she had dealt with anyone in quite this condition. She left the night-light on and walked back to the nursing station. She regarded the telephone for a long time before she lifted the receiver and dialed the number the transient had so carefully preserved.

There were a half-dozen rings before anyone answered. Not surprising, she thought guiltily. It was well past midnight.

"The White House."

Nurse Cullen gasped and hung up the telephone. She sat for a moment, heart pounding.

She almost leaped from her chair when the telephone rang under her hand. She picked it up and said shakily, "Spatha Station Hospital."

Bobby Lee Calhoun's soft North Carolina accents were on the other end of the line. "Miz Cullen?"

"Yes. Is that you, Bobby Lee?"

"Yes, ma'am."

Just then she was startled by a crash from the ward. On the telephone, Deputy Calhoun shouted, "What was that? Are you all right?"

"Yes, yes. Hold on, Bobby Lee, something has fallen in the ward." She left the telephone and ran, soundlessly on her rubbersoled shoes, down the hall to the ward. She snapped on the overhead lights.

The stand that held the IV bottle upright was on the floor, the flask shattered, saline solution puddled on the linoleum. Her patient lay sprawled beside it. He had apparently attempted to get out of his bed but had collapsed from weakness. His arms and legs made crawling motions, and he was moaning and calling out in Russian.

She knelt by his side and cradled his head tenderly, at the same time reaching for the call-bell that had been torn free of the bolster. "It's all right," she said in Russian. "It is all right, countryman."

He looked at her with dazed eyes. "Help me," he said.

Nurse Cullen did not attempt to lift him. She pulled a pillow from the bed and put it under his head. She pressed the call-bell again furiously and then shouted, "Clarissa! Clarissa, come in here! I need you!"

She lowered the man's head onto the pillow and stood. As Clarissa Washington appeared in the doorway, she commanded, "Stay with the patient, Clarissa."

Back at the nursing station she snatched up the telephone. "Bobby Lee? Are you still there?"

"Yes, ma'am. What's happened? Are you all right?"

"I am perfectly safe, Bobby Lee. Now, listen to me carefully. You must call the FBI in Raleigh immediately. They must come here right away. Understand, Bobby Lee? *Right away.*"

"But Miz Cullen—"

"Right away, Bobby. Just do it."

Chapter Twenty-five

Moscow/November 30.

The nation mourns a Hero of Russian Science.

—CAPTION ON IZVESTIA WIREPHOTO OF THE FUNERAL
PROCESSION OF MIKHAIL IVANOVICH ORGONEV,
RUSSIAN NUCLEAR WEAPONS DESIGNER.

THE CORTEGE MOVED SLOWLY AND DELIBERATELY down
snow-banked Kujbyseva Street, past the decayed rococo grandeur of the GUM department store, on to Red Square. The
deep winter wind lashed the mourners with an edge of steel
and snapped the red flags the military had massed.

The bone-chilling weather suited the mood of the Russian
President as he marched in the funeral procession for Mikhail
Ivanovich Orgonev. The only pleasure he felt today stemmed
from the scarcity of onlookers on the streets. Whether it was
due to the weather or the unwillingness of the citizenry to
salute a man who had designed so many instruments of mass
killing, Muscovites had stayed home for the most part. If ever,
Aleksandr Cherny thought, the Soyuz needed a lesson in the
attitude of the people of Moscow, this grand funeral for a

nasty, embittered, angry old man should instruct them. The procession was almost exclusively military. The crowds Soyuz had tried to muster to march along with the procession as a show of civilian grief had not materialized.

In melancholy grandeur, the contingents from the army, navy, air force, and security services paced ahead and behind the missile transporter carrying Orgonev's corpse. The dreadful old man lay in a glass-covered coffin, clothed in his old KGB general's uniform. The transporter was draped in funereal red, and the old man had been propped up so that his face could be seen, waxy and artificial, like a clothing store's mannequin. The coffin was as massive as an Egyptian sarcophagus. The President marched with the rest of the nomenklatura, perforce in the place of honor, an honor that he would have willingly forgone. He had despised Orgonev in life (the feeling had been mutual) and had no reason to respect him in death. Orgonev's contribution to the welfare of humanity consisted of design of the largest ICBMs ever built, together with a series of experimental warheads of such force that they could not even be tested safely.

Cherny glanced sidelong at the others in his rank beside the missile transporter. (Was there ever so appropriate a vehicle to bear the old curmudgeon on his journey into hell?) Piotr Kondratiev walked at the end of the rank nearest to the dead man, his medal-bedecked chest thrust forward aggressively. When Cherny had relieved Kondratiev of command of the Black Beret security battalions, their agreement had included terms arrived at after long negotiation. There would be no arrest, no open scandal, but Kondratiev agreed to stay out of Moscow. He would keep most of his perquisites. Admiral Aleyev and Yevgeny Suvorov, then Minister of Agriculture, had been the negotiators.

Like the Roman emperor Claudius, Cherny had wanted clean hands: no trials or executions when he assumed the principate. But one had to rely on the integrity of the man with whom one negotiated, or the result was failure. And here was

Kondratiev the hypocrite, resplendent in his old uniform, marching, head bowed as if in profound sorrow. That had been the excuse for his reappearance proffered by Aleyev and Suvorov: that Orgonev had been such an old and dear friend that it would be an insult to Orgonev's family were Kondratiev not to appear to pay his respects. Cherny was unconvinced. Kondratiev and Orgonev had long been rivals for power in the right-wing movement. No one had ever been an "old and dear friend" of either man.

"Could he have picked a colder day to be buried?" David Milstein walked beside the President. As Finance Minister, Milstein had been obliged to attend the funeral of a Hero of Socialist Science. The irony of his presence had a fine, piercing point. At one time in his life, General-Academician Mikhail Ivanovich Orgonev had tried very hard to purge all Jews from the Academy of Soviet Science. His plan failed, but he had continued to use his position of power to deny them rank and perquisites of academy membership.

"March in his cortege?" David Milstein had commented sarcastically when asked. "I would rather dance on his grave, the old Jew-baiter." But in the end, Milstein was present, as were all the officers of the state resident in Moscow for the winter.

Cherny felt a chill as he watched the rifle-balancing, goose-stepping Kremlin guardsmen under the personal command of their colonel in chief, Ivan Temko. Temko had made a great show of greeting Piotr Kondratiev, embracing him. Was Temko a recent convert, or a longtime member of Soyuz? He shivered, whether in response to the cold or to the thought of another entrant into the ring of hostile faces surrounding him day in and day out, he did not know.

The head of the procession entered Red Square, and the bells in the tower of St. Basil's began to toll. The great expanse in front of the church was almost empty. Ironies abound, Cherny thought. Orgonev had been a lifelong atheist and in the old days, a despoiler of churches. He had done so to abolish superstition, he said, in the name of Russian science. Cherny wondered how Orgonev's immortal soul would explain that at the gates of heaven, always assuming it could reach so high, weighed down as it was by so many sins.

The echoing clangor of the bells, the crack of ice beneath marching feet, the rumble of wheels across the cobbles—for an instant, the President felt the presence of all those who had gone before him, in this most Russian of places.

A flight of Sukhoi fighters roared low over Red Square, like birds of prey silhouetted against the steel-colored overcast. One of the aircraft pulled up sharply into the clouds in an elegant execution of the USAF missing man formation. Still more ironies, Cherny thought, the day abounds with them. Yuri Kalinin, the young air force general whom Cherny had newly appointed as Air Officer Commanding the Moscow Military District Air Defense, had chosen the romantic symbolism to honor Orgonev. But perhaps the old barbarian atop the flower-decked missile carrier would appreciate it. Who could tell?

"Very impressive," David Milstein murmured as the Sukhois vanished into the winter mist. "Does Kalinin know what that little gesture cost us? We could give shelter to a hundred homeless for a year with the price of the jet fuel."

Admiral Eduard Aleyev, his face flushed with vodka and his breath freezing on his mustache, glared at the Minister of Finance. Milstein ignored him, his gaze fixed on Cherny.

If I could only get him to move ahead on the cleanup of the nuclear power plants, or agree to the American oil companies' rescue of the Siberian oil fields, Milstein thought despairingly. We will never get our economy in hand until we have our energy shortages solved.

I should be content, Milstein thought, that Russia has an elected President, instead of the wrangling turmoil of the years since Yeltsin. But I despair of an end to the ethnic wars, all around the old empire, eating away at the very heart of the motherland. No one dares call them civil wars, but that is what they are.

He glanced at Aleksandr Cherny again. He is a comfortable man, a nonthreatening man, all that a schoolteacher should be, Milstein thought. Was that enough for the head of state at a time of continual crisis? Foreigners liked him, trusted him. But he had done nothing about the thunder on his right. The nationalists underestimated him, regarded him as a weakling, because Cherny never really finished off his opposition. He always softened before the final blow was struck, sought negotiation rather than continued confrontation.

In a strange sort of way, Kondratiev probably would never forgive Cherny for having stopped the buildup of Soyuz strength within his government without killing or imprisoning Kondratiev, as Soyuz's personification. He most probably considered it a personal insult, an indication that Kondratiev was no threat, either to Cherny or to the state.

When we tore down the red banners, Milstein thought, we did not imagine uncertainty would become a way of life for us. It all seemed so clear while we were waiting in the wings. There were times, Milstein feared, when his old friend's reasonableness and willingness to compromise was as dangerous as the conspiracies of men like Kondratiev. Nathan Abramov had been called back from New York by Yevgeny Suvorov on some flimsy excuse and would soon be in Moscow. At least he will meet with the President before he presents himself at the Foreign Ministry. If only I hadn't agreed to go to Ukovo with Aleyev, Milstein thought, I could be there, too, to discuss this with Nathan. He has a very clear understanding of the dangers we face. At Vienna, I did warn Vincent Kellner about Soyuz, but only in the most general terms. I should have been more candid. I shall send Kellner a more explicit message through Nathan, when he returns to New York.

Milstein stumbled slightly as the procession moved across the cobblestones toward the black marble mausoleum. He dreaded the prospect of the hunt at Aleyev's dacha tomorrow.

Deborah, his wife, was beside herself with worry. The air force band was playing Chopin's funeral march. The music lay heavy in the air, like a slow rain of black diamonds, dignified, grieving. Far too good for a man like Orgonev, Milstein thought.

Evidently others thought so, too, for suddenly a ragtag procession of young people came bursting out of 25th October Street. They were dressed in worker's clothes, some in western jeans and German parkas, others in the absurd motley of the recently very active Moscow street theater. They carried signs demanding immediate action on a multiplicity of things: relief for Armenia; the return of the army to Russia from all former republics; an end to the military draft; immediate nuclear disarmament and cessation of both the building of nuclear weapons and power plants; free tuition at Moscow University; a thousand percent increase in research money for AIDS. The young people of Moscow had taken to protest demonstrations with vast anger and enthusiasm.

Suddenly, counterdemonstrators, perhaps a hundred young men and women in the czarist uniforms favored by the right-wing organizations of Moscow, appeared, also from 25th October Street, marching in unison, singing and chanting Soyuz slogans, blocking any retreat by the first group.

The dissidents, absorbed by their own passions, paid no attention. As the Orgonev cortege reached the center of the square, they began to chant obscenities and wave their banners and signs.

Piotr Kondratiev called out in a commanding voice to Ivan Yulin, his replacement as the head of State Security. "Where are the militia?" he demanded loudly. "This is a state funeral! Is there no decency?"

The right-wing counterdemonstrators immediately took up the cry. *"Is there no decency?"*

As if at a signal, blue-uniformed members of the militia began to pour out of the Kremlin's Red Tower gate into the square. Some carried electric cattle prods, others were armed with AK-57 assault rifles. The militia formed in ranks, holding transparent plastic shields before them. The band played louder, repeating the march. The protesters in the original demonstration, frightened at the show of strength arrayed against them, milled around and began to look for avenues of escape, only now recognizing that they were in danger.

The militia marched in ranks past the cortege, across to the streets leading into Red Square, trapping the youthful dissenters in a smaller and smaller area. When they realized their predicament, the protesters began to fight back. They pried cobblestones out of the paving and threw them at random at the encircling troops, who protected themselves but did not make any overt moves to stop them. One of the stones went astray and crashed into the ranks of the band, hitting a tuba player in the face, injuring him. The musicians suddenly stopped playing, leaving only shouts and screams echoing in the square.

Now the young people in the czarist uniforms brought out weapons from under their voluminous clothing and attacked the disorganized dissenters with truncheons and steel bars. The militia stood watching, poised for attack, but for the moment did not interfere with the fighting between the two factions.

Milstein snatched at Cherny's arm. "For God's sake, Aleksandr! Give orders to Yulin to stop this before one of those youngsters gets killed!" When Cherny did not respond, Milstein turned away, seeking Ivan Yulin. "Vanya! Don't let the soldiers shoot!" he shouted.

It was already too late. Just as he spoke, the militia charged the dissidents. The phalanxes of policemen with their Soyuz allies and the young ragtag protesters merged into a club-swinging, rockthrowing mass. In the midst of the melee came gunfire, the popping sound of an automatic weapon. The protesters scattered in panic. Two bodies lay in front of the mausoleum. Their blood was brilliant red against the gray cobblestones. It steamed in the icy air.

As the young protesters ran toward the side streets, several units of Black Beret troops materialized in front of them. Within moments the dissidents were stopped, roughly subdued, and forced to lie face down on the ice-covered stones of Red Square.

Milstein grasped Yulin roughly by the shoulder. "What have you done, Vanya?" he cried in despair. Cherny stood watching as if in a trance, unwilling or unable to stop the carnage.

Ivan Yulin shook off Milstein's hand. "I had to be prepared," he said firmly. "They were trying to assassinate our President."

Milstein stared at Yulin in disbelief. Planned, he thought, this was all planned. He turned toward the two bodies, sprawled in the melted slush, unmoving. Their surviving fellows were being lifted one by one into black militia vans to be taken away. Are those children alive or dead, David Milstein wondered. He turned to protest to Cherny, but he was jostled aside by a protective convoy of Kremlin guardsmen, come to rush the President to safety through the Spassky Gate.

"This is insanity, Yulin," Milstein shouted wildly. "They had every right to protest."

"But not to threaten the head of state. It is time the hooligans are put in their place," the aged police chief said coldly, self-righteously. "The President must be protected."

Milstein looked about helplessly. Only now had someone from the police come to tend to the fallen demonstrators. They were hauled away like sacks, dumped into a militia van, not an ambulance, and taken from the square, sirens braying.

Suddenly Piotr Kondratiev materialized at the head of the funeral column. "Now, hear me," he commanded. "Let us forget this disgraceful affair and get on with the task of burying our comrade." He thrust his arm into the air, fist clenched. The bandmaster sprang to attention and waved his baton. The band began to play again. The cortege moved across the square at the mournful cadence, finally coming to a halt at the open grave that had been dug in the dead grasses under the Kremlin wall.

THE DEATHS IN RED SQUARE—confirmed within the hour—cast a blanket of depression over a shocked city. Orgonev's eulogy had been delivered by Admiral Aleyev, who had been just sober enough to be coherent. Now, at the reception in the rotunda of the Spassky Tower, Admiral Aleyev had remedied his state of sobriety, and he and the Minister of the Environment had fallen into a dispute, shouting coarse insults at one another.

Aleksandr Cherny was mortified, grateful that only a few members of the diplomatic corps were represented in the Spassky today. The sad truth was that Mikhail Orgonev, at one time or another, had managed to offend each of the diplomats stationed in Moscow. His manner had always been to bluster and threaten, and his extreme anti-Semitism had disgusted all but the representatives of the Arab nations.

President Cherny rubbed his forehead, trying to soothe his pounding headache. What if Yulin was right and those demonstrators had been trying to kill him? He had always believed that the people loved him. David Milstein, at Cherny's elbow, was continuing an outraged diatribe, always addressing Cherny as "Comrade President." How he dreaded being addressed as Comrade President by David Davidovich. Good God, didn't the man understand how difficult matters were in the Kremlin, with Kondratiev's clique gathered around him like a cadre of destruction?

He rounded on Milstein in sudden temper. "What would you have done, David Davidovich? Just tell me. It was unfortunate, but it wasn't Tiananmen Square, after all. There were no tanks. The hooligans started it, with their violence and their disrespect for the dead. Yulin was protecting me, protecting all of us, doing what he thought was best." He turned his back and walked a few steps away.

Milstein was silent, glaring across the sparsely populated

room, past the tables groaning with food and drink as usual. Food and drink, always available to us, while ordinary citizens go to empty shops, he thought angrily. Kondratiev was the center of a group standing by the windows, gesticulating as he spoke, his listeners nodding in earnest agreement.

As he watched, Milstein realized in horror that today was a turning point, that there was no time left to reason or negotiate with those monsters. Kondratiev and his Soyuz fascists were planning—not just planning, but *on the verge* of a putsch. Only the timing was still unclear, and chances were that it was imminent.

He chose a moment when Cherny was filling his plate at the buffet to approach him again. "Aleksandr," he said intensely, "that was no accident in the square. It was a test."

"A *test?* David Davidovich, have you taken leave of your senses?"

"The bastards wanted to see what you would do. They wanted to know if you would take command on the spot, forbid them to fire on unarmed demonstrators."

Cherny's broad face hardened. "You are upset. I am also." His voice was cold, warning Milstein.

Milstein's anger overcame his caution. "Damn you, Aleksandr," he said, "they're all corrupt: criminals, black marketeers, with every intention of overthrowing your government, even killing you, if that's what is necessary."

Cherny flew into a rage, unable to stand Milstein's incessant complaints. "I cannot—will not—believe the filthy gossip about these men. Aleyev and Suvorov are pressing for reconciliation between me and Kondratiev in order to heal the breach. That is why Kondratiev returned to Moscow, that and the funeral. They have capitulated, have given up their agenda, and promise full cooperation with me in the legislature."

"I can't believe what I am hearing, Aleksandr," Milstein said in dismay. "Reconciliation is impossible."

"Nothing is impossible if it means an end to this plot and counterplot." Cherny rubbed his forehead again, the weariness and strain showing clearly on his face.

My God, Milstein thought. *He is going to let it happen.* He is going to surrender to Soyuz and the fascists. "Please, my dear friend, do not allow this," Milstein said.

Cherny took hold of the minister's arm in a surprisingly powerful grip. His voice dropped to a whisper. "I don't know what they intend, Dovi, and neither do you. You have no proof. You and Abramov think you know what they plan to do. Thinking does not make it so. Get me *evidence*. That is why I asked you, why I need for you to go with those barbarians, to join them in the shooting party. If they want something from you, promise them the moon, if necessary. But find out exactly what they intend to do, and when."

Milstein stared at Cherny. I am no hero, David Milstein thought. Quite the contrary. Violence makes my knees tremble and my mouth dry.

"Don't worry; I gave my word, and I will do as you ask, old friend," Milstein said in an almost inaudible voice. He could not escape the feeling of impending disaster in the room.

Cherny's shoulders sagged, his broad face was pallid and damp with sweat. The overheated room rumbled with a babel of many voices. "Forgive me, Dovi," Aleksandr Cherny whispered. "I have nowhere else to turn."

Chapter Twenty-six

Flight Level 20/November 30

In order to enjoy the inestimable benefits that the liberty of the press insures, it is necessary to submit to the inevitable evils it creates.

—ALEXIS DE TOCQUEVILLE, DEMOCRACY IN AMERICA

IT WAS AFTER MIDNIGHT, and it had begun to rain again when Ave Peters's Cessna 310 lifted from the runway at Half Moon Bay. Anna Neville forced herself to watch from the small window as the airplane banked steeply over the sea and turned eastward. She had admitted it to no one, but since the crash in Canada, she had been afraid of flying.

She flexed her hands to relax them, wrapped herself in a blanket, and huddled against the thrumming wall of the Cessna's passenger compartment. Avery Peters's mechanics had put hot coffee and sandwiches aboard, but Anna had no appetite. The events of the last twenty-four hours had left her drained of energy. And of will? No, not that. She was more determined than ever to expose whoever it was who had killed Sean and Jake. She owned them that, she thought.

And sex with Morgan? Was that necessary to my survival? She closed her eyes, visualizing the scene with her father years ago, when she had come home after her first date. She'd been fifteen and had been invited to a school dance. Her father had embarrassed her by insisting on an eleven o'clock curfew. The boy—she couldn't even remember his name now—had brought her home a half hour late. He had been trying an awkward kiss, with his hand on her breast, when the door opened, and there was the Vicar. The boy fled.

The scene that followed was engraved in her memory. Her father had grabbed her by the arm and pulled her into the hall, slamming the door behind them. "Is that what you want? To be a whore, like your mother?" He pushed her ahead of him into the living room, his face deep red, distorted by rage, and she fell onto the chair nearest the door. "Your mother was the Whore of Babylon," he shouted, "and you are treading the same filthy path." There was more, a great deal more, most of it about the mistake he had made marrying a Catholic and the bad seed that had resulted from his sin.

Then for what seemed like hours, he had knelt at her feet praying to God for her salvation, praying that she would be pure, that she would live a Godly life, resisting all carnal temptation. When, exhausted by his emotions, he finally released her, she had crept up the stairs to bed, beyond tears.

Why am I remembering that, she wondered. Why am I thinking about my mother, whom I never really knew? Was her serial polygamy the same as my own promiscuity? Poor stupid women, hungry for overt signs of love? When I was small, a pat on the head was enough to assure me that my father loved me. But later, I hungered for the words, the embrace when I was sad, the time we could have spent together as a family. Now all I remember is the closed door to his study. I can still remember the carvings of angels on the panels. I can still feel jealous of those friends with whom my father laughed and joked, something he never did with me.

Anna could hear Morgan and Joe Ryerson arguing in low,

angry voices. They were sitting at the aft end of the cabin. She turned her head to hear more clearly what Ryerson was saying now. "This is kidnapping, plain and simple. I'll see you pay for it, Morgan."

"I'm taking you to the chaplain for a TS ticket. Tell him," Morgan said.

"I intend to tell everybody, everybody in the world. Vincent Kellner isn't God, you know." Ryerson's voice trembled with outrage.

"And you're not Walter Lippmann," Morgan said. "If I hadn't dragged you aboard by the scruff of the neck, you'd have given a year's pay to be where you are right now. With a little luck, on your own, you can get Anna Neville blown away while you watch. Think what a story that will make."

Ryerson, aggrieved, said, "You bastard, Morgan. I don't want to hurt her. I'm on her side."

"You're on no one's side but your own."

"Jesus, what sort of man do you think I am?" Ryerson protested. "I'm only doing my job."

"You don't want to know what I think," Morgan said, and left his seat for the cockpit.

Ryerson got up and made his way up the aisle to take the seat across from Anna. "Did you hear all that, Mrs. Neville? I want you to be a witness. Colonel Morgan seems never to have heard of the United States Constitution." He took a notebook out of his pocket and scribbled something in it.

Anna made no reply. Joe Ryerson sounded exactly like Jake. The blame was always on the other side, never a result of his own actions. She rested her head against the seat, too weary to answer. The Cessna twin was still climbing steeply. The sprawling lights of the Bay Area faded into the rainy night. Then those lights were totally snuffed out, and the airplane was in darkness. Through the rain-streaked window, Anna could see the reflections of the navigation strobes on the heavy could through which they were flying.

When she sat in silence for several minutes, still looking

out the window, Ryerson, who had been fidgeting in the seat beside her, spoke up. "Morgan expects too much," he said.

He sounded oddly plaintive. Everyone wants to be loved, she thought wryly. Even this sour man. "From whom?"

"From me. He expects me to wait patiently until he feels like letting me know what I can write about." He became more animated, more intimate. "And from you. He expects you to wait until he has time to arrange a cover-up for the people who killed your husband, and then to go along with it."

"Do you know who killed my husband, Mr. Ryerson?"

"If you mean do I believe your story, the answer is yes. I believe you saw an American submarine, and that it shot your plane down." The words smacked of peevish satisfaction.

"I came south with more questions than answers," Anna said. "Somehow, to those who say they sympathize with me, my questions have become accusations."

"You saw what you saw," Ryerson said, nodding.

"Yes, I did. But what was it?"

"I don't understand you."

"I saw a submarine. That's all."

"Well, then," Ryerson said. He took out his notebook again. "Tell me exactly what that sub looked like."

"Like any submarine, Mr. Ryerson. I'm not an expert."

"But what was its nationality?"

"It wasn't flying a flag."

"But you couldn't say it was *not* American."

"It was a submarine, Mr. Ryerson. That's all I know."

"What about pictures? Did you take pictures?" Ryerson leaned forward in his eagerness, his stale, cigarette-laden breath assailing Anna's nostrils.

She drew back in distaste. This conversation was all too familiar; wherever she went someone always wanted to hear her story again. Some of her interrogators in the Maritime Command Intelligence and the RCMP had been hectoring, disbelieving her; some had been sympathetic but doubtful. Those who had taken her under their wing for their own purposes, like the CCND, had not been so rigorous in their questioning. She sighed. She had no wish to go through it all again, not with this man whom she scarcely knew. Maybe it was time to turn the questions back on Ryerson.

"Colonel Morgan thinks you are irresponsible, Mr. Ryerson, and under the circumstances, perhaps dangerous. Why won't you tell him how you located us?"

"I can't reveal sources or methods, Mrs. Neville. If I did, who would trust me with information?" he asked smugly.

Anna remained silent. It seemed to her that this conversation was pointless. She and Ryerson seemed to be talking past each other.

"Surely you don't trust Morgan?" He was like a mosquito buzzing in her ear.

"Shouldn't I?"

"Our heroic colonel is a Marine. It takes a peculiar mindset to be a Marine, Mrs. Neville. All balls and no forehead. And he's crazy, you know," Ryerson said, confidentially. "A couple of nights ago in Leesburg he nearly killed me. He assaulted me with a pistol. He chased me through the woods. Naked."

Anna could not help smiling. "You, Mr. Ryerson?"

"Morgan, for Chrissake."

"That must have been quite a sight," she said. Then, more seriously: "Colonel Morgan saved my life. I owe him a great deal."

"Did he? Do you? Maybe." Ryerson's tone was skeptical, speculative. "How do you know he didn't set the whole thing up? He killed those people at Devil's Slide, didn't he? Maybe he did it to shut them up. I can't prove it yet, but if it's true, I will. The NSC should have learned some limits in the Iran-Contra affair." He leaned toward her again, lowering his voice. "Men like Morgan and Kellner never learn. They're dinosaurs, Mrs. Neville. The cold war is over, but they don't believe it. You need friends who can protect you. You frighten people in the Administration."

The plane struck turbulent air, dropping several feet before leveling off. Anna used it as an excuse for not replying. She closed her eyes and sat back. Morgan had all but convinced her that the American military was not involved in the murders of last winter. But was he right? Was he speaking the truth? She distrusted Ryerson, but he had raised her doubts all over again. Jake had despised men like Morgan. "They wrap their consciences in the flag," he had said contemptuously.

Ryerson persisted. "I could tell your story, Mrs. Neville. I could get some action for you. I have friends in Washington, powerful contacts."

"I don't want trouble. I want justice."

"In this country? That's not fucking likely."

Anna studied the homely, gaunt, hungry face, the slight frame, stooped at the shoulders. She'd read a great deal about the journalism of the glory days of newspapers, when a major city might have seven papers and editions were published morning, afternoon, and evening. In those days, the reputation of a journalist depended on objectivity, not advocacy. Or so she had been taught. Truth might be an abstraction, but the New Journalism, with its emphasis on personal bylines, opinions, and conjecture, seemed a poor substitute. "I'm sorry, Mr. Ryerson," she said, "but I don't want to tell my story again, and especially not to you."

"Well, if you feel that way," Ryerson said, stung by her curt reply. He snatched a blanket and returned to a seat at the rear of the cabin.

Anna sighed and tried to release the tension in her neck, rolling her head from side to side. Nothing made any sense anymore. Why was she in this plane? A feeling of panic overtook her. What if they crashed? She strained to see the instrument panel, not really knowing what to look for, but anxious for reassurance that the plane would not fall from the sky. Morgan turned and looked at her, then spoke briefly to Ave Peters. Their disembodied faces floated eerily in the reflected light from the windshield. What a wonderful picture that would make, Anna thought, her hand automatically reaching for her absent camera case. But every time she took photos now, all she could see in the lens was the black shape of the submarine, the brilliant flash of the missile. Unbidden, her father's voice echoed in her mind, intoning the text from Ecclesiastes 3:15, admonishing her not to rail against fate: "That which hath been is now; and that which is to be hath already been; and God requireth that which is past."

AVERY PETERS LEANED BACK against the cushions of the pilot's chair and lit a cigarette. "I was a kid in Laos when we bugged out on the Meo. Johnson Administration. I was in Saigon when we scrambled on the helicopters and left the South Viets to the Communists. Nixon Administration. I—we—left the Gulf without a backward look. To whomever can hold it. Bush Administration. What's a few hundred thousand Kurds, right? That's the way it *has* to be, Morgan. Get involved—but when it's time to bug out, don't look back." He made a small adjustment to the autopilot and throttles. The altimeter stood at 20,000 feet, the gyrocompass at 73 degrees. The radar distance indicator showed that the 310 had already covered 300 of the 2,400 miles between Half Moon Bay and Washington National.

Morgan, in the right-hand seat, stretched out his legs and looked at the darkness beyond the windshield. Ave was doing something few would attempt. He was offering Morgan advice. And he was talking about Anna Neville.

"You may work for Kellner," Peters said, "but you're in the spook business. It's safest to keep personal relations to a minimum. That way if the Caidin Administration says we walk away from this, you can follow orders."

"I don't think so, Ave," Morgan said quietly. "Not this time."

"You may be sorry."

Morgan grinned. "It wouldn't be the first time."

"How much does Ryerson know?"

"He, along with millions of television news viewers, knows what happened to Grau last night. What bothers me is that he knew where to find us. Someone's keeping him current."

"That's bad news. He could get you and the woman killed."

"That's why I'm delivering him to Kellner. Let the heavy hitters handle Ryerson."

"And Neville?"

Morgan did not reply. Presently he left his seat and said, "Can I get you something?"

"Coffee."

Morgan nodded and walked to the airplane's tiny galley. He returned with one of the thermos bottles Ave's crew had put aboard, opened it, and poured a cup.

"You're limping," Ave said.

"A nick."

"Want me to look at it? I'm good with nicks."

"No. If it gets worse, I'll have someone take care of it," Morgan said. "You want anything else?"

"No. Just take care, Bullet-stopper," Ave said. "I don't want to hear you've gone Elvis. Keep that temper under control. And keep Joe Pulitzer away from me."

"Done," Morgan said, clapping him on the back. He moved down the aisle, slipping into the seat next to Anna. "Why don't you try to get some sleep?"

"I don't need sleep. I need a change of clothes." She smiled at him. "Why did he call you Bullet-stopper? And what does Elvis have to do with anything?"

Morgan laughed. "Bullet-stoppers is what the navy types called Marines in the Gulf War, and 'gone Elvis' meant missing in action. Ave just wants us to take care." The tiny bright cabin light was shining directly on her, turning her eyes as blue as sapphires. Morgan studied her face with interest. She was far from being beautiful, but she was immensely appealing. He wondered about her reputation with men. A pang of jealousy stung him at the thought. He clenched his jaw. What right had he to such feelings? None. None at all.

"Something else, Morgan," Anna said. "I just have to say it."

"Else?"

"Flying terrifies me now."

"Ave will keep us safe," Morgan said.

"I keep seeing the flash, seeing us fall." She flinched as she spoke.

He noted the curve of her cheek, the way she held her head so that the light did not expose her scars, the soft luster of her redgold hair. Not beautiful. But engaging. Touching. And vulnerable. He said, "Nothing will happen to you that doesn't happen to me first. That's a promise." He was remembering Ave Peters's anecdotes of American betrayal and abandonment. Not this time, he thought. Not you.

Anna looked at him quizzically. "I'm not sure that remark is so reassuring, considering what's happened lately. By the way, why are you and Ave Peters so hostile to Ryerson?"

Morgan was silent for a moment. "Basic disagreement. Ryerson would sell us all for a story. That's his religion, what he believes in. I have other priorities."

"Is that fair? I have friends who are journalists and television news people. They're decent, patriotic folk. Every one of them would be horrified if they thought they were responsible for endangering lives. Even the lives of soldiers, fighting a war that they consider wrong."

"You give yourself away with that 'even.' It's easy to be against war, Anna. The 1960s hippies liked to say 'Peace is the natural order of things.' Jesus, even Jane Goodall finally discovered that her chimps fight their little wars, even kill for domination and turf. Does anyone read Clausewitz any more? About war being a human instinct gone political—the continuation of politics by other means?"

"*Why* can't we abolish war and killing and brutality? *Why* can't we spend our energies and our resources on making life better for everyone, everywhere? *Why* can't there be peace?"

Her voice rose with each passionate question.

Morgan said, "Believe it or not, I know very few professional soldiers who don't ask exactly the same questions. The closer to combat, the more often they ask. The difference between us is that I've had my reality check. You say, 'Why can't there be peace?' The soldier says, 'If we have to fight, let's fight to win.' Then peace will come."

"So that's it? That's reality? Is that all there is? Slogans and belligerent talk? It doesn't leave much to hope for."

"One step at a time. We're learning. The Russians thought a nuclear war could be fought and won. Then came Chernobyl. Most of them know better now. Small steps. Morsels of common sense, no matter how bitter. That's the way it works, Anna," Morgan said gently.

"I wonder if we will survive the learning," Anna said wearily. She pulled the blanket up around her shoulders and closed her eyes.

SHE SLEPT FITFULLY for about an hour, twitching and turning. When she woke, Morgan was beside her, holding a steaming cup of coffee. Anna sat up and accepted it gratefully.

Morgan asked, "Awake now?" When she nodded, he glanced back at Ryerson's seat. The only indication of the man was the wreath of cigarette smoke hanging in the air. Morgan turned back to Anna. "When Ryerson was talking to you, did he offer some kind of deal?"

"He said he wanted to tell my story to the world."

"I'll just bet he does," Morgan said.

"At least he seems to believe me," she said.

"Why not? I told you last night I believed you. I meant it." Morgan paused thoughtfully. "Did he ask about your photographs?"

"According to Maritime Command and the RCMP there are no photographs."

"You took some just before the crash, you said."

221

"My cameras were returned to me empty," Anna said flatly.

"They recovered all your cameras?"

"Two of them. The Olympus and the Hasselblad. I was using the Hasselblad when we were hit."

"No film in either of them when they were returned?"

"I'm a professional photographer. I don't carry cameras without film in them."

"No," Morgan agreed. "Of course you wouldn't. All right then. Tell me what Ryerson wants. Besides a peek at your vanished films."

"He asked me to describe exactly what the submarine looked like."

"Interesting," Morgan said thoughtfully.

"I think so. He wanted to know if I could definitely identify the submarine as American."

"He'd like that. Can you describe it?" Morgan asked. "There are differences between American and Soviet boats. Quite obvious ones."

"I have no idea what they are."

"Try to remember details. A professional photographer would have an eye for the details."

She sat silent, remembering. "Well, for one thing there was a kind of bulge just under the water ahead of the sail. I gather that's where the missile launchers are."

"Not on U.S. Navy boats."

"I was scared to death. I could have been mistaken."

"I don't think you were. I think that what you saw was a Hotelclass Soviet missile submarine. One that was supposed to have reached the yard in Murmansk, but somehow didn't."

"How can you be so sure, Morgan?"

"Because I saw photographs of that same boat. The pictures I saw were taken by the navy in the Yucatan Strait." Morgan stared straight at her. "I think the boat left Hudson Bay six days after it shot down your airplane. It steamed through Hudson Strait into the Labrador Sea, then south and west along the Atlantic coast into the Caribbean, through the Yucatan Strait, and when it was within sight of Cuba, it sank. By accident or design.''

''Is this all true? This isn't just some government disinformation you're feeding me?''

''I can't tell you why the Russian sub was in Canada, nor why it sank in the Caribbean. But that's the way it was, or damned close. When we get to Washington, we'll find out.'' He took her icy hand and held it. ''If anyone has a right to know what's going on, you do.''

Was that the answer she'd been looking for—a Russian submarine? She thought of all the interviews she'd endured, the eager faces of her advocates, the long, lined face of Pierre Grau. We were all quite sure who the enemy was.

Her hand felt warm now, cradled in his. Even though John Morgan might well be her enemy, she felt more comforted than she had in many days.

Chapter Twenty-seven

The Northwest Territories/61.07 N 89.90 W/November 30

The old Soviet science has come at last to a socialist ending. So far are we from excellence that we cannot build a harvester that functions as it should, let alone a computer. We cannot construct a submarine that is not more dangerous to its crew than to our enemies. And we should be grateful to Providence that the intercontinental rockets our leaders once boasted of have never been fired in anger. One Chernobyl is enough.

—ACADEMICIAN VITALY CHURKIN,
JOURNAL OF RUSSIAN SCIENCE

IN THE AIR ABOVE THE BLACK WATER there are snow flurries. Surface ice forms, cracks, breaks, and melts to form again as the northeasterly gale drives long rollers toward the shore. The height of the waves from crest to trough at times exceeds twelve feet, and when this happens the nose cone of the Device is exposed to wind and wave. The water is too shallow to let the entire Device remain submerged in such violent weather, and the steady battering of the waves is taking a toll.

The Eighth Day of the Week

The water around the Device is lethal, polluted with plutonium oxide. Water has penetrated the casing, flooding the guidance and control system, rendering it useless. Soyuz will never fly.

The timer and launch sequencer are powered by a special set of nickel-cadmium batteries. The only requirement of the sequencer system is to count the days and hours. But the lower stages of the Device are all powered by ancillary equipment dependent on the plutonium reactor. It is this reactor, already faulty while the Device was still aboard the Pravda, that exposed the vessel's crew to high doses of radiation.

The jolt of being expelled from a launch tube and dropped to the floor of the bay has inflicted further damage to delicate elements in the reactor, and the opening, followed by the imperfect closing, of the hatch from which the message buoy was ejected has allowed more water to flood the guidance system.

The gyrostabilizer, spinning at a rate of 22,000 revolutions per minute, has been slowing as the power diminishes. The wave action and the wind blowing against the exposed nose section of the erect Device make impossible demands on the gyrostabilizer system.

As the timer inside the warhead changes from 00:13:09 to 00:13:10, Universal Time, the gyro tumbles. There is no longer an analog of the horizon for the onboard computer to use as a reference. The swiftly turning gyro wheel screeches to a halt, smoking and sparking against its stainless steel casing. The Device is now balanced only on the bracing struts. And the struts are anchored only in the alluvial sea bottom.

A seventy-mile-per-hour gust of wind catches the Device on the exposed nose, swiftly followed by the heavy impact of a block of sea ice thrusting its weight against the exposed casing, crushing it.

The Device leans and then topples into the darkness. It smashes soundlessly into the mud on the bottom of the bay. The white, decomposed carrion of fishes, eels, and crustaceans swirl inside the cloud of black, given a kind of brief life before the mud begins once again to settle. The rotting skeletal corpse of a once large Ling cod spins and spirals in the murk, shedding slivers and shreds of itself as though to bestow a deadly sustenance on the microscopic creatures of the cold inland sea.

The Device rolls into slightly deeper water and slowly comes to a stop. Inside the warhead, the faithful mission timer's digital readout records that the warhead is now seven days, ten hours, twenty-seven minutes, and eighteen seconds from detonation.

Snow and sleet lash the bay and the lonely shore. The Air Command aircraft, which has been searching the Hudson Bay coast hereabouts for a radiation source, are grounded and waiting for a break in the storm.

DECEMBER

Chapter Twenty-eight

New York City/December 1

"Who was the political leader you mentioned in the telegram?"

I decided to stall for time. "Which telegram?"

"The telegram that defames the KGB," the man behind my back roared.

"I'm not trying to defame anyone," I said, seeing that the game was useless. "I only wrote what I had learned from an American politician. If this information is correct, those who have arrested Sinyavsky and Daniel have put a slur on our country's prestige and have simply fallen into a trap."

"It's a slander!" bellowed the man sitting on the table.

—YEVGENY YEVTUSHENKO, IN *SOVIET LIFE*

THE DISTINCTIVE SOUND of a call from the downstairs security desk woke Charlotte Conroy at three in the morning. She came awake immediately, her heart pounding, sat up, and reached for the telephone. She cleared her throat before she spoke,

229

Alfred Coppel

hoping that the voice on the other end would be that of Nathan Abramov; that he had changed his mind about returning to Moscow. She was overcome with a feeling of apprehension.

The voice of Otis Washington, the security guard at the lobby desk, was apologetic. "Sorry to wake you, Dr. Conroy, but there's a foreign woman here who says she must see you. I told her I couldn't disturb you at this time of night, but she insists. I remember what you told me when I first came to work here, Doctor: 'First say no, then listen hard.' So I thought I had better wake you. She says she's from the Russian Mission. Here, Dr. Conroy, she wants to talk to you herself."

Charlotte Conroy disliked the impersonality of the official ambassadorial apartment in the Waldorf Towers, and so she spent what she called "private time" at her own co-op apartment close to Central Park. It was within earshot of Fifth Avenue, but the morning was as nearly silent as early mornings ever were in New York. Sleety rain fell on the terrace outside her bedroom, and Charlotte could hear the hiss of tires on wet pavement as New York's night people drove by the building.

A woman's voice came on the line, heavily accented, one that Charlotte recognized from the brief meeting they'd had earlier, when Nathan's letter had been hand delivered. "Madame Ambassador, here speaks Olga Vetsayeva, personal assistant to Ambassador Abramov. Please forgive intrusion, but is only time I can get away."

Charlotte Conroy's pulse raced. "Do not apologize. I understand, Miss Vetsayeva. Put the security gentleman on again, please." When Washington's deep voice answered, Charlotte said, "Bring her up at once, Otis."

"Right away, Doctor."

Charlotte rose and walked into the dressing room, her mind spinning with speculation. She splashed cold water on her face, brushed her hair into its usual silvery cap, and put on some lipstick. She put on a lace-trimmed satin robe and slippers and headed for the tiny kitchen. Her live-in maid, Rosa Gonzales, heard the commotion and opened the door of her room off the kitchen, blinking sleepily at the light.

"*Qué pasa, señora?*" Rosa asked.

"Nothing for you to worry about, Rosa. I'm making a pot of tea, that's all. Go back to sleep." Charlotte smiled at her reassuringly.

A look of profound relief passed over Rosa's face. "*Gracias, señora,*" she said, and closed the door before her employer could change her mind.

Charlotte filled the teakettle with water and put it on the stove. She rummaged in the cupboard for the tin of dark, strong tea, brought back from a trip to Moscow in the spring. She hoped it would help her to put Olga Vetsayeva at ease at once. Nathan Abramov's messenger must be received with warmth and attention.

When the doorbell rang, Olga Vetsayeva stood at her door, escorted closely by Otis Washington. "Thank you, Otis," Charlotte said, smiling at his doubtful expression as she escorted her latenight visitor inside.

Olga was young, blonde, broad-faced, and gray eyed, a Great Russian. She wore a cheap but stylish belted black raincoat over a gray-taupe skirt and blouse, severely tailored, probably the outfit she wore at work. The black tights that covered her sturdy legs blended imperceptibly into black running shoes. Olga would be very hard to spot on a dark, rainy street at night. Charlotte resisted the impulse to go to the window to check if someone were standing on the street below, watching her apartment. That only happens in B movies, she thought uneasily.

"Madame Conroy, I am happy to see you again, but I am sorry to disturb you at so late hour. Ambassador Abramov assured me you would forgive." Olga's voice was low and pleasant, but it betrayed her extreme nervousness.

"Yes, my dear. Come sit down. Take off your coat. I am making us some tea."

Olga did as she was bid. She eyed the deep-cushioned velvet sofa longingly, but instead chose the straight chair at the Hepplewhite desk, close to the door. She held her handbag, a bulky satchel of imitation leather, with both hands across her lap. She cast a sweeping glance around the room, appreciative of the beauty and luxury surrounding her. She was trying to remember Ambassador Abramov's exact words. Her lips moved soundlessly.

When Charlotte returned with the tea tray containing a silver teapot and two silver-handled glasses, Olga half-rose from her chair. In so doing, she dropped her handbag, out of which spilled a bulky envelope. She stooped swiftly to retrieve it. Charlotte placed the tea service on the coffee table in front of the sofa and beckoned Olga to join her. She poured the tea, giving the nervous girl time to recover herself, fearful of what she would have to say.

Olga sank down uneasily on the sofa and picked up the glass with a shaking hand, then put it down again. "I am clumsy, Madame Ambassador—"

"Be at ease, Olga Vetsayeva," Charlotte said in Russian.

The sound of her own language had a firming effect on Olga. She took a deep breath and said, "Before he left, Ambassador Abramov said I was to come to you."

"Yes. He told me of the arrangement."

The girl's face crumpled. "He has been arrested," she said in a desolate voice. "The moment aircraft reached Moscow, he was arrested." She caught her breath with difficulty and rushed on. "And Minister Milstein, his closest friend—he has been killed in hunting accident."

Charlotte suppressed her shock and fear, asking evenly, "How do you know this?"

Olga lifted her square chin proudly. "In my country, Madame Conroy, many truly believe in freedom. We have been promised democracy. Officer of militia witnessed arrest of ambassador at Sheremeteyvo and used Ministry of Foreign Affairs wire to send message here to Mission. Official announcement about Minister Milstein was in intelligence bulletin." She spoke agitatedly, articles and pronouns vanishing.

"How was a militiaman able to use the Foreign Ministry wire?" Charlotte was puzzled, wary.

Olga's face showed her distress at Charlotte's reservations. "Foreign Ministry communications person send message. All persons who know and admire Ambassador Abramov. Some are members of his old discussion group from even before perestroika. Some former students. Is truth. Even among police can find democrats," she said proudly.

She opened her purse and produced her precious burden, the envelope she had previously dropped. It was closed with red wax seals. "Ambassador Abramov entrusted me with this. He said, 'Give this to Ambassador Conroy in event of arrest, Olga.' Please accept, madame."

Charlotte accepted.

Once relieved of the envelope, Olga sagged back against the cushions, weary beyond belief. Only her affection and respect for Nathan Abramov had driven her to carry out such a dark and probably dangerous task. She was afraid that the days ahead would be just as stressful. And she would have no one to protect her, now that Ambassador Abramov had been arrested. Who knew what questions might be asked of her? But she would never tell anyone of the last task she had performed for the ambassador.

Charlotte looked at her with sympathy mixed with sadness. "Have you slept at all tonight, Olga?" the older woman asked.

"No, Madame Ambassador."

"What will you do now? Would you like to stay here with me? Or will you return to the Mission?"

Real fear flared in Olga's pale eyes. But she said firmly, "Yes, of course I return, Madame Ambassador. It is where I belong."

Charlotte put three teaspoons of sugar in Olga's glass of tea and handed it to her. "Drink it, my dear," she said. "You need something hot and sweet." As she watched Olga sip the beverage, Charlotte Conroy thought ruefully that Diet Pepsi would be more her style than sugared tea in the style of her homeland. The world really was growing smaller. "Please remember that you are welcome to stay here. It might be safer until we can make other arrangements for you."

Olga had drunk about a quarter of her glass of tea, then put it down, pushing it away. She said firmly, "I follow instructions of my ambassador, Madame Conroy. Only that. I do not defect."

"Of course. I understand. But will you be safe?"

"Yes. I hope so. My friends have helped, so that no one knows of my visit." She stood, still nervous, anxious to be gone. A fearful thought struck her, and she asked urgently, "You will not tell, please?"

"No. I will not tell. Thank you, Olga," Charlotte said.

"Good morning, madame." She paused for a moment and then asked in a far less certain voice: "Did I do correct thing, Madame Ambassador? I want to help Ambassador Abramov."

"You did exactly the right thing," Charlotte said. "Nathan will be grateful." She felt as if a hand had squeezed her heart. *If he is still alive,* she thought.

WHEN THE GIRL WAS GONE, Charlotte Conroy went swiftly into her study and seated herself at her desk. She looked at the envelope Olga Vetsayeva had brought her for a long moment before she broke the seals. As she read, chills ran up and down her spine.

When she had finished, she reached for the telephone and dialed the duty officer at the United States Mission at the United Nations.

"This is Ambassador Conroy. Get me a flight to Washington on the early shuttle and then put me through directly to Dr. Vincent Kellner's home. I want the call to have top security." She was amazed at how calm she sounded, under the circumstances. Nathan, dear Nathan . . . Then she cast sentiment aside. Her professional responsibilities came first now. Her task at this moment was to announce to her colleagues in the Caidin Administration that a period of Russian-American cooperation was coming to an end.

234

Chapter Twenty-nine

Washington, D.C./Cyrandell Valley, Virginia/December 1

A man had rather have a hundred lies told of him than one truth which he does not wish should be told.

—SAMUEL JOHNSON, *BOSWELL'S LIFE*

A man had rather have a hundred lies told to him than one truth which he does not wish should be told.

—VINCENT KELLNER, *MEMOIRS*

VINCENT KELLNER CLOSED the red-banded file cover on the intelligence estimates for the last twenty-four hours. There was a hard knot in his stomach. The conversation with Charlton Fisk two days ago in this office had suddenly become far more than just an argument about turf. It had become prophecy.

The Central Intelligence Agency was every bit as feeble these days as Fisk had said. It had not been an accusation Kellner was pleased to accept. It was, after all, his own Administration that had starved the CIA into its present state of near impotence. He had been accused by bitter ex-Company men of aiding and abetting Cole Caidin in his austerity program because it would make the National Security Council more important, more powerful. For a moment Kellner was tempted to discount the accuracy of the daily estimate, but his innate probity rejected that course of action. Moscow station was struggling to gather intelligence on the Russians with totally inadequate resources. The estimates showed this. Reports that used to run twenty to thirty pages now consisted of single pages and outlines. Marshall Gray, the CIA caretaker, took a perverse pride in the brevity of the Russian documents. And until today, Kellner had shared that attitude with the director of Central Intelligence. Despite his familiarity with international affairs and his years in politics, Vincent Kellner still shared the intellectual's conviction that, in the absence of proven hostile intent, spying on a friendly power was dangerous and unrewarding.

Until this very day, Kellner had also clung to the intellectual's ability to hold two or more contradictory opinions on any subject and act on whichever was expedient.

But the first day of December was a day the National Security Adviser would not soon forget. It was the day the Moscow station chief included in the national intelligence estimates the information that David Milstein, Finance Minister of Russia, had died in a hunting accident in Ukovo.

Kellner sat at his bare desk and closed his eyes. Did I cause his death? He asked himself the same question a dozen times. A *hunting* accident? Did Dovi Milstein hunt? It was not the sort of sport Kellner could imagine him enjoying. Milstein was a book man, a computer man, an economic theorist. How much time did a career like his allow for murdering wild animals?

The digital clocks on the wall snapped to the hour position. Four o'clock in Washington, eleven o'clock in Moscow. Nathan Abramov must be there by now. Learning what? Who was to blame for Milstein's death—if Milstein was, in fact, dead.

Again Kellner thought: An accident? Never. Then why? The answer was obvious, and it sickened Kellner. Fisk had warned him. What had he said? Spying is no game for amateurs, or something like that. Was it so simple? Had Milstein betrayed himself to the Soyuz right-wingers? To Cherny?

Or had he been betrayed? By someone who had discovered his activities and sold him to the Russian Intelligence Directorate?

He pressed a call button. "Come in here, please, Camilla," he said.

When Camilla came through the door, Kellner was surprised to see that she was dressed to leave the office. Boots, raincoat, gloves, and hat. "Leaving at four?" The event was so rare Kellner felt compelled to remark on it.

"Didn't I mention to you I was leaving early today, Vincent? It's my symphony night at Kennedy Center." Her face seemed more than normally pallid.

"Sit down, Camilla," Kellner said, "I won't keep you long."

Discussions that did not directly apply to work had become increasingly difficult between them in the last six months. Kellner did not know to what he should ascribe this change in their association. Their sexual relationship had ended long ago, but Kellner had always assured himself that they were good and intimate friends. In point of fact, Camilla Varig was the only woman he could call a friend.

He said, "Did you by chance look at today's intelligence estimates?"

"I never do that, Vincent, unless you specifically ask me to." She sat on the edge of her chair, seemingly edgy and anxious to go.

"David Milstein is dead," he said.

Did she flinch? Eyes widen ever so slightly? If she did, it was imperceptible.

"He was a friend of yours, wasn't he?" Her voice was level, apparently only slightly interested.

237

"You know all my friends, Camilla," Kellner said. "But yes, I knew him." Why am I doing this, he wondered. I certainly never discussed my arrangement with David Milstein with anyone, let alone Camilla. She had no need to know. But *had* she known? He decided to test the waters a little further.

"I am troubled, Camilla," he said. "Charlie Fisk thinks we have a security leak in this office. Until today I would not accept that possibility. But we have staff in and out all day. Have you heard any talk, any gossip?"

"About us? Never, Vincent."

"I've put it off too long, but now I intend having the ferrets in. I have to be sure."

"Of course, I understand and agree," Camilla said.

Kellner waited, watching her. Over the years she had grown more sophisticated, more assured. She would never be a beautiful woman, but she had become the doyen of the NSC office. And she had grown impenetrable to his gaze.

"Was there anything else, Vincent?" she asked.

Speak to me, damn it, Kellner thought. Reassure me that all is as it should be, as it has been for all the years between us. "No,"he said wearily. "Enjoy the symphony."

Camilla Varig stood and crossed to the door, holding her hat and gloves. "I am sorry about your friend, Vincent," she said.

CAMILLA KNOCKED SOFTLY on the door to the room on the second story of the Forest House in Cyrandell Valley. She had originally hoped and planned for a lover's meeting with Marina, but her conversation with Vincent had radically changed her intentions.

She was badly frightened and angry. It was, she had concluded on the drive from Washington, her own fault. She had been so loftily boastful, so full of herself and her special knowledge the last time she spoke to Marina. "*A minister of the Russian government was an American spy*—" How could anyone wishing to be paid for valuable information be so dolt-

238

ish? Of course Marina had unraveled what little mystery Evangeline's boast presented, and now David Milstein was dead. What hope was there now to be paid the quarter million dollars she had so airily demanded?

Worse still was Vincent's reaction. He *knew* there was something wrong in the NSC office. He had to know that she was privy to almost all his secrets. That was what all that soft probing had been about. The Farmer of Grand-Pre was not so foolish as he had seemed only yesterday.

But Camilla's greatest shock came when she entered the room and encountered a totally new Marina.

The Russian woman sat on the edge of the bed with a bottle of Stoly on the nightstand, a glass in her hand, and a silenced automatic pistol on the pillow beside her.

She was dressed in black, her hair tousled and neglected, and on her face was a look of cold loathing. "So, you've finally come," she said.

Camilla stole a glance at her Rolex. She was six minutes late. Matters were not going to go well. Act natural, she admonished herself, don't let her see that you're upset. "I heard about Milstein," she said. "I was foolish, wasn't I?"

"Not foolish. Stupid," Marina said bluntly.

Camilla sat in a chair, unwilling to be intimidated. "I suppose there is no question of payment now," she said.

"Not a prayer," Marina said. "The account is settled." She regarded Camilla contemptuously.

How could I have thought she loved me, Camilla wondered. For that matter, did I ever love her? How could I have imagined that the excitement, the thrilling sense of danger, could go on indefinitely? Reality had returned with a vengeance. She began to think in terms of escape. Not openly from this room, from the Russian woman who boasted she was an assassin, from the pistol on the pillow, but from Washington. I must start to liquidate my possessions, she thought, those not already in the Cayman Islands bank. And somehow I must allay Vincent's suspicions, at least long enough to get away safely.

And how long would it take Vincent to forget all the years they worked together, slept together, planned and schemed together.

Marina was exactly right. Camilla Varig, in grasping for that one last big prize, had stupidly overreached herself. "Did the Russians already know about Milstein?" she asked.

Marina shook her head. "I told them."

"I see."

"You see nothing. They would have killed him anyway. Soon."

"Why soon?"

"Why not? He was a Jew and a traitor." Marina picked up the pistol. "Now, you—you are not a Jew, but you are a traitor. Maybe I should do your secret police a service."

"You don't frighten me, Marina," Camilla said in a thin, timbreless voice. She hugged her elbows against her body to keep from shaking. "I've taken precautions, of course."

"Don't I? How odd. Your face is pale. You look frightened. What is Evangeline afraid of, then?"

"Vincent is close to the truth about you and me," Camilla said.

"Close."

Camilla managed a shrug. "Soon now," she said.

"You still want money."

In spite of herself, Camilla said with urgency, "More than before."

"Running money."

"Yes. We always knew it would probably come to this," Camilla said, trying to sound resigned and calm.

Marina drank vodka and refilled her glass. "Money for information," she said. "That is all. And the information must be absolutely true."

"What a surprise," Camilla said. I'll never let you know how much you frighten me, you Russian psycho bitch, she thought bitterly.

"A Russian scientist named Arkady Karmann will be arriving in Washington soon. He may already be here. I must know where he is now and where he is going, the exact itinerary. Ten thousand dollars cash. Not in Grand Cayman. In Washington.''

"I have heard nothing about any Arkady Karmann."

"Then see to it that you do hear. Very soon. And that's all the money you'll get. Your goods are being remaindered, Evangeline. The value will not hold up for long."

Camilla Varig stood. Her knees were trembling. "Goddamn you, Marina." She winced when the cold voice spoke again.

"Also." Marina had picked up the pistol and sighted along the barrel. "Colonel Morgan of your office. And the woman Anna Akhmatova Neville. I want to know everything about them—where they are, where they have been, and where they are going."

"Is that all?" Now that she was about to escape Marina's presence, Camilla's anger surged to the surface.

"No. Give me your NSC identification."

Camilla was stunned for a moment, then took the folder from her purse and threw it at Marina. She strode toward the door with a bravado she was far from feeling. "I'll call you at the Georgetown number to tell you what you need to know." Now who's stupid, she thought; she can wait for that call until the cows come home.

Still sitting on the bed, bare legs crossed, pistol back on the pillow, Marina finished her vodka. "Close the door on your way out."

Chapter Thirty

Washington, D.C./December 1

Only our nuclear weapons confer power. In order to realize our world mission we must take risks.

—GENERAL PIOTR KONDRATIEV IN A LECTURE TO
    OFFICER CANDIDATES AT THE HIGHER INTERNAL
    SECURITY COLLEGE AT KRASNOGORSK (PRIOR
    TO HIS DISMISSAL BY PRESIDENT CHERNY)

CHARLOTTE CONROY WAS ESCORTED past two sets of federal marshals (who looked as tired as she felt) and through the metal detectors into the White House Situation Room, which bustled with an unusual level of early morning activity. She recognized two junior members of Kellner's National Security Council staff, a bespectacled woman wearing a National Security Agency White House pass and a uniformed officer each from the army, the navy, and the air force, all at work around a map table and at computer terminals. Did all this stem, Charlotte wondered, from her early-morning call from New York? She had been unwilling to discuss Nathan Abramov's arrest over the telephone, and even more unwilling to speak of the information he had sent her by the Vetsayeva girl. Yet there was already a crisis atmosphere in the White House. That was ominous.

Vincent Kellner came forward to greet her.

Charlotte said, "Thank you for seeing me so promptly, Vincent. I've received very important information. You will have to decide how important it is."

"First come look at this," Kellner said. He led her to where the analyst from NSA and the military officers were piecing together satellite images bearing the top secret Observer Office stamp. They showed a coastline and what appeared to be a wilderness of taiga in remarkable detail.

"Hudson Bay?" Conroy asked.

"Yes. The last clear weather images we have. Taken November 19," Kellner said. "The Canadian Ministry of Health is in a funk. Something has contaminated the waters around Eskimo Point with plutonium." He pointed out the location on a satellite image. "There have been three deaths so far."

"Could the Neville woman have been right?"

"It depends what you mean by right, Charlotte. Obviously there is something in the water up there." Kellner regarded her soberly. "We have been asked—unofficially—for help by Ottawa. No accusations. Just a friendly request. We're cooperating, doing a thorough investigation from our end. And we have queried Moscow. All right, then. What brought you down from New York so quickly?"

"Is there somewhere we can talk privately?"

"Follow me." Vincent Kellner led the way to a small interview room furnished with a table and two chairs. Charlotte glanced at the metal walls, which were insulated with soundproofing. "This is secure," Kellner said. "Now, what did you bring?"

Charlotte opened her slim briefcase and laid Nathan Abramov's documents on the table. "Nathan has been arrested," she said without preamble. "The minute he arrived in Moscow he was taken into custody by Intelligence Directorate agents.

I don't know where he is now, but I would guess he is in Lefortovo.''

Kellner nodded noncommittally.

"The rumor was all around New York that David Milstein was killed in an accident," she said.

"A hunting accident," Kellner said.

"But he never hunted. He hated guns."

Kellner's face seemed carved in stone. Milstein's death had affected him deeply. Charlotte had never seen him so grim and withdrawn.

"What is this?" Kellner asked, touching the file folder she had brought with her with his fingertips.

Charlotte opened the file to show the double-eagle insignia of the Russian UN Mission. "You read Russian. Take a look." She sat back in her chair and waited.

Kellner read the pages carefully. When he had read them through, he began again, reading even more slowly and deliberately. At last he looked up, gray-faced. "*Jesus Christ!* . . . Do you believe that all this is true?''

"Nathan believed it enough to gather those documents, and I believe Nathan. Can they possibly do what they plan?"

"If no one prevents them, the short answer is yes."

"And how does one prevent them?"

"The first thing to do is find what it is that Soyuz planted in Canada. Abramov barely mentions here that Soyuz plans a 'distraction.' But we have to assume that by 'distraction' he means whatever the Russian submarine left in the waters of Hudson Bay. If they believe it will stop us dead in our tracks, keep us from reacting in any way when they move on Cherny, it has to be a Pulse weapon. No other single device would be of any use. Even so, even the placement of a weapon is unbelievably dangerous. And firing the weapon is technically an act of war against Canada. Canada is a member of NATO.''

"And the Nevilles and their pilot stumbled on them while they were doing whatever they did in the bay."

"Bad luck for the Nevilles."

"But the risk they're running, Vincent. Is Russia as unstable as that?"

"Russia is always unstable, always has been. That's why they settle on totalitarian governments, no matter how good the revolutionaries' intentions. When a great empire disintegrates, the temblors go on for years. If they can seize Moscow, they can manage the rest."

"Can Soyuz govern?" Charlotte asked.

"Do you mean can Kondratiev and his friends form a government? With military help and some luck, yes. The military has been dissatisfied ever since the USSR dissolved. Soldiers are living in shacks and packing cases. Men who were officers and unit commanders are panhandling on the streets. But if you mean can Soyuz put together a real government and then rule Russia, the answer is no. Not even if Kondratiev plays Stalin and brings back the Terror. Cherny has built on all the hard realities of the years since the eighties. They actually are almost on the verge of some economic success—that light at the end of the tunnel people are always invoking. But paramilitary rebellions don't have futures. They succeed or fail day by day. That means every morning conspirators wake up in a desperate condition."

"I am terribly worried about Nathan," Charlotte said.

"We will do what we can, Charlotte," Kellner said grimly. "But it won't be much. Thank God he warned us. But he may pay for it. You have to be prepared for that."

Charlotte remained silent.

Kellner returned to perusing the Russian papers. "Kondratiev doesn't surprise me. He's been a fascist for years. But Suvorov. My God, I would have expected better sense from Yevgeny Suvorov. And Kalinin. The man has just been appointed Air Defense Commander for the Moscow Military District. He has three regiments of fighter-interceptors in his command. His forces might tip the balance, if they're willing to follow Kalinin."

"What about Aleksandr Cherny? Why hasn't he acted to stop them before this?"

"Ignorance. Weakness. Reasonableness. Denial. Probably all of those. He's a schoolteacher by trade, Charlotte. An intellectual, an idealist, not a man of action." Kellner paused thoughtfully. "He is not the type to challenge the group, most of whom he has considered colleagues up to this time. Remember how horrified he was when Yeltsin blew the first parliament out of the White House with artillery? If Cherny knows of the plot, he'll try to handle it by diplomatic means, secretly."

"Will he succeed?"

"He can try," Kellner said. "But I suspect the Soyuz crowd learned something from the Yaneyev attempt in '91. There's an old proverb in almost every European language that says 'If you strike at a king, make damned sure you kill him.' The Yaneyev conspirators dithered, and Boris Yeltsin climbed up on a tank and faced them down. Kondratiev won't make that mistake."

"Then President Cherny must be warned. The plotters may have isolated him, cut off his political intelligence. We have to alert him."

Kellner regarded Charlotte Conroy evenly. "If we do that, we may cause Abramov's death. Do you understand that?"

Charlotte sat for a moment in silence. Then she said slowly, "Nathan sent me these documents. He intended for me to make the best use of them."

"We must show them to the President," Kellner said. "He's been very concerned about Mrs. Neville's odyssey, thinking as we all did that it was only a propaganda effort, a political ploy." He sat for a moment in thought, his face drawn, pale. He reached over to open a wall panel and lifted a telephone handset from it.

Presently he said, "This is the Adviser. I have Ambassador Conroy with me. We need to see the President at once. Please arrange it."

He broke the connection and held the telephone in his hand for a full half minute.

"Vincent? Are you all right?"

Kellner expelled a breath and said in a quiet voice, "Quite all right, Charlotte." Then he spoke again into the telephone, in the voice of a man who has just made a hard decision: "Get me Charlton Fisk. If he's not in his office yet, get him at home or in his car."

They waited in anticipatory silence. Charlotte's eyes remained fixed on Kellner's drawn, bleak face. She realized that she was holding her breath and made an effort to relax. She'd need all her strength in the hours ahead.

Another minute passed and then Kellner said, "Charlton. Camilla Varig has not come in yet this morning. Find her, Charlie." A pause, and then in a voice that seemed to come from the grave, he said: "I would say the charges are breach of security. Espionage."

He replaced the handset in the compartment and closed the panel. "Let's go now, Charlotte. The President will be expecting us."

Chapter Thirty-one

Washington, D.C./December 1

Four more deaths due to acute radiation exposure have been reported in the Canadian Northwest Territories. Prime Minister Ian Halloran has run to Washington looking for answers.

—CCND NEWSLETTER

IN HIS GUARDED ROOM at Bethesda Naval Hospital Arkady Karmann lay breathing with difficulty beneath the crackling clear plastic of an oxygen tent. His symptoms had slightly ameliorated after massive infusions of blood plasma had been poured into him by the military paramedics aboard the navy helicopter that had brought him from North Carolina.

He no longer felt that he could suffocate at any moment. His limbs felt warmer than they had since crossing the Rio Grande at Brownsville. In the guarded room, a machine monitored his vital signs, and every fifteen minutes a naval officer nurse looked in on him.

The prize GKNT defector, Karmann thought. Is that what these Americans saw, why they took such good care of him?

His recent memories were scrambled. He remembered the crossing from Mexico into Texas. Before that there had been the Mexican coyotes. And long, long ago, there had been the steaming heat of the Mosquito Coast and Russian bodies floating in the sea among feeding sharks.

He sometimes wondered if those memories were real. Certainly the *Pravda* was gone, and with it, all those murdered shipmates. How could it have happened? Far, far away, in another life, he had been a marine biologist, a diver, a scientist. He remembered that clearly, and yet how was it possible? This room, this place, was in America.

Somewhere to the north, in deep, dark water, there lay a monstrous thing that he had helped to put there. He could not remember why he had done this terrible thing. Since the shark had taken his hand, he had been beyond memory, almost without identity. But he remembered the look of the great dark thing at the bottom of the bay. He had helped to awaken it. Now it must be killed.

Karmann closed his eyes and dozed fitfully. His dreams were haunted by images of Krasny, shooting at him from the sail of the doomed submarine. In each dream, he threw himself into the water to escape the bullets, only to be faced with the horror of the sharks, circling, frenzied, in the bloodstained water. Each time, he saw with dread that it was his own blood—*his*—staining the sea. He forced himself to stay awake, hoping for surcease from the terror.

But soon he slept again, and this time he dreamed of the illegals drowning in the flash flood, the hovering helicopter with its spear of blue-white light . . . He came awake with a strangled cry, only then realizing that the sounds he heard were made by the machine monitoring his vital signs.

Sick as he was, he had accomplished a very difficult thing. He had survived Krasny, survived the sea and the sharks, survived the weeks on the Mosquito Coast, then three thousand kilometers of solitary travel. He had done it, mostly without funds or assistance, save from unsavory characters like the coyotes who abandoned the illegals near Brownsville.

But it was now the first of December. Rain froze on the windowpanes, like his hopes. If someone in authority did not appear soon, Soyuz would change the world.

AVERY PETERS SWUNG into the seat next to Anna Neville on the ride from National Airport to the White House. Across the aisle, Morgan stared moodily out of the window at the dark, wet countryside. Joe Ryerson sat in the rear of the van, flanked by two granitefaced air force police. His tape recorder and notes had been confiscated. Ryerson was silent now, after his first protests. He was saving his breath, planning his legal challenges.

Anna Neville was uncomfortable to find herself the object of Ave's scrutiny. "Is something wrong, Mr. Peters?" she asked.

Ave's weatherbeaten face broke into a mirthless smile. "I'd say so, Mrs. Neville. There usually is when people like me and like you find ourselves going in the same direction."

Anna turned to face him. She and her friends had always regarded the Avery Peterses of this life, if they thought about them at all, as men who lived outside the pale of civility. They were capable of breaking any law, committing any misdeed, and rationalizing their behavior in the name of national security, or the government, or their own safety, if it came to that. But Anna found herself in a dilemma. In truth, Morgan frightened her more than did Peters. Ave Peters was just a large, gruff man who had always been on the other side, and would remain so. But Morgan, the man of few words, something of a loner like herself, was a different matter.

"Adversity is a great matchmaker," Ave said. "In more ways than one. You and me. You and Morgan." He dropped his voice and said softly, "Go easy on him, Mrs. Neville. I mean it. John's a good man, and lonely, so he's ripe for the plucking from someone like you—someone who knows all the tricks." When Anna tried to interrupt him, Peters gestured to the city beyond the river and said in a louder tone, "So, here we are." The Capitol dome and the Washington Monument stood out against the sleeting dark of the December morning. Early Christmas decorations lent a forlorn touch of tattered gaiety to the landscape.

Anna sat for a moment, trying to figure how best to show Peters just how rude he had been. She decided that indiscretion was the better part of valor. "I do appreciate what you have done, Mr. Peters, but—" Anna stopped. She had been about to say, "Stay out of my private affairs, please. I am convinced that you have used unacceptable means to save my life. Therefore I reserve the right to disapprove of what you have done, regardless of the fact that I am alive to disapprove because of it." Sincere or not, it would make her sound like an ungrammatical, ungrateful prig.

Ave's expression was quizzical. It gave him a curious (and totally spurious, Anna thought) innocence. "Are you still suggesting that less violent methods could have been used to save you? Even our prize turkey Ryerson doesn't believe that." His tone was just this side of contempt.

"I have no way to judge the methods, since I have had no prior experience of this sort of danger," she said, thinking, My God, I really do sound like a prig. How can I change the subject? "What happens now?"

"You have a complaint, lady, one that you wanted the brass to address. I suspect you're about to get your wish."

"I mean after that."

"I'm not sure, Mrs. Neville. How resolved are you to see this through to the end? You began it, after all."

"That's not fair," Anna protested hotly. "I didn't ask to be put in a hospital for six months, nor to be a witness to a murder, nor to have grenades thrown at me."

"Point taken," Ave said calmly. "But none the less, I suspect that your resolve may be put to the test. What are you going to say when it's proved to your satisfaction that the Russians are up to their asses in alligators?"

Anna lost her temper and turned on him. "My God, can't you blame anyone but the Russians? It seems to me that even American reactionaries would get tired of stirring the embers of the cold war."

Ave rolled his eyes up to heaven. "Jesus Christ, lady, you haven't been listening to me at all. What will it take to convince her, John?" he asked.

Morgan had risen to stand in the narrow aisle, watching and listening to the two of them argue. He settled into the empty seat ahead of Anna and Ave, turning to face them. "Settle it later. Right now we have another problem."

"I'm not surprised," Ave said. "This operation isn't exactly a Swiss watch."

"I think there's a leak in the NSC office. A bad one."

Ave said, "Shit. So that's how the little turd knew how to find you."

"I think so. No one else knew except for Charlotte Conroy."

"UN Conroy?"

"Yes."

"She could have leaked. The UN wallahs love to run off at the mouth."

"But not to Ryerson."

"True." Peters paused. "Kellner will shit a brick."

But the information on Morgan's whereabouts could *only* have come from the NSC office. When I talked to Hardy, the duty officer, Morgan thought, I gave him time and location. We were shopped almost as soon as I'd hung up the telephone, he thought bitterly. The question was, by whom?

Anna listened with growing unease. "Are you sure you're not just playing a cloak-and-dagger game?"

Ave threw up his hands. "You are a gem, lady. Beyond fucking price. Spoken like Jake Fucking Neville."

The van was slowing to stop at the White House gate.

"I told you that you might be in over your head, girl, but you don't believe me. All right. You're going to learn all kinds of things that will make your lefty upbringing scream for mercy,'' Avery Peters said. ''This isn't a time for summer soldiers, Mrs. Neville.''

Anna said angrily, ''Don't moralize, Mr. Peters. And remember, I am not ashamed of what you choose to call 'my lefty upbringing.' I am a Canadian, Mr. Peters, not a paranoid American. And summer comes late in Canada.''

''Yes,'' Ave said sardonically. ''If it comes at all this year, Mrs. Neville.''

Chapter Thirty-two

Moscow/Washington, D.C./December 1

> *On our crowded planet there are no longer any internal affairs. The Communists say, "Don't interfere in our internal affairs. Let us strangle our citizens in peace and quiet." But I tell you: Interfere more and more. Interfere as much as you can. We beg you to come and interfere.*

> —ALEKSANDR SOLZHENITSYN, 1975

ALEKSANDR CHERNY LOOKED WEARILY at the stack of papers that needed his prompt attention and closed his eyes to hide the sight. He rose from his chair behind the vast, antique table that served him as a desk in his Kremlin suite and walked across the parquet floor to the window overlooking the inner court of the citadel. On the horizon a low sun had broken through the gray sky of late afternoon, shining a golden path across the perfectly smooth coating of snow covering the cobblestones. From where he stood he could not see the ugly tracks left by the departing Mercedes limousines of the members of the Council of Ministers, nor could he see the sandbagged machine-gun emplacements that Colonel Temko, the

Kremlin guard regiment commander (and Kondratiev's good friend), had suddenly insisted be placed at intervals around the outer walls. By stripping myself of the three rings of security devised to protect the presidency, I proved nothing except my naiveté. I have allowed the Kremlin to revert to its original purpose, Cherny thought. It is again a fortress, not against an external enemy, but to guard its privileged denizens.

How could the government that he headed have come to such a state? He had done his best to govern in an enlightened manner, to pry open the cracks in the dishonored authoritarian regimes that had preceded his, letting in modern thought and modern economic methods. All for the good of the Russian people, not for personal gain.

Cherny stood looking down at the untrammeled snow with tears in his eyes. It was because of me, my caution, my fears, and my sins of omission that Dovi Milstein, companion of my university days, supporter in exile, coworker in the chaotic fields of Russian politics, confidant and adviser, faithful friend, was dead. Cherny broke down and wept freely, mopping at his face with a large white handkerchief. There would be no state funeral, no open casket, for David Davidovich Milstein. His ascetic face had been destroyed by the explosion of one of Admiral Aleyev's costly British Purdy shotguns.

My God, he thought bitterly, did that group of murderers really imagine he would accept an explanation for Milstein's death so transparently false? Kondratiev and his adherents had purposefully killed Dovi, just as certainly as he, Aleksandr Cherny, who stood here alone, with the last light of the dying winter's day on his face, had sent him to his death at their hands.

The insufferable arrogance of those bastards, he thought, as they feigned sorrow at my bereavement. Not ten minutes ago they had gathered in this very room, crying their crocodile tears, then trying to bully him into naming one of theirs as Dovi Milstein's replacement. Now that Cherny and Kondratiev had reconciled, Kondratiev, or someone he nominated from

Soyuz, should inherit the Ministry of Finance, they argued, in order to "save the Russian motherland from the conspiracies of the American and European bankers."

He was at once consumed with an icy rage and, at the same time, truly frightened. The plotters were far ahead of him. They were very close to isolating him, leaving him with no one to speak to the people or to those in the parliament who supported him, now that Milstein was dead.

Kondratiev's vision of the future under the governance of Soyuz was that the President of Russia be only a figurehead, bypassed as though he were an obsolete strongpoint on some fluid war front, where battle was dark, and dubious, and far from heroic.

What were the lines of that Englishman's poem?

And we are here as on a darkling plain,
Where ignorant armies clash by night.

How well he put it, Cherny thought. It was the chilling ignorance that was so frightening. Through the high window he watched a soldier of the guard walking his post on the Inner Kremlin wall. He felt an insane impulse to call to the man, to ask him if he were guarding his chief of state, or if he were confining him. How surprised the soldier would be, how silly he would think the President. He would tell all his fellows about it when he was off duty. Our President is a fool, he would say, and he would be right. Only a fool could have managed not to see and to understand all that was going on, right under his nose. It is my nature and my training to consider, to ponder, to speculate, to discuss, and to do nothing for fear of making things worse.

What was it that Freud had said about intellectuals? Oh, yes; that the intellectual has no direct contact with life in the raw, but encounters it in its easiest synthetic form—the printed page. It has been my blessing and my curse, Cherny thought. Now, I must fight, whether by myself or by summoning those who will fight with me. I cannot allow my country to fall to Soyuz and the new Oprichnika. Czar Ivan the Terrible's black state within a state had been reborn once with the Communist party and blighted Russia for seventy years. It must not come again.

> *And what rough beast, its hour come round at last,*
> *Slouches toward Bethlehem to be born?*

It must be *my* rough beast born, and Dovi's, not Kondratiev's, Cherny thought passionately. We can never again slip into barbarism.

He walked purposefully back to his desk and picked up a telephone. "Connect me with the Defense Office," he said. He waited while the surprised and confused operator did as he was told. It was unusual for this President ever to call the Defense Office. Aleksandr Cherny had never been interested in military deployments. Until today.

When the duty officer answered, Cherny closed his eyes for a moment, then spoke in a firm voice: "Connect me directly with General Lieutenant Komarov of the Thirtieth Shock Army at Stavropol."

"At once, Mr. President."

The Thirtieth Shock was a people's army, one of the last to be withdrawn from Eastern Europe. They were not the Kremlin guards, goose-stepping like Prussians in front of the Spassky Gate and the mausoleum. Vladimir Komarov had spoken out with enthusiasm about the new Russia. Milstein had trusted him. But enlisting any active duty officer of the armed forces in such an enterprise as Cherny had in mind might be risky. Perhaps Kondratiev had already approached Komarov, persuaded him to follow Soyuz. While he waited, he ticked off members of his cabinet who were increasingly restive, showing that their sympathies lay with Kondratiev. Yevgeny Suvorov, who apparently confused his authority as Minister of Defense with that of the President, for one, and of course old

Yulin, who was terrified of street demonstrations and wanted to turn the security forces loose on the "hooligans—*all* the hooligans." He dwelt constantly on the deadly confrontation on the day of Orgonev's funeral, even though it had been his troops who had done the killing. The rest of the Council of Ministers appeared to agree with Yulin, heavily influenced by the warnings from Kondratiev's supporters. They claimed that only repressive measures would save the state—or was it their hides they were worried about, if a putsch succeeded?

He was startled out of his reverie by the sound of a clipped military voice on the telephone saying, "V. A. Komarov here, Mr. President. At your service, Excellency."

Cherny cleared his throat and squared his shoulders before speaking. There is no going back now, he thought. The battle begins.

"General Komarov," the President said firmly. "I order you to come here to the Kremlin at once, by the swiftest means available. I wish to confer with you personally. You may bring an aide. No one else. And your mission is secret. Is that understood?"

Which road would Komarov choose, the new—or the old? He is a hard-bitten, professional soldier, Cherny thought. He held his breath, awaiting Komarov's answer.

Komarov's voice was firm. "Yes, Mr. President."

Cherny let out a great sigh of relief. Thank God, he thought. "Come at once, General," Cherny said, and broke the connection.

For a full five minutes Cherny sat at his littered worktable, gazing at nothing. His heart beat heavily in his chest. He could feel the pulse behind his eyes. He could see it, as well, together with swimming dark spots at the edges of his field of vision. *By Jesus the Christos and his Holy Virgin Mother,* he thought, *am I having a stroke?*

The telephone on his desk rang urgently, just once. He stared at it blankly. There was a five-second pause, then it began to ring again, this time with the urgent bell tone, the tone used only for emergency calls. He picked it up gingerly, and said, "Yes?"

It was the duty officer at the Communications Center, a captain of the security forces. She said, "Washington has informed us that the White House will be calling in five minutes, Mr. President."

Cherny's mind went blank for a moment. With everything he had on his mind, the informal message Ambassador James Rankin had brought from the American President had been almost forgotten. Besides, the premise in the message was preposterous—Russian submarines and nuclear missiles and dying Eskimos. His automatic response to the duty officer was a pedagogic rebuke. "The White House is an inanimate object, Captain. It calls no one. Who in the White House is calling? Is it President Caidin himself, Dr. Kellner, his National Security Adviser, or another of the President's aides?"

"The President himself is on the line, sir."

God, he thought exasperatedly. What could the importunate Americans want at this moment that could not wait? To Cherny's mind, Cole Caidin was still an adolescent, a beautiful, youthful television era President, more concerned with image than with substance. He started to ask the captain to call Foreign Minister Mirisov to join him before the call went through, but realized with a shock that he was unsure of the man's loyalties. I am alone, he thought, no matter what President Caidin had in mind, and I must act alone. "I will come straightaway, Captain."

THE CAPTAIN ON DUTY outside the Hot Line Room to whom Cherny had spoken was a woman in her forties, plainly proud to be in such a position of trust. She stood stiffly at attention as Cherny entered.

Cherny nodded, then said, "Captain."

"Sir?"

"Please forgive me for my rude remark about the White House. It was ungracious."

Alfred Coppel

"Yes, Mr. President. Thank you." The astonishment in the woman's voice and on her face was clear.

She sees me as an idiot, he thought. An idiot and a weakling. As I probably am. It is time to find out if there is a better man, a stronger man, able to cope with the danger ahead, lurking deep inside this soft body. Red-eyed with grief and loss of sleep, weighed down with fatigue and worry, Aleksandr Cherny walked across the long room to the elevator. Dovi, he thought, how I wish you were here.

In the Kremlin, the Hot Line Room was deep below ground, in a structure that had been hardened in an attempt to protect it from a thermonuclear attack on the city. Of course, the newest weapons would most probably destroy it, just as an attack on the American Command Center at Cheyenne Mountain in Colorado would demolish that useful but also semi-obsolete facility. The shelter lay directly under the Spassky Tower, thirty meters down, and one entered through two sets of vanadium-steel blast doors and past three guard posts. The security arrangements for the direct line between Moscow and Washington had not changed appreciably since the days of Leonid Brezhnev. The original teletype machines had been long ago relegated to backup duties. The current state-of-the-art audiovisual links now terminated in large, high-resolution television monitors with stereo pickups and players.

Cameras and television screens occupied the end wall of a cramped and cheerless room a dozen meters in length, filled with mainframe computers of French manufacture, obtained by a barter agreement—Soviet oil and gas for French technology.

Aleksandr Cherny sat down at the console and signaled his readiness.

IN WASHINGTON, Cole Caidin was suffering from severe shock, compounded by throbbing pain from a bad toothache. His handsome face was marred by a massive frown and a swollen jaw. The documents that Charlotte Conroy and Vin-

260

cent Kellner had brought him appeared to be irrefutable. He had stared at the English translations of Nathan Abramov's papers uneasily, finally flinging them back across his desk at Kellner. "We haven't got time for me to read these—just give me the gist of what Abramov claims is happening." The skepticism in his voice indicated how seriously he took Abramov's message.

However, as Kellner outlined Abramov's documentation of the extent of the Soyuz plot and the possibility that General Kondratiev would soon try to overthrow the legitimate government of Russia, Caidin's skepticism turned into anger and frustration.

"Goddamn it, Vincent, it's a hell of a time for you to dump this mess in my lap. The Egyptian ambassador is due to present his credentials, and Ian Halloran is coming in from Ottawa tonight about the business with the submarine. Someone from State should be here to help handle it, but Jannings is in intensive care at Bethesda. The doctor says he has only days left." The President shuddered. "He looks like a skeleton, and he drifts in and out of consciousness. I should never have named him to State. That's what I get for being so damned nice to those people, and they're still screaming that I'm insensitive to their feelings."

Caidin rubbed his jaw gently. "I was up all night with this lousy toothache, and I'm running a fever. I feel terrible. Are you sure that I need to speak to Cherny personally? Are you sure he doesn't know what's going on under his nose? If Abramov is right, and Milstein's death wasn't accidental, even Cherny must be getting the picture."

"Were I to be the bearer of such a message, it would never have the same gravity as it would coming from you, sir." Vincent Kellner spoke softly, suppressing the anger and anxiety he felt so deeply. It was true that Caidin didn't look well; he had circles under his eyes, and his face was flushed.

Charlotte Conroy said urgently, "Please, Mr. President. It must come from you, and you alone."

Alfred Coppel

Caidin rubbed his forehead and sighed deeply. "All right, then, let's get with it." He set his lips and frowned, then walked to the console and sat down. "I'm ready."

The head and shoulders of Aleksandr Cherny suddenly appeared on the screen before them, larger than life. He was a true Slav, with a broad face and a rosy complexion; his usual expression was cheerful, friendly, and slightly quizzical. Today his face was gray and drawn, and his thinning hair was rumpled. His pale blue eyes were swollen and red. He had never been a fashion plate, but his clothes looked as if they had been slept in.

Charlotte drew in her breath; this man was under great emotional strain. Part would stem from David Milstein's death, the rest possibly from some knowledge about the conspiracy. Cole Caidin could advise Cherny tactfully of the full scale of the Soyuz plot. But her heart sank when she heard the tone of voice Caidin adopted to address the Russian President.

"Mr. President," Caidin said, leaning toward the camera for emphasis, "I am dispensing with diplomatic niceties today, because a crisis is pending in your country. You may believe that we are interfering with a matter that is strictly internal. But I would like to make it clear to you that American interests are deeply involved, as well."

The expression on Cherny's face changed from weariness to irritation. Vincent Kellner winced at the hectoring tone of voice Caidin was using. You'll only make it worse, you fool, he thought angrily. Kellner knew what Caidin had never realized: that Cherny had never felt an affinity with Cole Caidin. They were of different generations, different backgrounds.

Cherny said in his precise, heavily accented English, "I am listening, Mr. President. Please tell me what it is that so engages your concern that you should call at this hour."

"Are you satisfied with the security of your communications arrangements, Aleksandr Borisovich?" Caidin asked abruptly.

When Cherny stared back without answering immediately,

262

Kellner whispered to Charlotte, "My God, I'll bet he isn't sure. I wonder if his internal security people have pledged loyalty to Kondratiev and Soyuz?"

"My arrangements are excellent, thank you," Cherny said, his expression forbidding further discussion. This exchange was not starting well.

Caidin sat up straight and said, his voice equally cold, "Very well, Mr. President . . ." Then he plunged ahead. "We believe that another coup d'état is about to take place in Russia, that your government is in imminent danger of being overthrown."

Cherny stiffened perceptibly. Behind him, the communications technicians and his personal interpreter, who was standing by in case Cherny's English abandoned him, looked up, their faces reflecting shock and surprise.

The Russian smiled and spoke calmly. "I must have misunderstood you, Mr. President. What is this nonsense? How can you know this?"

Cole Caidin rubbed his swollen jaw again and winced at the pain. "It is not nonsense, sir. I meant exactly what I said," he stated with a new edge in his voice. Caidin was not fond of foreign policy matters. He was more at ease with domestic concerns; hence his almost automatic delegation of his authority in foreign affairs either to State or to Kellner. When he had been awakened this morning at the crack of dawn with the awful news that the cold war might be on again, he was furious. Goddamned devious Russians, he thought bitterly, and after all I've done for them. All that time, all that money, all those votes in the World Bank and the UN just to give them enough time to save their treacherous hides.

Now Caidin glanced over at Charlotte Conroy, then said to Cherny angrily, "The information reached us through one of your own men."

Charlotte Conroy's eyes widened. She reacted to that statement with a half-suppressed "Mr. President!" but Vincent Kellner's gesture warned her to be quiet.

"He has to be told the truth," Kellner whispered.

At that moment, Cherny turned away from the console and signaled for everyone but the chief communications technician to leave the room. The Americans watched them file out, faces full of suppressed excitement and worry. As soon as the staff and the interpreter had gone, Cherny said grimly, "Now. Be more explicit, Mr. President." He sounded angry, and slightly contemptuous.

A pose, Kellner wondered. Or to gain time?

Charlotte crossed her fingers, awaiting the next exchange. Don't make things worse, she pleaded silently.

"The coup is being planned by General Kondratiev, Admiral Aleyev, and their nationalist confederates. The name of their organization is Soyuz. Our list of the men involved is available to you, if you want it," Caidin said. His face was very flushed now, his manner deliberate, his eyes glittering.

Cherny sat, impassive, uncommunicative.

"You will recall that Ambassador Rankin gave you a message from me two days ago, about the plutonium contamination in Hudson Bay. We have had no response at all from you to date. Now we have concrete evidence that a Russian naval vessel has engaged in illegal operations inside the territorial waters of Canada, a NATO ally of the United States. These activities may be connected to the conspiracy against your government. If not, I would have to believe that these illegal operations were ordered by you. A thorough investigation has begun here. Am I making myself clear, Mr. President?"

He rushed on, not waiting for an answer. "Are you aware that Nathan Abramov was recalled to Moscow by Foreign Minister Mirisov, and that he was arrested the moment he arrived at Sheremeteyvo?"

Kellner had never admired Aleksandr Cherny more than he did at that moment. It must have taken every bit of his self-control to keep silent in the face of these surprises and bitter accusations.

Then Cherny spoke, slowly and deliberately. "You are mistaken, about both matters, Mr. President. I asked Ambassador Abramov to return for consultations myself," Cherny said, his voice steady, but the quality of his English deteriorating. "I cannot imagine source you heard Abramov is detained. I assure you, you make mistake. I have appointment with him in morning." His voice rose in outrage. "And your other business is preposterous—preposterous, do you hear?"

Cole Caidin seemed on the verge of shouting back at the screen when Vincent Kellner's hand closed on his arm, warning him. Caidin paused for a swallow of water, then said harshly, "If you are resolved to deny everything, determined not to believe us, Mr. President, that is your choice. We cannot force you to face the truth, nor to acknowledge the seriousness of our situation here in North America, if the plutonium contamination is the result of a Russian missile. But I speak now in my capacity as leader of the government and the people of the United States."

"I hear you out, Mr. President." Cherny's expression was every bit as stony as Caidin's, and he was obviously outraged. "But I do not accept premise. You are telling untruth. And *I* speak on behalf of Russian people."

"We have initiated this call in the spirit of friendship and concern," Caidin said, his voice rising. "Three American presidents have committed themselves to helping the former Soviet Union transform itself from a despotism feared by the world to a democratic state acceptable in the society of nations—"

It was true enough, but Cherny flushed at the insult.

"You prefer not to accept our friendship nor to understand that we offer it in good faith," Caidin went on. "Since the end of the Gulf War, the United States has been engaged in a steady reduction of its conventional military power. We have deactivated air wings and army divisions, and we have mothballed ships. At our last meeting, as you know, we agreed to reduce our land-based missile force to zero before the end of this year. Under the circumstances, we are entitled to hear the truth from you—''

As Caidin's words grew more harsh, Vincent Kellner rose from his seat and walked to the side of the room, frowning at the President, trying to calm him.

Charlotte Conroy was alarmed at the tenor of the President's message. Stop, be careful, she implored silently. A lesson of her childhood sprang to mind—when playing crack the whip, the person at the end of the line must remember to take very small, very cautious steps, or be flung out into the unknown. She couldn't bear to watch the exchange any longer; she left the room altogether.

But Cole Caidin shrugged off Kellner's murmured warning. He had sincerely come to believe that he and Aleksandr Cherny were friends, personal friends. This friendship, and the attendant diminishment of superpower tensions, had been a central feature of his Administration's policy, one that had garnered much praise around the diplomatic world. Now his goodwill was being met with ingratitude and, by inference, humiliation and betrayal. Caidin was absolutely convinced of his righteousness.

"Since you refuse to accept my warning, President Cherny, let me make my position clear. No matter what threat we face from you, the United States cannot and will not accept a radical change of government in Russia, a fascist regime.'' The President touched his jaw again. The throbbing pain stiffened his resolve. "We have approached you in friendship, to give you vital information that you choose to ignore. If a weapon was emplaced in Hudson Bay, it indicates that a Soyuz government armed with nuclear missiles is an unacceptable risk for the United States—''

Vincent Kellner closed his eyes and shook his head, knowing what came next, appalled at the outcome of this encounter.

"Therefore, Mr. President," Caidin said heavily, "it shall be the policy of the United States of America that any unlawful change in the government of Russia will be considered an act of war against the United States. So that there will be no possible misunderstanding, I suggest you inform General Kondratiev and his associates that I am ordering United States strategic forces to defcon two at once. I have nothing more to say."

Aleksandr Cherny controlled his anger. Pride and prudence struggled for precedence as he listened. Pride won. He lifted his chin. "Very well, Mr. President," he said. "I do the same with my forces. Again, I tell you truth. This so-called weapon you describe could not have been placed by any Russian, Soyuz or not. May God—if He exists—deal with us cautiously, and with mercy. I speak with you again, very soon."

"That would be wise," Cole Caidin said.

The monitor went dark.

THE INITIAL CALL from the White House to the Pentagon telling the Joint Chiefs that the President of the United States had accused the Russian government of planning an act of war against his country, and hence had declared defense condition two, was received with shock and surprise.

The repercussions of that call echoed throughout the halls of the huge building.

"What is it with that bastard, anyway?" General Laurence Collingwood said angrily. "As the head of the Joint Chiefs, am I not supposed to be consulted at least, before our President, God bless him, goes off half-cocked?"

"I didn't hear that," murmured his aide. "Just hope your office isn't bugged, sir. By the way, the shelter in the Catoctin Mountains is almost completely shut down, thanks to this year's military appropriations and the Office of Management and Budget. They convinced Congress and the President that we didn't need such an expensive facility any more—no external threat, and all that. Therefore, do you think that defcon two means that we'll have to reactivate the Looking Glass?"

"That damned plane, that 707, is obsolete, to begin with, and we haven't time to get all the electronic gear back on it,"

Collingwood said, pacing agitatedly back and forth. "Call Andrews and see if there's even a possibility of cobbling something together in the next couple of days. Our fearless leader didn't say when he expects to be attacked, did he, by any chance?"

Like many Pentagon officers, the Chairman disliked Cole Caidin, who was reputed once to have said that he "loathed" the military. "I'm told that bad temper is what got our commander in chief in so deep, that and his aching tooth. Sort of like the theory that Woodrow Wilson got us into World War I because his feet hurt all the time. And just think how much more you can pry out of Congress next year if he's right. Remember, our boy is up for reelection next November. Can't you just see the headlines now? 'Unprepared!' shouts the *New York Times*. 'Unconscionable!' yells the *Washington Post*. We might even be able to convince the bean counters that Star Wars should be revived."

"Caution is the watchword," Collingwood said, smiling. Then he sobered. "Let's get to work. We've got a crisis on our hands, even if it is only practice. One day, you wait and see, one day it'll be all too real."

Chapter Thirty-three

Washington, D.C./December 1

The most dangerous time for a bad government is when it starts to reform itself.

—ALEXIS DE TOQUEVILLE

THE MARINE GUARD led Morgan and the others into the Executive Wing and down the stairs into NSC country. The young corporal addressed himself to Morgan as though the trio of civilians accompanying him were troops under the colonel's command.

"Please wait here, sir. Dr. Kellner is next door with Ambassador Conroy, but he has asked to see you before the meeting starts." He indicated where they were to wait, then hurried off.

Camilla Varig was not at her desk, Morgan noted. Probably in with Kellner, he thought. But time passed and Camilla did not appear. Varig was never sick, never late, rarely absent. Yet her desk and console remained unattended.

Joe Ryerson, who had been reasonably cowed by his escort and silent on the ride in from Andrews, began once again to

269

Alfred Coppel

complain that he was being detained illegally.

Morgan, tired and exasperated, said sharply, "Oh, shut up and sit down." Seething, Ryerson did as he was told.

Anna looked done in. Her face was so pale that the shadows under her eyes were like bruises against her cheeks. The fact is, Morgan thought, we are all exhausted and tempers are short. Even the usually unflappable Avery Peters looked worn out by the long flight.

Morgan got up and paced the room. The heavy silence was heightened by tension. He looked speculatively at Camilla Varig's empty chair, watching the access light blinking on the computer's display. Lights on the telephone console were also flashing. Someone elsewhere was answering calls to the Adviser's office. So where in the hell was Varig?

Ave joined him and whispered, "Where's the wicked witch?" nodding at Camilla's desk. Morgan whispered back, "Damned if I know."

Staff members hurried by, looking neither right nor left, coming and going, clutching papers and briefcases, civilian and military. The uniforms were an unexpected note in Cole Caidin's ordinarily purely civilian White House. Morgan looked at Anna, Ryerson. They felt the tension, too, he thought. Anna's eyes met his across the room. Are you sorry you began this crusade, Anna Akhmatova, he wondered.

So in my heart the past loses its power;
I'm almost free; I'll forgive anything. . . .

No, Morgan thought, that might be Akhmatova's way, but never her namesake's. Anna was not so irresolute. The past had lost none of its power over her. Morgan found that admirable, but, in his present state of mind, he also found it exasperating. In circumstances like those into which they had stumbled, time and events telescoped emotions. The fact is, Anna, he thought, that right now I would rather lie beside you again in Ave's raunchy bed than carry a spear in your crusade.

270

So much for Morgan, the mighty warrior, he thought. Semper fi, Mac.

Vincent Kellner and two of his administrative aides came out into the anteroom. Kellner appeared calm, but there was a tight look around his eyes that suggested he had not slept enough in the last twenty-four hours. Morgan looked inside Kellner's office, still expecting to see Camilla Varig hovering in the background. Instead, he glimpsed Charlotte Conroy through the open door, a telephone receiver to her ear, listening for a moment, then speaking urgently to whoever was at the other end of the line. Her face was like a thundercloud. Whatever was going on when I left, Morgan thought with a prickle of apprehension, has escalated, gone ballistic. He braced himself.

The two aides with Kellner were members of the NSC's intelligence committee; both were lawyers, three-piece suit men, with inscrutable faces. A female colonel of the Canadian armed forces, wearing the wings of Air Command and the braided bullion shoulder cord of an aide-de-camp, followed close behind. Only a high-ranking Canadian official would rate a colonel as an aide. So, Ian Halloran was in Washington, Morgan realized. That meant the Canadians had come around at last.

Dr. Kellner said briskly, "Welcome back, John." To Anna he offered a brief smile, almost a grimace, and introduced himself before Morgan could speak. "Mrs. Neville. I'm Vincent Kellner. I'm pleased to see that you're safe."

Anna looked at him in weary silence. Kellner gestured to the Canadian colonel to come forward and said, "Mrs. Neville, this is Colonel Heloise Duquesne of Air Command. Please accompany her. She'll take you along where you can freshen up, then bring you back here. President Caidin and Prime Minister Halloran are pressed for time, but they both want to meet you."

Anna shot a look of dubiety at Morgan, then stood up. Colonel Duquesne, neat in her well-pressed uniform, obviously

Alfred Coppel

well washed and groomed, nodded and reached out to shake hands. Anna vainly tried to look as if she were totally comfortable in her rumpled state, but failed.

Colonel Duquesne said formally, "Be good enough to follow me, Mrs. Neville."

Morgan watched Anna go, limping slightly as she moved, his mind sorting out the possibilities involved. It looked as though Anna's crusade was being co-opted by higher authority. How will she react to that, he wondered. She had come a long way in a short time. She was learning the rules. She knew she had rights, even some clout. She was that rara avis, an eyewitness to a crime, untainted by any stain of belonging to "the establishment." He heard Kellner talking to Ave Peters, asking him if he was still helo qualified.

Ave's lined face showed his surprise. "Yes, sir," he said.

"You are now restored to active duty until further notice, Mr. Peters. Is that agreeable to you?"

"Have I a choice?"

"You do not." Kellner's voice crackled with strain.

Another indicator, Morgan thought. Peters was a CIA asset, and ever since the Iran-Contra mess, the CIA had been kept at a discreet distance from the White House. Now, suddenly, there seemed to be full cooperation between NSC and the CIA, organizations that were natural rivals by the very nature of their work.

"Then I accept," Peters said dryly.

"Keep yourself available," Kellner said. "I want to speak with you privately when these meetings are over."

Kellner next addressed himself to Joe Ryerson, who had moved to the doorway, peering inside with curiosity to watch Charlotte Conroy. "Now I shall dispose of you, Mr. Ryerson." His voice had gone icy cold. "I want you and these gentlemen here—" He indicated his aides, the two men from the legal staff. "—to have a thorough discussion regarding highly classified information, and the misuse thereof."

272

As always, Joe Ryerson reacted with bluster. "Hold on, Kellner—"

"No, Mr. Ryerson. *You* hold on. I can have a warrant for your arrest here in ten minutes, and I am not bluffing."

"Arrest? On what charge?" Ryerson protested, backing away, his face pale.

Kellner said coldly, "The charge will be for a crime not covered by the First Amendment. We are speaking here of espionage, Mr. Ryerson."

Ryerson looked as if he were going to faint.

"Information has reached the FBI that you have met regularly with a member of my staff and with a member of the Russian mission. Does the mention of a townhouse in Georgetown ring any bells?"

"The Bureau had me under surveillance? I'm a journalist, for God's sake!"

"Surveillance of foreign agents is routine, even in Washington," Kellner said. "The Bureau suggests that you may have been a courier. Not a very exalted position, Mr. Ryerson. But if you cooperate now, it will be to your advantage. If not, there are two FBI agents in the hall, ready to take you to the U.S. magistrate and then to the stockade at Fort Myers. Decide."

Ryerson's face showed that he understood the weakness of his position. Bluster wouldn't do here. Whatever else Joe Ryerson was, he was not stupid.

Kellner said to the lawyers, "I want a complete statement from him. Wait for me in the legal counsel's office." The three men moved off down the hall, the aides conferring, then one turned back to Kellner for an answer to a last-minute question.

While he waited, Morgan considered the unpleasant scene he had just witnessed. There had been a personal note of cruelty in Vincent Kellner's attack on Joe Ryerson, and that was unlike the Adviser, who prided himself on his rational behavior. That could only have had to do with Camilla, Morgan thought. Kellner had said "a member of my staff and a mem-

273

ber of the Russian mission.'' It had hardly been necessary to suggest Ryerson talk to the FBI. Charlton Fisk and his people had been way ahead of everyone on the NSC roster. *Everyone.*

Kellner turned back. ''Go on inside, John,'' he said. ''I'll be right there.''

Morgan found Charlotte Conroy still on the phone. She nodded briefly, then ignored him. ''Look,'' she was saying angrily, ''I've had about enough from State about this. The declaration of a defcon two may have been unwise, but it was the President's decision. He told Cherny, face to face, that the possibility of a coup d'état in a fragmenting nuclear power was such a danger to the world that he felt he had to act immediately.''

Morgan froze in his tracks. His mind was racing. *Defcon two.* What coup and where? What had gotten into Cole Caidin, the pacifist President? He almost missed Charlotte Conroy's next words.

''Yes, we know that, now,'' she was saying. ''There has been a serious leak here. Milstein's murder and Abramov's arrest make that clear. Vincent now considers the probability, even the certainty, that information held closely in this office has reached Moscow within hours of its discussion here. I—'' She listened for a moment and shook her head, obviously disagreeing with what she was hearing.

''What I was going to say, Gerald,'' she finally said in exasperation, ''is that Ian Halloran is here now, at Blair House. They're in an uproar at home about the nuclear contamination in Hudson Bay, and he's leaning hard on the President. But we have found a defector, a GKNT man, or rather, he found us. He's ill and in the hospital at Bethesda, with what looks to be plutonium poisoning, so we're quite sure he's real.''

Charlotte Conroy looked over at Morgan, who stood transfixed at the news he was hearing. ''Don't worry,'' she said into the phone. ''We have just the man on hand to find out.'' She noticed Kellner returning and said, ''I'll be in touch, Gerald. I'll call you as soon as I have more complete information.

The press release you have in mind will have to be coordinated with the State Department, and then the President must see it. Work it up, and you can read it to me when I call again.''

Morgan turned to find Kellner at his elbow. ''Is the defector the Russian from Mexico City?''

''From farther away than that, John. A helo is on the South Lawn, waiting to take you to Bethesda. I want to know what he knows. Talk to him, then get back here as fast as you can.''

UNDER AN OVERCAST SO HEAVY it left the city in a leaden twilight, the Marine helicopter lifted from the South Lawn of the White House with Morgan the sole passenger.

Rain had begun to streak the helo's cabin windows as the pilots circled to land on the helicopter pad at Bethesda. On the shiny streets below the morning traffic jam coming in off the Beltway was near gridlock. Headlights reflected from the wet pavements. The dark morning grew even darker as a line of squalls moved up Chesapeake Bay and on into the capital. Turbulence shook the descending chopper, and to the south-east could be seen streaks of lightning.

The helicopter landed in a swirling storm of spray from the rotor downdraft. A gray utility vehicle waited close by, head-lights on, blue and red strobes flashing. The helo's flight engineer, a Marine warrant officer, appeared in the passenger cabin and unlatched the door. A shore patrolman waited on the helipad at the foot of the ladder. ''Colonel Morgan, come with me please.'' He gestured at the van.

Morgan followed him across the rainy, windswept space to the vehicle for the short ride into the basement of the Bethesda Naval Hospital. The SP pointed out the elevator and said, ''Deck Three, Colonel. You're expected.''

When the elevator deposited Morgan on the third floor, a middle-aged woman in starched whites with the stripes of a U.S. Navy Nurse Corps lieutenant senior grade on her cap stepped out from behind the counter of the floor station to meet him.

"Colonel Morgan?" She spoke sternly. "I am Harrelson, the nursing supervisor. Mr. Karmann is out of intensive care now, but still critical. Please keep your visit with him short."

ANNA NEVILLE CAST A GLANCE at herself in the mirror of the powder room as she swallowed her pain pill. I look like hell, she thought, more like a bag lady than someone about to confront two heads of state. Here I am, in the White House, and I'm too tired even to look around. What I wouldn't give for a half hour in a wonderful hot bath and at least two days of sleep. She could feel the disapproving, impatient presence of Colonel Duquesne, barely able to refrain from hustling Anna along. Damn you, Madame Colonel, Anna thought defiantly, I'm not one of your Quebecoise recruits. Her body ached all over, but particularly her right leg, the one that had never healed properly.

She straightened her shoulders, wincing, and took one last look in the mirror. The pill had better work, she thought. Otherwise, she would never make it through the remainder of the day.

At the door to the Oval Office, an American air force military aide wearing a brigadier's stars and an earnest-looking young man in a gray suit and heavy horn-rimmed glasses joined the two women. The civilian introduced himself simply as Jamison, a deputy press secretary to the President, and the general turned out to be the presidential aide from his service.

Jamison spoke in a hushed voice, filled with his own importance, "Before we go in, Mrs. Neville, I shall brief you on what we Americans already know about your accident last December. Colonel Duquesne can tell you what Canadian Forces have discovered since you left to go on your tour. It's best you have this information before speaking with President Caidin and the Prime Minister."

They're going to tell *me* about my accident, are they, she thought. What arrogance. She had found a sort of second wind now and wondered at her self-possession in such a politically rarified atmosphere. Her life with Jacob Neville had not prepared her for meetings with presidents and prime ministers. It had always been Jake's feeling that important politicians were chauvinists, that they felt more at ease dealing with men. Therefore, on their photographic assignments involving heads of state, Anna had always been relegated to the role of silent assistant.

"Your talent is nature photography," Jake had said. "Mine is sons of bitches. Be satisfied." As she remembered his condescension now, she felt anger at her passivity. She had been conditioned to survive among strong, opinionated men, and part of survival in such circumstances was stoic endurance of opinions with which she disagreed.

But that was the past, and in many ways it was receding from her consciousness. Now that she had time to consider it, both her father and her husband had behaved much like men in tribes wherein woman's menstruation was considered unclean, and the woman must be cast out until she was healed.

Jamison was pressing her again. "First of all, Mrs. Neville," he said, "I must entreat you to keep all of these conversations—with all of us here, and with the President and Prime Minister—totally confidential. Otherwise we could all find ourselves in a very bad situation." He waited expectantly.

"I thought the situation was already very bad, Mr. Jamison," Anna said.

"It is, Mrs. Neville, and getting more so by the hour. President Cherny, if you'll forgive me, is up to his ass in alligators right now. I'll let General Bolton tell you what we know for certain. General?"

General Bolton, who seemed far too young for his rank, flashed her a bright white smile and said, "Let's make ourselves comfortable over here, until the President is ready to see Mrs. Neville." He led the way to an alcove with couches, chairs, and a magnificent Louis XV table.

Anna's fingers itched to caress the tabletop. The elegance of the furnishings of the White House made her think of the

Red Vicar ostentatiously selling off his possessions (some of which were surely Anglican church property), announcing that the proceeds would go to feed and clothe the poor in his parish. It was a very early memory, and literally forced her to wonder how many homeless could be housed, and for how long, for the cost of the royal French table around which they had gathered. For some reason, the thought made her want to giggle. It must be the pill, she thought, trying to compose herself.

General Bolton leaned forward and said to Anna, "One of our satellites tracked a Russian missile submarine from Hudson Channel to the Caribbean last January, Mrs. Neville."

He seemed to be waiting for some comment from her, so she said, "Colonel Morgan told me of that sighting, General."

Bolton looked discomfited. "Yes. Well. The main point is, we believe that this submarine was the same boat that you and your husband discovered in Hudson Bay, and that shot you down."

"That may or may not be so, General. It is true I saw a submarine before we were struck. I'm not sure even now of its nationality. Pierre Grau, my lawyer, was convinced that it was American."

Bolton's voice rose. "Your lawyer was a Russian-trained, dues-paying member in good standing of the Canadian Committee for Nuclear Disinvestment—which is, as I am sure you know, a clone descendant of the Committee for Nuclear Disarmament, which spent most of the years of the cold war trying to strip the West of weapons that we needed to confront the threat posed by the Russians, Mrs. Neville."

Anna looked at him with distaste. "General Bolton, Pierre Grau is dead. He can't defend himself."

"General Bolton is telling the truth, Mrs. Neville. Pierre Grau has been known to us as an agent of influence, a secret member of the Communist party of Canada, for a long while," Heloise Duquesne said. "It is a fact."

Two against one, Anna thought, ganging up on me. Calm

down, Anna. "Please go on, General," she said quietly.

"Since your plane went down, there have been a dozen deaths among the Inuit along that coastline where your aircraft was shot down," General Bolton said somberly. "The deaths have been investigated by officials of the Health Service and found to be radiation sickness fatalities, Mrs. Neville. There are several possibilities as to the cause of whatever is spewing plutonium into the environment. All but two have been ruled out. The first possibility is remote—that an unknown country wanted to dispose of the nuclear reactor from an old submarine and chose to dump it on the bottom of Hudson Bay. Don't look so shocked, Mrs. Neville. The Russians have been dumping their old subs and other nuclear waste into the Arctic Sea since about 1956."

He paused before continuing. "The second possibility is the worst, and the one I personally believe to be responsible for the plutonium. That the Russians—some Russians, I should say—have deposited a nuclear weapon on the bottom of Hudson Bay. Possibly they were putting the weapon in place just as your pilot flew your plane over that area of the bay."

"That's absurd," Anna said angrily. "Your hypotheses are both absurd. That's the sort of thing that happened under Stalin. It simply couldn't happen under Aleksandr Cherny."

"Nothing is impossible, Mrs. Neville. You and I both know how many hard-liners, how many old Communists, are still in the government of Russia, how a good portion of the armed forces is disaffected. Russians have always had an inferiority complex about the West, and the U.S. in particular. They considered it an insult to be offered a chance to be part of the Marshall Plan. And didn't Khrushchev say that they'd bury us?"

"But he didn't mean that literally," Anna argued. "He meant it metaphorically."

"The Russian weapons designers took a terrible psychological beating, both in the war in Afghanistan and in the Gulf War, Mrs. Neville," Bolton said. "In the Gulf, our smart weapons beat their smart weapons at a rate of a hundred to one. Or better. We developed nonlethal technology, lasers and ignition killers and chemicals that turn tarmac roads into rivers of oil slush. These weapons were very costly. The Russian designers—Orgonev, for one—replied in their usual fashion. What technology and money do for the United States, brute force has always done for the Russians. They concentrated on high-yield weapons. Twenty-five megatons. Fifty. A hundred. Once you have the plutonium bomb trigger, size and yield are open-ended." He smiled a death's head grin. "Just add tritium and stir. It's possible that's what you saw them planting in Hudson Bay almost a year ago to the day. But why? Surely they wouldn't have gone to all that trouble to kill some poor damned Inuits and a hell of a lot of fish. What are they up to? And no matter what they're up to, what has gone wrong, if indeed it has?"

Anna was stunned into silence. She and Jake had done a feature for the *New York Times Magazine* on the children of Chernobyl, children with leukemia, some with severe birth defects. Farm animals had suffered the same fate. Anna knew. She had seen the half-living babies, held them, photographed them.

"It's all true, Mrs. Neville," Bolton said urgently. "In at least one Inuit family, the parents and all the children have died, and the flying doctor and his wife who made the discovery are contaminated. There are others. Maritime Command is searching the waters up there and they've found several patches of lethal concentration. The fish and seabirds and the shore mammals are all affected. The Inuit are eating food, fish and game, that is killing them."

Anna's revulsion and pity had overcome her antagonism. "How long has Ottawa known about the contamination? And can anything be done medically for these people?"

Colonel Duquesne said heavily, "Time for blame comes later, Mrs. Neville. The problem is that we still aren't positive what the source of the plutonium is. Maritime Command has plotted the area of greatest contamination, but we're waiting for a remotely piloted vehicle that is reasonably impervious to the radiation in the water. Getting the RPV up there isn't easy. It has to be flown there by a plane that can carry very heavy cargo, and the airports at Eskimo Point and Churchill are both too small to handle an aircraft that size. Canada's Mobile Command is trying to lengthen and reinforce the runways, but the work is taking far too long. For one thing, the crews have to be flown in and out for safety's sake, according to the time spent on the scene and proximity to the contamination.'' She looked at General Bolton and said, ''She'd better be told the rest.''

''All right,'' Bolton said. He glanced at Jamison.

Jamison dropped his fussy manner and said quietly, ''The President has ordered American forces to defense condition two, and he has advised President Cherny of his order. The Canadian forces are about to take the same posture. The President and Prime Minister may tell you why. The point is that we *require* your cooperation. My choice of words is deliberate, Mrs. Neville. We are within hours of preparing to go to war with the Russian republic.''

Anna could only stare at the man, speechless.

Jamison favored her with a bleak smile. ''In spite of what you may think about Americans, Mrs. Neville, we are not eager to declare martial law, nor are we eager to suspend the Bill of Rights, and, most particularly, we do not want to go to war with Aleksandr Cherny's Russia. But if you choose to believe the worst of us, let me remind you that despite all the ethnic and financial troubles the Russians have had since Gorbachev stepped down, the Russian Strategic Rocket Forces have not been reduced; indeed, they've been increased. Their strategic forces alone still have 10,000 nuclear warheads aimed at North America, without counting those in the Ukraine and the other former Soviet republics. Those missile forces are modern, and if used, will be *effective*.''

Jamison paused, looking at Anna searchingly. ''So when

you speak with the Prime Minister and the President, remember that as an inhabitant of North America, you have your part to play to keep my country—and yours—from becoming a radioactive desert. You may be able to help us save half the population in the Northern Hemisphere, including you and me, from dying a horrible death.'' He stood up. ''Now, shall we go in, Mrs. Neville?''

Chapter Thirty-four

Bykovo Air Base, Russia/December 1

> *If you ask a Russian serviceman which was the most memorable day of his life, he will say that it was the day he took the Oath of Allegiance. And that is quite natural, because it is a solemn pledge of loyalty to his Homeland. As soon as a man takes it, he assumes responsibility for the fate of his country and people, he swears he will defend them to his last breath, to the last drop of his blood.*

> —COLONEL G. KOBOZEV IN
> *RUSSIAN MILITARY REVIEW*

AIR REGIMENT COMMANDER LIEUTENANT COLONEL SARUNAS DANIUS of the 875th Interceptor Regiment of the Russian air force peered anxiously through the windows of the ready room, watching the armored limousine arrive with a flourish, the rank flag of a general officer flying on its standard at the left front fender. He turned to gesture at the room full of pilots, trying to silence the everyday uproar. Regimental headquarters had passed along the word that this new general was a tiger

283

Alfred Coppel

and in a position to reward or to punish. I told the men, he thought. More than that I am unwilling to do. Danius's transfer from the air force to Aeroflot was still hanging up in the bureaucratic thicket, and he did not need any of this political nonsense. Colonel Bukharin insisted that membership in the new political group headed by General Kondratiev would be advisable for all pilots. "They'll judge you by the number on your card, Danius. The lower the number, the more status you accrue immediately on the day Soyuz becomes the supreme power in the land," Bukharin had said. But Danius had procrastinated. One learned to be cautious in these troubled times.

The door was flung open and, along with a blast of cold air, into the room strode the new commander of the Moscow Air Defense District, General Yuri Kalinin, accompanied by an aide. "Attention!" Danius shouted, and the regimental officers came to a semblance of order.

The general's cold eyes regarded Danius, discarded him as inconsequential, and moved on to the others in the room. A karakul-collared greatcoat worn loosely over his shoulders was shrugged off and into the waiting hands of the obsequious aide. A handsome and blond Great Russian, Kalinin conformed perfectly with the Ministry of Information's poster image of the ideal fighter pilot: tall and erect with piercing blue eyes. He was resplendent in full service uniform and eight rows of medal ribbons. Danius raised his hand and again shouted for silence from his officers.

"Gentlemen, gentlemen! This is General Yuri Kalinin, chief of the Moscow Defense Command, come to speak to us on a most important matter." The pilots ceased most of their rowdy chatter and focused their attention on their guest.

Kalinin had been looking over his audience of aviators speculatively while Danius struggled to quiet them. What an undisciplined lot they were; they would have lasted less than a week in Afghan bandit country, or in Star City. They wore their uniforms carelessly, their hair was too long, and their manners were insubordinate.

It had been Colonel Bukharin who had asked General Kalinin to address his men. "Speak to my men, Excellency," Bukharin had told him confidently. They are eager to be part of the coming New Order in Russia."

Kalinin's misgivings grew. This did not appear to be an audience prepared to hang on his every word. The remembrance of Eduard Aleyev's ignominious departure from the Morskaya Pristan Naval Base was very clear in his mind. He had promised General Kondratiev that he would succeed with the airmen where Aleyev had failed with his naval officers. But these New Order Russian warriors, lolling in battered easy chairs or sitting on tables or even on the floor, were unimpressed by their visitor.

Kalinin fixed his restless audience with a glare until they quieted down a little. "I have come here informally to speak with my fellow fighter pilots." Now he smiled at them, showing them that in spite of his lofty rank, he was sympathetic to their concerns. "I invite you to join the greatest adventure of your lives," he said in a very loud voice. "It will bring glory to every one of you, but the grandeur of her past will be restored to Mother Russia."

When he paused to see the impact of his words, the ingrates began to talk among themselves again. We need these damned hooligans, Kalinin thought, enraged, and that is the most maddening part. Having a regiment of Sukhoi fighter-interceptors with us would not only put on a brave show; they could inflict terrible damage on any troops foolish enough to stay loyal to Aleksandr Cherny. But the spirit of levity in this ready room appalled Kalinin. Were all the elements of his Moscow Air Defense command so slack, so indifferent?

Kondratiev should have come himself. People responded to the general, sometimes viscerally, never indifferently. But Piotr Kondratiev, who obviously held no high opinion of the air forces, had said that these men were unlikely to welcome anyone—no matter what age—from another service, or from the security forces. "They will come round only if spoken to

285

by an aviator,'' he had said, putting his arm around Kalinin's shoulders confidingly. "You must stop the rot in the air forces." It was hard to misinterpret such a directive, Kalinin thought. So here I am.

He began again, even louder, so as to be heard over the hum of conversation in the room. "I am here to remind you of the price our ancestors paid for the Russian earth, which we are all sworn to protect. From the Revolution, the Great Patriotic War, through the cold war years, the air forces have done more than their part to ensure the safety of our people, our blessed land. I invite you to join a movement that will restore Russia to its greatest glory. I now will take questions.''

A lieutenant standing against the wall spoke up and said almost lazily, "Tell me, General, as a student of this glorious Russian history—is there any truth to the stories I have heard? That our planes and tanks and artillery pieces and missiles are being sold to our potential enemies at bargain prices?''

Kalinin was horrified. Had the word gotten out? It was true that Minister of Defense Suvorov had been quietly selling armored vehicles and surface-to-air missiles to the Chinese and to India for hard currency, but the knowledge had been held to a very few in the government. "That is a treasonous question,'' he snapped, "and totally out of order.''

"Nevertheless, General. The Western press carries stories about our best remaining technology going to both the Chinese and some Arab countries,'' the lieutenant said.

"The Western press lies, has always lied, about us.'' Kalinin's face reddened.

From the other side of the room another flyer drawled, "At Frunze, we were told that we taught the Iraqis all they knew about military tactics and strategy. Is that true, General?''

Kalinin said sharply, "We cannot be held accountable for the incompetence of Arab soldiers.''

"Has anyone explained that to our client states, those we have armed and advised for years past, General?'' the flyer, eyebrows raised, asked, to general laughter.

"Are you Soyuz, General?" another officer asked. "Is joining Soyuz required as the first step in this great adventure of yours?"

Kalinin glared across the room at Danius. These men were trying to humiliate him, and Danius knew it.

The regimental commander shrugged. "It is no longer against military regulations to ask questions, General," he said mildly.

The great porcelain stove in the far corner seemed to swell with radiated heat. Kalinin ran his finger around his collar, then checked himself. He could not sweat in front of this uniformed rabble. What on earth could he say now that would bring them to order? His anger was mixed with strong feelings of anxiety. The Soyuz plan would take exquisite timing if it were to succeed. And if it did not succeed? What if the Americans, or the Chinese, or anyone, were to attack the motherland when she was weakened by disorder? How long, he wondered, would it take these undisciplined air regiments to scramble? The Strategic Rocket Forces to empty their silos? Russia was naked if this regiment was typical of the military. Things had seemed much simpler in Sochi, listening to Kondratiev as he outlined his elegant plan, unencumbered by details.

Outside, seen through frosted windows, lines of MiG-37 fighters stood on the flight line, the new flag and double eagle insignia on their fuselages splashes of color in the gray landscape. On the fighters' stubby, swept-back wings the snow and ice were a thick blanket. In an emergency, those aircraft could not fly without thirty minutes of defrosting. As interceptors they were worthless, almost as worthless as these so-called aviators.

Kalinin shouted "Quiet!" and the hooligans were so surprised that they shut up. He said brusquely, "I am speaking of love of country, patriotism. Do they still teach *that* at the air force higher schools?"

A ground-service officer standing in a far corner spoke up. "Patriotism is always in our hearts, Your Excellency." A wave of laughter swept the room.

"What is your name and duty, Lieutenant?"

"Vilnius, Your Excellency. Morale officer."

Another damned foreigner masquerading as a Russian. *Patriotism is always in our hearts.* What dogshit. Since the August 1991 coup, no one lectured the troops on the glories of the Revolution, socialist centralism, and a Marxist empire. Instead, lecturers spent their time making speeches about soldiers' rights. Soldiers had no rights, Kalinin thought angrily. Soldiers did not need rights. For the man under arms there was only duty.

Soyuz was coming not a moment too soon.

This whole trip had been useless. Let these ruffians do as they pleased. He comforted himself with the thought that, in the end, all that was needed for Soyuz to succeed now was the loyalty of the troops in Moscow. He ticked them off: Colonel Temko and his Kremlin guards regiment, a few others. One could count on them. The officer corps of the Kremlin guards consisted of sons of the nomenklatura, men whose families had lost, and were still losing, perquisites and privileges, as the poverty-stricken Russian democracy staggered from crisis to crisis. Three in five of the unit commanders of the guards were Soyuz. Two others were members of Pamyat, a right-wing group even more fiercely nationalistic and anti-American than Soyuz.

Handpicked Kremlin guardsmen had manned Admiral Aleyev's Ukovo dacha when the Jew, Milstein, was liquidated. The old KGB had always been willing. Almost the entire command staff of the headquarters at Teplyy Stan were committed. Yulin, nominally in command of the security forces, was still too frightened of what might happen to his own skin to commit to Soyuz openly. He would pay for that.

Kalinin motioned to his aide to hand him his broad-crowned, blue-banded cap and put it on. The aide slipped in behind the general, holding his greatcoat. The fliers, sensing release, came to their feet and headed for the coffee machine.

Danius, feeling somewhat abashed at the rudeness of his men, started to ask the general if he wished for any refreshment, but his voice was drowned out by the thwacking sounds of the blades of a large helicopter overhead.

Kalinin frowned. He had not requested a helicopter. He looked to Danius for an explanation, but Danius avoided his eyes.

The helicopter, bearing the flag and double eagle insignia, landed in a whirl of mist on the ice-coated tarmac just outside the hangar. Soldiers, a full company of them, wearing battle gear, spilled from the aircraft and formed a column to jog toward the air regiment's ready room. An army colonel was at their head. Kalinin recognized the uniforms and collar tabs; the newcomers were members of the Thirtieth Shock Army, one of the last units with-drawn from eastern Germany and now based at Stavropol.

Everyone in the room rushed to the windows to see the strangers. Soldiers of the shock armies, heavy infantry and tankers, were a rare sight near Moscow, and a particularly extraordinary sight on an airfield. As the detachment reached the ready room, their commanding officer barked an order, and the soldiers fanned out to form a cordon around the building. The pilots were chattering like excited adolescents. Kalinin felt a deep chill.

A short, squat shock army colonel, attended by two very hard-looking sergeants armed with assault rifles, stomped into the room. They brought with them a sharp draft of icy winter air. The colonel advanced purposefully toward Kalinin, ignoring everyone else in the room. "Yuri Kalinin?" he demanded gruffly.

The general drew himself up to his full height and glared down at his interrogator. "I am General Kalinin. Who are you?"

"Colonel Ulyan Zenobiev, of the 56th Provost Battalion of the Thirtieth Shock Army," the stone-faced officer said. "I have orders to place you under arrest and fly you immediately to Moscow. Surrender your side arm.''

Kalinin's aide tried to bolt from the room, but was quickly subdued. The general stood frozen for a moment. He found it difficult to breathe. Then, slowly, he unbuckled his holstered pistol and handed it to one of the soldiers accompanying the colonel. He felt the weight of his greatcoat on his shoulders. Colonel Danius had placed it there.

"Thank you, General Kalinin," Danius said sardonically, "for your inspiring visit. The 875th Interceptor Regiment will remember this day for a very long time."

Zenobiev said brusquely, "Come. You are expected in the Kremlin at once. Do not keep the President waiting."

Chapter Thirty-five

Washington, D.C./December 1

> *The first nuclear age is drawing to a close, along with the cold war that it grew up with, but the arsenals remain at absurdly high levels, 8,000 or more warheads for each superpower, deployed variously on land-based ballistic missiles, sea-based ones, cruise missiles and manned bombers. More than enough, even after START, for the United States and Russia to destroy the other ten times over.*

—LONDON REVIEW OF FOREIGN POLICY

IF JAKE WERE HERE, he'd be angry, lecturing, hectoring his listeners, Anna thought. Across the table were two of the politicians he had most despised in the world, one of whom was certainly the most powerful. No one yet had gotten around to telling her why she had received this signal honor; they were all too busy to pay her any attention. The pain pill she had taken was working all too well at the moment. Perhaps it was the combination of stress and far too little sleep, which had, in concert with the pill, made everything seem so disconnected

Alfred Coppel

and unreal to her. The horrifying information about the nuclear contamination with its attendant possibility of nuclear war came and went in her mind like little stabs of reality. Those horrors meshed in some peculiar underlying manner in her consciousness with the remembrance of bursting grenades and broken windows, Pierre Grau's body rolling over and over across the hood of that Bronco. I'm going to have to come to terms with all this, Anna thought, but not right now.

Masses of very tense people seemed to be rushing into the room, conferring quietly with one or more of the very tense principals, then going away in a flurry of activity. She looked around the Oval Office, admiring the President's desk, and stifled a laugh. She was still paying more attention to the furniture than to the matters at hand, whatever they might be. Her part in all this turmoil was unclear.

She squirmed in her seat, trying to smooth her skirt, tuck in her blouse a little better. The leather had been totally scraped off the toe of her right shoe. She'd showered in Avery Peters's fiberglass bathtub forty-eight hours ago, but it seemed much longer. I hope I don't smell as bad as I must look, she thought.

The room grew misty again. To keep awake, she forced herself to try to place everyone she'd met so far. The handsome, voluble, and angry woman in the room when Anna first arrived had turned out to be the U.S. ambassador to the United Nations, Charlotte Conroy. A woman had rushed in and handed her a message of some sort, and Ms. Conroy made her apologies and left almost immediately.

"Ambassador Conroy is going back to New York to brief the UN," President Caidin had explained, smiling at Anna, his even white teeth gleaming, his brown eyes locked on hers, his famous charm on display. I suppose I should be impressed, she thought, persuaded that I am *the* most important thing in his life at this moment. If so, he's got a surprise in store. I hate professionally charming men with a passion, even those with acquiline features and broad shoulders and lots of power.

"She has some damage control to do in New York before the NSC meeting in—" Caidin had glanced at his gold Rolex, brushing back a boyish lock of hair. "—twenty-seven minutes." Judging from Caidin's frequent looks at wall clocks or his wristwatch, these particular heads of state were operating on a tight schedule. And the President had the appearance of an impatient and impulsive man being forced to move much more slowly than he wished.

Vincent Kellner, the President's National Security Adviser and John Morgan's master, was the tall man at the end of the table.

Ian Halloran, the Canadian Prime Minister, had been sitting across from Anna on Cole Caidin's right. Anna had seen him several times, always at large environmental gatherings. Halloran was a bull of a man, built like an athlete, with powerful sloping shoulders. However, his speech and manners were more those of a Cambridge don, Anna thought, even when he is in the midst of an argument. At least he looks like a person, not like a slightly used clothing store dummy.

One of the ambulatory aides had entered, whispered something urgently in Halloran's ear, gotten an expletive-filled answer, and then left. Immediately, Halloran had gotten up, beckoning to Caidin to come with him. Then they signalled for the young man who was Caidin's aide and Vincent Kellner to join them at the opposite end of the room, theoretically out of earshot. Now all except Kellner were shouting at each other and gesticulating, red faced and full of frustration.

"What do you mean, the Ministry of Health knew about this as early as the twenty-ninth? And the assholes *didn't tell anybody?*" Caidin stalked over to the desk and threw himself down in his chair, the others following, continuing to argue. "—send our Seals—" Caidin said, but Halloran shook his head vehemently. "—our turf—under our command—"

Anna blinked her eyes, uninterested in their quarrel, trying to clear her vision. She felt as if she'd had three drinks before dinner, and a bottle of wine with it, she thought longingly.

Ian Halloran continued arguing some point with vehemence, his face flushed. ''—berserk—Cherny—holocaust—never stand for it—not at all wise—'' She should be listening carefully, but his words ran together, without meaning. He was a product of western Canada, one of the few Westerners ever to succeed to the post of prime minister. His Irish ancestry had given Halloran a florid complexion, reddish hair, and a spray of freckles across the nose not unlike Anna's own. He was a man of extremes, known as much for his fits of anger as for his charm. Canadian women tended to adore him, and he had a considerable following among younger Canadian men, But the ''Canadian question,'' as it had for so long, loomed in the background—the new constitution, and what it meant to the provinces as opposed to the central government in Ottawa— with not much progress being made. And the Quebecois ''distinct society'' mess, now taken up by the native tribes. How had Mordecai Richler described himself? Montreal born and bred, religion Jewish, but in the Quebecois nomenclature, a nonvisible minority Anglophone. Ludicrous. Problems without solutions, she thought wearily, paralyzing the political process.

Anna looked at President Caidin with curiosity. A sellout to the establishment, Jake Neville had called him. Once Caidin had been an avowed student radical and idealistic progressive. Under that facade, Jake had contended, the man was only an American political hack, an empty vessel for any idea that appealed to powerful segments of the voting public, a pollster's dream. So far, neither man had impressed her with his wit or wisdom. American politics appalled her. The police actions in Grenada and in Panama, the air raid on Libya, all seemed gratuitous brutality, pure adventurism. Surely each of those situations could have been solved by skilled diplomacy, rather than by force. The Gulf War with its periodic reignition was another example of the failure of reason.

Morgan was absolutely wrong, she decided, thinking back to their conversation about the role of the military. If you had it, you would use it, as the saying went, or lose it. If no one on the face of this earth ever made another weapon, we'd all be the better for it.

She jumped when, across the room, the President exploded. "Damn it, no, Ian," Caidin shouted, pounding the desk in front of him. "We had to lay it on the line with Cherny. There's no time for waffling." His face was as red as Halloran's now.

Vincent Kellner moved quickly to insert himself physically between Caidin and Halloran. "I agree, Prime Minister, with the President," he said smoothly. "Now I suggest that we tell Mrs. Neville all the facts. I'm sure she'll cooperate."

Behind Kellner's stolid expression Anna thought she could see exasperation, perhaps even anger. The mention of her name brought her out of her haze. She sat up straight. What facts? Why was she, Anna Neville, being mentioned in the same breath as the president of Russia? Possibly now she'd find out why she was here.

The President, the Prime Minister, and Dr. Kellner were bearing down on her. Anna braced herself for what was to come. The three men sat down across the table from her, and Vincent Kellner began to speak.

What he was saying was bald, stripped of the solicitous, almost unctuous, charm both the President and the Prime Minister had tried to display. "We have no Official Secrets Act in this country, Mrs. Neville," Kellner began. "Occasionally, I wish we did. Because of what General Bolton and Mr. Jamison have told you, and what you are about to be told, you will be privy to state secrets of enormous sensitivity. This information is dangerous, explosive. War and peace literally depend on its confidentiality."

Anna drew a hard breath, forcing herself to concentrate, and said firmly, "I am not a believer in government secrecy, Dr. Kellner, for whatever reason, however melodramatic. In fact, I beg that you leave me out of any further deliberations on the state secret level. All I ask, all that I ever asked, is that the United States government explain what part, if any, it may have played in the accident that has changed my life radically—''

''Yes, yes, we know that,'' Kellner broke in impatiently. ''But your accident has turned out to be only a small part of a very dangerous situation, one with world-shaking consequences. Should you disclose, purposefully or carelessly, anything you might hear today, it would only make this situation much worse. It is my understanding that several news organizations have discovered your whereabouts and would like to interview you, as they say, in depth.'' He paused, and his lined, ascetic face took on a death head's cast. ''They pay well, I am told, for a good story.''

Anna, disbelieving what Kellner was saying, looked at Caidin and Halloran. They were nodding agreement with Kellner as he spoke, bodies tense, foreheads furrowed with worry and strain. She cleared her throat. ''First, I suppose I should tell you that I am not for sale, Dr. Kellner, no matter what you may think of me and my actions personally.'' She was pleased to see him flush at the contempt in her words. ''Now, to the important part of all these secrets, so-called. I thought that the plutonium contamination in Hudson Bay was bad enough. Isn't it about time you told me what more there is to all this? Truthfully.''

Kellner took a deep breath and continued: ''I apologize if I gave offense, Mrs. Neville. The military forces of the United States are in defense condition two, with specific regard to the armed forces of Russia.'' He stopped for a moment to sip from a water glass beside him.

Anna knew no reply had been expected from her. Caidin and Halloran, their eyes cold and calculating, disturbed her at first. Then she thought, damn, I wish I had my cameras. What a marvelous picture those two would make, for once apparently forgetful of self.

Vincent Kellner said, ''At defcon two, the Stealth bombers are airborne and the ballistic missile submarines are alerted by ultralow frequency radio. One hour after that, the bombers will begin to orbit outside Russian airspace. Should conditions so warrant, and the President decide to go to defcon one, the missile silos begin their countdowns. Am I making myself clear, Mrs. Neville?''

Anna was aghast. She could feel her heart pounding in her chest. The rush of fear finally cleared her mind of all its cobwebs. ''Dr. Kellner,'' she said quietly, ''what you say terrifies me. That was the intention, I suspect. Why? I cannot believe that anything I can say or do would affect such decisions.'' Her voice trembled, but she did not avoid meeting Kellner's eyes.

President Caidin broke in. ''Mrs. Neville, you and your friends came to this country specifically to accuse the United States Navy of sailing illegally in Canadian waters and of shooting down your plane when discovered, an act that killed your husband and your pilot.'' She could hear the rising impatience in his voice. ''That is so, is it not?''

''Yes, Mr. President,'' Anna said, facing Caidin squarely. ''I have since heard a different version of the episode, and I concede I could have been wrong. But the alternative explanation that I have been given, that the submarine was Russian, is very hard for me to believe.''

''It is nonetheless true,'' Prime Minister Halloran said, his voice firm, ''and what's more, we can prove it. Just one hour and twenty minutes ago, a Canadian Maritime Command icebreaker located a lethal device that we believe to be the source of the plutonium contamination in the area, on the bottom of Hudson Bay, in almost the exact place where your aircraft was lost.''

''You found a nuclear weapon?'' Anna asked in horror.

''It is a nuclear device. At this point, that's all we know. We have no actual sighting, because the water in the area is turbid and badly contaminated with plutonium,'' Ian Halloran said, his face at last showing the depth of his feelings. ''You know of the illnesses and deaths among the local Inuit people. More will die. No matter how you view it, either politically or environmentally, the situation is a nightmare. The submarine you saw was almost certainly a Russian vessel, manned by Russian sailors. And the photographs you took confirm it."

Anna Neville gasped in shock. "You have my pictures?"

"Yes." Halloran's face was again impassive.

Anna rose to her feet in outrage, ignoring the pain in her stiffened muscles. "And you let me come down here and accuse the American navy?" Suddenly she tasted bile, the flavor of her stupidity and their betrayal. "You and your psychiatrists—how did you get them to sell out, get them to try to convince me I was hallucinating?" She sank back into her chair.

President Caidin looked over at Ian Halloran with an expression of injured self-righteousness, the look of the unjustly accused. Anna could imagine how their earlier discussion of this point had gone—Halloran on the defensive, Caidin outraged and demanding, both playing a game that had already turned deadly.

Halloran said in exasperation, "Mrs. Neville, you are naive. We couldn't accuse the Russians of so provocative an act. We had only two clear long-range photographs, which you had taken at a time of great stress. There is nothing in either picture to prove that the craft was in Canadian waters, after all. The Russians could wriggle out by saying it could have been taken anywhere in the Arctic."

Anna could not help saying caustically, "Of course you knew where I was; wasn't that proof enough where it was taken? And then you let me accuse the Americans? Because you knew they wouldn't attack, and the Russians might? By the way, would the film have been more acceptable as proof if it had been taken by my husband?"

"When the Americans showed us their satellite images," the Prime Minister said, ignoring her thrust, "we knew a Russian boat had actually been in Hudson Strait. And your photographs had to be enhanced and studied."

"For a *year*, Prime Minister?" Anna asked bitterly. "And

when did you start to investigate the contamination? Or was that all handled as skillfully as the rest?''

Vincent Kellner intervened. ''We are asking for your absolute silence, Mrs. Neville, until this issue is resolved. After a suitable interval, you will be free to say or do whatever you think best.''

''I'm to exonerate the United States Navy?'' Anna demanded. ''After what I've been told, *and if it is true,* of course I must make a statement, but I should do it right away—''

''Stop there, Mrs. Neville,'' Kellner said. One of his hovering aides slipped a paper into his hand as he spoke. ''The situation is so delicate now that no one can issue any statements. We must await resolution of the situation.''

Anna felt a sudden rush of anger and outrage that overwhelmed any discretion she had been feeling in this powerful company. ''Dr. Kellner,'' she said in a voice that quavered with fury, ''do you mean that war with Russia is a proper resolution of 'the situation,' as you put it, and that anything I might say will precipitate it? That's the most offensive suggestion I have yet received.'' Her blue eyes were brilliant with unshed tears, and she dashed them away. ''I made the accusations, now I must tell the truth.''

''If it's that offensive to you, Mrs. Neville,'' Kellner said coldly, ''I don't know whether to congratulate you or pity you. You don't seem to realize that none of us know exactly what your famous 'truth' is right now. You seem to be thinking only of your own image in the eyes of your advocates. What of the consequences to the public, the panic it could cause?''

Anna pushed her hair back from her forehead, her mind whirling. ''But what about President Cherny? Does he know? Surely he can't be responsible.''

President Caidin had long since lost his patience with her. He began pacing up and down, glaring at Anna. ''For God's sake—'' he began.

Vincent Kellner stepped in. ''I think anyone who is a member in good standing of the Canadian Committee for Nuclear

Disinvestment is unlikely to accuse me of being overly solicitous of the Russians, Mrs. Neville. Rather, you see me as paranoid, demonic.''

Anna said firmly, "I am *not* a member of the CCND. I agree with many of their policies, and they have been very helpful to me since my husband was killed. Stop trying to stereotype me. I am an individual, a whole person with a mind of my own. You haven't told me the full story. Do it now. Then I'll decide whether or not to cooperate with you.''

Vincent Kellner said in a rush of words, "Mrs. Neville, the missile in Hudson Bay was planted by dissidents in Moscow, who would overthrow Cherny's government. Just what part it is or was to play, we don't know. The murder of Pierre Grau and the attempts on your life were also ordered by the same cabal, by the way—for which I offer my country's most profound apologies. President Caidin, as commander in chief, has warned President Cherny of an impending coup by a faction hostile to continued rapprochement with the West. Should they succeed in their plot, we will consider it an act of war.''

Nuclear war, Anna thought in a daze.

"So you see, you have no other alternative but to remain silent. Should you disregard the request, the resultant uproar might well bring on just the consequence you least desire," Kellner said.

"You don't understand women very well, Doctor," she said. "There is *always* another alternative.''

Kellner said quietly, "What if the existence of this missile becomes general public knowledge? That not only did the Russians place it in Hudson Bay, but that they bungled it?''

Anna glanced at Ian Halloran and noted that a film of perspiration had formed on his upper lip. It was not that warm in the room. The Prime Minister of Canada was afraid. For his political life? No, for the world, if what she had been told was true.

"The Canadian armed forces do their best, Mrs. Neville,''

300

he said wearily, "with damned little public support and less money."

Sometime during their three days together Morgan had said wonderingly that "Canada's Air Command consists of the Snow Birds and two obsolete tactical fighter squadrons stationed in Europe." She had happily photographed the dismantlement of NATO's continental air bases. The Canadian force was, now that she thought about it, a pitifully meager force with which to protect the territorial integrity of a nation a third again as big as the United States. She had always been proud of that fact, convinced that it showed the superiority of the Canadian system over the overbearing American bullies, who were always armed to the teeth.

"You can't keep this story quiet, Prime Minister," she said urgently.

"I am not suggesting a cover-up in perpetuity, Mrs. Neville," he said indignantly.

"It's time the NSC meeting got started, Vincent," Caidin said impatiently. "I want Mrs. Neville sworn to silence by the time it's over. Bolton or Jamison can take care of that."

The door to the office opened, and an aide beckoned to General Bolton, whom Anna had almost forgotten. He and Jamison had been sitting close to the French windows, listening carefully, but not entering the discussions. The general then whispered to the President, who said exasperatedly, "Yes, yes, all right. Vincent, you have a call from Colonel Morgan at Bethesda. Take it here."

Morgan's call to Kellner was brief, but Anna had never before seen so profound a change in a man. Kellner listened, responded in monotones Anna could hear but not decipher, and seemed to change from a man of flesh and blood to one of stone. In a slightly more audible tone he said to Morgan, "Can he make the journey?"

He listened to what Morgan replied and then said, "Attend to it. Peters can fly the helo we have up there." Then he replaced the telephone in its cradle and spoke to the ever more impatient President. "A moment, sir. And you, Prime Minister."

The three men formed a tight huddle at the far end of the room. Anna sat in silence. Kellner's air of strain immediately infected the other two men. The dangerous matters under discussion must have gone from the troublesome to the terrifying.

Cole Caidin's face blanched at what he heard. He said harshly, "Damn! All right, Vincent. The Joint Chiefs must be informed." He signaled for General Bolton. "Take the Prime Minister over to Blair House, General, and see to it that an open line is maintained to us here in the White House at all times. I want you close at hand, Ian," he said to Halloran. "You'll keep me informed about Hudson Bay?"

When Halloran nodded, Caidin said, "Vincent, come with me now. We have to start counting every goddamned minute." He looked abruptly at Anna Neville as though he had forgotten she was in the office. "Mrs. Neville, you'll go with Jamison. I'll expect an answer from you, the one I want to hear."

Anna sagged with weariness, not sure if she could last until the President returned, if indeed, he did so. So the CLA was to be her watchdog for the indefinite future. What had happened to Morgan at Bethesda to ratchet up the tension to this degree?

Jamison stood and said politely, "Will you come with me, Mrs. Neville?"

Anna followed the CLA man into the main part of the Executive Mansion. Jamison took care not to make it appear that she was under any duress, but she knew better.

Jamison led her into a small, charming room, one that belied its rather grand title of "the White House Library." He explained to her that this retreat had been created by the workers and artisans who remodeled the White House during the Truman Administration. Once part of the basement, it had been walled with panels made from the old timbers removed from the floor above, when the great old house was given a modern steel frame.

"That red tole and crystal chandelier was once owned by James Fenimore Cooper. I think the Indian portraits were, too," Jamison explained, giving her a mini-tour of the room. Then he added solicitously, "Are you sure you don't want me to have something brought, Mrs. Neville? You haven't eaten breakfast. Sandwiches, coffee?"

"Thank you, no, Mr. Jamison."

Anna chose a seat on a banquette beneath the Indian paintings and fell silent. Mr. Jamison did her the courtesy of matching her mood, no more small talk. A Herman Miller grandfather clock, made in the style of the early Federal period to fit into this twentieth-century replica of a room, ticked loudly. Anna sat, head back, eyes closed, thoughts churning. I'm coming back to life, she thought wonderingly. I'm not there yet, but it's close. And an odd time it is for me to find myself. She fell into a reverie and listened to the clock tick and strike for an hour and a half.

SHE WAS HALF ASLEEP when the door to the library opened and Vincent Kellner reappeared. His face looked drawn, his eyes sunken and burning; here stood a man who had just received a shock, Anna thought. What had Morgan said to him on the telephone?

"All right, Jamison," Kellner said. He paused before going on, his lips set in a thin line. "Thank you. You can go back to Langley now."

"Yes. Yes, sir. Mrs. Neville." Jamison nodded to Anna and departed hurriedly.

Kellner sat down and looked bitterly for a moment at the faces in the paintings on the wall. Algonquin, Mohican, Niagara. "They lost their world to treachery and an advanced technology," he said somberly, as if to himself. "I wonder if we aren't repeating their fate." Then Kellner focused on Anna, as though abandoning some bleak inner vision.

He said, "Here's the rest of the story, Mrs. Neville, a piece that just fell into place today. A Russian GKNT technician has defected to us and is recuperating at Bethesda. Academician Arkady Karmann was aboard that submarine you saw in Hudson Bay. In fact, it was he who initialized the systems on the device now poisoning the environment up there. That submarine was scuttled—sunk with all hands in the Caribbean, except for Academician Karmann, who by some miracle escaped. The man had a profound change of heart and somehow managed to travel to the United States on his own, determined to find and warn the authorities in Washington. To me, that is a measure of his credibility.

"Now," Kellner said, "Karmann has informed Colonel Morgan that the missile he planted and armed in Hudson Bay is probably damaged and cannot fly, but that its warhead is still alive. It is worse than we suspected, Mrs. Neville, a very large missile with a nuclear warhead. The device was timed to launch, then explode in space over the North American continent on December 7, the day of the planned coup in Moscow."

He stood up, tall, thin, and almost cadaverous, Anna thought. He resembles an Old Testament prophet. Jeremiah, the purveyor of doom. Her mouth was dry.

"Our defcon stands—it must, because we have to be prepared for whatever might happen if the device in the bay really does explode," Kellner said evenly. "There are already arguments upstairs about whether or not all this is not just some deceptive Russian scheme, *maskirovka*, to frighten the American government into submission. If you think we have diehard cold warriors in this country, you should meet those in Russia, in Moscow. They're still yearning after the old glory days, when they had full access to the purse strings, to absolute power." He ran a hand over his mouth, pulling absently at his cheeks.

"Morgan, Arkady Karmann, and Avery Peters will be flying north as soon as transport can be arranged. Canada is sending a team of divers. We have six days to find and then to disarm that warhead. We are demanding that a Russian team of nuclear ordnance people fly over. And we *must* use Karmann, we have no other option. Morgan was once a Seal, so he'll work with the Canadians, as an observer only. The Prime Minister won't have it any other way.'' Kellner's features twisted into a bitter smile. ''A matter of sovereignty, you understand.''

Anna stiffened. ''But didn't you say the water is contaminated?''

''Yes.'' Kellner stood silent for a moment while Anna caught her breath. ''There is no margin of safety now, Mrs. Neville. I ask that you never reveal any of the information you've heard today.''

Anna looked straight into Kellner's pale eyes. Her heart was pounding; she was not absolutely certain why. She felt a wrench at the thought of Morgan, on the scene of the disaster, standing beside the polynyas of a wintry, contaminated Hudson Bay. The utter stupidity of it all. There was no way she'd let Morgan go without her. ''A bargain, Doctor,'' she said.

''What sort of bargain, Mrs. Neville?''

''My word to be silent, in return for two things: a seat on the aircraft taking Morgan and the Russian to Canada and, second, the right to use my cameras without interference during the operation. If Canadians and Russians and Americans are cooperating in the face of this disaster, some day the story will be told. It should help deflect some of the hysteria you anticipate from the public at large. History needs to have a record of it,'' she said firmly. ''Those are my terms, Doctor. There are no others, but I will accept nothing less.''

Kellner said courteously, ''You have me at a disadvantage, Mrs. Neville. You're right, we must have a record of what occurs up there, one that even the CCND will accept. I'll allow you to accompany the team we're sending north. Planned departure is tomorrow afternoon.''

He changed the subject abruptly. ''Until tomorrow, we will accommodate you at Blair House, along with the Prime Minister's party. We've managed to retrieve your baggage for you, your clothes and your camera equipment—you'll find it waiting for you.'' His pale eyes grew steely. ''A word of warning. Do not attempt to leave Blair by yourself, Mrs. Neville. We cannot guarantee your safety when not under guard.''

She shrugged off the warning. ''Dr. Kellner? Where is Morgan?''

''On his way back from Bethesda, Mrs. Neville. You'll see him tomorrow. A member of my staff will escort you to Blair House. Now, I bid you good day.''

Chapter Thirty-six

Washington, D.C./December 1

Almost from the day of their inception, nuclear weapons were regarded in two distinct ways. On one side there were those who regarded them as qualitatively different and, therefore, too terrible to use for any other purpose except deterrence pure and simple. On the other, there were those who conceived them as fundamentally similar to, if much more powerful than, all previous weapons.

—MARTIN VAN CREVELD, TECHNOLOGY AND WAR

VINCENT KELLNER SAT AT HIS DESK, staring at the opposite wall, the disaster facing the North American continent almost forgotten at the moment. A more personal calamity overwhelmed him. Fisk had been both right and wrong. It had not been a leak, but a river. The immensity of the betrayal stunned and bewildered him. *What could I ever have done to Camilla, when could I have angered her, or hurt her enough, to cause her to turn traitor?* The President would have to be told, and Kellner burned with the humiliation that would entail. He would write out his resignation immediately.

And where was Camilla now, how far and how fast had she run? The FBI would find her, no question of that. It had been obvious since Charlie Fisk first mentioned the leak that he'd been watching everyone in the office—even me, Kellner thought bitterly, and rightly so. But that would only be the beginning of my own private hell.

Camilla, you bitch, he thought. You killed David Milstein. No one had yet said so, but it was obvious whose hands were bloody—mine for accepting his offer, hers for telling the Russians, and theirs for the actual killing. Did she realize what the eventualities would be? Did she care?

The end of my dreams, my ambitions, my hopes of serving in some higher capacity. He rubbed his burning eyes.

He straightened in his chair, looking across the desk at Charlton Fisk's sympathetic expression. *I have always been too prideful, too sure of my own capacities in judging people,* he thought. *It's been a long time since I had to face the consequences of my arrogance.*

Fisk regarded the President's gray-faced Adviser with interest. Kellner appeared composed, but his insides must be burning, Fisk thought. The blow must be almost devastating. A resignation was a certainty. "It would not be amiss, Vincent," Fisk said, "if you were to allow me to protect you—at least until we sort everything out."

Kellner said, "Oh, yes."

"I mean it."

"I understand that you do. It is kind of you to be concerned. But there is the larger matter in Canada to consider. I can't go into isolation."

"Understood. We'll take care of you wherever you go for the next few days. Right now, the President needs you."

"Quite," Kellner said.

"This business in Canada is out of my league, Vincent. I've been a big-city cop by trade. Nuke doomsday machines are a bit out of my experience."

"Out of everyone's, Charlie."

Fisk did not hesitate as he asked, "This Marine of yours. How good is he?"

"At what?"

"At whatever he'll need to do. Spokesman, debater, diplomat, diver—I understand the Canadians are dead set against an American solution to the problem."

"They have the divers. We're supplying the transport, John Morgan is watching out for the President's interests."

"What about the Russians?"

"We've asked, then demanded help, but we'll have to see what they have to contribute. They may balk at helping."

"Which brings me back to your Marine. I hear rumors."

"Such as?"

"Such as he's not exactly impartial when it comes to dealing with the Neville woman—that he's very taken with her."

Kellner frowned. "What do you suggest? Thumbscrews?"

"Come on, Vincent. I know you've had a shock, but don't set yourself up for more problems."

"My impression of Anna Neville is that she is an intelligent woman, and will be a cooperative one. But just in case, Morgan will be watched, and Anna Neville will be watched. Remember, Ave Peters will be with them."

Fisk said, "I hoped you would say that. I have nothing against her, but the stakes are too damned high for tender hearts."

"Who should know that better than I?"

Fisk remained silent for a tactful moment and then said, "When we pick up Varig, the first thing she'll say is that she must see you."

Kellner shook his head. "Absolutely not," he said. He made a pained, dismissive gesture. "Not until later, when it is necessary that I do so." He asked hesitantly, "What specifically do you know about her Intelligence Directorate contact?"

"Some, but not much. We won't know until we have Varig in hand, singing away. Suslova is flashy, very good looking, very noticeable, but she's been surprisingly invisible most of her time here in Washington. If it's any comfort, there are going to be heads rolling up on Mount Alto over this submarine business.''

''It's no comfort, Charlie. It's not even something we want to think about until that thing in Canada stops ticking.''

''How bad is it, Vincent?''

''As bad as it can be,'' Kellner said soberly. ''The world is looking down the barrel of a very big cannon. That should terrify you, Charlie. It does me. And the only people who know that right now are here and in Moscow.''

''I hear the rumors. Another Chernobyl?''

Another Armageddon, Kellner thought. ''The Canadians say it's possible,'' he said. ''We're sending a military and scientific pickup team north tomorrow, along with Morgan. It's in their hands from then on.''

''And welcome to it,'' Fisk said.

''Yes,'' Kellner said heavily. ''If you're a God-fearing man, start praying now.''

''It's a deal.'' Fisk leaned over to shake hands before he left. ''Oh—what'll we do about Ryerson?'' he asked. ''My people have finished questioning him for now. I can only hold him a little longer, unless we charge him with something.''

''Leave him to me. I'll handle it. Keep him overnight.''

''Take care. Don't let him near any of his newsy friends.''

''I doubt he has many friends. He's a corrupt man,'' Kellner said, his jaw set. ''Corrupt men are useful.''

''Remember the First Amendment, Vincent.''

''I wouldn't dream of forgetting it,'' Vincent Kellner said.

The light indicating that someone was at his outer office door turned red. The voice of the pool secretary temporarily replacing Camilla came from the intercom. ''Colonel Morgan is here, sir.''

''YOU LOOK TIRED,'' Kellner said with unexpected solicitude.

''It's been a long three days,'' Morgan said, stretching his

310

back before he dropped into a chair. "You've got a line on the skinheads who killed Grau?"

"We know who they were. Was it necessary to kill them?" Kellner asked abruptly.

"Yes."

"That's it? Yes. No further explanation?"

"They knew where we were, they had lots of firepower, they were ready to use it on Anna and me after they killed Grau, and they had us in their sights. I was lucky enough to get the drop on them, otherwise you'd be at my funeral about now."

"All right, I accept your premise. Now, tell me about the Russian. Is he real? The Company man I talked to thought he might be a ploy to distract us. Was he lucid? What did he tell you?"

Morgan said, "The whole story—except for the ending, that is. No man would undergo what he's gone through just for their precious *maskirovka*. He's an underwater specialist, sometimes for civilian projects, most of the time in the military. He headed the team that deployed the goddamned thing. He calls it the Device, with a capital letter. He spent three hours describing it and how the Device might be defused. I've passed the sketches on to the Canadians. Orgonev designed and built it. He called it *Soyuz*."

"How touching."

"The December 7 date for detonation is a nice touch," Morgan said. "It shows great sensitivity to American history."

"The Russians are a sentimental people," Kellner said.

"During the deployment, Karmann says, two Russian navy divers were killed by mines they set in the water around it. The mines must still be active. He says the whole project was strictly clandestine, poorly planned, done on a shoestring. The warhead leaked plutonium oxide aboard the *Pravda*. Two-thirds of the crew were already sick when the captain scuttled the ship. The Device is cobbled together from bits of ICBM warheads and rated at eighty to a hundred megatons. They

Alfred Coppel

aren't quite sure because they could never test any of the components."

"My God."

Morgan said relentlessly, "The intention was to launch the missile, let it climb to the proper altitude, then detonate in space above Omaha. It's dicey exploding a nuclear warhead over your antagonist's homeland. But if it's done properly, it fries every piece of electronic gear in the hemisphere, and, at least theoretically, you spare the lives of the people underneath. If at the same time we were blinded Soyuz moved to take over the Russian government—" He shrugged. "I don't know. It still might work."

"Yes," Kellner said intently. "It would work. Soyuz would have taken over the Kremlin and we wouldn't know—we could do nothing. We would be helpless, without command and control of our own forces." He sighed. "The President tried to warn Cherny of the plot, but Cherny stonewalled. Cherny may already have been aware of the possibility of a coup, but can't control events. Caidin lost his poise and his temper, insulted Cherny, hence defcon two."

He opened a locked drawer in his desk and withdrew a redbanded folder. "Study this. It's a file on a diving suit for work in contaminated water. It's been developed by a Canadian marine biologist named Doris Waymer. She's been fretting for twenty years about the nuclear wastes dropped into the ocean since the fifties. She claims her suit will protect a diver in a lethal environment up to half an hour. We've bought three of them for testing. The Canadian underwater team is bringing a dozen more Waymer suits."

Morgan said, "My last open water dive was five years ago."

"There really is no need for you to get into the water with the Canadians. They worry so much about sovereignty, let them exercise it. This is a Canadian operation, with the cooperation of the NSC. The President has promised Halloran full support. We'll borrow what we need from the Pentagon."

312

"There's no way you can keep this secret, you know," Morgan said. "I'll bet the presses are hot now."

"We have to try," Kellner said. "At least until it's over."

"Vincent," Morgan said, "I do hate politics. Look what they get us into, time and again."

"In five days, politics might not matter," Kellner said.

Chapter Thirty-seven

The Kremlin/December 2

The plane has taken off and a section of the public still believes it will land in Paris or Stockholm. But, in fact, the course has been set for Brazil, or even Nigeria, since this airline and this make of plane does not fly to the West at all.

—BORIS KAGARLITSKY, DISINTEGRATION OF THE MONOLITH, 1992

IT WAS LATE NIGHT when the staff car carrying Air Force General Kalinin and Provost Colonel Zenobiev drove across the floodlit expanse of Red Square and into the Spassky Tower Gate of the Kremlin. Snow was falling lightly, giving the illuminated roofs and towers of the Kremlin a fairy-tale look, brightly colored against the dark winter sky.

When shall I ever see all this again, Kalinin wondered. The smooth plain of white snow, the red brick of the Kremlin wall, the squat black marble of the mausoleum. It was only six days ago that he had stood there with his peers, exulting in his new rank, to watch the National Day parade.

Do they know about my part in the missile sales abroad? Surely Aleksandr Cherny would not execute me out of hand for something so common, he thought hopefully. A man must look to his future, and, of his own knowledge, he could name at least a hundred military men who had done the same, including Kondratiev.

Kalinin glanced at the expressionless peasant face of the provost officer who had him in charge. Zenobiev gave him no clue as to what came next. The limousine rounded into the parking area behind the bell tower. Kalinin's heart sank. Instead of the familiar uniform of the men of the Kremlin guards, the regiment had all been replaced by a very hard-looking detachment of soldiers from the Thirtieth Shock Army, dressed in full battle gear, including flak vests and steel helmets. The showy guards were nowhere to be seen. Kondratiev had once scoffed at them, called them "chocolate soldiers," and he had pressured old Yulin to replace them with a regiment of Black Berets, Ministry of the Interior security troops. But Yulin, as present commander of the security forces, had dithered over the order until it was too late.

Looking at the shock army soldiers standing guard now, Kalinin was envious. Oh, how I wish the air force regiments had troops like these instead of insolent bastards like those at Bykovo, he thought mournfully. It might have made all the difference in the world. Kondratiev should have struck that bargain with the Communists, combine forces. He could have dealt with them later, after the takeover.

Was it also too late to get himself out of this mess? Success of the Soyuz putsch had depended almost entirely on secrecy and surprise. Perhaps, when pressed, he could confess the sins of the plotters, with the full understanding that the guilt lay with Kondratiev and the others, not with an upstanding, patriotic officer like himself. Could he convince them that he was just an innocent bystander, somehow drawn into the plot against his will?

The car had stopped and Colonel Zenobiev held the door

open. "Out, General," he said in his scratchy voice.

Zenobiev led the way into the base of the Spassky Tower. Two shock army soldiers with assault rifles at the ready fell in behind. Kalinin noted that the interior halls of the Spassky were well guarded by at least twice the normal number of troops. So Aleksandr Cherny wasn't the fool the Soyuz conspirators had believed him to be. Once alerted to danger—by whom, Kalinin wondered—he had moved decisively.

Kalinin kept pace with the provost colonel. If Cherny knew about the plot, did he know about the Device? Kalinin swallowed hard. His throat felt dry. The missile was to have been in readiness to fire even before Kondratiev arrived in Moscow for Orgonev's funeral. The time for it to launch itself was now five days away. That close we came, he thought bitterly. Soyuz as a movement was dead and buried. The conspirators were still above ground, but for how long?

Zenobiev signaled for the elevator to take them into the upper Spassky Tower. When the lift reached an intermediate story in the Spassky, Kalinin was led into a bare room containing one piece of furniture, a chair. Colonel Zenobiev said, "Sit. You will be called."

Without waiting to see that his instructions were obeyed, the colonel turned and marched from the room, closing the door behind him. The two troopers who had accompanied them into the tower took station on either side of the single door, their Kalashnikov rifles held across their broad, peasants' chests. Their faces were immobile. Kalinin addressed them in Russian.

"I want to smoke."

They gave no indication of having heard him. He tried to remember what he knew about the Thirtieth Shock Army. Very little, actually. It was not a military formation of distinction, but the kind that was good only for high-casualty battle. It was, in fact, exactly the sort of unit Kalinin had intended weeding out of the Russian army once the Soyuz troika had appointed him Minister of Defense.

He moved to take from his pocket a silver case containing Cuban cigarillos. With dazzling swiftness, the soldiers responded by assuming a firing position with their weapons leveled at his head and chest.

Kalinin very cautiously placed his hands on his thighs, in plain view. Time appeared to have slowed down to a painful crawl. His bladder was full and there was no chance that he could convince these outland brutes to let him find a toilet. He looked at his expensive Japanese watch, a gift from Igor Ligachev in the old days, when Ligachev was Party Chief of Ideology, and there had been some hope that Mikhail Gorbachev was going to become an unmourned memory.

The time was twenty minutes after two in the morning. A time for ghosts, he thought. A time for executions of the old Stalinist style—a walk through the concrete tunnels below the Lubyanka and a pistol round in the back of the neck, the dyevyat gram so beloved of Dzershinsky's and Beria's thugs.

One of his guards was eyeing his watch covetously. *Could I bribe him with it? But to what end? If he and his friend are not impressed with the fact that I am the Moscow Air Defense Commander and a general of the Russian air force, they are unlikely to let me wander out of the Spassky Tower like some itinerant tourist. They are more likely to take the watch and have done with it.*

Provost Colonel Zenobiev reappeared. "Follow me," he said.

"I need to piss," Kalinin said.

"Later. Follow me."

Kalinin was close to weeping with discomfort and frustration, but he had enough sense to do as he was told. He again pridefully kept pace with Zenobiev, breathing hard, the pain from his full bladder increasing. What a perfect way to demean a general of the Russian air force, summoning him into Cherny's royal presence with his trousers wet. Kalinin had a rebellious urge to pull out his penis and hose away at the parquet floor. But he was prevented by the degrading thought that his

317

once pillarlike manhood now probably resembled a shriveled turnip. Fear had that effect.

Yet if he wasn't granted relief soon, there was going to be humiliation enough to go around. It was absurd to spend what were probably his last moments on earth brooding over urination, but it came as an epiphany that some of life's most elemental demands wiped the mind clean of other, loftier thoughts.

To distract himself, he concentrated on the unfamiliar soldiers guarding the passageway. So, the President had replaced the security forces guarding the Kremlin—all of them. An act totally out of character, if General Kondratiev were to be believed. Until this black morning, Kalinin thought, I would have agreed with him. Every time I saw Cherny, he behaved like no more than a gassybrained academic.

A second elevator loomed at the end of the corridor. When the door opened, Kalinin and Zenobiev got in, followed by all of the soldiers who were guarding them. The elevator was so small and so full that the soldiers' equipment struck the varnished walls with hollow, drumlike sounds. The car began to move with paralyzing slowness.

The rank smell of sweat and damp wool was redolent in the enclosed space. Only the scent of blood is missing, or I'd believe I was back doing interrogations in Afghanistan. I've been too long in Moscow, Kalinin thought, away from soldiers in the field and the filthy, primitive way they live.

The elevator stopped and the door opened onto a small, octagonal room. A six-foot-square table stood near the far wall, where long draped cloths covered the windows closely. Stacked papers, bound documents, and a cocked and charged Kalashnikov assault rifle were visible on the table.

Large, high-backed upholstered chairs surrounded the table on three sides, three at the head, two at each side, and all empty at the moment. On the fourth side sat three low, scruffy, metal chairs, paint chipped, hard and uncomfortable. Slumped in one of them was the familiar figure of Admiral Eduard

Aleyev. Kalinin could smell the vodka all the way across the room. My colleague, he thought angrily, my partner in crime. Kalinin could stand it no longer, and shouted, "Damn it, I have to piss."

Aleyev gave a grunting laugh. He turned around to look at his fellow prisoner with red, watery eyes. He is totally disgusting, Kalinin thought.

"Let the flyboy piss, Colonel," Aleyev said mockingly. "For the fucking honor of the air force, man. He'll spoil his fancy pants if you don't, not to speak of what he'll do to the rugs."

Aleksandr Cherny heard Kalinin's plea as he entered the room. "There." He nodded impatiently toward a narrow door in the far wall of the octagon. "Go with him, Zenobiev."

Aleyev said in a thin, shaky voice, "Kalinin, thank the schoolmaster nicely."

The old drunk still shows some spirit, Kalinin thought with surprise. That gave him hope. Perhaps between the two of them, Cherny could be handled.

"Come," Zenobiev said curtly, obviously annoyed by the order. He escorted Kalinin to the door, opened it, and pushed him into a tiny room containing a galvanized bucket in a wooden commode. He left the door open.

Kalinin opened his trousers and, knowing that the sound of his urine striking the bucket could be heard in the outer room, with some difficulty began to piss. Humiliation after humiliation would be the pattern tonight.

When he reappeared, Zenobiev led him to a metal chair next to Aleyev. While he was in the other room, several people had arrived and were seated at the table—in the good chairs. He recognized two of them, Lykov and Yadanov, from the GKNT, fussy and self-important technocrats, but rather subdued tonight. They were seated together on his right, Cherny's left, closest to his side of the table.

Sitting to the right of President Cherny was a man named Gallikov, a youngish pedantic bureaucrat, who always parroted

Cherny's words to those not fortunate enough to be close to his hero. Gallikov, as an aide to Cherny, had fought Kalinin, as Moscow's Air Defense Commander, tooth and nail when the military budget was being considered. He is my natural enemy, Kalinin thought. On Cherny's left sat Natalya Renkova, a judge of depressing rectitude from the Ministry of Justice. Cherny had appointed her to the Supreme Judicial Council, a group of time-wasters who had been fumbling about since Yeltsin's era trying to amend the new Russian constitution to no one's satisfaction.

I'll get no mercy, Kalinin thought despairingly. Not from that dried up old sow, nor from a friend of the Jew so recently planted in the Kremlin wall. And certainly not from Cherny. I wonder if he knows that Kondratiev intended to get rid of him, execute him.

Marshal Suvorov, the Minister of Defense, of all people, was just seating himself in the first chair on the side of the table to Kalinin's left. What was he doing here, apparently and implicitly supporting Cherny? General Kondratiev had as much as promised that Suvorov was a member of the conspiracy. Had he turned when he saw that Cherny knew of the plot? If so, there was no hope.

Two chairs remained empty, one beside Suvorov, beckoning in its upholstered comfort, promising safety, the prospect of seeing the dawn in freedom. But for whom was the third metal chair being held?

Cherny regarded Aleyev and Kalinin gravely. "You know Judge Renkova. She will be my adviser. Academicians Oleg Yadanov and Stepan Lykov, members of the Russian Academy of Science and consultants to the naval cadre of the GKNT."

Kalinin caught his breath in despair. Now he understood why these two were here. Not only did Cherny have knowledge of the planned putsch, but the Soyuz Device had been compromised. Aleyev expelled a long, fetid sigh and tried to get up. "I should be in Vladivostok," he mumbled.

Cherny gave him a frigid glance. Zenobiev materialized behind Aleyev and shoved him roughly back down into his chair.

"Welcome to Judgment Day," Aleyev muttered to Kalinin.

Cherny frowned at the two Soyuz conspirators. "I want you to listen carefully to what Yadanov and Lykov have to say. It may give you some notion of the degree of your guilt." He turned to Yadanov. "You say, Academician, in your written statement, which I have before me, that the submarine *Pravda* was to be dismantled but by special order was reassigned to be modified as a GKNT research vessel?"

"Yes, Excellency."

His companion, Lykov, spoke up swiftly. "That is correct, Excellency. But you must realize that the GKNT design team was only carrying out the orders of the navy."

Aleyev snorted his derision but said nothing.

"No comment, Admiral?" Cherny asked.

"None," Aleyev said heavily. "Why not end this farce?"

Kalinin thought, In God's name, you old fool, don't be so eager for the neck-shot.

"Yet we have searched everywhere and we find no written records of the change, Academicians," Cherny said grimly. "No naval architect's drawings, no signed authorizations, either from the GKNT or from the Bureau of Ships." His tone was frigid. "*Pravda* might never have existed."

"That is true, Your Honor. But—"

"A moment," Cherny said. "I have a question for Admiral Aleyev. I want to know why Captain Kolodin, the admiral's own choice for this peculiar project, was so anxious to get out of Kola that he dispensed completely with the customary sea trials."

Yadanov said unctuously, "I know what you are suggesting, Your Honor. But the Design Cadre cannot be held responsible for the loss of the ship. We grieve for the men lost, but the boat put to sea on the verbal orders of Captain Kolodin and a former political officer, Viktor Krasny."

321

"Have you anything to add, Admiral Aleyev?" Cherny asked.

Stepan Lykov spoke up nervously. "The submarine was obsolete, Honorable President, destined for destruction in Murmansk. It was declared available for modification as an ocean environmental research vessel by the Ministry of Marine." There was suddenly a sheen of sweat on his face.

"On whose authority, Academician Lykov?"

"Admiral Aleyev's, Excellency."

"Well, Admiral?" Cherny asked, regarding Aleyev.

"I didn't steal the goddamned submarine, Aleksandr Borisovich," Aleyev muttered. "Nor sink it."

"Watch your manners," President Cherny said, bristling. "Tell me what was done with it, and for what purpose."

"Go to hell," Aleyev said. "Excellency."

Cherny said bleakly, "If what I have been told is correct, there is a very good chance we shall all go there. And soon." He turned to stare coldly at the two men from the Naval Design Cadre. "The *Pravda* was modified to carry a single very large ballistic missile. Is that not what you have buried here in almost unreadable technical jargon?"

"Well, yes, Your Honor. That is what was done," Lykov said faintly. He thought, the man has the report I wrote, intended only for General Kondratiev's eyes, after the triumph of Soyuz.

"General Orgonev's Nuclear Weapons Development Bureau delivered such a missile to the submarine at Kola. Is *that* not so?" Cherny pursued.

The two academicians spoke at the same time. Then Yadanov yielded to Lykov, who said pleadingly, "You must realize, Excellency, that the Design Cadre's work covers a great many projects. Authorization is automatically sent down approved from the Bureau of Ships with the authority of the general staff of the navy."

For the first time Cherny looked at Marshal Suvorov, who had been sitting silently, staring at the tabletop. "How much

322

of this did you know about, Yevgeny Pavlovich?"

"None of it," the old marshal spoke up firmly. "I would never have permitted any of it."

Cherny said, "Ah, but you *did* know, and you *did* permit it to happen. These two pillars of patriotism from the GKNT are right about one thing. Authorizations for all kinds of black programs were sent to Kola with your approval. And yours, Aleyev. Fortunately, those documents have survived."

Aleyev cackled happily. "Come round here, Yevgeny, join us in glorious disgrace." He patted the metal chair at his side. Suvorov closed his eyes.

"Go on, Lykov," Cherny said. "We know that a missile was taken from the inventory of the Strategic Rocket Forces. Tell me why. Was it to be fired from the submarine? And if so, at what target?"

When Lykov began to fumble with his papers, Cherny interrupted him. "You'll find nothing there, Academician," he said. "Written records of what was done to the *Pravda* are scarcer than the teeth of birds. I am certain that does not surprise you. Just tell us what you know."

Lykov sat in frozen silence.

We have a penchant for confession and self-incrimination, Kalinin thought. Cherny is counting on it with all in this room. The Bolsheviks made use of it during the purge trials, with old comrades fighting one another for priority in confessing capital crimes. Is that what happens now? Cherny's version of the Stalinist terror?

Cherny addressed Admiral Aleyev. "Eduard Sergeivich? Tell us why you lent yourself to this scheme."

"It was best for Russia," the old man mumbled.

"I can give you a better answer than that. I believe all your illegal manipulation of naval assets was part of your activities on behalf of Soyuz." Cherny paused for a moment, looking intently at the faces of his adversaries. "I should tell you now, all of you, that your leader, General Kondratiev, has been taken into custody. He is on his way here to this room, and will arrive before this hearing is concluded. Now—tell me why the *Pravda* was sunk and what has become of the missile it carried. Is it safely at the bottom of the sea?''

With drunken defiance, Aleyev raised his head and shouted, "The Device is where it is intended to be. The Device will do what we intended it should do."

Cherny's face seemed paler than before. "Hear me and understand what I am telling you. A Canadian woman claims to have been an eyewitness to the sighting of a submarine in Hudson Bay at approximately this time last year, that the airplane in which she was a passenger was shot down by that same vessel. Are you aware of that? Yes, I see you are. I believe it was the *Pravda*. What I did not know until the Canadians and the Americans approached me this very day for 'a Russian nuclear accident team,' was that there has been widespread nuclear pollution in the precise location where the submarine was seen last year. Now goddamn you to hell, Eduard Sergeivich, tell me what you and your fascist Soyuz friends have done and why."

Aleyev, his moment of defiance over, closed his eyes and said nothing.

Cherny turned to Yadanov. "Describe the modifications that were made to the missile that was put abroad the *Pravda*. Don't look in your notes. Just speak."

"Yes, Mr. President." The man's skin was the color of chalk. "Ah—according to General Orgonev's design—we, ah—enlarged a surplus SS-18 and fitted it into the modified missile bay of the *Pravda*. The mirved warhead was removed and replaced with a single warhead—ah—that had been— ah—enhanced. The yield was increased to an estimated eighty to a hundred megatons, Honorable President, suitable for detonation in space as a pulse weapon."

Cherny leaned forward. "A pulse weapon? To be used for what purpose?"

"A large detonation at the proper altitude—very high— would render an enemy electronically deaf, dumb, and blind for an indefinite period, until the electronic systems components burned out by the gamma pulse could be replaced. It would completely destroy an army's command and control systems." When he saw Cherny's expression, he hastened to add, "And without a single death on the ground."

"I am moved by your delicacy of feeling, Academician Lykov," Natalya Renkova said sardonically. She had been silent to this point. Lykov looked at her, startled, his face flushing a deep scarlet.

Kalinin spoke up brusquely. "This man is dreaming. There is no such weapon as an eighty-megaton warhead in the Strategic Rocket Forces inventory."

Lykov rushed to defend Yadanov's testimony. "A thermonuclear warhead is simple to enhance—it is merely a matter of adding tritium oxide."

Cherny addressed Kalinin. "I put it to you, General, that such a warhead was, in fact, assembled and mated to a very special SSN-18 missile. When the job was completed, your leader, General Kondratiev, at that time commander of the security forces, had those who had worked on the missile, a hundred in all, arrested and sent to Camp 166 on the north coast of the island of Novaya Zemlya. All but three of those arrested died there."

Marshal Suvorov stirred in his chair. "I had nothing to do with that," he declared thickly. "I am a soldier, not a policeman."

Cherny said bitterly, "I appreciate the distinction, Suvorov, but it is a distinction without a difference. Nevertheless, there is a second company of ghosts to join those sent to Novaya Zemlya, to haunt you, and you, Admiral, and you, General Kalinin," Cherny said bitterly. "Your fellow military men— the Russian sailors of the crew of the submarine *Pravda*. The sole survivor will testify what happened."

Aleyev drew in his breath sharply. "The *Pravda* was lost at sea. There *were* no survivors," he declared.

"One," Natalya Renkova said in her low, carrying voice.

Alfred Coppel

"He is in American hands, in an American hospital."

Aleksandr Cherny closed his eyes for a moment. "The astonishing thing is that you three and your mentor, Piotr Kondratiev, have so little knowledge of the world. The American President has discovered your intentions. He has ordered an alert at the level of defense condition two while lecturing me as if I were a child still in school. Their submarines are already putting to sea, their strategic bombers are already on air alert, and their missile silos are manned and ready to fire. The crucial element of surprise in your plan has been lost. In fact, they have declared that any attempt at an illegal change of government in this country will be considered an act of war. And now we are required to supply a disaster response team, to be sent to Canada by tomorrow. The team is to find the missile in concert with the Canadians."

Aleyev blurted arrogantly, "You agreed to this, Aleksandr Borisovich? This is not the Persian Gulf, and we are not Iraqis. The Americans' golden weapon systems will be jammed, unusable. Our Device is safe on the bottom of Hudson Bay. They'll never find it. It will launch itself no matter what the Americans say or do."

Boris Gallikov, silent to this point, said harshly, "Honorable President, that's not so. I have looked into the technical side of this missile very thoroughly. If Eskimo are dying of plutonium poisoning in Canada's Northwest Territories, that is evidence the Device is leaking. If so, the chances of the missile launching itself are remote."

"Well, Lykov? Is that true?" Cherny demanded.

"Yes." Lykov's reply was almost inaudible.

Time seemed to pass very slowly in the hot, paneled room. "*Go on,* Lykov," Cherny said. "*Now.*"

The weapons man spoke haltingly, "He is right. A launch failure will not deactivate the warhead, Excellency." Lykov's voice dropped to almost a whisper. "The device is one designed to detonate a given number of seconds after the designated time of launch. It was made so in order to prevent anyone but our technicians from deactivating the trigger mechanism. Two minutes—no, two minutes and thirty-seven seconds—after initialization, the warhead will detonate.'' He looked around, pleading for understanding. ''It was to have flown so high, they said. They said it wouldn't hurt anyone, only the machinery.''

For a moment, everyone and everything in the room was absolutely still and silent.

Cherny felt as though a fist had struck him over the heart. His mind whirled. An eighty-megaton nuclear explosion underwater in central Canada? The blast would kill or injure almost everything within a hundred kilometers of ground zero. Fish, game, birds, and human beings within twenty kilometers of the explosion would die at once. Beyond that radius, the secondary effects would kill more slowly. There would be a lethal column of steam, mist, and debris, boiling into the stratosphere, to be caught by the jet stream and carried across eastern Canada, the northeastern United States, the Atlantic, the British Isles; then across the Channel to northern Europe, to Germany, to Poland, and finally, into Russia itself.

It would be a disaster, Chernobyl a thousand times over. It would brand the Russian people as the greatest mass killers in human history, pariahs forever.

Oleg Yadanov said eagerly, ''The warhead *can* be deactivated, Honorable President. We had the forethought to provide a mechanism that allows for the timing device to be turned off. Of course, it would be difficult. But if properly briefed, one trained diver could do it.''

Lykov chimed in eagerly, ''It is dangerous, of course, but technically possible. That must be why the Americans and Canadians are demanding a Russian nuclear accident team.''

Cherny glared at the two academicians. ''How clever of you to make the connection.'' He spoke sharply to Colonel Zenobiev. ''Put our prisoners into isolated custody, Colonel, including Marshal Suvorov. They are to speak to no one, see no one. This hearing is recessed for three hours.''

I must call Caidin immediately, Cherny thought, as the shock army colonel and his men took custody of the prisoners. And I must speak with Ian Halloran. For some reason, fear had gone, and his mind was working quickly and clearly. "Gallikov, have we any personnel qualified to disarm the missile at our mission in Canada? Or Washington?"

"No, Honorable President. Only at the Kola Naval Base."

"Very well. Order Kola to assemble an underwater nuclear weapons disposal team and fly them to Montreal at once. Then convene a consultation with your best experts about how best to deal with this abomination."

"Sir."

The soldiers guided Aleyev, Kalinin, and Suvorov, along with the two academicians from the Design Cadre, out of the door, but paused there in confusion.

Cherny pushed his way past the prisoners into the anteroom. There, in the custody of four of the shock army guards, stood General Piotr Kondratiev. His Black Berets uniform was rumpled and showed evidence of a struggle upon his arrest, but he seemed unperturbed.

"I heard what you said just now, Aleksandr Borisovich," Kondratiev said, laughing. "You had better go to your shelter and allow the state to be run by those competent to do Mother Russia's business."

For the first time, Aleksandr Cherny's anger and contempt overcame his diffidence when dealing with Kondratiev. "You egotistical bungler, this disaster is on your head, yours and your stupid sycophants." He waved at the guards. "Take this—this—murderer—away."

One of the soldiers shoved Kondratiev so hard that he almost fell, then grasped him by the coat collar to pull him upright again. As his guards began to hurry him back along the corridor, he shouted over his shoulder at Cherny, "I'll not do you a favor like Sergei Akromeyev did for Gorbachev and hang myself. I'll not shoot myself like Boris Pugo, nor jump from a high window like Nikolai Kruchina—unless, of course, your thugs here defenestrate me.''

The last words Cherny heard as Kondratiev disappeared from view, surrounded by his escort, were: "I'll outlive you, you son of a bitch, just wait and see!"

Chapter Thirty-eight

Andrews AFB/Washington, D.C./December 3

The subject of today's press briefing at the White House was expected to be the latest fine-tuning of the National Health Insurance Act.

Instead, Presidential Press Secretary Bob Stover spent most of his time trying to quell rumors of trouble brewing to the north. No one seems to be quite clear about what the trouble is, and, of course, Prime Minister Halloran and President Caidin deny any disagreement vigorously. But something is cooking, children. You don't suppose that we're back to "54-40 or Fight" after all these years?

—LIZ SCHORR, IN THE
"WASHINGTON INSIDER" COLUMN

AN ICY WIND BLEW across Washington and the temperature dropped steadily into the twenties. Sleet-laden rain slashed at the windshield of the air force van taking John Morgan and Arkady Karmann to Andrews Air Force Base. The driver, a baby-faced sergeant, was forced to slow to a crawl in the heavy traffic.

The atmospherics were as cold inside the van as they were outside, Morgan thought, glancing at Karmann. The Russian sat, eyes closed at times, staring out the steamy windows at others. He was ill; perhaps, Morgan thought, he had made a mistake by spiriting Karmann out of Bethesda in secret. But if the word had spread about Karmann's whereabouts, the man might be in great danger. Morgan had questioned the nurses, asking if anyone had been nosing around, anyone claiming to be either a friend or an official, but he'd been assured he was the first visitor. And no reporters had called—yet.

The Russian-American nurse in North Carolina had undoubtedly saved Karmann's life, given him a respite at least. The flight he and Morgan must take into the Northwest Territories was surely not what the navy doctors would prescribe for a return to some semblance of health. It might be the death of him. Yet Karmann was determined to repair the damage he had done. I don't find that decision so strange, Morgan thought. What I can't understand is why he made his original choice of action.

Morgan leaned his head wearily against the seat. My God, I'm tired, he thought. Karmann stirred, but did not speak. Morgan watched him speculatively. How deeply was he involved in the plot, how committed? Had he been promised great rewards if he cooperated, only to be betrayed, to see his shipmates slaughtered? The daily intelligence summary provided to Kellner had described the ongoing street disturbances and arrests in Moscow. All diplomatic meetings with members of the Cherny government had been canceled or postponed.

"What time is it?" Karmann's hoarse voice startled Morgan. It was the first time he had spoken since they left the safe house where he had spent the night under Morgan's guard. "Why do we go so slow?"

"It's just after seventeen hundred hours," Morgan said. On the third day of December, a date that now had some significance. A chill ran through him. Three and a half days left.

Alfred Coppel

Karmann said the launch was automated, set for the seventh, at 0830 local time.

The Canadians were arguing back and forth about the feasibility of evacuating everyone within a 200-kilometer radius of the live warhead in the bay. But it would be like trying to bail out a sinking boat with a teaspoon. Between 61 degrees north, 90 degrees west, and along the Canadian Atlantic coast, there were perhaps two million Quebecois, and at least a quarter that many isolated Newfoundlanders. Who could evacuate them, and how? The total air, land, and sea lift capabilities of the United States and Canada might manage it—in a year. It had taken five months for the U.S. Army and Navy to get a half million troops to Saudi Arabia.

And God help the poor jokers running America's answer to disaster—the Federal Emergency Management Agency, Morgan thought. It was one thing to plan for a nuclear attack, as the agency had been formed to do, and another to deal with the actuality of it. In the last few years, years in which floods, earthquakes, and hurricanes had ravaged large areas of the United States, critics had complained that Washington should have been better prepared for coping with those emergencies. Morgan wondered if anyone had told the agency honchos that their time had come with a vengeance.

Goddamn it, the Russians did this, he thought with a surge of anger. His grandfather had trained Russian pilots to fly American airplanes during World War II. He often told the story of one almost disastrous training flight. On a first takeoff in a Lend-Lease B-25, the Russian had attempted a slow roll at twenty feet. "I was scared shitless," Gramps had said," and I snatched the controls out of the fucker's hands. And you know what he said to me, laughing his head off? He said 'What's the matter, Amerikanski? You 'fraid to die?' "

Afraid to die, Morgan? You're damned right I am, Morgan thought. And I'm no saint. There is a kind of primeval, savage satisfaction in knowing that if a storm of radioactive debris killed a million or so Canadians and Europeans, the fallout plume would still be deadly when it passed across the heartland of European Russia.

Arkady Karmann knew that Morgan had rarely taken his eyes off him, eyes that burned through bone and flesh, asking why had he helped in this criminal act. Karmann shivered. How could he explain? I don't know myself, to tell the truth, he thought.

The plan had seemed so plausible when it was explained to him. If the missile exploded its warhead high in space, as it was designed to do and as its creators had intended, no one would have been killed, only greatly inconvenienced. Public anger in America would probably demand "proportionate retaliation," which might or might not ever take place. Certainly any American attack would have been greatly delayed by the electronic blackout the Device would have caused. But if the warhead exploded under the water and killed a million North Americans, the anger would become rage and the demand would be for a full-scale nuclear strike against Russia.

Our world is collapsing around us, and we are hungry for self-immolation. Stalin lives, Arkady thought. Stalin and all those like him *always* live.

But it was far too easy to blame it all on dead Stalin. After all, he was near to half a century in his grave. For myself, I am German as well as Russian. Doubly damned, he thought with a burst of laughter.

Morgan stared at him.

"It's all right," Karmann said. "I haven't gone mad."

The hitherto silent sergeant jerked the wheel of the van sharply and let out a stream of curses at the incautious driver who had cut in front of him. Sleet smeared the windscreen and loaded the streets with frozen muck. The weather was growing worse.

How is the weather at Eskimo Point? Morgan wondered. Anxiety was building. Karmann's bitter laughter had shaken him. I am ninety hours from being vaporized into an unimportant part of a cloud blowing across the world on the jet

333

stream, and one of the people most responsible for this potential catastrophe sits beside me, laughing like a crazy man.

Karmann said abruptly, "You look at me as though you would like to kill me."

"There's no point in talking about it," Morgan said curtly, turning to regard the slowly moving traffic around them. The van window was higher than the car next to them, a Porsche. The driver had his seat belt buckled, but his trousers belt undone, a victim of vanity over comfort, obviously. A boomer apparatchik, car phone to his ear. A prick, Morgan thought. How fast does that Porsche go, Mac? It doesn't matter, because three times faster still wouldn't get you out from under the fallout of an eighty megatonner.

"They amuse you, your countrymen?" Karmann asked.

"Was I smiling? No, my countrymen do not amuse me. No more than yours do." Morgan found it difficult to be civil.

Karmann nodded at the stream of cars. "I sailed once with an East German naval commander who was convinced that all the colorful and neat cities full of modern cars and prosperous-looking people that appeared on Western television were *maskirovka,* all pure propaganda, meant to deceive the people in the East. He stopped watching years ago, even though he loved the television story about Dallas. Watching Western programs corrupts the socialist soul, he said. Imagine that."

I suppose Karmann is trying to tell me something, but I'm damned if I'll listen, Morgan decided. Instead, I'll let myself think about Anna. What would life have been like in the house in Leesburg with Anna there? He tried to imagine it, to see her meeting him at the door, feeding Tripoli, watering the shaggy garden, making love with him in his bed, sheets rumpled and warm, laughing and crying and just plain living together.

But Joan's face kept intruding on the domestic images, and the pain of her loss was as strong as ever. Anna Neville was not a domesticated woman, and Morgan doubted that she ever had been. Her life had been so different from his that they had little common ground. Except for here, and now, in this time of great turmoil. I'm not good at chasing off after dreams, he thought a little sadly, especially not dreams that could never come true. Still, for the next four days he might have reason to be grateful for a lack of imagination.

The cellular telephone next to the driver buzzed for attention. The airman answered, listened, and said, "It's for you, Colonel. The White House duty officer."

Morgan took the handset from him. "Morgan."

"Duty Officer here, Colonel. You just had a telephone call from Bethesda, sir. Odd call. It was one of the senior nurses, named Harrelson. She said to tell you that a woman who identified herself as Camilla Varig, who works at the NSC for Dr. Kellner, was at the administration desk with a request to see the Russian about twenty minutes ago. When they told her you checked him out last night, she left. The nurse gave a pretty good description of the woman. Any instructions?"

"Yes. Locate the Adviser and give him this information. Then call the Shore Patrol and have them try to find her. If they locate Varig, she is to be held until she's cleared by Dr. Kellner."

"Yes, sir."

Morgan looked over at Karmann. The man had fallen asleep. The sleep of exhaustion. The sleep of the dead. Tell him about his putative visitor, Camilla Varig? Never, he thought. Never in a thousand years.

IT WAS AFTER 1800 HOURS when the van deposited Morgan and Karmann on the apron at Andrews. Two of the hangars across the field were brilliantly lit, the planes inside swarming with mechanics. Trying to get Looking Glass, or a reasonable facsimile, back up in the air, Morgan thought. More likely the facsimile. Cole Caidin was getting quite a lesson in the false economics of sudden disarmament.

One of the hardened airplanes assigned to Air Force Special Operations Command waited on the apron, a black-painted

Hercules C-130H with its boarding ramp down. A half dozen people in civilian clothes stood around a stack of equipment, bright lights illuminating the gathering darkness. A detachment of Air Force Special Operations troops guarded the plane. Members of the flight crew were engaged in running up the turbofans, blowing the icy rain and sleet into a knife-edged blizzard. A USAF full colonel in flying coveralls walked over to Morgan. "Colonel Morgan? From the NSC? I'm Benson."

"Colonel," Morgan said, nodding. He was too impatient for pleasantries right now. "How soon can we get under way?"

The colonel's coveralls were a blaze of colorful patches, one from the Combat Command Wing at Seymour Johnson Air Force Base in North Carolina. "Hell, I'm not driving the truck. Those are my birds over there." He indicated a flight of four F-15 Eagles with their canopies raised, three pilots aboard, ground crews ready to start engines.

"Why do we need an escort?" Morgan demanded.

"Don't ask me. I just follow orders. We go as far as the border, anyway."

Morgan shook his head in exasperation. The presence of the Special Operations troops and the F-15s betrayed an incipient turf battle inside the Pentagon, Morgan thought, all the better to screw things up. An air force captain with Special Operations Command patches on his flight jacket came trotting over from the Hercules. He asked the Eagle pilot, "Any word yet, Colonel?" He stared at Morgan, at Karmann, back to Morgan. "Are you the White House honcho? The Agency pilot is already aboard. We're almost ready. Any orders?"

"Yes," Morgan said. "Get the people on and let's haul. Is there a medical team on board?"

"We always carry one," the captain said.

Morgan said to Karmann, who stood shivering beside him, "Get aboard. Go with this officer." When the captain hesitated, Morgan demanded, "Well, what now?"

The captain grimaced. "There are supposed to be two more of you. Our orders are to wait for the rest of your White House people."

Morgan looked at his watch. Daylight was gone. Who else was going with them? He looked again at the huge plane and was struck by a thought. "Can you get that thing on the ground at Eskimo Point?"

The captain looked offended. "We'll get you there safely, Mister Morgan," he said.

"*Colonel* Morgan," the fighter pilot said sarcastically. "This is a genuine Marine half-colonel, son."

"Right," the captain said, unimpressed.

It began in the service academies, Morgan thought. And it took years to cut out the trade-school bullshit and learn to work and fight together. But the Canadian version of a single armed force with commands seemed to work no more smoothly. From all indications, their performance in this mess was far from exemplary. Air, Maritime, and Mobile Command each wanted a share of catastrophe.

Two White House limousines appeared driving up the concrete ramp led by the airdrome officer's blue staff car.

"Saddle up, Colonel," Morgan said to the fighter pilot.

"My pleasure." He sauntered back toward his flight. Had anyone briefed him on why he had orders for Eskimo Point and what was happening there, Morgan wondered. Did any of these people hastily gathered here? Probably not. One of the heavily tinted windows of the lead limo opened and Vincent Kellner's head appeared. "Over here, John."

Morgan trotted through the rain to the car. Kellner opened the door and said, "Get in."

Anna, wearing an air force flight suit and parka, was in the car, to his mingled pleasure and surprise. When he saw what she was wearing, it dawned on him that she planned to go north with the plane.

Kellner said, "Ryerson is under guard in the other car. He's going with you. His presence is one of the bargains I mentioned to you. There's no argument, so don't waste time on it. He has been told he can write the official version of this enterprise. Ryerson will be the pool reporter."

"*Ryerson?*"

"Mr. Ryerson will do his part, believe me."

Morgan looked at Anna. Her face was expressionless, guarded. She had two bags of photo equipment at her feet. *Goddamn, that's what she had in mind.*

"What did Ryerson give you in return?" Morgan asked.

Kellner's voice was quiet. "Camilla. All the proof we need."

Morgan said, "I had a call in the van from the duty officer, about a woman looking for Karmann. I told him to call you."

"I know. He reached me on our way here."

"It may not have been Camilla," Morgan said.

"Then again, it may have been. Never mind. You have enough on your plate. We'll handle my old friend. Everything she values is within thirty miles of this place. She won't go far."

"I still think taking Ryerson is a terrible idea," Morgan argued, without much hope of persuading Kellner. "Anna—"

Anna spoke up. "Don't go male chauvinist on me, Morgan," she said. "There has to be a record of this, and we can't leave it to the creative pen of Joe Ryerson, or any other reporter. If we succeed, my photographs will record everything that goes on up there, and no one will be able to deny them."

"You don't know what you're facing." He glared at Kellner. "Does she?"

"She knows. It's her choice to make."

"Her choice or yours?" Morgan was very angry. He said harshly, "What did she have to promise for the privilege of risking her life?"

"That's enough, Colonel," Kellner said. "Mrs. Neville made her decision. That's the end of it, unless you feel you cannot continue with the mission. In which case, you have only to say so and you will be replaced."

"Anna," Morgan said pleadingly.

"Someone has to do it, Morgan," Anna said. "And I've been in on this since the beginning. Vincent Kellner or Ian Halloran or Cole Caidin might skew the facts to save their own skins. Someone has to document the truth. We have to let people know what really happened. The fascists in Russia are trying again, and we have to stop them, have solid evidence, so they can't manipulate the truth. That's worth doing, Morgan."

Should he remind her, Morgan wondered, that if the warhead exploded while she was anywhere within a dozen miles of it there would *be* no record? Quite possibly no world. But she knew that already, of course.

He looked at Kellner and shrugged. "I hope you know what you are doing," he said.

Kellner replied in his most ironic tone, "That's a hope I share, Colonel."

Kellner picked up the radiophone and spoke into it. "Mercury, this is Gray Eminence. Take Ryerson to the aircraft and turn him over to the Special Operations troopers."

To Morgan he said, "Yes, I know there are already too many people involved in this operation. Too many services. And the Canadians will be nominally in charge at the Eskimo Point base. Remember, you're our official observer only. The sooner you're on your way, the better, John. And look at this."

He unfolded an extra edition of the *Washington Post*. The giant headline taking up half the front page read: ERRANT NUCLEAR BOMB IN CANADA? There were six columns of wild speculation on the front page, and more inside, no doubt.

"Christ," Morgan said. "Jesus Christ. Who did this?"

"It doesn't really matter now. The President has decided to roll with the punch. A press plane will be leaving for Hudson Bay first thing tomorrow morning."

Kellner looked ancient, Morgan thought. Drained of life. There was only intellect left in him now. The authority and confidence seemed to have leached away.

"Avery Peters is already aboard. He will fly you from the base camp to the diving site. The Russians and Canadians are sending diving teams."

"The *Russians?*"

"Remarkable, isn't it. Aleksandr Cherny is suddenly the most amenable of men, offering anything and everything we ask. Do try to keep them away from our defector. I don't want anything untoward to happen to him."

"Sir," Morgan said heavily.

"Thank you, John. I would have managed tactical command badly at my age, I fear. One thing more. We've been on the hot line to Cherny, and will be again tonight. In spite of his change of heart, defcon stays at two until this matter is cleaned up." Kellner's tone softened when he saw the strain on Anna's face. "Just remember, Mrs. Neville, that in 1790 John Adams was severely criticized for saying that irrational rather than rational forces shape history. There's nothing new in this mess. Let's hope that, like the British, we'll muddle through somehow."

The wind battered at the limousine, shaking the heavy car on its suspension. Morgan opened the car door and the cold penetrated like a storm of spears. He looked at Anna, resigned to her presence, and said, "It's time to go."

Together, bowed against the gusts, they made their way to the waiting C-130.

Chapter Thirty-nine

There are times when fear drops below the threshold of the mind; never beyond recall, but far enough from the instant to become a background. Moments of great exaltation, of tremendous physical exertion, when activity can dominate over all rivals in the mind, the times of exhaustion that follow these great moments; there are occasions of release from the governance of fear.

—WYN GRIFFTTH, EX-ROYAL WELSH FUSILIER

MORGAN FELT THE HERCULES begin its long descent. Even at 41,000 feet, the turbulence had remained severe until the aircraft flew out of the cold front and its parade of line squalls marching across the continental United States and Canada. The front was only the first of several, driven by the winter jet stream. It was a weather pattern that assured a lethal distribution of radioactivity over the northeastern United States if the Russian warhead could not be defused. Morgan realized that he had begun to distance himself from the scene. It was a familiar feeling, one he always experienced in the face of imminent danger.

Anna had fallen into exhausted sleep, wrapped in blankets and curled into the canvas sling seat like a little girl. Morgan's heart stirred as he watched her. He admired courage, and there was no lack of it in Anna Neville. She had other qualities he could barely name, and some he could not stand, but she had qualities he knew were precious in a woman, even if that sounded chauvinistic. Anna Neville was remarkable.

He looked out of the small window. Occasionally the wing-tip could be seen in the darkness of cloud and storm. The ride grew smoother, for the moment less violently turbulent. Morgan turned to look back at Arkady Karmann, expecting him, too, to be asleep. But the Russian sat staring out at the night, his face pale, that grotesque hook resting on the back of the seat ahead. He hadn't responded when Morgan tried to question him about the design of the fuse. The man was totally uncommunicative and steeped in Slavic melancholy. Will we ever know him, Morgan wondered. We had better begin. Our lives depend on him.

Such high stakes involved in this, he thought, higher than any I've ever experienced before. Each one on this plane is coping in his or her own way. Karmann was a scientist. Did his lethargy stem from illness mixed with guilt? Or was that melancholy a kind of Valium that took the sharp edges off reality?

It could be the end of *our* world, Morgan thought, thinking of the men and women aboard the aircraft. This band of strangers, all skilled in the arts of war, most of them volunteers, brought together to save lives. Morgan looked at Anna's sleeping form again. I wonder if she'll see our little group as saviors, or if she will never perceive that we're all on the same side, just using different techniques, he thought.

He rubbed his leg gingerly. It was still sore to the touch, but what part of his body wasn't these days. He slept poorly, ate quickly, feeling that he needed every minute available so he could be fully briefed by the Canadian scientists in charge of their part of the mission. They had got themselves organized with a speed that did them credit, though the personnel mix of their team made Morgan uneasy.

There were four ocean divers from Maritime Command, two from the Department of the Environment—which Morgan regarded as a nice touch, considering that the CCND had demanded, and had been granted, permission to send two observers on the press plane.

From that Morgan assumed what had been a leak to the *Washington Post* when they left Andrews was now a torrent. A Colonel Newton of Air Command assured Morgan that the airspace at what they were calling Site X would be rigidly controlled by a Canadian component of the North American Air Defense Command.

What did that mean, Morgan wondered. A continuous air cap? Or just a squadron of Magisters warning interlopers away? The Air Command colonel did not elaborate.

He did inform Morgan that the Russian team—composition unknown—was due in Montreal momentarily and would emplane for Site X immediately upon arrival in Canada. A dozen of Dr. Doris Waymer's special diving suits—all that existed, save for the precious pair aboard the Hercules—had been loaded onto the Starlifter cargo plane, which would follow as soon as the Russians arrived.

"And, oh, yes, Colonel Morgan," Newton said, "there is a possibility—only a rumor right now—that your President and our Prime Minister will be arriving in Montreal the day after tomorrow. The fifth of December."

"Jesus Christ," Morgan exploded. "They aren't coming up here, too, are they?"

"There is some argument going on about that now in Washington. I hope it's only a public relations ploy. Your military and Secret Service are adamantly opposed, as is our military. The Canadian Internal Security Ministry is held by a Liberal member of the coalition cabinet. I understand the CCND is pressing him to go north and 'oversee' the proceedings. They feel that his presence would ensure that we warmongers do the right thing. I suppose they envision all of us jumping up and down in ecstasy at the thought of the missile exploding right before our eyes. Fortunately, the Minister would prefer not to be anywhere near—''

''At last,'' Morgan said. ''A man with some sense.''

''CIA informs us that the estimated time of detonation remains the same. December 7 at 0830 local time. Wasn't that the time of the Japanese attack on Pearl Harbor?''

''It was.''

''Someone had a nice sense of history.''

''What is the status of the press and television? Where are you quartering them?''

''Ah, the press and the telly. We've had an earful of demands for accommodations, but not so many firm reservations. We're cobbling together a tented enclave for them as far from the water as is feasible. They'll encounter a problem, though, one they may not appreciate. Electronic communications from Site X are very dicey right now—very stormy, you know. One press plane is weathering over here until this storm front moves on east. Another will depart early tomorrow if it's needed.''

''I suggest, Colonel, that you tell the newspeople that they'll have to work with a pool reporter, one who's come on our plane.''

''They won't like that much.''

They'll like it less when they find out the pool reporter is Joe Ryerson, Morgan thought. Well, he wasn't going to sweat that now.

''The Russians are also sending reporters. From Izvestia. Ah, the wonders of a free press,'' the Canadian said dryly.

''It's a peculiar world, Colonel.''

''But the only one we have. Let's keep it that way. Good luck to you, Mr. Morgan.''

''They're not really going to try evacuating the people downwind of us, are they?''

''The machinery is beginning to turn. Your FEMA people

are trying to help, but if you want my personal opinion, no one with any sense thinks an evacuation is possible. We are simply going to have to stop the bloody thing from detonating.''

At that point, the Canadian's voice grew thin. Morgan understood only too well. Each mile the Hercules covered through the ice and winds of the storm brought all aboard closer to a different storm—a mortal storm of fire and dirty radiation. What did Robert Frost have in mind when he wrote those lines about promises to keep and miles to go before he slept, Morgan wondered. Nothing like this, certainly. And yet, poets sometimes had the gift of "the long sight." Morgan's grandmother had believed that with all her Welsh soul.

What else did Frost say? Something apropos of the world ending in fire or in ice. Well, there was fire enough to set the world alight under the ice of Hudson Bay.

"You're looking very sad, Morgan." Anna regarded him sleepily from her nest of blankets.

Before he could answer, Avery Peters emerged from the flight deck and leaned over Anna to speak into Morgan's ear. "We're almost there. We just passed over Eskimo Point."

Morgan glanced at Anna. How would she react? Her husband and her former lover lay somewhere below, on the black, muddy bottom of a northern inland sea.

Anna threw off her blankets and looked past Morgan, trying to pierce the darkness outside the window. The air turbulence increased as the C-130 descended through layers of cloud and broke into clear air over Hudson Bay. This December, she'd been told, was much colder than last winter had been. The great bay and its surroundings would be in the hard grip of an early winter, with fewer polynyas and a great deal more ice. They must already be north of latitude 61. The Arctic Circle was nearer to their destination than the United States border.

She knew this land, one of cruel beauty. This was the region of permafrost. Here the hostile earth grudgingly accepted the

345

yearly blanket of snow and ice, and became home to the snow
hare, the arctic fox, and the shaggy winter-coated caribou. But
there was death under the ice, ready to erupt into raging fire
and poisoned steam.

"Look there," Morgan said, and pointed. "I think those
lights are on the *Trudeau*." Maritime Command had named
their big, costly, already obsolete icebreaker after Pierre Elliott
Trudeau. The problem with the icebreaker was that she was
diesel powered rather than nuclear, and therefore as much at
the mercy of the polar winters as any icebreaker built in the
previous century. The CCND had left its mark on the Canadian
outlook, of that there could be no doubt.

Now they could see lights lining a long dock, leading into
the water from the shoreline, some four thousand yards from
where the *Trudeau* and several smaller ships clustered around
her were anchored. Well back from the water Morgan could
make out three clusters of inflatable arctic emergency shelters,
large ones, and at least a dozen smaller ones. But of traffic on
foot between the encampment and the shore, or between the
shore and the ships, there was none. It looked as though all
operations had come to a halt. Time, Morgan thought. They're
wasting time, the one commodity in shortest supply.

The Hercules descended further, circling the anchored flo-
tilla at a thousand feet, then turning once again north by northwest toward Eskimo Point.

Anna loaded her cameras and rose to cross to the opposite
side of the plane, hoping to get a shot of the lights of the
settlement at Eskimo Point. Morgan moved over into the aisle
seat and glanced back at Joe Ryerson. He was surrounded by
airmen and soldiers, and not enjoying their company one bit.
No Ernie Pyle-type newsman is our Joe, Morgan thought sardonically. He wouldn't have been interested in slogging across
Europe and the islands of the Pacific with the troops. Possibly
wars seemed less righteous these days, Morgan thought. Or
possibly, newspeople now thought of themselves as citizens
of the world, with no sentimental bonds to one country, no

matter the color of the passport. Some stayed in the enemy's territory once hostilities broke out, posing before the cameras in the very spot that was to be targeted by American missiles. That might well muddy one's perspective.

The Hercules banked sharply under a layer of low cloud as it flew over the airstrip at Eskimo Point. The whole strip from one end to the other, as well as the taxiway, was brilliantly lit. Here at least they were not wasting time. Calculating by the number of lights bordering the runway, it was even shorter than Morgan had expected. Some twenty feet from the end was an Air Command Starlifter, bogged down in the muddy taiga. One wingtip rested awkwardly on the frozen ground, and an engine nacelle had been damaged. The Canadian pilots had discovered, obviously too late, that the strip at Eskimo Point could not accommodate a Starlifter. But the loading ramp of the damaged airplane was down, and a crew was at work assembling a large American helicopter, an MH-53J.

The C-130 made a single broad circuit of the airstrip, then settled into a steep final approach. Morgan watched the spoilers emerge from the wings like metal fences, steepening even more the Hercules' approach. At no more than fifty feet, the pilot flared the big airplane sharply, and a moment later the wheel trucks were on the ground, and the comforting sound of the tires rumbling over the uneven surface thrummed through the cavernous interior of the fuselage.

As the Hercules turned to taxi back to the half-cylindrical Quonset hut that served as a field operations office, Morgan could see the Canadian and American crew climbing all over the helo. At the moment the machine did not look as though it would be ready to fly in a week, let alone in a day. But crews working in places like this had a surprising record of successes.

An all-terrain vehicle driven by an Air Command enlisted man appeared beside the C-130, guiding it to its designated parking place. As the ATV swung in close to the fuselage,

Alfred Coppel

Morgan could see that the driver was wearing a radiation dosage badge. A big one.

Anna asked, "Is that what I think it is?"

"It is."

No sooner had the aircraft come to rest than the jumpmaster came down the aisle with kits, a requirement for all aboard before disembarking. The selection of equipment in the kits was not calculated to build confidence. There was a yellow plastic antirad suit, called a banana suit by those working in radioactive areas, a dosimeter, gloves and boots of light vinyl, goggles and fiber filters for nose and mouth, and a stack of paper hats, suits, gloves, and boots for keeping clothing free from any radioactivity around the camp.

"There's no reading outside, Colonel," the jumpmaster said, anticipating Morgan's unspoken question. "But a quarter mile closer to the shore the count starts climbing."

"Pass the word, Master Sergeant," Morgan said. "There will be a general briefing of all personnel at 2000 hours."

"Right, sir."

The rear ramp dropped with a crash. First off the plane, escorted by the air force surgeon and nurse, was Arkady Karmann. He was being treated as fragile and very, very valuable.

A squad of Canadian armed forces police appeared and took charge of a furious Joe Ryerson. "The little shit doesn't like that, does he?" Avery Peters had appeared at Morgan's elbow, and his voice was filled with satisfaction. "I'll go over straightaway to the helo and see if I can help. Christ," he said, zipping his parka as the wind blew through the open cargo door. "It's freezing here. I'm a desert rat at heart." He strode down the ramp and vanished in the direction of the wrecked Starlifter and damaged helicopter.

Morgan and Anna followed the Rangers and Special Ops men onto the hard-packed gravel parking ramp. The ground crunched underfoot, frozen to a depth of six feet. Banks of snow lay all around, soiled and unmelted in drifts and piles under the dark gray sky.

An Air Command major appeared and saluted formally. "You would be Colonel John Morgan. I'm Evan Harris. And you are Mrs. Neville? I've heard of you."

Anna aimed her camera at Harris and clicked the shutter. "No doubt, Major," Anna said. "I'm official, by the way. So please tell your men not to interfere when they see me taking pictures." Anna's voice was as cold as the wind.

"We all understand that," Major Harris said. "And may I say we are impressed by the hell you have raised, and damned grateful you did. I'm only sorry no one paid attention to you sooner."

"I'll need transport for Mrs. Neville, Academician Karmann, and myself," Morgan said. "How near to airworthy is the MH-53?"

"There's about four hours left to do on the rotor hub. It got bashed about rather badly when the Starlifter ran off the strip. Then there's another six or eight hours to install the floats," Harris said. "Don't worry."

"That thing in the bay goes off at 0830 hours local on the seventh, Major."

The Canadian's easy manner vanished, along with most of the color from his face. "Holy Mary, Mother of God. No one has bothered to tell me that bit."

"Your diving crew is on the ground in Montreal waiting for a team of Russian divers to join them. By the way, I heard a horrid rumor—"

"You must mean the one about the PM and your President being silly enough to come see for themselves. No problem. That was just talk."

"Good," Morgan said, with a great sigh of relief. "Now, can you take us to the commo section? I need to call Washington."

"That part, at least, is easy," Harris said. "It's all the rest I worry about."

Chapter Forty

The Kremlin/December 4

Comrade Stalin,

I am sending for your approval four lists of people to be tried by the Military Collegium:

List No. 1 (General)
List No. 2 (Former military personnel)
List No. 3 (Former personnel of the NKVD)
List No. 4 (Wives of enemies of the people)

I request sanction to convict all in the first degree (death by shooting).

—Yezhov, Purge Commissioner, 1937

IVAN YULIN, dressed in full security forces uniform and wearing all his old army and political medals, paused before the narrow pine door of the President's Kremlin retreat, the small office built for Boris Yeltsin facing the inner Kremlin garden during Yeltsin's tenure. Cherny, as Yulin well knew, was not self-indulgent. In fact, he was troubled when circumstances demanded that he exercise the privileges of his office. Yet Cherny did not always scorn luxury and perquisites. This ambivalence, Yulin thought, was surely sharpened by the certainty that he was being measured by some unreachable standard of purity and would eventually pay dearly for any human weakness. Whichever group succeeded Cherny in power, Yulin believed, sooner or later would hold Aleksandr Borisovich up to public obloquy. Possibly punishment, as well. Yulin also believed that Cherny was prepared for this fall from grace. It was, after all, the fate of all Russian politicians since Stalin.

The last twelve hours had been the worst in memory, both for the security forces and for Yulin himself. Pacing his office in the Lubyanka prison, he thanked God that he had never fully succumbed to Piotr Kondratiev and his grandiose blandishments, even when presented with the most sacred of Soyuz's royalist awards. He fingered the small white fragment of the cross, erected over the site in Ekaterinburg where the czar and his family were slaughtered and said to be miraculous. Should he—? No, he decided, it was too dangerous. He took the tiny piece of wood and smashed it, then threw it into the wastebasket. Nothing tangible now, nothing with which Cherny could hang him.

But who could ever have imagined that the commander of the security forces, under the cold supervision of selected officers—yokels, every one—of the Thirtieth Shock Army, would have to prove his loyalty to President Cherny by carrying out the arrests for treason of the entire hierarchy of the Soyuz movement? Yulin did not know General Kalinin well, but Aleyev and Suvorov were old comrades. Now Kondratiev was in custody and the entire Soyuz dream of a new, but old, Russian Empire seemed far, far away.

The arrests of the plotters must now be tempting Cherny to do as Mikhail Sergeivich Gorbachev had once done: to declare for himself the absolute dictatorial power to rule by decree.

Alfred Coppel

Martial law was always available, like a sword in a scabbard, on the books.

Ivan Yulin had been badly shaken by the shock army soldiers' insistence that he, a man far above them in rank, swear the oath of loyalty to the government that common soldiers swore on their enlistment day. These bumpkins were deadly serious and suspicious of everything and everyone in the capital. The question he needed answered was, did they behave this way because they were naïve and ignorant men or because they suspected his loyalty?

The chief of the Intelligence Directorate and the commander of Kremlin Security had been required to swear the oath as well. Never mind, thought Yulin bitterly, that Aleksandr Borisovich had never allowed either of them to carry out their duties properly. Yulin well remembered him saying, "I don't need three agencies surrounding me, keeping me away from the Russian people. I love them, and they love me." Sentimental slop. Who knew if it was really so? If given a choice between Cherny and Kondratiev, whom would the masses have chosen? For that matter, which one would *I* have chosen?

The President knew that Ivan Yulin was a member of an Old Guard that had served in the Politburo for many years before Yeltsin had begun to dismantle state and party. Cherny had chosen Yulin to preside at the dismantlement of the KGB apparat for exactly that reason. "Our new thinking must never allow us to forget the dynamism of the old regime," he had said, as recently as last year, to a session of the Congress. At the time he had made the speech, he claimed that the deputies should remember that though he was a "liberal," he was also the heir to all the power of the state, and capable of reprisals against his enemies. No one had believed him; in fact, they had laughed at him behind his back.

But a new phase in the long battle for change in Russia had begun with the arrests of Aleyev, Kalinin, and Suvorov.

* * *

The Eighth Day of the Week

YULIN TAPPED ON THE DOOR and waited for it to be opened by one of the shock army soldiers who now overran the Kremlin. Inside, he found Aleksandr Cherny standing at a frosted window, through which could be seen the snow-covered garden. In one corner of the room a porcelain stove radiated heat. In another, a table with the remnants of a meal stood. A samovar steamed nearby. To Yulin's surprise, a bottle of French brandy stood open. Cherny rarely drank—setting an example to the people, he called it, railing against the Russians' fatal addiction to vodka and other hard liquors.

Cherny turned. General Yulin was shocked at his appearance. He had aged perceptibly. He held a glass of tea in both hands, as though he required the heat of it to warm his hands, even in this stifling room. Without preamble, Cherny said, "We have captured the head of the beast, but there is worse to come."

Is he testing me, Yulin wondered. Is he asking for advice or only probing at my loyalty? Cherny's gaze was full of suspicion and hostility.

"Kondratiev strutted into the Spassky Tower with all the hubris and arrogance of a folk hero. After what the son of a bitch has done, I wanted to kill him with my bare hands." Cherny almost spat out the words. "How is it that the security forces did not warn me of his presence?"

"You must remember, sir, that the abilities of the former KGB are much degraded," Yulin said stiffly. "Some units are unreliable, and others no longer function. We are in the process of dismantling the entire internal security apparatus, Excellency—at your orders."

"Did Zenobiev brief you?"

"Yes, Excellency. But surely you can't believe Russian renegades planted a nuclear device in Hudson Bay? Or that it was done on General Kondratiev's orders?"

Cherny cut him off. "I *know* it, you idiot. Stop arguing and listen. We have less than a day and a half before the thing detonates." He slammed his glass down so roughly that it spilled some of its contents on the lace cloth. "I want you present when Suvorov, Aleyev, and Kalinin are questioned further, particularly when we examine Kondratiev," Cherny said, enunciating very carefully. "He must be under no delusions about your loyalty and the loyalty of our state security forces. Is that clear?"

Yulin nodded, trying to conceal his fears. When asked, he had refused to join the Soyuz conspiracy formally, but he had made no attempt to betray it. That single fact, that prior knowledge, of which Piotr Kondratiev was well aware, could cost him his life. In these circumstances, he, Ivan Yulin, must be more orthodox than the Metropolitan of Moscow, more chaste than the Virgin Mary. Death was ghosting through the Kremlin.

"Colonel Zenobiev—" Cherny began to issue an order. Yulin, startled, turned to see the provost colonel of the Thirtieth Shock Army in the room. "Are the prisoners here?"

"They are, Your Excellency." The colonel's voice echoed and reechoed harshly in Yulin's ears. The motherland had come far since the days when Stalinist gunmen stalked the corridors of power in the Kremlin. Nathan Abramov, now in a cell at Lefortovo (perhaps he would be released immediately?), often said about Russia that she took two steps into the light, then one and a half back into the darkness, wracked with suspicion about what the light would illuminate. Cherny, the almost foolishly benign liberal, was becoming a new Stalin before Yulin's very eyes. Somehow, some way, he must be placated.

To Yulin, Cherny said, "Are you aware that there are Soyuz street demonstrations in St. Petersburg and Gorkiy? A few thousand people, the militia say."

"I have not seen today's internal security precis, Your Excellency," Yulin said apologetically. It was true; he always left such things to his subordinates. What one did not know, one could not act upon. He was, after all, only a caretaker, not a policeman. Aleksandr Cherny himself had stated that his task was to dismantle the secret police apparatus, not to use it. But that was two months ago. An eternity.

Cherny's face was suffused with an almost unbearable melancholy. "Our world may vanish, Yulin, if Orgonev's device succeeds in detonating. The Americans and their NATO allies will retaliate instantaneously, destroying our cities, our beloved land, a thousand years of Russian history. Over. Finished."

"The West would not dare attack us, Excellency," Colonel Zenobiev spoke up bravely. What a fool, Yulin thought. Did he really believe that? Since the Gulf War, no Russian should doubt that an American President had the power to tilt the world into a holocaust.

"Do not deceive yourself, Colonel. The American forces are on alert," Cherny said, "and President Caidin knows that I have done the same with our forces. God forgive me, I could do nothing else. If the device in Hudson Bay actually detonates in the water, the last war on this earth will begin."

Yulin looked at Cherny in dawning horror. It is not a hoax after all, he thought. I thought it must be a hoax, that even Kondratiev would not threaten the very existence of our world with his Doomsday Device. I must gather my family, Yulin thought frantically, and get them into the bomb shelters under the Kremlin. Then he remembered that the shelters had been essentially abandoned. What supplies were still in them were old, the water stale, the rooms dirty and unkempt. It had been years since any Russian had actually feared nuclear attack.

There was a sharp rap on the door, then it opened. "The prisoners are waiting in the Spassky Tower, Excellency," an officer of the Thirtieth Shock Army announced.

Cherny arose and said, "Come, then, Ivan. It is time."

ALEYEV, KALININ, MARSHAL SUVOROV, AND PIOTR KONDRATIEV stood shackled against the side wall of the tower room, each with a guard. The table had been moved to the center of the room, and against the big upholstered chair reserved for the President a military Kalashnikov assault rifle rested. A sign of how the power had shifted, Yulin thought.

"Bring them to the table," Cherny ordered. "Seat them across from me. You, Yulin, sit beside me."

"I'd rather stand, sir," Yulin said, positioning himself to the right and behind Cherny. He folded his arms across his chest, head up, chin out, the very picture of integrity.

The prisoners were roughly shoved over to the metal chairs now four in number and pushed down into them. Their guards wore field kit and carried sidearms. The show of weaponry made Yulin caress the grip of the Makarov pistol in his uniform's polished leather holster.

"What now, Aleksandr Borisovich? I demand to be set free!" Marshal Suvorov growled irritably, still resisting complete surrender. "I have done nothing—it's all lies."

Aleyev, for once sober, and appearing much the worse for it, peered past Cherny's shoulder to look at Yulin and said, "Are you content? See what you have brought us to with your treachery!" He spat at Yulin's feet with great accuracy.

"How typical of you to try to put the blame elsewhere. You brought this on yourself with your fascist dreams," Yulin shouted defensively.

Kalinin ignored his fellow prisoners. He spoke directly to Cherny. "I joined Soyuz less than ten days ago, Mr. President. I was not involved in the initial planning, nor was I ever entrusted with any primary task. I—"

But Cherny was concentrating on Piotr Kondratiev, watching his reactions. The former KGB general said scornfully, "The hero of Afghanistan speaks."

Aleksandr Cherny said slowly, still looking at Kondratiev. "You are under sentence of death. All of you. But I would prefer not to take your lives. Tell me now how deep the rot has gone within my administration, and without. Who else is involved—what troops?" Kondratiev looked back at Cherny in silence, shoulders slumped in a fusion of willfulness and resignation.

The Eighth Day of the Week

"Siberia is out of style, I understand," Admiral Aleyev said. "Too bad, I might see some old friends there."

"For Russia, Piotr Ivanovich," Cherny said, almost entreating. Then, when Kondratiev continued his silence, he said heavily, "It is on your head, if the device detonates on December 7."

No one spoke. Kalinin and Suvorov don't yet grasp the full danger. Aleyev doesn't give a damn. Kondratiev's arrogance feeds his ego, and he still thinks he can win. Not one of them believes him, Ivan Yulin thought; they think he is too weak, too soft. But they will eventually talk, in Kondratiev's case if only to brag. They will admit everything. They will talk, and then those who dreamed of Soyuz's success will be lost.

I will be lost.

"How brave you all are with your schemes," Cherny whispered. "How clever. Cleverer than poor Milstein. Cleverer than I." He reached down beside his chair and lifted the assault rifle off the floor, handling it awkwardly.

Yulin watched with horrified fascination. *He won't do it. He can't. Men like Cherny don't kill.* Yulin searched the expressions on the prisoners' faces. They ranged from fearlessness to terror. Kalinin was weakening. And it would only take one to bring me to ruination, Yulin thought. He moved swiftly around the table behind the prisoners, motioning to the guards to step back.

As Yuri Kalinin opened his mouth to speak, almost without pause, General Ivan Yulin unholstered the service automatic at his waist and fired a bullet into the base of Kalinin's skull. In rapid succession, he shot Admiral Aleyev, then Marshal Suvorov, and finally Piotr Kondratiev.

The room exploded into bedlam. The prisoners' guards leveled their Kalashnikovs. Ivan Yulin threw his weapon to the floor, raised his hands above his head, and cried out, "I acted for Russia and for my President!"

Aleksandr Cherny looked at the carnage, unbelieving. As he sat, unable to move, a hand descended upon his shoulder.

357

Alfred Coppel

He looked up to see General Komarov, smiling at him, nodding his approval at Yulin's act.

"Don't worry, Little Father," Komarov said gruffly, and he seemed to Cherny to speak with the voice of all the generals and marshals who had ever served Holy Russia. "Don't fret. We," and he looked over at Ivan Yulin, "we will always be right behind you to do what must be done."

Chapter Forty-one

The Northwest Territories/December 5

Six months ago we estimated the number of people affected by Chernobyl's radiation to be near a million. But those figures appear to be far too small. It may be in the multiple millions.

Stories of incredible environmental radiation disasters and explosions are surfacing. . . .

A man who fought the fire at Chernobyl claimed, "When I started feeling sick last year, I came for medical help. . . . but they told me they could not help me because I was a volunteer and not assigned to put out the fire." Others told of leaking radiation surfacing from secret, underground reactors, which have since exploded. . . .

—LETTER FROM MICHAEL MARKHAM,
INTERNATIONAL RELIEF FUND,
IN NEZAVISIMAYA GAZETA,
MAY/JUNE 1993

EKATERINA MARCHENKA, more commonly known as Marina Suslova, sat on a hard metal seat amid piles of tied-down equipment in the cargo bay of a Canadian C-130. The air was cold and she could hear hail battering the thin metal of the airplane's fuselage. The crew had overwhelmed her with attention, dressing her in arctic gear, plying her with hot drink and tasteless food.

The other passengers, a motley troop of reporters and television technicians, including five other Russians, all men, had separated into cliques by race and by nationality. Marina recognized only a few faces among the Americans, familiar to her through Washington newscasts, but by and large it seemed that the first-line network people had not volunteered in great numbers for this assignment. I shouldn't wonder, Marina thought angrily. I should have been on my way to Moscow by now, only hours before the warhead was to detonate, to Moscow and safety. But the meaning of the order from Kondratiev had been inescapable: Do whatever you must do, anything. *But liquidate the traitor Arkady Karmann.*

The failure at Bethesda rankled. No one at the hospital had questioned her credentials as Vincent Kellner's assistant, Camilla Varig. It wasn't all her fault, she thought self-righteously. Kellner's Marine colonel had been a step ahead, and he had taken Karmann out of the hospital before she could act. Too bad she hadn't been able to meet this Colonel Morgan, persuade him that his interests lay on the other side. What a double agent he would have made, she thought.

As for her present situation, posing as a media person was nothing new to Marina. She had used the same cover several times, and had never been compromised. Nevertheless, she was relieved that she recognized none of the other Russian journalists. Once aboard the Canadian Air Command Hercules, she had maintained her distance from the newspeople by flirting with members of the crew, asking silly female questions to account for her presence among them. The five Russian reporters regarded her with suspicion and perhaps talked about her among themselves. But being Russians, they said nothing to any of the Canadian authorities on the plane.

Marina could only hear snippets of conversation among the reporters. The major topic was, of course, the pending disaster in Hudson Bay. But the Canadians were questioning the Russians about rumors of a purge in Moscow. The Russians were taciturn, but that didn't mean the rumors were not true.

For heaven's sake, Marina thought angrily, be specific, damn it. Are you talking about a purge of Cherny's government by Kondratiev and his followers? Clearly, she must kill Karmann as soon as possible, and then she could return to Moscow in triumph. The piss-faced reporters now ignoring her would be interviewing her, kissing her ass. *But,* if the Cherny government was purging itself of those who belonged to Soyuz, that was a different situation. Well, Marina thought ironically, as she had warned Evangeline, nothing was forever. The dangers of the secret game were in part, at least, its rewards.

A camera team from South Africa seemed deep in murmured discussion about how ad hoc this entire operation appeared to be. It was, and that was a fact, Marina thought. It was interesting to note that the "efficient" Westerners, Canadians and Americans, when caught unawares, were as capable of incompetence as anyone.

But for the first time in her life, Marina Suslova had to acknowledge, she was truly afraid. All the toys she'd had at her disposal while she was in Washington, all the authority she had wielded, had disappeared into nothingness. It was as if the power she had been enjoying now was balanced on some great scale by the prospect of imminent death, a flaming, flashing death. Her options were limited and her time was short.

She wondered where Evangeline was at this moment. It had been a treat to watch her face that last night, when she realized the end had come. The last word Marina had received from her aide at the Mount Alto compound was that Camilla Varig, Vincent Kellner's personal assistant, was on the run. The gossip about her disappearance was all over Washington. But where could Camilla run to if she decided to disappear? Had she planned for this contingency? Marina knew just how much money Camilla had received—she knew to the penny, since she had disbursed it. And, at least to date, Camilla hadn't any other grateful patrons; Marina had made sure of that. No, Camilla didn't have enough money to be impervious to danger, only enough to indulge her childish greediness. She would run for a day, a week, perhaps even a month. But she would be caught, indicted, and convicted. Vincent Kellner's few friends would mourn and, at the same time, his many enemies would rejoice in his downfall.

Marina craned her neck, trying to hear what the Englishman from the BBC was asking about this rumored purge in Moscow, but the noise in the plane made it impossible. She could have screamed in frustration. Who had been supposedly purged, and by whom? She tried to comfort herself by deciding that Soyuz must have succeeded. For one thing, Kondratiev's orders had not spelled out his usual organized listing of specific tasks to be carried out. His only requirement was the elimination of Karmann. He had not even specified the method she should use. The most important hour of his life was swiftly approaching, and Piotr Kondratiev was ready for it. For the first time, she wondered what sort of quasi-czar Kondratiev would make. She shuddered, and not entirely from the cold that pervaded the interior of this rattling tinplane.

The Canadian officer had explained that the press plane would land at the Eskimo Point airstrip, close to the hastily built camp at Site X, today, December 5. They could look around everywhere at the camp except in the most dangerous areas and interview those who were involved. An official briefing as to what the device was and how it could be defused would be held tomorrow, December 6. Those who came in today, plus any others scheduled to leave prior to H-hour, would be flown out of the site to safety in the very early morning hours on December 7. That was the day the Russian and Canadian diving teams were to attempt to deactivate the mechanism.

December 7 was also the day, ironically enough, when Joe Ryerson would become the one pool reporter, remaining on site to write the story. Hearing his name mentioned when the reporters were boarding the plane gave her quite a turn.

I should have had someone take care of him—he might talk, admit all the telephone calls that allowed her to trace the movements of the Neville woman and Morgan after Grau's death. No, she decided. If Ryerson disclosed his indiscretions, he would be finished in journalism. Still, Marina crossed her fingers. His very presence at Site X showed a side of Ryerson Marina had not known existed. The man she had known must be terrified—she could hardly credit him with having noble motives. But with the key to fame and success in his grasp, he dare not refuse to use it. So, Marina thought, Ryerson's equation was: Greed and Ambition neutralize Fear.

She resolved to avoid him as much as possible while she was there. An encounter with him would require far too many explanations to the officials, and it would be dangerous. But then, it would be dangerous for Ryerson to acknowledge that he knew her, as well. If Ryerson pressed the point—She momentarily considered killing Ryerson either before or after killing Arkady Karmann. What do the British say? "In for a penny, in for a pound." She even felt a premonitory thrill at the thought of isolating Ryerson, seducing him, killing him.

But caution warned that the potential hazards were far too great. Better simply to avoid him. Then, if Fate decreed that Ryerson was meant to die, let the Device kill him.

JOE RYERSON, exercising his limited freedom of movement in the camp, stood in the muddy track camp officials called a street and stared malevolently at the computer tent complex. Morgan and the others had been working in there for an hour, but the Special Operations troops acting as police had refused him press access. His mind darted, back and forth, between worry over any possible danger he might be in and anger over his continuing ignorance as to what the Ops people were planning.

The irony of Ryerson's situation was that his mortal enemy, Vincent Kellner, had assured his fame and fortune by making him the pool reporter for this venture. It was the chance he'd always dreamed of. Naturally, he was getting what pool reporters usually got: a mess of restrictions. It had been that way in the coalition's press pools in the Gulf, and it appeared it would continue to be so forever. The stupid public didn't understand how difficult it made his job; they had simply refused to respond to the media's complaints during the war against Saddam Hussein, or after it was over.

Thus far, Ryerson had learned two things. One was that the Canadians and the Americans knew there was something dangerous in the water, on the bottom of Hudson Bay, allegedly placed there by the Russians. The second thing he'd learned made his hair stand on end: that whatever the thing might be, it probably was radioactive, as evidenced by the antiradiation kits handed out so freely, even to him, by the crew chief on the Hercules. He'd almost forgotten to wear his protective paper zipper suit when he started on his rounds today. He pitied the crew that had to collect them and dispose of them at the end of each day here.

It was obvious that the whole camp's level of anxiety was rising in geometric progression. He kept hearing talk about December 7, just two days from now. Some sort of deadline? And Morgan and his buddies had hinted that the thing in the water was a nuclear device. That was impossible, of course, if the Russians had been the culprits. Aleksandr Cherny's government would never do such a mad thing. The Americans—well, possibly, but that would be so unutterably stupid that even the American military brass couldn't be guilty.

And yet, what about Captain Hook, the Russian who looked like the wrath of God come to earth in mortal form? He was with Morgan and Neville and Peters all the time, but not of their little group. Ryerson had never seen them in intimate conversation. In fact, they hardly spoke at all to one another. But the Russian obviously had some special knowledge of the missile, or the officials wouldn't be deferring to his judgment all the time.

Major Harris, the Canadian who was Ryerson's only contact with Operations, had assured him "it," meaning the radioactive something, would be taken care of. That was the Canadian's own phrase. Taken care of. At least he didn't say "piece of cake." Jesus, Ryerson thought, I have this huge story on my hands, but I don't know exactly what "it" is, how "it" got here, or how they mean to take care of "it." Other than that, I'm in clover. And the little voice in the back of his mind kept asking, would Joe Ryerson, or anyone else on the site, survive to tell it?

Head retracted into the hood of his GI parka, he walked restlessly through the blustery wind and falling sleet toward the airstrip, unwilling to retreat to his tent, sure that he was missing some vital item of news. That's just what that bastard Morgan would like me to do, I'll bet, he thought, go to my tent and stay there. When he reached the edge of the airstrip, Ryerson could see the big helicopter, its crash damage repaired, ready to fly. The big Starlifter remained bogged down at the end of the steel mesh runway. Nothing sadder than a big bird like that, sitting wounded and unflyable. He walked along the side of the runway, his footsteps crunching in the snow, peering out at intervals from under his hood.

I wish I could go out to the water tomorrow, Ryerson thought morosely. He had heard talk of bringing in a research submersible to look for "it" when he first arrived, but had heard no more of it—that idea appeared to have been discarded. Dammit all, he thought, you're operating on guesswork. Go back to the beginning, and see if you can put a few pieces together.

It had all begun a year ago, really, when the Nevilles' plane crashed. Every event since then—Anna Neville's crusade, Grau's death, Morgan's revenge killing of the skinheads in

San Francisco—they all stemmed from that one happening. At first, he had agreed with Grau and Neville and the CCND that the crash had been caused by an American missile. Now that he thought about it, however, Marina Suslova had been very curious, too curious, about Morgan and Anna Neville and their travels. When he'd called from Frisco to tell her what had happened, she'd turned coy on him about the Bronco. When she got cute it meant, he had learned over time, that she probably already knew more about events than he did. That fact made Morgan's insistence that the Russians had shot down the Nevilles' plane more plausible. Not probable, just yet, but plausible.

Damn, Ryerson thought, if only I'd paid more attention, done a bit more digging before I came up here, checking out the movements of American ships and so on. But no, he'd been sunk in a funk over his bad luck in losing his job. Now that he was on the scene, he'd better be alert, receptive to every bit of information he could gather.

The camp now held almost five hundred people. Not one of the fuckers wanted to spend a few minutes with him, explaining just what the hell was going on. He kicked the edge of the airstrip's steel webbing viciously with his boot.

An armed sentry stood at the ladder to the improvised control tower, watching Ryerson's approach with a typical kind of blank stare. They all hate me, Ryerson thought, aggrieved; I'm the token journalist, and I'm not to be trusted. But it was only partially personal, he knew. The military's distrust of the media had begun long ago, in Vietnam—a war that most military men, some of whom were now generals and admirals, thought was lost when the press made a separate peace with the enemy and turned public opinion against the war. Considering the manner in which the politicians ran that war, choosing bombing targets in the Oval Office and micromanaging every move the military made, Ryerson thought, the accusation was unfair. But there it was, and that resentment had continued to color military thinking.

He kicked out again at a grimy drift of snow and turned to go back to his tent when he heard the sound of engines over the wet warbling of the wind. It was the unmistakable sound of another C-130 Hercules approaching the camp. It must be the press plane. The sound, together with the hope he might finally learn something from the newcomers, soothed his anger, and Ryerson turned back to wait for the plane to land.

The Special Ops soldier approached him and said stiffly, "That's far enough, Mr. Ryerson. The airstrip is off limits."

Ryerson gritted his teeth. "Is there any rule against me just standing here?"

"No, sir. Just so you go no farther."

"Thanks for nothing."

"Mr. Ryerson, sir. You aren't wearing your dosimeter badge." The youthful face under the blue beret was earnest. "It should be worn at all times, sir."

"So I forgot," Ryerson said. Stupid kid, probably scared out of his wits at being here. Then he looked more closely at the dosimeter badge on the soldier's uniform. The reading reflected a low level of radiation exposure. He blurted out in alarm, "There's something hot out in the bay, isn't there?"

"You must get your information from Major Harris or Colonel Morgan, sir. Orders."

Not for the first time since he had arrived, Ryerson wondered if he'd had the best of his bargain with Kellner.

A Hercules appeared just under the low clouds, leveling off for final approach, lights on in the murk. The big plane landed, rolled to the end of the strip, and turned onto the taxiway, coming to a stop near the low control tower. As Ryerson watched, the rear cargo door opened, and the ground crew ran out to help the aircrew begin their usual tasks of unloading gear.

An aircrewman emerged from the plane's cockpit door and fastened a ladder to the side. From the cantonment area a Hummer came racing through the mud and puddles to draw up with a flourish just at the bottom of the ladder. Ryerson recognized the ubiquitous Major Harris, who swung out from behind the wheel of the Hummer and trotted toward the plane to greet the motley score of bulky, bundled figures disembarking.

Ryerson counted the bodies getting off and snickered a little. Not too many brave souls, I see, he thought. A lot fewer than I figured would come. Four-by-fours and Hummers congregated to carry away the mountain of television equipment and baggage coming out of the rear of the plane.

As he watched the reporters disembarking, the one at the top of the ladder just emerging from the plane threw back her parka hood, looked around, and smiled at the person just below when offered a helping hand. Ryerson drew in his breath, almost in shock. It was Marina Suslova. What in God's name was she doing here? Was she looking for him—had she followed him all the way to this misbegotten place? Did she know that he had, so to speak, spilled the beans about her activities in Washington? If so, she could be damn dangerous.

Ryerson's heart was beating rapidly and he was sweating in the icy air. He drew back into the shadows by the tower, confused as to how to act if Marina should spot him. But she seemed to be completely absorbed in greeting Major Harris, not in looking at either the landscape or its few occupants. Harris gallantly ushered Suslova into his Hummer, got into the driver's seat, backed up, and drove swiftly away from the strip toward the admin tents. Ryerson winced as the Hummer's lights sought him out momentarily where he stood by the tower. For some reason, he was convinced that Marina had seen him and recognized him in that split second as the Hummer passed. Her gaze had lingered, looked away, and then on past him, as though he were a total stranger. Ryerson's gaunt cheeks paled. You bitch! I fucked you upside down and sideways, he thought, enraged, and you diss me?

There were a thousand reasons why it would be wiser if no one knew of any relationship between himself and Marina Suslova, not the least of which was that she worked for the

GKNT. But Ryerson could not bear the slight. He stood watching Harris's Hummer race back toward the cantonment area.

"We'll see," he murmured. "We'll see, won't we, you Russian whore."

Chapter Forty-two

The Northwest Territories/December 6

Thus, to date, the fear that all nuclear weapons would be unleashed if even one were used has meant that none has been used. This, however, is not to say that their existence has not affected the conduct of war. On the contrary, war has been revolutionized by them.

—MARTIN VAN CREVELD, *TECHNOLOGY AND WAR*

IT TOOK A LITTLE TIME to get everyone settled down so that the briefing could begin. Anna was talking to one of the photographers, swapping stories, comparing lenses. She was particularly interested in his Panasonic video camera—something about an MH stabilizer, Morgan thought the man said. Morgan had just come into the tent after another planning session and looked for her right away. He found her at the back of the tent, absorbed in examining the camera. Anna was animated in a way he had never seen her, confident, recognized, and admired as a fellow professional by her colleague in the business. Morgan was getting a glimpse of the real Anna Neville for the first time, Anna without all the emotional baggage that had so burdened her since they met just nine days earlier.

She caught sight of Morgan at the entrance, shook hands with the photographer, and headed toward him, smiling that luminous smile that made her almost beautiful. Oh God, Morgan thought, what have I got myself into? Of all times and of all people—He rubbed his eyes, weary, but so charged with adrenaline that he was unable to relax. He remembered reading a fantastic story long ago, by an Argentinean writer named Borges, about a man who had the experience of encountering everything in the world, all at once, even to seeing the circulation of his own dark blood. That's how it is right now for me, Morgan thought, dizzy with the enormity of it all. Anna's touch on his arm sent a thrill through him, and he smiled back at her, wondering if she could sense how he felt.

The Canadians running the show dimmed the lights and started up the videotape player. Morgan spotted Ave Peters and Arkady Karmann where they were already seated, and led Anna over to join them.

THE IMAGES EMANATING from the videotape player were repeated twelve times on the screens of large television sets that had been strategically placed across the far end of the large, shabby Quonset hut where the press briefing was being held.

The hut was crowded with men and women in heavy winter gear; the indoor air was hot, smelly, and humid. Outside, the gusting wind had dropped the temperature to minus twenty degrees Celsius, but the gale had also swept the sky of clouds. The stars shone with diamond brightness, shimmering and twinkling in the wind. A sliver of moon cast a pallid light over the frozen tundra. After a day and a half of delay due to the late arrival in Montreal of the Russian contingent, the Air Command Starlifter carrying the Canadian and Russian diving teams was reported inbound.

The Americans sat in a group toward the front, with Arkady Karmann seated between Ave Peters and Morgan, and Anna Neville on Morgan's other side. Joe Ryerson was not seated

Alfred Coppel

with them, but in the midst of the section in the rear of the hut reserved for the newly arrived press representatives. Although there had been room for more in the press plane, only some thirty reporters had flown in, including those from Russia, obviating the necessity for a second plane. Most of them were still complaining about the lack of a full briefing before their hasty departure for Hudson Bay.

When the American reporters, even those from television networks, had been told that much of their news was to be filtered through Ryerson, as Ryerson himself confided to Morgan before the briefing session, "The shit really hit the fan." And when they found out their stories couldn't be filed from the scene, but would have to wait until they got back to Montreal, the Canadians had a hostile, adversarial audience on their hands.

The Canadian Maritime Command officer, the media relations officer assigned to the remotely piloted vehicle team from the *Trudeau,* was interpreting the RPV's videotape on the monitors. Commander Amalie Hebert, a plain, solidly built young Quebecoise, spoke with a French-Canadian accent.

"You can see the deployed airlift from the deck of the *Trudeau* moving into position over the missile," she said. "Air Intelligence has determined that it is without question of Russian design, a modification of the Soviet SSN-18."

The members of the Russian news contingent, five men and a woman, received that statement with considerable skepticism. A young Russian representing Izvestia questioned Commander Hebert's assessment. "It seems to me that the missile could have been provided by any one of a number of nations," he argued. "China, for example. North Korea, for another. Or even Iran."

"Sorry, sir, I cannot agree. Only wait; you can see in the next sequence, when the RPV was close enough so that they could be recognized, the Cyrillic ideographs on the warhead," Commander Hebert said positively. "There, on screen now."

They all watched intently as the airlift on the RPV, a tube

372

about ten centimeters in diameter through which water was pumped at high pressure, had cleared mud and sediment from around the hull of the missile, which lay on its side in sixty meters of water. A hum arose from the audience in the hut at the sight. The five Russian men clustered together, arguing angrily among themselves.

Commander Hebert asked, "Any other questions, sir?"

The Izvestia man said sullenly, "No," and ruffled the pages of his notebook. After a few moments of silence, a television director standing at the rear of the hut amid the massed TV cameras asked if copies of the tape they were watching would be made available to the world networks.

Commander Hebert assured him that the tape was being processed for general distribution. Someone in the back of the hut said loudly, "Who the hell d'you think's going to be around to watch it?"

The hum in the room became a loud buzz, as the video continued. Its murky pictures were illuminated by underwater floodlights. At the head of the airlift could be seen a dark, sediment laden swirl of disturbed water.

"Ordinarily we would not use so gross a method of uncovering an artifact of value under water. But we are not constrained by archaeological standards here. Our intention is to present the divers with a clear area in which they can work tomorrow," Commander Hebert said, raising her voice.

"Question?" One of the American reporters was on his feet, waving his notebook. "Ron Blair, of the *Washington Post,*" he said. "The whole thing is very confusing to me. I've done a little research on Mrs. Neville's accident, and she apparently told the Canadian authorities about her plane being shot down while she was in the hospital. That was a year ago. Didn't you believe her? Didn't you even try to check her story out? And why didn't you start to deal with this missile sooner? One day seems to be very little time for the diving teams to prepare for so hazardous a mission."

The buzz became individual voices, agreeing with Blair,

Alfred Coppel

demanding an explanation, and then a blur of questions, shouted out at the briefing officer.

She raised her hands in a plea for quiet. It took several minutes before the group obeyed her request. "That is true. The plane carrying the divers has been delayed for various reasons, mainly weather. If you have a complaint about that point, I suggest you take it up with the Lord, Mr. Blair. He makes the weather, not I."

"But surely, a day or two here would be prudent while the divers study the conditions they'll face—And you haven't answered my question about Mrs. Neville's accident."

"Mr. Blair and ladies and gentlemen, please quiet down, or you'll get no answers at all. If you will examine the release prepared jointly by the Department of Defense and the Department of the Environment and read it carefully, you will see that the device was originally intended to deploy in space as a pulse weapon, destroying, or at least crippling, communications on the whole North American continent. As for your other questions, I am a sailor, not a politician, so I will refrain from making some very obvious judgments. But now the point is that the warhead will detonate tomorrow at 0830 local time if it is not deactivated." Commander Hebert's manner was calm, but her face was pink with suppressed anger. Morgan could see she had been well trained for her job. These lions would have a hard time chewing her up and digesting her.

For a moment, the room fell absolutely quiet as her listeners absorbed the import of her words. The disdain in Commander Hebert's voice was evident. "You in the press needn't worry. You will all depart on the press plane at 0600 hours for Montreal. After that, media coverage on the scene will be handled by Mr. Joseph Ryerson as pool reporter. There will be no, repeat *no*, live television coverage."

The already edgy reporters began to complain all at once, and soon the room was in an uproar, until someone who was watching the television screens surrounding them yelled out, "Shut up and take a look," shocking them into relative silence. They turned to watch the questing vacuum intake tube of the airlift working on a long sedimentary ridge in the sea bottom caused by the missile's slide toward deeper water. Wherever the tube touched, an instant depression in the sediment was formed, as silt was sucked into the airlift. Now they sat transfixed, watching as mud and debris were drawn up from the bottom of the bay and the rotting white carcasses of fish swirled, spun, and then were consumed by the searching mouth of the airlift.

Morgan was watching an even more important item, the heads-up readout of a radiation counter, superimposed on the upper right-hand corner of the picture. The count hovered near 2,200 roentgens. The water flowing through the airlift tube was lethal, and few watching knew how deadly. Nuclear radiation exposure was measured in millirems, and U.S. law limited it to no more than 5,000 millirems of radiation a year. This count was 400 times that level.

But the RPV officer brought the counter to general attention, and her voice reflected her respect for the presence of the enormous killing force lying in the silt at the bottom of the bay. "Judging from the bottom traces and a radiation trail detector," Commander Hebert said soberly, "we conclude that the missile was originally deployed closer to shore. And from intelligence supplied—very late, I must say—by the U.S. Navy, we conclude that the device was emplaced last December." She turned an angry, but contained, glance on Arkady Karmann. "This information has been confirmed by one of our Russian experts, Academician Karmann, as was the preset time of detonation. More on this later, Colonel Morgan?"

"Definitely later," Morgan said. Washington and Ottawa had been undecided about the advisability of letting members of the joint task force know of Arkady Karmann's part in the deployment of the device. Among the Canadians present at this briefing were local people, Inuit, who were suffering personal tragedies caused by the plutonium contamination in the water. With tensions this high, everyone in officialdom was concerned for the Russian's safety. Keep it quiet, they had decided, for now. Afterwards—well, who knew?

Karmann's primitive prosthesis lay in his lap. Like the mark of Cain, Morgan thought, unforgivable and unforgiving. Even if he should survive this deadly errand, Karmann would carry that mark until the end of his days.

Commander Hebert stopped the tape. "If you will look at the upper right area of the frame, you'll see a damaged metal protrusion. Academician Karmann confirms it as a component of the erecting system, which has failed catastrophically. There are two others like it, buried in the bottom silt. In other words, the missile was initially deployed in a horizontal position, and after a programmed time interval, it began its move into an erect firing position. It is difficult to say if it ever achieved erection—"

The tension had grown to the point that several people laughed uncomfortably, and one gross wag in the press corps made a vulgar comment. Amalie Hebert looked at him coldly and continued. "If it ever reached an upright position, which is doubtful, at some later time the lifting mechanism collapsed. Very likely internal power to the gyroscopes fell below the required limits and the device toppled, causing it to roll and slide into deeper water. It now rests at a depth of sixty-one meters."

Hebert nodded in the direction of the Americans and said, "For our American press colleagues, that is about 120 feet, or sixty fathoms. Not a dangerous depth, as such things are ordinarily measured." The smile faded. "But then, we do not find ourselves in an ordinary situation, do we?"

Her audience was quiet, recognizing the difficulties in defusing the device the divers would encounter. She restarted the tape, only to stop it again two dozen frames on. The airlift had cleared away much of the silt at this point, and the curving flank of the missile was exposed, revealing obvious damage. A long opening in the metal skin curved around and down into the muddy bottom. The hull was badly breached, the interior corroded by salt water. The interface between the missile and the warhead was a shambles.

A soughing sound, something like a groan of anguish, came from the group.

FROM HER SEAT at the rear of the Quonset hut, Marina Suslova watched the back of Arkady Karmann's almost totally bald head. He must have been exposed to an extraordinarily large dose of radiation aboard the *Pravda*. His hair had fallen out in an odd pattern. Why wasn't he dead now? He looked so ill that he must be running on sheer force of will. Die, damn you, Marina thought, and I can escape this hellish place.

Commander Hebert caught her attention as she pointed a laser light at the tape frame. "You can see that the original design flaw in the system that damaged the power source was probably made much worse by the fall. The interface is badly shattered." Now a light from the RPV shone directly into the opening in the metal skin of the missile. The interior of the device revealed a tangle of metal plates, cables, and printed boards. The steel containment of the nuclear power source for all the missile's ancillary devices—the inertial navigator, the various clocks, the imploders surrounding the warhead, and the timers that had been substituted for the failsafe trigger locks—lay in a salt-corroded mess.

"Now you are looking at the source of the plutonium contamination," Hebert said. "The plutonium in the water does not come from the warhead. There, the metal is pure, machined into two fitted hemispheres that must be exactly compacted by implosion before a chain reaction can begin. The contaminant in the water is plutonium oxide from the power source. When used as an energy source, plutonium in this form—dust, actually—is convenient to handle, but *very* dangerous. Twenty or more years ago, a Cosmos satellite fell in north central Yukon. The extent of contamination was never fully admitted to the public by the Trudeau government for diplomatic reasons, but it was substantial. Plutonium oxide is, plainly speaking, deadly. The divers, both Russian and Canadian, are volunteers who have been fully informed and understand the risks involved. As does Dr. Karmann.''

The assembly stirred, and a murmur went around the room. Avery Peters, sitting directly behind Morgan, muttered, ''Better you than me, Ivan. After all, it's your baby.''

Morgan glanced at Karmann. The Russian sat so still that he might have been sculpted, his eyes on the Canadian officer, his pallor and his half-bald head betraying how ill he really was. It must be sheer willpower holding him up.

Anna clutched at Morgan's hand with her icy one, her eyes still fixed on the screens. At her touch, Morgan again felt a sexual urge more powerful than any he could remember. She felt it, too; he could read it in the tenseness of her body, the tightness of her grasp. When death comes sniffing around like a jackal in the night, the urge to affirm our place in life becomes almost overwhelming. *We will be lovers again before morning.* She knew it as well as he did. A sheen of perspiration lay on her upper lip. The scar on her face was white, etched against the warm flesh tones of her skin. Wisps of hair clung to her damp cheek. Outside the wind raged and rattled the fabric of the old Quonset.

Commander Hebert said, ''That's all the videotape that actually shows the missile. I urge you to be sure to take all precautions when walking outside, and be sure to dispose of your paper suits properly. I must tell you that we have already had two cases of radiation sickness, primarily because of carelessness about wearing protective clothing. The names of the men afflicted are Leading Seaman Reese and Lieutenant Muldoon, both of the Environmental Monitoring staff. Their white count is up sharply and they show the classic symptoms of radiation sickness: fever, diarrhea, weakness, nausea. We are prepared to care for casualties, of course, but only on a temporary basis. The plan is to fly cases of radiation exposure to the closest large hospital, which is in Winnipeg, as quickly as we can. From there, they'll be transported to a unit specializing in nuclear medicine.''

Marina Suslova sat up straighter, her mind made up. This whole affair was more than she had bargained for. Had Kondratiev sent her here to her death? She would do her best to carry out his wishes, but she *must* be on that press plane leaving at 0600 tomorrow.

What was happening in Moscow? She was afraid to ask the Western reporters for fear they would wonder why she didn't know, and she couldn't ask the Russians. Damn Kondratiev, damn them all, what had gone wrong? A deep anger stirred in her. She felt sweaty, uncomfortable, and pushed her hair away from her damp forehead with both hands. Was she too warm, or was it fear?

The audience had grown increasingly restless with the end of the briefing, gathering in small groups, comparing notes. One of the reporters asked Commander Hebert, ''When are the divers expected?''

She raised her voice to be heard by all. ''The divers arrive at 2130 hours. Weather permitting.''

''Fuck the weather,'' murmured Ave Peters. He was right, of course, Morgan thought. The diving teams were being flown in on a Starlifter, an aircraft already shown to be far too large for the primitive steel mesh strip. And the plane was coming—and would land—regardless of the weather. The warhead in the bay offered no options.

Major Harris took over from Commander Hebert, thanking her for ''a superb job of briefing us all.'' She nodded with relief and headed for the table in the corner holding a giant coffee urn and stacks of paper cups.

Harris said over the din, ''Please, please, ladies and gentlemen, I realize we are all concerned about the arrival of the diving teams, but Ops informs me that the Starlifter is on time and not encountering too much bad weather. But this is the Northwest Territories, after all. I suggest you television people set up now at the airstrip. You will want good photos of the

379

Alfred Coppel

people who will be diving tomorrow.''

Anna, who had been refusing any interviews, sat slouched in her chair behind her three companions until the noisy group of reporters and technicians had pushed their way out of the hut. To Morgan's surprise, Arkady Karmann stayed as well. When their little group walked out, he went with them, saying, ''I think I try to sleep for few hours.'' He raised his steel hook in mock salute. ''Mrs. Neville, gentlemen,'' he said politely, and strode off.

Ave Peters said, ''You know, they call the hotdog stand in the middle of the Pentagon's courtyard Ground Zero. Always gets a big laugh when you show it to the tourists. It doesn't strike me so funny tonight, somehow.'' He sighed. ''Well, three's a crowd. See you first light.'' He waited a moment, then followed Karmann.

Morgan and Anna stood in the icy wind, looking at the northern stars.

''So beautiful,'' Anna whispered. ''So cold. So close.''

Morgan put his arms around her and held her, feeling the warmth of her body under the heavy parka she wore.

She asked, ''Do you need to meet the aircraft coming with the divers?''

Morgan shook his head.

Anna said, ''They gave me a tent to myself. Come.''

THEY UNDRESSED QUICKLY and stood in the half-light that shone through the Dacron fabric of the tent. In spite of the biting cold Morgan held Anna by the shoulders and said, ''Wait. Let me look at you.'' As if it were for the last time, he thought.

She stood with her hands at her sides, her face lifted to his. He ran his hands down her flanks. He could feel the ribs under her skin, the flare of her hips, the soft, fleshy curve of her buttocks and thighs. He drew her against him, feeling the soft breasts of a mature woman against his skin. Such a human thing, lovemaking, he thought. When we are most threatened, hunger for life takes this form and we are back at the beginning.

He picked her up, left forearm under the bend of her knees, right arm about her body, hand spread to the swell of her breast. Even in the icy air of the tent there was a sheen of dampness on her skin, her belly spasmed with a near orgasm. It was more than simply lust, although it was certainly that. It was sexual hunger, terror held at bay, an anger at fate, a need to *live*. He felt himself risen, hard as a spear as he sank to his knees on the open sleeping bag.

She stretched out on her back, spread her thighs, palmed her pillowed breasts. He kissed her, tasted her skin, mouthed her nipples, cupped her buttocks. He felt a driving need to know every part of her before the darkness fell. There was no speech. None was needed. They functioned at the deepest level of ancestral memory. Men and women had coupled this way behind the embers of the cave fires while the tigers and dire wolves hunted in the night.

Anna encircled him with arms and legs so that he slid into her vagina without guidance. A hot, urgent thrust into the depths of her. She strained against him, her calves against his buttocks driving him into her deeper, deeper still. He heard her cry out and the night, the world, everything, began and ended here. Even if sunbright death should suddenly blossom on the seafloor, they had this. They were alive, right now. They were human.

At midnight, Anna, lying tight against him in the sleeping bag, put a thigh over his so that he could feel the warm dampness of her mons.

Morgan kissed her scarred face. He began to make love to her again, slowly, then with increasing desperation. There were eight hours of darkness left. So little time.

Chapter Forty-three

The Northwest Territories/December 7, 0215 Hours

The worst friend and enemy is but Death.

—RUPERT BROOKE, "THE SOLDIER"

ARKADY KARMANN SAT on the edge of his cot listening to the regular breathing of the two navy corpsmen who shared his tent. They were large men, apparently with little imagination, supremely confident that even here, even now, with the Device counting steadily down a kilometer from where they slept, they would survive whatever came. They had been peacefully asleep since midnight, when they had rolled in from the Canadian lines, smelling of whiskey and sex.

The only effect of the bomb in the bay on the men and women in camp was a prodigious urge to fornicate, Karmann thought scornfully. If they thought the act of screwing was going to assure the survival of their genes, their species, they were mistaken. Even if they did live, if the bomb was defused, chances were good that their progeny could look like some of the Chernobyl babies. Or was he faulting the others because he felt too ill for any such activities?

He looked again at his watch. It was now 2:15 in the morning, on the seventh day of December, the anniversary of the Americans' "Day of Infamy." He was restless, ready to dive right now. The plane from Montreal was late, five hours late. I only hope, Karmann thought, that the crew coming in are capable divers, able to take over if the effort is too much for me, or rather what is left of me.

What had become of Captain Krasny? Karmann pictured in his mind his last glimpse of Krasny as he was dragged aboard a Cuban gunboat just as *Pravda* rolled into its last deep dive to the bottom of the Caribbean. One year ago, such a long year. Wherever the bastard is, Karmann thought, I wish him torment and a lingering death. No fate Karmann could imagine could be bad enough for Captain Krasny.

Karmann closed his eyes and with his left hand held tight the steel frame of the cot, feeling the edge press into his flesh. The prosthetic hook grated against the metal when he moved it, reminding him of that late afternoon on the Rosario Bank, where he left a part of himself in the belly of a shark.

Now Karmann tried to remember Ekaterina Marchenka. One of the young Canadian corpsmen had slipped him a note from her. A classmate of his all those long years ago, her message had said. He had observed her from a safe distance when she arrived, and her face had stirred his memory. If Marchenka was the girl he was thinking of, she had earned her high grades in the professors' beds. Her father had been a mid-level party functionary. Was the handsome woman with the Russian press contingent the girl he vaguely remembered? He could not recall any sign that she had had any interest in journalism, or any other academic subject. It would have been out of character for that girl to risk her life.

Yet she was a countrywoman and he owed her the courtesy of a meeting if she wanted one. The other Russians all looked to be wet behind the ears. None of them had requested an interview. They seemed to be more interested in when the press plane left than in talking to a sick man. Karmann tried to get up, lost his balance, and fell back onto the cot. He held his breath, but the Americans snored on.

He came near to weeping at his physical weakness. And, Karmann thought, my mental state. I hadn't realized how near I am to the brink of despair. I am ill and disheartened, he thought, and I have lost any real hope of survival. The Device has already killed Arkady Karmann, Karmann the drunken fool, who decided, when offered the chance to join the crew of the *Pravda,* that any job was better than no job at all. I was wrong, and because of it, I am dead. The plutonium I ingested aboard the *Pravda* is my death. But perhaps I might be comforted, having my last words with a countrywoman. Perhaps I can tell her something of what is in my heart, my sorrow and my guilt. I simply cannot speak when I face Morgan and the other Americans. The words will not come out.

God, but it was cold.

His heart labored in his chest, and he tried to take a deep breath. A yearning of almost unbearable intensity suffused him. He tried to remember how it felt to be healthy, to draw air into undamaged lungs, to feel red blood in strong veins and arteries. How I wish that I could go home, home to Russia, to die there, rather than here in this wasteland.

Karmann gathered the sheaf of notes he had made while he had been studying drawings of the systems inside the Device and put them into his briefcase. Bad weather lessened their chances of success, good weather strengthened them. The diving teams should have been on hand two days ago, studying the site. But the crash of the original Starlifter, whose crumpled corpse lay at the end of the steel runway, had frightened the Canadians into delaying one day while the engineers lengthened the runway a pitiful few meters because the ground under the mesh was so swampy. And then the Russians had not arrived in Montreal until another ten hours had passed. Enough of what had gone awry, Karmann thought. If they will follow my instructions, we can defuse the bomb.

He lay back on the cot, trying to rest, until 0230 hours, then rose and quietly prepared to leave the tent, pulling on his USAF parka and a new set of the awkward paper suit and boots. It's too late for me, he thought, but I should wear them to spare my tentmates the same type of death. This was an odd hour for a meeting, but then, the press plane left in three hours. Marchenka probably had chosen it because it was the only convenient time for her. He stepped out into the arctic night.

The fall of wet sleet and soft snow had stopped, and the sky was partially clear of clouds. Thank God for that, he thought. The first good sign. The plane could land more easily. He felt a little ray of hope. Arctic stars shone with a peculiar winter intensity. The drifting clouds parted, and Orion the Hunter dominated the zenith, his belt of diamonds—the birthplace of stars, the astronomers said—glittered with a hard, cruel light. For a moment Karmann stood with upraised eyes, looking at the starshot vastness. How easy it was at such a moment to assess the works of man at their true value. He stood as in a dream staring into a past so distant he had no means to estimate it. The light striking his eyes had left the dimmer stars a million years ago. In the presence of such grandeur, how could he, or anyone, believe that what was happening here was important?

He walked slowly down to the makeshift dock at the water's edge. Out at the anchorage, the sodium vapor deck lights of the *Trudeau* and the working platform gleamed bright yellow, out of place on that icy sea. A Canadian sailor on guard stepped from his shelter and challenged him. "Who is it?" Then, recognizing him as the camp's weird "tame Russian," he said in surprise, "You're up very late, Dr. Karmann."

"I need ride to icebreaker." He knew better than that. "I need a ride to *the* icebreaker," Karmann said carefully.

The man said doubtfully, "Nothing's going to begin out there for another two hours. Everyone's worn themselves out clearing the missile for the divers."

"I need to go there, please," Arkady insisted. "I have re-

Alfred Coppel

membered important information, necessary to make measurements before morning. Divers will be here in an hour, and I must tell them.''

"Well, all right," the sailor said doubtfully.

Arkady felt suddenly weak and very tired, almost disembodied. As he looked over at the deck of the icebreaker, for a moment he could see a girl, a young girl waving at him, beckoning him to come to her. It is my sister, he thought, and at first tried to wave back. But it couldn't be Ilena, he thought in confusion, it was not possible. She had died of meningitis at sixteen, when they lived in Leningrad. Am I dreaming?

Karmann squeezed the steel hook at the end of his arm with his good hand, causing sharp pain. Stay alert, Arkady, he thought. You have no time for memories. Stay awake and meet a beautiful Russian woman with whom you have an assignation.

Overhead the clouds were closing in again, darkening the night.

"Get aboard the *Zodiac*," the sailor said grudgingly. "I'll run you out to the *Trudeau*."

MARINA SUSLOVA FELT she had been waiting for hours before she saw the two men get into the *Zodiac* and leave the jury-rigged jetty. So much depended on whether or not the note she had written piqued his curiosity enough to get him out here at this hour. He would never recognize the name—Ekaterina Marchenka was the cover she always used when posing as a journalist. From this distance, it was hard to be sure that Arkady Karmann was the passenger. "Come on, you bastard," she breathed, watching the little boat's progress across the water. "I don't have much time."

Marina stood on the working platform in the deep shadow between a tied-down portable generator and a stack of spares for the RPV. Much of the platform was empty, garishly lit by banks of sodium vapor lights powered from the nearby *Trudeau*. The circular metal deck was rusted and uneven, showing

386

the scars and wear of twenty years' hard usage. It had been towed to Eskimo Point from Winisk, in Polar Bear Provincial Park, three hundred kilometers to the south. The tugboat that had brought it was long gone, dispatched south to safety.

She had hung back at the end of the journalists' final night tour of the icebreaker. The executive officer had been busy answering technical questions from the reporters, and she could see that he was exhausted. The rest of the reporters were bored and anxious to check on the Starlifter's new arrival time, exasperated that the plane carrying the divers was so late. It had been easy to slip away when it was time to board the *Zodiac* to return to shore, hoping that in the dark, and in his present state, the officer would not count heads. She could use one of the small craft moored to the platform to escape from this empty, abandoned deck when Arkady Karmann had been dispatched to his fate.

Above Marina's head, the flank of the *Trudeau* rose into the night like a steel cliff. Fenders fashioned of pairs of huge truck tires squealed softly to each other as the wave action moved the ship and platform. Now the brilliant gleam of stars had vanished, leaving a wet, icy darkness. Another cold front was moving east across the Northwest Territories to the bay, bearing with it a promise of more nasty sleet storms and blustery winds. She could only hope that the weather wouldn't delay the departure of the press plane.

Marina scanned the perimeter of the work platform again. It was fully a hundred meters in circumference. The supporting gear for the remote vehicle was stacked near the gangway to the icebreaker, as was the large suction pump that powered the airlift. The Canadians had done their work properly, all right. The missile was clear of the bottom mud. It lay directly below the platform at a depth of nineteen meters. Fallen, damaged, leaking plutonium into the water—and still very much alive. I simply must get out of here, she thought, suppressing a feeling close to terror.

Now Marina could hear the burble of the approaching *Zo-*

diac's outboard. The watch on the *Trudeau*'s bridge was unlikely to challenge. The *Zodiac* had made several trips to the platform since the briefing. One more would not attract attention.

From inside her parka Marina took a slender, silenced Colt Woodsman. She ejected the magazine and inspected the bullets. Twenty-two long rifle bullets, express loaded, with hollow points. Silent, powerful for a light gun, and deadly at close range.

A last quick glance at her watch: 2:40 now. Ample time. The Canadian Hercules on which she and the others had come was departing with all "unessential personnel" at six o'clock. Organization, Marina thought. The cardinal virtue.

The murmuring *Zodiac* reached the platform and she heard the exchange between Karmann and the boatman, Karmann telling the sailor that he would signal across when and if he needed to be picked up and returned to shore. Then Karmann climbed onto the deck alone.

Marina was wholly concentrated on her task now. Piotr Kondratiev had told her all about Arkady Karmann, a man who claimed to be Russian, but who was really a German and a dirty Jew at that. It stung her pride that she had failed so signally to kill him the first time. It was Karmann's fault that she was here, damn him, she thought angrily. It was his fault that she was not in Moscow, safe in her own bed, ready to enjoy the fruits of Piotr Kondratiev's triumph and ascension to power. She cradled the assassin's weapon to her breast and waited as the *Zodiac* pulled away, heading back to shore.

When Karmann seemed to hesitate for a moment, she moved forward out of the shadows to catch his eye. "Arkady Karmann," she called out in a low voice, speaking in Russian. "Over here. I am waiting for you." She gripped the Colt as thought it were a part of a lover. "I have something special— a surprise for you, countryman."

Chapter Forty-four

The Northwest Territories/December 7, 0250 Hours

*Soviet science did not fail, it was betrayed by so called
scientists who were unwilling to take the risks needed to
grasp world leadership. We loyalists were forced to
work with inferior minds and materials. Now, even our
proud name is to be taken from us.*

—MIKHAIL ORGONEV, IN HIS LAST SPEECH
TO THE SOVIET ACADEMY OF SCIENCE

JOE RYERSON STOOD SHIVERING in the shadows of two huge
water tanks placed just behind the dock's jerry-built guard
shack. The giant hoses attached to the tanks on the water side
were for the purpose of washing any radioactivity off the divers the moment they came out of the water, and before they
went into the decompression chamber on the *Trudeau*. The
wind had risen. He could hear its eerie sound over the chug
of the generators. The cold burned his eyes. Ice crystals, wind-
driven, shone eerily through the pools of light from pressure
lanterns placed at intervals on the dock.

For Ryerson the scene was all too familiar. He could have

been looking at the farmhouse from the barn on a stormy night, sent out to make sure the animals were safe before going to bed. Brought up in Wisconsin by his maiden aunt, a God-fearing woman who trusted no man, let alone one just into puberty, she had impressed upon him the icy hell he would be cast into if he indulged his carnal appetites, or any other vices he might encounter. The hellish flames preferred by most other religious people he had met had never struck him as half so terrifying as the thought of being thrust into some great ice cave and abandoned there, unmoving, for eternity. Was this the place, was this the time for Joseph Ryerson to meet the fate his aunt had prophesied so long ago?

He moved along the hilltop, trying to throw off the feelings of foreboding his memories had brought him. But it was damned hard to think of anything positive right now. For one thing, the plane bringing the divers from Montreal had not yet appeared, and H-hour was only a little more than four hours off. He knew that all the other reporters were heading down to the airstrip to wait for the plane. Interesting that Anna Neville, who had been blatting to the whole world a fortnight before, now refused to give interviews. Morgan kept a pretty close eye on her, and she seemed to like it.

Interviews with the diving teams were the last item on the agenda before the press plane was to leave. He should be there on the strip, but he felt uncomfortable with the other newsmen. Most had heard of his disgrace, for one thing, and tended to rag him about it. For another, they all resented his so-called favored role as the pool reporter. Favored, indeed, Ryerson thought. I'm the only newsman who'll be around when the goddamned device goes off. They'll all be home, writing my obituary. I wonder why that doesn't bother me as much as it should, he thought, surprised at his own equanimity. Is bravery catching? All these stiff upper lips around here must have gotten to me.

He had shaken off his own minder easily. The kid was exhausted and scared, happy to find a bunk in the press tent alongside Ryerson's so he could get some rest. Ryerson had pretended to go to sleep, then slipped away when the kid started snoring. Then he set to work trailing Marina Suslova. At a distance, of course. One of the crewmen on the press plane told him that the Russian woman was some kind of a reporter, and man, would he like to fuck her. The kid was still in that dazed state Ryerson knew so well, after Suslova came on loud and strong to you. It was a message no flesh-and-blood man could resist.

Then he had mingled with the Russian media people and discovered that there was no such person as Marina Suslova on the list of Russians in the camp. His informant, a young television technician, had told him that the woman he described was Ekaterina Marchenka, the representative of *Komsomolets Rusiya,* a former Ukrainian Young Communist publication now sustained at subsistence level by the state. "By the Intelligence Directorate and the security forces," the technician grumbled. "Or so most of us think. No one has ever read a copy of her magazine. We doubt anyone ever will."

Suslova had seen him following her, talking to the other Russians. Clearly, she knew he was here. And as clearly, she made it plain that she had no inclination of acknowledging that they even knew one another. He could almost hear her. "Do not be silly, Yosip. Neither of us has anything to gain by betraying the other. Actually, you have more to lose than I." Thank God she didn't know how much he'd told Kellner about her and Camilla Varig—fuzzed up, of course, to hide how involved he'd been with Marina.

She must have some errand here; she never did anything without a damn good reason. Her cover as a journalist was thin. But then she and her handlers probably hadn't had much time to create what the spooks called "the legend."

Ryerson had almost frozen to death waiting outside Marina's tent to see if she had any special mischief in mind. He had followed her to the dock, watched while one of the sailors from the *Trudeau* had ferried her out to the diving platform. Very soon his patience had been rewarded by the appearance of Arkady Karmann, Morgan's pet Russian, the gray-faced specter with the dramatic steel hook for a hand. The man who had flown north on our plane, with me and with Morgan and Anna Neville and the rest. The First Team, he thought proudly, the VIPs who had arrived from Washington on the Air Force Special Ops C-130.

What the hell was Karmann up to? And arriving so soon after Suslova. Here was a new angle, very suspicious. The two of them must have had a very strong reason to meet on the diving platform, the most dangerous place at Site X, and getting more so every minute it sits over that fucking missile. He had watched while Karmann argued softly with the watch, using his authority as *the* expert to overcome the man's reluctance, Ryerson realized. Then one of the dock guards had taken Karmann out to the diving platform on the *Zodiac,* left him there, and returned alone to the dock.

The platform was moored alongside the *Trudeau,* so perhaps Marina and Karmann had gone aboard the icebreaker. Doing what? Sabotaging the ship? It was due to leave at the same time the press plane left, to steam as far from the missile as was possible. Looks like two spies for the price of one, he thought ironically. Maybe Kellner and his boys are right, maybe the cold war isn't over. Ryerson shivered with cold and excitement, and his paper suit crackled loudly. A story—a good story—always affected him that way. It gripped his throat and his balls. Should he go now to tell that prick Morgan that the Russians were on the platform? He decided against leaving. Better stay and see when they come back, and where they go then.

He stomped his feet and waved his arms to keep warm. I'll never last, he thought despairingly. Even all this GI arctic wear isn't enough to keep out the cold. He inspected a large wooden crate on the ground between the tanks. It was empty. He pried at the board on the side toward him and found an opening large enough to wriggle inside, out of the wind. The board creaked loudly as he climbed in, but the guards didn't look in his direction, thank goodness—too much background noise. He fixed his attention on the dark shape of the diving platform. Goddamn, he thought, what the hell is going on? It was some time since Karmann had been ferried out there. There was no use whatever asking for information from the sailor on duty. Military cretins, Ryerson thought. Junior John Morgans.

Ryerson began to consider the idea of abandoning his watch. Who could know how long they would be out there? Was that a splash he heard over the hum of the generators? Had they thrown some key equipment overboard so that the dive couldn't take place? But that didn't make sense, if Karmann was going to dive with the teams. He decided to stay, at least a little longer. He'd give his eyeteeth for a cigarette, and of course that was impossible. No, it was stand and shiver until either Marina or Arkady Karmann came ashore. Then, if it was Marina, perhaps he could milk some real information from her.

AT 31,000 FEET the Starlifter Alpha Bravo shouldered its way through repeated ranks of thunderstorms. In the passenger bay of the big transport a team of sixteen Russian divers and half that many Canadians braced themselves in their seats fighting off airsickness caused by the extreme turbulence.

On the flight deck, Wing Commander Ian Ahlgren, Officer Commanding Number 7 Transport Wing, Air Command, flexed his aching fingers and made ready to take another turn at the Starlifter's controls. The autopilot had packed up well and properly thirty minutes out of Montreal and the wing commander and his first officer, Flight Lieutenant Mark Macpherson, had been alternating half hours battling the yoke and rudder pedals as the aircraft worked steadily northwest toward Site X.

It was 0250 hours on what had turned into one of the most spectacularly nasty nights ever to engulf the Northwest Territories. Fortunately, the Starlifter was not heavily burdened. It had been laid on rather than a Hercules because Air Command had not been told in advance by the Russians how many passengers and how much equipment they were bringing to Montreal aboard their great beast of an Antonov. That had been the good news. The bad was that there was already a Starlifter on the ground at Site X, the one the American cousins had managed to run off the steel mesh and bog down at the end of the strip. It made Ahlgren uneasy about his ability to land the big airplane on the primitive runway, and in this weather, without duplicating the Americans' embarrassing mishap.

Ahlgren checked the position on the inertial navigation display. Alpha Bravo was now forty miles southeast of her destination, flying in extremely turbulent air over southern Hudson Bay. Air Command Tactical Air Control's operator had been calling Alpha Bravo every ten minutes since the departure from Montreal. The much delayed departure, Ahlgren thought, with more than his proper share of anger and irritation. It was his experience that if an operation did not keep to its planned timetable, it was almost certainly heading for assorted troubles. Ahlgren was a firm believer in Murphy's First Law, the one that stated simply that if anything could go wrong, it would.

The late arrival of the Russians destroyed the timing of the mission immediately, and there was no possibility of postponing the flight for better weather. Ahlgren did not know why it was not possible, but his superiors had made it clear that more delay was not an option.

A series of brilliant lightning bolts flashed through the line of thunderheads just ahead. Hard ice and freezing rain slashed at the Starlifter's windscreen.

"Alpha Bravo, we copy you thirty-two nautical miles from Site X. Begin your descent now."

Supervision so precise, Ahlgren realized, meant satellite surveillance. The Americans were putting plenty of assets in this flight, he thought. That was reassuring. One could feel damn lonely in the storms above the Northwest Territories.

"Flight Engineer, reduce power twenty percent."

"Twenty percent, sir."

Neither Ahlgren nor Macpherson could take their hands off the control yokes to make the power reduction. Pilot Officer Winthrop, the token female member of Ahlgren's crew, performed the pullback and resetting of the throttles. Mary Winthrop was good at her job, but Ahlgren had never become accustomed to mixed-gender flight crews. Too near retirement to worry about it now, he thought. Six weeks to go and counting to be free of worries like tonight's.

Another voice came through the radio link. "Alpha Bravo, this is Site X approach control. We have you on radar. You are above the glide path. Correct and steer right to a course of 355 degrees true."

"Understand, 355 true," Ahlgren said.

Macpherson set the correction into the directional gyro. The Starlifter literally crashed through another line of high, icy squalls. The pilots could hear the airframe creaking and complaining.

"Call the stewards and see how the passengers are doing," Ahlgren ordered.

"As well as can be expected," Macpherson reported back. "Clancy and Johnson want to know if it's going to get rough."

"Fun-nee," Winthrop said.

"Not with two dozen sailors upchucking all at once back there," Macpherson said.

"Pay attention, Flight," Ahlgren snapped irritably.

"Alpha Bravo, this is Site X approach control. You are on glide path and on course. You are now nineteen miles from touchdown. Advise you will be landing east to west. The head of the strip is obstructed."

"Alpha Bravo." Thanks to our bloody Yank cousins, Wing Commander Ahlgren thought. His back and arms ached. He hoped to God they had someone at Site X capable of repairing the autopilot. He didn't fancy facing a return to Montreal horsing this heavy motherfucker all the way.

"Alpha Bravo, this is Site X approach control. You are slightly below glide path, on course, eight miles from touchdown. Do not acknowledge any further transmissions from approach control."

"Hold the bitch, Flight." Ahlgren released the control yoke and flexed his arms and shoulders for a moment, then clutched the yoke firmly. "Okay, I have her. Gear down."

The plane buffeted as the wheels extended, destroying aerodynamic integrity. Ahlgren said sharply, "Make sure all the sheep are belted in back there. It's getting rougher."

Pilot Officer Winthrop flashed the seat belt warning light in the passenger bay.

"Alpha Bravo, Site X approach control. You are below the glide path, repeat, *below,* five miles from touchdown. Be advised we are showing wind sheers on radar."

Ahlgren advanced the throttle quadrant to forty percent power. He turned on the landing lights, hoping for a sight of the ground. The altimeter showed 800 feet. The Starlifter was still in heavy cloud and rain.

"Lights ahead," Macpherson said. "Looks like a ship. It's the *Trudeau.* We're low, skipper."

The lighted ship, indistinct in the mist, disappeared under the nose. Ahlgren advanced the throttles to fifty percent, but the descent continued. Son of a bitch, Ahlgren thought. Ice. Lots of it.

"Alpha Bravo, approach control. You are too low. Do you read? Power up and go around again." The tone changed to one of sudden alarm. "Alpha Bravo, go around. *I say again, go around!*"

Ahlgren, a veteran pilot with ten thousand hours in the air, muttered a curse and swept the throttles forward to the stops. The aircraft surged forward and upward, until it struck the wind sheer. The right wing dropped steeply. The pilots reacted as one to apply opposite aileron so as to lift it, to level out. The wing was finally rising when the red obstruction lights on the grounded Starlifter appeared out of the rain and mist.

THROUGH THE INTERSTICES OF WEATHER and the noise of the electrical generators, Ryerson heard the whisper of an approaching jet airplane. The Starlifter carrying the divers, he thought. And about fucking time. That thing in the water must be ticking away the seconds, minutes, hours. It was damn late for the diving teams to arrive. The approaching aircraft was flying low, probably trying to stay under the cloud cover. Electronic navigational aids were not always to be trusted this far to the north. Ryerson reluctantly crept out of his sheltering crate and looked over in the direction of the airstrip. Three of the lights outlining the runway were not operational and had been replaced by barrels of oil, now set ablaze. The dancing red and gold flames contrasted sharply with the immobile cold white lights on either side of them. Windblown ice crystals swirled in the illuminations. Blinking red obstruction lights had been placed on the mired Starlifter at the end of the strip toward Ryerson.

The Air Command transport now swept over the *Trudeau,* whose lights reflected on the airplane's undersurfaces. Jesus, Ryerson thought, it's a big son of a bitch. No wonder the other one crashed. And I thought it was just evidence that the U.S. Air Force was incompetent. But a Starlifter actually in the air, this low and this slow in the dark sky over the camp, was a daunting sight.

As he strained to see the onrushing Starlifter almost above him, a severe wind gust sent him staggering back against the crate. Jesus, he thought, the damn wind has changed direction. He had never been the slightest bit interested in becoming a pilot, but he was an experienced air traveler. And that Starlifter was coming in to land east to west, directly over the grounded American transport. I hope the bastard knows just how short that strip is, Ryerson thought.

The big airplane's landing lights bathed the camp in brilliance as the Starlifter swept over the shoreline, jets hushed, wings rocking in the heavy turbulence. Now it passed over Ryerson's head.

The engines doppler-changed in pitch as the jet swept by. The pilot evidently intended to use every foot of the steel mesh runway. The airplane sank lower, too low. It seemed to Ryerson that he could have reached up and touched it. Suddenly a wing dropped precipitously.

Oh my God, Ryerson thought. He's going to hit the other plane. *Can't the bastard see it?*

He could hear the engines utter a gasping roar. The drooping wing began to rise. But not far enough.

First came a dull, tearing sound, then an ominous rumble, and the morning dark exploded into flame as the drooping wing of the descending aircraft struck the tall tail of the wrecked Starlifter. Ryerson watched in horror as both airplanes crumpled into a single, vast fiery ball of metal and burning fuel. There was a noise like a massive blow on a loose-headed drum. The fireball grew, expanded in two directions, diagonally away from the strip into the taiga, and skyward into a towering mushroom of oily fire.

Ryerson stood stricken, paralyzed, while all around him the tents and Quonsets of the camp vomited people and the emergency vehicles on the airstrip began their futile wailing chase down the broad path of fire that lighted the camp, the *Trudeau*, the platform, and the storm-troubled December morning.

THE SOUND OF THE EXPLOSION woke Morgan from a troubled sleep. The interior of Anna's tent was lit with a sullen orange light.

Anna sat up and said sleepily, "What is it?"

Morgan rolled from the cot and pulled on his pants, threw a parka around his shoulders, and stepped through the flap into the flame-lighted night. "Holy Mother of God!" The almost forgotten oath of his Catholic childhood was ripped from him by the pillar of fire he could see roiling up into the sky from the airstrip. There could be no mistaking what it was. The incoming Starlifter had crashed and was burning, lighting the surrounding area. The underside of the low, wind-driven clouds was a brilliant crimson, streaked with black.

From the main compound and the flight line came the familiar shrill and desperate clangor of emergency vehicles demanding the right of way.

Anna, in boots, parka, and a blanket, was suddenly beside him. "It's the plane from Montreal," she said in horror. "The two observers from the CCND who missed the press plane were to come in on it."

"Yes," he said absently. "And the divers." Well, that's it, he thought. The only ones left are Karmann—and me. A Hummer sped by, driven by an officer of the American medical staff, accompanied by three corpsmen. Morgan said, "I have to go find Karmann." He went back into the tent, reached for his weather gear, and finished dressing.

Anna followed and watched him, still clutching the blanket. "Does this mean—" She fell silent. I know exactly what this means. What more could go wrong, she thought. Are the Inuit right, and has this become an accursed place?

"Worry about that later. Dress."

"Yes. I'll get my cameras and join you."

Morgan finished dressing and burst from the tent, only to turn around, come back, and hold Anna tightly for a moment. She clung to him. There were no words.

The fireball burned fiercely just beyond the fabric of the tent roof, but no heat reached them.

"Damn it all, Anna," Morgan said past clenched teeth. "I love you."

Chapter Forty-five

The Northwest Territories/December 7, 0433 Hours

I asked our scientific program director why the most primitive and simple variant had been chosen. He explained that it was essential to demonstrate as soon as possible that we had a bomb; besides, we knew the size of the hatch of the Boeing that had dropped the bomb on Hiroshima. Our device could easily go through that hatch.

When the first successful test was carried out, everyone cheered up no end; people were embracing everyone around them, even Beria.... It was Beria's creation, made and serviced by thousands of slave convicts.... In the final analysis the project itself was designed to cause untold destruction.

—MATHEMATICIAN PROFESSOR LEV ALTSCHULER
IN LITERATURNAYA GAZETA

THE EMERGENCY MEETING IN THE ADMIN TENT was one of the few points of relative calm in the midst of the general chaos following the crash. It combined the characteristics of a wake

400

and a war council. Upwards of fifty people, most of them trained to respond to crises, had crowded into the enclosure to hear Major Harris, standing on a box for better visibility, tell them the facts. They were grim.

The Russian and Canadian divers had all died in the crash of the Starlifter, together with the crew. The only survivor from the plane was a badly burned woman, one of the two CCND members scheduled to observe events at Site X, both of whom had missed the press plane.

To compound the tragedy, many of the Russian and European newspeople had gathered to greet the Russian divers at the end of the steel runway, or at least so they had thought. There was no protection from the sleet and the driving wind there, and the small hut used as a control tower was only large enough for two. Anticipating that the plane would land at the opposite end of the runway, as theirs had, many in the group had sheltered from the weather under the wings of the grounded Starlifter, against the specific advice of the airmen on the scene. But the shift in wind direction had changed the landing pattern to the exact opposite of that experienced in previous flights. The onlookers were trapped, although a few tried to run. The pilot of the big plane, knowing it was too low to begin with, fighting the wind sheer, had tried desperately to skim over the sister ship, and failed. The descending Starlifter had flown into her sister ship and disintegrated into a ball of oily fire.

Some twenty media people were in the direct line of the crash, reporters, technicians, cameramen. Ten were dead at the scene, six were critical with burns and other injuries, and four were missing, either blown to bits by the explosion or unrecognizable as human remains. The ten who had not been at the runway were in the admin tent, very distraught, demanding to know what could be done about their situation.

"So now you all know what we know to date," Major Harris said somberly. "We think everyone in the Russian contingent died. We have so far counted six survivors of the press group, all in critical condition, mainly from burns. My executive officer has a list of the names available. There are four members of the press unaccounted for: Ballantine of the *London Times,* Higashi of *Asahi Shimbun,* LeClerc of Montreal Public Television, and Marchenka of *Komsomolets Rusiya.''*

''I think I speak for all of us who survived,'' said an American TV reporter, his face white under its pall of gray-black soot, ''when I say that we don't want to wait for six o'clock to get the hell out of this hellhole. We want to leave as soon as possible—the sooner, the better.'' His colleagues agreed vociferously.

Harris looked at the reporter in astonishment, embattled but dogged. ''It was my understanding that you were all volunteers, and that you knew what a dangerous situation you were coming into. Now, if there is still any doubt among you as to why we are here, I'll lay it out for you in plain language. Even if we could get a plane out now, which I very much doubt because the runway is blocked, we can't spare anyone to take you. You haven't asked, but I should tell you that twelve Canadian airmen also were injured and/or burned, including one in our temporary control tower. The tower itself is nonoperational at the moment.''

The wind flapped the fabric of the tent and made a drumming sound. Fire images still lighted the walls from the persistent flames outside. ''We are here in this godforsaken place because there is still a nuclear device in the bay, cocked to go off at 0830 hours. The loss of the divers hasn't changed that. Understood?''

An uneasy rustle ran through the crowd. One of the Canadian reporters asked angrily, ''Why didn't you take us out last evening, before the storm, Harris?''

''I was informed in no uncertain terms, by you and several of your colleagues, *Mr.* Bartlett, that you press people wished to stay as long as possible, right up to the attempt to defuse the missile,'' Harris said, trying to control his temper. ''If I'd had my way, you wouldn't have been here in the first place, getting in the way. We certainly had no way of knowing that the wind would change and the plane carrying the divers would crash. As Commander Hebert so succinctly put it, the Lord makes the weather.''

"You mean that the plane that brought us here is too big to land on the part of the runway that's not blocked? I want to get out of here. I have a story to file,'' the American reporter said passionately. "Are you sure that the press plane can neither land nor take off?''

"That's about it, sir.''

"I thought you said the divers were all killed,'' Bartlett persisted, in spite of Harris's rebuke. "Does that mean we're all trapped here, just waiting until that damned thing blows us to eternity?''

"The Russian and Canadian divers were killed,'' Harris said. "Fortunately, we have backup right here for the dive. Colonel John Morgan and Academician Arkady Karmann are prepared to go down and defuse the warhead in the bay. The remote vehicle team will support them with the robot.''

Standing near the desk beside Morgan, Anna closed her eyes.

"How do you spell the Russian's name?'' The questioner was immediately shouted down by his peers.

"You can't mean the guy with the hook? He's sick as a dog, for God's sake.'' The American reporter was not going down without a fight. "What good would he be?''

Harris said, "If our expert, GKNT consultant Academician Karmann, cannot dive with Colonel Morgan for some reason, we have his notes and sketches. We—Colonel Morgan and the support team—will do whatever is necessary to complete the mission here. In the meantime, those of you service personnel without specific December 7 assignments, please return to your quarters and await further instructions. The medical teams can use help, but wait until they come to get you. And as soon as the wreckage cools, we'll need people at the crash scene.''

He consulted with a member of the medical staff standing behind him and said, "We may run short of whole blood. The doctors can use blood for the burn victims, especially type O and type A. If you are willing to donate, please report to the medical compound. I think that's all for now."

Harris clambered down from the box and said to Morgan, "Have I forgotten anything?"

"Probably," Morgan said. He could feel the heavy beating of his heart as he contemplated descending into the dark, icy bay. "Like, where is Arkady Karmann, for instance. Hasn't anyone seen him?"

"No, damn the bastard's bloody eyes. We've got several people out looking for him. As far as we can tell, no one saw him at the runway."

"I can't believe he'd run out so late," Morgan said, "but then the man's an enigma. We still don't know why he joined the group of thugs. It's more obvious why he betrayed them."

Anna's hand closed on his arm. Morgan turned to her and said, "It would be better if you stayed as far away from the dive platform as you can. They really do need people to help with the injured." His face was strained, worried.

"No," she said firmly. "That was settled in Washington."

Commander Hebert appeared at the tent door and beckoned to Morgan and Major Harris.

Avery Peters had been silently watching the proceedings, standing with arms folded at the back of the tent. He strolled forward to Anna's side and asked her, "Everyone else is ready to run. Why aren't you?"

Anna held back an attack of angry tears. "You shut your mouth, Mr. Peters," she said. "You still don't know the first thing about me."

"So, the lady has teeth. I was beginning to wonder," Ave said. He paused, then went on, "It isn't that I don't like you, Mrs. Neville. It's that I'm a hardscrabble guy, like our friend, the good Colonel, there. I knew his dad, who died a hero, saving three little kids from mines laid by those simple peas-

404

ants in their black pajamas. We haven't any fancy, convoluted reasons to do this, or not do that, no excuses. I guess you would say we see things in black and white. I assure you that we see shades of gray, too. We live by simple rules. Wave the flag and we salute and charge."

He looked at Anna sideways, judging her expression. "You and yours despise us for that, I think. Maybe that's not the politically correct word. Bourgeois chauvinism is the current expression. Now, you, lady, you spend your time on some cloud up there out of our reach, chasing rainbows. We suffer wounds. You suffer moral dilemmas. Do you understand what I'm trying to say?"

"You seem to think I'm dangerous, twitching my ass and waving my tits at every man who goes by," Anna said passionately. "Look at me, damn it—I'm plain, I'm not beautiful. I'm going on middle-aged. And I really care about John Morgan."

"Unlike some of the others?" Ave said, one eyebrow raised. "Sorry, that was uncalled for. All I want is for Johnny Morgan not to get hurt, pardon my grammar. He loved his wife dearly, and since she died, he's been at loose ends."

"What was she like, Mr. Peters? What was her name? I've never had the time or the chance to ask."

"Joan. She was a sweetheart, a wonderful wife for a man in the service." Ave's voice was wistful. "A little thing physically, but strong on character. She couldn't have kids. When she went to the doctor to find out why—that's when they discovered the cancer."

Anna looked at him in astonishment. Were his eyes wet?

He went on briskly. "Enough of all that. Actually, I'm paying you a kind of compliment. You're staying at ground zero with us peons, not crying in your beer like those brave newsmen here this morning. Welcome to the world, Anna Neville."

Morgan had finished his discussion with the Canadians and came back over in time to hear Ave's last words to Anna. Then Ave turned to Morgan and clapped him on the shoulder.

Alfred Coppel

"I'll fly the helo just the way that son of a bitch in the White
House basement meant for me to do all along. And I'd better
tell you, this being no time for girlish secrets: Kellner asked
me to watch you and keep you in line."

Morgan's face paled with anger.

"He could see how the lady was affecting you. Listen, I'm
only telling you. You have a right to know, and I wanted it
off my conscience. Speaking of which, where is the little shit,
Ryerson? You don't suppose he and Karmann have run off
together, do you?"

Just then, Dr. Doris Waymer bore down on Morgan, ignoring everyone else in her single-minded concentration. "What
size are you, Colonel—six feet, 180 or so?" She inspected
him closely. "We have two antirad diving suits, one smaller
and one considerably bigger than your size. We'll modify the
big one for you, Colonel Morgan. Please come along."

"How long will it take?"

"An hour."

"Too long." Morgan rubbed his forehead wearily, fighting
off a headache. "I need time with Karmann's notes. Where
the hell is he? And what time is it now?"

They all looked at their watches, driven by a single instinct.
It was 0507 hours.

"Just a moment while I get some measurements, and we
can work on the suit while you're getting together with the
Russian. Cuts the time I'll need you in person in half," Dr.
Waymer said, whipping out a tape measure.

Harris fidgeted while Dr. Waymer used her tape, then insisted, "Karmann's notes, Colonel Morgan."

"Let's go look," Morgan said. The air inside the admin
tent was cold, moist, and pungent with the smell of fear. he
looked at Anna. "All right? Any regrets?"

"None," she said. "Not one."

JOE RYERSON STOOD, breathless, outside the admin tent. He'd
missed the briefing. The air was freezing, laced with snow and

rain, but he was drenched with sweat. He had spent the last three quarters of an hour searching for Marina, who now called herself Ekaterina Marchenka, and who was missing.

It was possible that she had returned ashore from the diving platform in the confusion following the crash on the airstrip, but if she had, Ryerson had been unable to find her. That placed her either on the platform or the *Trudeau,* and the ice-breaker had cast off for a destination as far away as possible an hour ago, after the plane crash. Surely Arkady Karmann wouldn't have gone with the *Trudeau,* and neither would Marina. There's no place for them to hide, he thought, without freezing to death in the process.

He had heard Harris paging Karmann repeatedly over the camp bullhorn. But judging from the number of times the message was being repeated, the Russian was nowhere to be found either. Ryerson was certain he had not come ashore.

And now, God help me, he thought, I have to gather my wits and act like I'm not scared shitless.

It was suddenly 0555 hours, just two and a half hours until blastoff. The time the press plane should have been leaving. Nothing in this whole damn mess has gone the way it was planned, he thought miserably. If Morgan really pulls this dive off, I'll owe him an apology. Not that I'd ever actually do it, but I definitely would owe him.

Where is Marina Suslova?

ANNA HUDDLED IN THE CORNER of the crowded troop compartment of the helicopter, wrapped like an astronaut in her cadmium-impregnated antiradiation suit. It seemed to her that it had taken much too long a time to load the helo. Five of the remote vehicle team were aboard, the others were on the platform operating the remotely piloted vehicle. Two of the RPV crew on the helo were wearing ordinary diving gear under their antirad suits, but she had heard Morgan giving them express orders not to enter the water. A large tank of fresh water took up most of the space near the door. A hose a good

twelve inches in diameter and connected to the tank was coiled
beside it. The two RPV crewmen would use a high-power
spray to wash the radioactivity off Morgan's diving suit,
when—and if—he came out of the water safely.

In the center of the compartment, already breathing oxygen
from a rebreather, John Morgan stood, swaying with the motion of the helo as it flew low over the water toward the group
of flagged buoys ahead.

Anna checked the radiation counters affixed to the padded
bulkheads of the compartment. They showed a steep rise in
gamma ray concentration, close to the point at which it would
fog her film. She realized that she was holding her breath, and
exhaled, trying to breathe normally, and stuffed her cameras
into their protective pouches without regret. She had pro-
claimed her right to take pictures of these heart-stopping moments "for posterity." Somehow, here and now, that boastful
right no longer seemed important. She didn't even know if
any of the pictures she had taken over the last few days could
be developed. And if the warhead went off, she and her cameras would be blown up. Even if they survived the blast by
some miracle, who would be around to see them?

She could catch only glimpses of Morgan between the bulky
bodies that surrounded him. It was hard to reconcile her tender
lover of last night with that armor-clad being making ready to
dive into the poisoned sea below. He loves me, she thought
with some astonishment. He said so. Why does that simple
statement make me so uneasy?

Anna's fears had made her initial concern about Arkady
Karmann's absence into an obsession. Everyone else was too
busy to be concerned by the disappearance of Arkady Karmann and Ekaterina Marchenka, they were all absorbed in the
task at hand. Morgan had been impressed by the scope of
Karmann's notes. But the Russian was gone. Was that a sign
that Karmann had lied about the missile? About where it was
and how it could be disarmed? God, I haven't had a headache

like this, Anna thought, since I woke up in the hospital all those months ago.

It was ten minutes before eight in the morning, still very dark, especially since the fire had almost burned itself out on the runway. Deep beneath this assemblage of hopeful souls was the damaged missile. Its microchip brain would decide in forty minutes if, in pursuit of its merciless mission, the warhead should be in the proper position over North America. Whether the warhead was twenty miles up in the stratosphere or fathoms below in the waters of Hudson Bay, if that electronic brain was satisfied, the warhead would detonate. And within seconds of that explosion, American warheads might retaliate over Russia.

The *Trudeau* had cast off from the platform and was steaming at flank speed away to the south. The icebreaker and those aboard were connected to the platform, the RPV, and this helo by microwave links bearing television pictures.

I still can't take it in, Anna thought, and I suspect none of us here really have the ability to imagine disaster on a thermonuclear scale. She thought about Ave's comments to her and flushed. *We have wounds. You have moral dilemmas.*

Jake and Sean lay somewhere on the muddy bottom of Hudson Bay very near here. And what if we had not flown over this spot, she wondered. The submarine would have slipped away unseen, its later loss unquestioningly attributed to a bungled mutiny. Poor Pierre Grau. Poor CCND observers on the Starlifter, one dead and one dying. In a way, Pierre and the whole group of well-intentioned activists would never have guessed the Canadian Committee for Nuclear Disinvestment had stumbled into a very high-stakes game—stakes higher than anyone could ever have imagined. Site X. What an uncommunicative name. The trail of individual deaths began here. The scale of impending death was much, much larger.

UP ON THE FLIGHT DECK Avery Peters struck the landing alarm. The air was bumpy and the water would be rough. He glanced out of the left-hand window at the jury-rigged floats and hoped they would bear the weight of the heavily loaded machine. A swim in the contaminated water would almost certainly be fatal to anyone in ordinary-issue antiradiation gear.

Ave was very uneasy, wondering if he had run out of luck on this one. He hated operations controlled by politicians, and it was clear that this one was tainted by politics from start to finish. It had the stink of Desert One. At least he wasn't listening to the President's voice in his ear, telling him when to go up and when to go down. If Morgan failed to deactivate the warhead, it was over. This part of Hudson Bay and an unknown number of miles of shoreline would simply boil away into the stratosphere, together with everyone on the scene.

The realization shook him to the core. He had always known that thermonuclear weapons were open-ended systems. It was possible to enhance a hydrogen warhead, raising the yield exponentially. Nikita Khrushchev, operating on the Russian peasant's dictum that more was always better than enough, had ordered some fifty- and a hundred-megaton devices built and tested at Semipalatinsk. The ensuing detonations had frightened scientists on both sides of the Iron Curtain so much that no warheads of over two megatons had been built since. Most weapons in the Russian and American arsenals were two to five kilotons in yield. The really big bombs had remained hidden and unacknowledged. Until now, Ave thought bitterly. These fucking fanatics had deployed a great fucking monster on the fucking seabottom, not more than a thousand fucking yards, give or take a few, from where he and a helo of fucking heroes were at this very fucking moment.

He brought the MH-56 into the wind and landed it delicately on the water inside the circle of red-flagged buoys. He was aware that it might well be the last helicopter landing he ever executed, and by goddamn, he wanted it to be perfect. It was.

* * *

The Eighth Day of the Week

THE RPV TEAM HEAD BANGED Morgan on the back and said, "Ready, Colonel."

Morgan felt the blow and heard him faintly through the dive helmet and hood of the Waymer suit. He nodded. "Right, Chief," he said. "Let's do it."

The clock on the bulkhead showed 0759, local time. For a moment he had a sick pang of uncertainty. Jesus, was there going to be enough time? Only thirty-one minutes. The time had been figured narrowly, in order to limit his stay in the contaminated water. Doris Waymer's creation was experimental, after all, but Dr. Waymer was positive it would protect him. He just had enough time, if everything went right.

Only it never did.

Murphy's Law applied to underwater work just as it did to everything else men did.

He looked beyond the divers at Anna. She was looking back at him. He could see her face, dead white behind the Lexan of her antirad suit's mask. She should never have been allowed to come back to this place of death, he thought. But, by God, he was glad she was here. He raised a gloved hand to her in a mute gesture of love, then moved toward the open door of the compartment.

Six feet below the edge lay the turbid water of Hudson Bay. The polynya stretched out toward the eastern horizon, a narrow reach of green water etched with wind-driven whitecaps. The *Trudeau* was out of sight.

It was exactly eight o'clock. Morgan, filled with a dread he dared not show, heaved himself awkwardly forward to the pontoon, caught his balance, then made a somersaulting entry into the murky, green water.

AS MORGAN HIT THE WATER, the helicopter, hovering over his head, simultaneously lowered a sonobuoy. Even through his arctic dry suit, the shock of the bay's temperature was greater than he had expected. His helmet light illuminated the area close around him. The thermometer strapped to his left wrist

411

Alfred Coppel

showed a swift drop from four degrees Celsius to minus ten.
By rights, the water through which Morgan was sinking now
should be frozen into hard, saltwater ice. He watched the thermometer and saw that the temperature rose slightly as he settled deeper into the sea. The visibility was very poor. Morgan
could see no more than two meters though the deepening green
murk. The work of the airlift and the remotely piloted vehicle
had continued throughout the night and morning, leaving the
sediment stirred into solution. He should watch for antipersonnel mines here. Karmann had said two sailors had been
killed by mine mishaps during the deployment. Goddamn it,
Arkady, he thought angrily, why did you come so far, under
such great difficulties, and desert me now?

Morgan kept to the agreed upon procedure exactly, following the anchor line of one of the flagged buoys that thrashed
about in the sea and wind on the surface.

Now the bottom of the bay materialized out of the murk.
Despite all the mud moved by the airlift, the sea bottom was
littered with pallid, half-eaten dead fish. Close by was what
looked like the rotting remains of an arctic seal. A small school
of fish darted about in the semi-darkness, scavenging on the
corpses. Morgan waved his arm, chasing them away. Welcome
to your death, you simple creatures, Morgan thought. See what
modern science has brought you.

Just as Morgan had begun to worry that Karmann had lied
to him, the long, ominous shape of the Device began to materialize ahead, in the gloom of two dozen fathoms. It was like
meeting a fabled enemy at last.

The elapsed time dial on his watch showed that he had been
underwater for three minutes and seven seconds. He felt a stab
of near panic. Time was slipping away, and he was just pad-
dling around, doing nothing here in the icy depths. For a fleet-
ing moment, he considered surfacing and demanding that Ave
fly them all as far from here as he could manage in the time
remaining. Too late, Morgan, he thought, even if you fry.
Would the troops waiting above break and run? Morgan

thought not. They were all professionals, all of them volunteers who knew the dangers before they agreed to come. The Device had to be met and defeated.

He was almost over the warhead now. The cold had worked its way deeper into Morgan's inner being. It was more than a physical cold, it was an awesome sense of what could happen here and what it would mean all across the planet. He had a momentary vision of Oppenheimer dramatically quoting the Bhagavad Gita in the New Mexico desert. Surely he had never envisioned the world ending on such an absurd note as this.

Morgan swam down to the broken missile. At six minutes and nine seconds elapsed time, his light pierced the silty gloom in which the Device lay, looking like an innocent section of pipeline, beginning nowhere and ending nowhere. Deep pits had been excavated around it at two-meter intervals by the airlift. In some of the deeper diggings, it appeared that he could probably, with some effort, pull himself under the missile to the other side for inspection.

"I am approaching the warhead," he reported to the surface. At this depth his voice was a burring drone, like the sound of an insect. He swam down into still deeper water, his fins disturbing the silt and whatever other detritus lay on the bottom. The bomb was indeed a modified SS-18 ICBM, monsters built by Nikita Khrushchev, deployed by Brezhnev. "We will bury you," Krushchev had said. When Gorbachev appeared, young, vigorous, we wanted to believe the world could be a better place, Morgan thought. The world gave Gorby a Nobel Peace Prize—and now the world was in a reality check.

"Colonel?" The sonar phone carried the acting divemaster's voice. "Everything all right?"

"Fine, Chief," Morgan said. "Stay cool."

As he swam down the length of the Device, he caught his breath. There was something primitive, savage, about a ballistic missile of this size, Morgan thought. It was a wonder that the *Pravda*, once it had been extensively—and imprudently—modified to make possible carrying this monster, could have put to sea, let alone make its long voyage. If the submarine had not been scuttled, it might very well have succumbed to the wounds inflicted on it by the idiotic architects of the Kola naval base.

Some fifty meters away, almost lost in the murk, a small, moored, antipersonnel mine swayed in the current. He ignored it. A light patch ahead captured his attention. As he swam toward it, the sonar phone burred the note agreed upon to mark the first ten minutes. Twenty minutes left now. The divemaster would now sound the sonar phone every five minutes, then in the last five, every minute, and finally, every second. Countdown to oblivion, Morgan thought.

The bitter cold of the water seeped through his heavy cold-water gear and the metallic weave of the Waymer suit. His legs felt leaden. The watch on his wrist stood at 0811, local time. Only Arkady Karmann had any practical knowledge of the nuclear weapon down here in the murk. Without him, the operation was a pure gamble.

Morgan made his way along the side. Just ahead, the missile's skin had crush-ripples in the thin metal. The collapse had bent the head of the missile to one side.

"Divemaster," he said into the sonar phone. "I have reached the warhead. I see the access plate."

The blurry voice in his ears said, "Four-oh, Colonel. Understand, you are at the warhead."

Morgan snapped on his second helmet light and detached the tool he needed. Bits of debris floated through the beam.

He began to work on the fasteners with the dzus wrench, which ordinarily was a simple matter of inserting a broad blade into a slot and twisting the spring-loaded fasteners. But they resisted his efforts. The American tool did not fit the Russian slots exactly.

He controlled his breathing with an effort and applied pressure more carefully, this time with more success.

The radiation card taped to his forearm was darkening all too quickly, moving though the dangerous to the lethal hue.

The Eighth Day of the Week

Dr. Waymer, Morgan thought, *I hope you knew what you were doing when you made this armor I'm wearing.*

He blinked and swam up to straddle the missile. The warhead was six feet in diameter and slick with the residue of a year in water. It was difficult to maintain his balance, but he freed the last fastener. The inspection plate fell out of the light and vanished in the gloom.

Inside the warhead, nested among pipes and braces, lay the digital windows of the timing mechanism, and they were just as Arkady had described them, over and over. But—no they weren't. God, he thought, the glowing digits had the right year and month, but the hours and minutes did not match those on his watch. The timer on the Device announced that it was 0821, *just nine minutes to detonation.*

The discrepancy shocked him into a momentary stumble. He lost his balance on the slippery metal and fell, twisting, two meters to the bottom, where he sprawled, disoriented, surrounded by a cloud of disturbed mud and sediment.

Chapter Forty-six

When the reactor of a Soviet nuclear submarine suddenly went haywire in 1961, Captain Nikolai Zateyev sent 22 volunteers to their deaths in a heroic struggle to save the ship. . . . The K-19 was a major technological advance for the Soviets, and engineers were so eager to launch the sub that they installed no backup cooling system. . . . During . . . construction, a welder dripped solder onto a pipe carrying coolant to the reactor, causing a microscopic crack. On June 4, 1961, while K-19 was hiding in the North Atlantic from Soviet diesel subs, the cracked pipe burst. . . . Zateyev organized three-man brigades of volunteers to work 5 to 10 minutes each. Protected only by raincoats and gas masks, they were ordered to weld a new cooling system. . . . Of the 130-man crew, 22 died of radiation poisoning, 8 within a matter of days, the rest within two years. "Right on the spot their appearances began changing. Skin not protected . . . began to redden, face and hands to swell. Dots of blood appeared on their foreheads, under their hair. Within two hours, we couldn't recognize them."

The Eighth Day of the Week

. . . People died fully conscious, in terrible pain. . . . The government . . . ordered them not to discuss what had happened, and their medical histories were falsified. Doctors wrote that they had "damage to the peripheral nervous system."

—MATT BIVENS, ASSOCIATED PRESS, 1993

AT AN ALTITUDE OF 412 NAUTICAL MILES above *the capital of Russia, a KH-13 satellite's imaging cameras zero in on the city below. It is night and Moscow lies under a winter storm. But the KH-13's infrared images are bright and clear. They are stored as digits in the satellite's memory.*

At 1729 GMT the KH is traversing the high American latitudes over Valdez, Alaska; by 1740 it is overflying Manitoba and Ontario. This KH makes no effort to record the activity in Hudson Bay. Other satellites, both American and Russian, are doing that.

At 1750 GMT, the Moscow images are downloaded to the National Security Agency station at Wallops Island, Virginia. They show no aircraft incoming to Sheremeteyvo, and all roads leading out of Moscow clogged with civilians, either in vehicles of all kinds or on foot and carrying their belongings, in the time-honored, war-weary tradition of twentieth-century Europe. The apparent evacuation sets off warnings at the North American Aerospace Defense Command Center in Cheyenne Mountain, where the banked supercomputers have long been programmed to watch for these exact images. The alert spreads to the Blue Cube Satellite Control Facility at Sunnyvale, California, and into the Gold Room at the Pentagon. Other military satellites are repositioned to overfly Moscow. The National Command Authority is alerted.

AS HE WAITED FOR THE HELICOPTER, sent by the President to take Vincent Kellner from the pad near his house at Fort Myers, he looked off to the northwest, then glanced at his watch.

417

He was on his way to an emergency meeting at Andrews Air Force Base. The President was due to take off in the substitute Looking Glass plane at nine o'clock, at the same time that Morgan, so many miles to the northwest, went into the water. The Joint Chiefs and a clutch of others vital to the governing of the United States were gathering at Andrews, preparatory to joining the President aloft.

The duty officer at the Pentagon had notified Kellner of the crash at Site X at five in the morning, Washington time, four A.M. at Hudson Bay. At 5:40 the Canadian Major Harris had called personally to report on the tragedy at the airstrip, telling Kellner that Morgan and Anna Neville were all right, but that Arkady Karmann was missing and possibly killed, along with many in the group of newspeople waiting at the airstrip when the Starlifter crashed. "Your Colonel Morgan is our last chance. He'll make the attempt to deactivate the nuclear device in the bay—alone," Harris had said wearily, the weight of the world on his shoulders.

I'm on my way to Andrews for the last time, Kellner thought. Everything I do, God willing that Morgan succeeds, will be "for the last time" in the next few days. Here in Washington, the sky was winter blue; the fitful, squalling weather of the last few days had turned into a beautiful cold morning, sharp and clear.

Just minutes before the call from the Pentagon had come the call from the FBI, from Charlie Fisk. Bless Fisk, Kellner thought, for having the kindness to tell me himself that Camilla Varig had been apprehended. I was right about her, at least in one way. She had come back to her apartment to claim her possessions, Charlie said. They'd found her with suitcases open, throwing everything in her closets into them with abandon, all her jewelry and a large sum of money in her purse.

I'll have to see her face to face, he thought, hear her out. I already know what she'll say—that I used her when I needed her, and left her to her own devices when I didn't. That I never loved her, and that she hates me. She's wrong about the second one, Kellner realized with a deep pang of regret. I did love her, as much as I'm able. Not so much for the sexual part, but for her keen mind. She could always keep up with me, sometimes get ahead, in these mental and psychological games we play in this town. I could bounce ideas off her and get an instantaneous, logical reaction. In some ways, she is responsible for many of the Agency's secretive successes.

That's over, except for the regret, he thought. The reports he had read about Camilla's liaison with the Russian woman, Suslova, still sickened him. Kellner closed his eyes. This is the thing that hurt the most, Camilla's betrayal. But all things shall pass, so they say.

For the first time in days, Kellner thought, I have almost achieved peace of mind. The incessant scramble for control of every situation and for the attention of the President is over; I have come to realize that we only deceive ourselves when we believe we can control events. Odd that this peace should come now, when the country I love, as well as many of its people, is at risk. At a moment when my career—my life, for that matter—is in ashes. When a man, under my orders, is in great personal danger and is about to risk what I have *never* risked—almost certain death.

Two things have brought me to this pass, he thought. One stems from ill-considered action by men I never knew except as names on an intelligence document, and the reaction— which I would never have expected—from the man I serve in the White House. The second stems from my own hubris.

Today's decisions will be my last, no matter what Cole Caidin says now. He will accept my resignation, and be very glad he did so when the jackals come after us, Kellner thought, his face twisted in a grimace of pain. I am ready to take the blame; it's only fitting that I do. No matter what happens in the next few hours and minutes this December 7, I shall no longer influence the future of the United States.

Kellner shook off his depression and turned to practical considerations. The Russians had declared a news blackout, and it was succeeding to a great extent. The Pentagon had received scattered reports about a purge in Moscow, in the Kremlin. Had Cherny used the information they had given him to save himself and his government? Was the purge more widespread, or confined to the capital? How can we analyze this situation properly with no human intelligence from Russia since David Milstein's death? Satellites could relay only that which had already happened, not why or how it happened—the most critical information.

The few newspaper accounts from correspondents in Moscow that had come out before the blackout was imposed said unequivocally that Marshal Suvorov, Admiral Aleyev, and Air Force General Kalinin had been executed on Cherny's orders. What of Kondratiev, the Security Service chief? Earlier reports claimed that Kondratiev was recruiting for Soyuz among the services. The armed forces, except for the nuclear units, were pitifully weak, Kellner knew, and very poorly paid. Senior officers sometimes had to perform menial tasks, like guard duty. Entire units had declared independence and often refused to fight in the brushfire ethnic wars, even those in Russia. Almost half of those conscripted into the army avoid service, Milstein had said. But all it would take was one or two tank units and an air force squadron to follow the rebels, and civil war could break out in the heart of Moscow. One of the strangest accounts Kellner had heard came from a Swedish correspondent, who had left the country on one of the last flights before the blackout. He claimed that Lenin's mausoleum had been dynamited by the insurgents, who then had been attacked by elements of the army and routed. If it is true, Kellner thought wryly, those who had expected Soyuz to reinstate the Communist party were wrong. Again.

What else was happening there? Was Aleksandr Cherny still in charge of Russia—or, in any real sense, did Russia still exist? Russian TV and all the Western networks' Moscow bureaus had been shut down completely. Russia was cut off from the rest of the world. In this most dangerous moment, communications had ceased. How the cold warriors would howl now, Kellner thought. Was it possible that the Russians had sabotaged the whole rescue mission, crippled the Canadian Starlifter carrying their own divers? Then they might say: "We did our best. Your allies bungled the effort to get us to the device in time to prevent detonation."

Or was that the most monstrous paranoia yet?

Kellner had immediately notified President Caidin at Camp David about the disaster at the airstrip. He had assumed that Caidin wouldn't require his services. He had already tendered his resignation as chairman of the National Security Council to the President, together with a full accounting of the reasons for it. And Caidin had other advisers, good ones, who could counsel him in the coming hours.

But Caidin had said only, "One more day, Vincent. You owe me that much."

His reverie was broken by the clacking sound of the helicopter readying to land. He grasped his briefcase firmly, bent over to dodge the whirling blades above, and climbed aboard.

As they took off, the capital was spread out before him, bright sunlight revealing the beauty of L'Enfant's visionary plan. None of the human flaws that were so painfully clear at ground level were visible to Kellner looking down from above. He took a look around, then closed his eyes for a moment, struck with a feeling hard to describe. There is nothing I would not do to save this country, he thought. Nothing. The red light on the communications unit began to flash. Kellner picked up the handset.

A distant voice said, "Hold for the President."

Kellner glanced in the direction of Mount Alto. The compound there bristled with antennae, and he knew the Russians on the hill were listening.

"Vincent."

"I am here, Mr. President," Kellner said.

"Where is here, Vincent?"

"Just taking off from Fort Myers, Mr. President."

"You should be here in minutes, then. The sooner, the better. I want you to come with us in Looking Glass."

Kellner tensed when he heard the strain in the President's voice. Pray God that Cole Caidin did not have something in mind as foolhardy as his diatribe to Cherny and the attendant escalation to defense condition two had been. "What's happened now, Mr. President?" Kellner asked, dreading the answer.

"Our networks have canceled regular programming and gone to nothing but so-called news, raving on about the blackout in Moscow. They've got a bunch of self-proclaimed experts on, hour after hour, doing their thing, spreading rumors and confusion, speculating. Remember those 10,000 body bags that were supposed to come back to the U.S. during the Gulf War? Well, those same prophets are outdoing that prognostication by miles.

"The newspapers are putting out extras, also full of rumors. They only know there's been a revolt in Moscow and a news blackout there. They've just begun to tie it in with the *Post* story about the 'errant missile,' as they called it. And of course everyone's blaming us, the Administration, for the whole thing. They're attacking *me.* The people are panicking, coming out in the streets. The White House phones are jammed. I'll probably have to declare a state of emergency, get the police and the National Guard out to thwart any troublemakers. We're too damn close to a state of war, Vincent."

I'll speak my mind, if he goes off again, Kellner decided. I am freed of ambition at last. I do not serve *this man,* I serve the *presidency.* "You do realize that you'll have to give some thought to how to handle the aftermath when John Morgan succeeds in defusing the device, sir." His voice was calm, assured. "Who is there with you?"

"Marsh Gray and the head of the Russian desk at the CIA, Collingwood, General Talbot is here for the army—the other Chiefs are on their way. Charlton Fisk is here ready for any contingency. Kruger from the House Intelligence Committee,

Senator Marcus from Armed Forces. Any others are coming on a need-to-know basis. But they're all just blathering on, fighting the same old turf battles. And no one wins this one if that damn device goes off." Caidin sounded on the verge of exhaustion.

"We shouldn't be discussing this on an open link, Mr. President," Kellner warned automatically.

"Open link, shit, Vincent. Because Mount Alto is listening? I want those motherfuckers to be absolutely sure that what happens to us, happens to them if that beast goes off in Canada. There's no place for them to hide. The fallout will sail all the way to Russia and douse their people, just as it will ours. Halloran just called. He's thinking again of ordering an evacuation of Ottawa."

"That would be worse than useless, Mr. President. Why save only Ottawa? There are some sixty-five million Americans in the northeast, where do we send them? It's too late—it has always been too late. If we'd known the extent of the threat two weeks ago, that would have been another matter. If he orders it now, hundreds of thousands of people will be on the roads with no safe place to go."

"Ian confirmed that bastard Karmann is missing. I never trusted him. And NSA says the Russians are evacuating Moscow and St. Petersburg. Get here fast."

Kellner looked at his pilot, who pointed at the buildings at Andrews looming up ahead. The pitch of the rotor deepened, and the helicopter began its turn. "We're just now ready to land, sir."

"Good. I want you here," the President said insistently. "You must be a witness if I have to open the nuclear codes." Caidin sounded as if he were speaking from a great distance, his voice as bleak and as cold as the half-frozen Potomac or the icy waters of Hudson Bay.

"Yes, Mr. President," Kellner said soberly, and returned the headset to its rack.

"Dr. Kellner? Sir?"

The second pilot was speaking to him through the open door to the flight deck. ''We have just received an emergency notice to airmen, sir. All civil aviation north of 41 degrees 30 minutes and east of 78 degrees 30 minutes is temporarily prohibited by the National Command Authority, beginning immediately. That means north of Poughkeepsie and Scranton and east of Buffalo, sir, to give you the parameters.''

Kellner looked at his watch again. He felt almost preternaturally calm. Words no longer counted in this immediate battle, only the actions taken, far from the reach of the President. Morgan had started his dive by now. Vincent Kellner was not a religious man, almost an agnostic, in fact. But now he bowed his head, closed his eyes, and began praying.

Chapter Forty-seven

We scrutinize the dates
Of long-past human things
The bounds of effaced states,
The lines of deceased kings;
We search out dead men's words,
and works of dead men's hands

—MATTHEW ARNOLD,
"EMPEDOCLES ON ETNA"

MORGAN WAS STUNNED BY HIS FALL, and disoriented by the roiling mud and debris he had disturbed when he struck the bottom of the bay. Slowly, the current cleared the water around him. He found himself sitting, half-caught under the curve of the missile's flank, one hand resting on something soft and yielding, somehow loathsome. He twisted around, directed his helmet lights downward, and sucked in his breath at what he saw.

His hand rested on a woman's breast. A few inches above his gloved fingers, he could see her blue-white neck, torn and

425

distorted by a steel hook. Its point was embedded deep in the stretched muscles, but its pad and the lacings that had once held it fast to Arkady Karmann's arm stump had been ripped free by an unbelievably strong, desperate force. Framed by floating black hair, the dead woman's face was a mask of terror. She had been slashed across one cheek. Her mouth gaped in a silent scream, her eyes were wide, protruding and dulled by immersion. Morgan pulled his hand away as though the dead woman's flesh had burned him with icy fire. The corpse, disturbed and dislodged, rolled free from beneath the missile and into the path of the gentle current on the sea bottom. The current caught the body and moved it along the length of the missile's flank. As it moved, buoyed by internal gases, it rose above the floor of the bay, steel hook still embedded in its neck. Morgan had seen death often, but not like this. The parka the corpse wore stood away from the torso, ripped where the steel hook had caught a fold before penetrating the throat.

Arkady Karmann had killed this woman, whoever she was. Could she be the Russian woman Harris had listed as missing, possibly killed when the plane crashed? Arkady had killed her; he must have died at the same time, since he'd not been seen since the first briefing for the press. Morgan stared, transfixed, as the woman's body slowly disappeared into the murk, her clothing billowing about her, showing dull flashes of white thighs and booted legs

The loud burring sound in his helmet phones startled Morgan. Had he missed any time signals while he sat, stunned by murder, on the sea bottom? He looked at his watch. No, thank God. He had to warn the team on the surface of the nine-minute discrepancy between the time originally estimated for detonation and the clock on the warhead. *My watch says 0815, the missile computer says 0824, and Peters thinks I still have fifteen minutes. Ave needed to move the copter away, away from ground zero, as far as he could take it in six minutes.*

Morgan kicked off from the bottom, reaching for the missile. At the same time, he activated the sonar phone. *"Hear this! There are six minutes left. Repeat, six minutes. This is an order for Peters. Take off and move south. Now, Ave. Now."*

He heard a burr of protest.

"DO IT!"

He seized a handhold, then another, and clawed his way back to the open warhead.

Another signal. Damn them! Ave hadn't followed his orders. The helo was still hovering right above. He didn't have time to argue anymore.

Five minutes. Less, now.

He braced himself atop the warhead. The luminous numbers counted down, seemed to flow before his eyes. Four minutes, twenty seconds. Nineteen. Eighteen.

Morgan fought an urge to attack the recalcitrant timer with his diver's knife, with a weapon, any weapon, with his gloved fists.

Another time signal. Damn Peters. Three minutes, five seconds. Still no progress. Two minutes fifty, forty-five, thirty.

Morgan's fingers were clumsy in the reinforced gloves. In desperation, he split the Velcro fastener on his right glove and discarded it. The icy, contaminated water burned his hand. All feeling began to vanish, but at last he caught hold of a terminal lead connecting the timing mechanism to the implosion module, the trigger, the heart of the warhead.

He tugged at the wire, the effort making his pulse pound in his head. His hand strength was weakened by the cold. His movements were lazy, imprecise, in slow motion.

Another time signal. *One minute.*

He began to count to himself. Fifty seconds. Forty. He reached for the wire clippers in his tool pouch, closing his frozen fingers around the grip. Thirty. The burring time signals were coming every second now.

Morgan cut the wire.

The timer lights went dark.

427

Morgan held his breath. Killing the timer didn't always mean that the detonation of an explosive device had been stopped. Quite often the timing device included a revenge circuit, a secondary trigger, which would set off the explosion seconds after the first timer went dead.

Morgan closed his eyes and waited.

A last time signal came from the sonobuoy—then silence.

Morgan gasped for breath and released his weight belt from around his waist. His muscles were like water; he hadn't the strength to swim to the surface. He allowed his suit's buoyancy to carry him upward, toward the light.

WHEN HE REACHED THE SURFACE, in the wintry light he could make out the helicopter. Ave had landed it on the steepening waves. He raised his ungloved hand to wave, wondering as he did if he had killed himself because of his clumsiness.

Too late now to worry about it.

The helicopter crew was firing repeated green flares. Signals to the *Trudeau*. Now it moved back directly over him, lowering a sling for Morgan to fasten around his body, preparatory to being pulled out of the water. It took a few tries before he could fasten it properly. The grinning faces of the RPV crew in the helo showed their glee as they winched him up a few feet. Ave gently backed the craft toward the dock, where Morgan could see hats thrown in the air, usually staid figures capering about clumsily in excitement, mouths moving in dumb show.

When the helo was within a dozen feet, the RPV crew on the dock aimed their hoses at Morgan, dousing him and washing him down with heavy sprays of fresh water, sending him spinning around in the sling. A rubber boat set out from the dock to retrieve him. Morgan lay back in the sling, his mind blank, numb with adrenaline overdose, and waited to be reborn.

MAY

Chapter Forty-eight

Washington, D.C./Memorial Day

What makes this century worse than those that came
  before
In fumes of care and sorrow that we feel
It penetrated to our deepest sore,
A wound so black it could not heal.

And still Earth's brilliant sun is shining in the West;
There, city roofs glisten with every ray. . . .

—ANNA AKHMATOVA

ANNA BURNED HER HAND on the hot handle and dropped the pot back onto the stove. Morgan, leaning against the door into the kitchen, laughed, then looked apologetic when she glared at him.

"Don't laugh, damn it," she snapped. "This breakfast is supposed to be a festive occasion, with good food and drink and good companionship—a reunion before the great celebration. And so I burn the eggs, forget to buy frozen orange juice, and I don't think I have enough bread for toast. I'm not good at this, Morgan."

"There're only six of us. Let's see what you have in the freezer," Morgan suggested. He opened the door and began rummaging. "Waffles, croissants, some fake egg stuff—and a loaf of French bread. Hell, that's a feast. And in the back here is a can of apple juice. You can see what my years as a bachelor have done to make me into a food scrounger. A man can eat only so much pizza, so I got pretty good at throwing stuff together."

Anna kissed him lightly and helped spread his loot out on the counter. "So what do I do with all this?"

"Turn on the oven. Heat the waffles and the croissants. Get a flat bowl for the egg guck. Mix in a bit of vanilla. Slice the bread and soak it in the bowl for French toast. I'll microwave the bacon and mix the juice. No syrup, I see. Heat up this strawberry jelly, and use it." He turned and caught her around the waist. "I miss you," he said. "Leesburg is so quiet I can hear the grass grow."

"I miss you, too," Anna said, and this time kissed him properly. "But this is only a sublet for six months. It's just until I get the photographs sorted and indexed and an outline of the book finished for my publisher. It's easier to get to the airports from here when I give lectures to what you call the Little Groups of Earnest Thinkers. And I do have to make a living. You know there was no place for me to work at your house. Besides, Tripoli seemed to think my manuscript box had been put on the table just so he'd have a place to sleep, and he makes me sneeze."

Morgan released her. "I apologize for Tripoli," he said.

The doorbell rang, and Anna and Morgan went together to greet their guests. After the flurry of hellos, she excused herself and went back into the kitchen. It's really Morgan's day, she thought, or else I never would have invited Vincent Kellner or Avery Peters. Morgan is the Rose Garden hero today. A Distinguished Service Medal from the President. He seems pleased. Why am I not? Is the ghost of the Red Vicar leading me still?

The Eighth Day of the Week

Evan Harris and Amalie Hebert had come down to Washington as representatives of the Canadian contingent to receive the gratitude of the people of the United States for their part in averting the Soyuz disaster. And I'm to get special mention, whatever that is. Anna looked helplessly at the ingredients for the French toast. The food police in the next apartment would approve of the cholesterol-free egg mixture, she thought. She read the directions on the carton and set to work.

"SO THESE ARE the famous Watergate apartments," Lieutenant Colonel Evan Harris said, peering out the window toward the river. "Where all the President's men went walkabout, is it?"

"Glad to see you got your promotion, Evan," Ave Peters said, joining him, gin fizz in hand. "Me, on the other hand, all I got was the chance to go back to my charter service in California. Do you know, I haven't put a foot outside Half Moon Bay since I got home?" He gave a mock sigh. "How about you, Amalie? How did they reward you?"

Amalie Hebert laughed. "I am now in charge of public relations for Maritime Command." Her accent sounded much softer to Peters today than it had at that tense briefing at Site X.

"I propose a toast," Harris said, suddenly serious. "To everyone who was with us in that great adventure. To those who still toil at Site X, cleaning up the mess. It's going to take years, and many, many volunteers to finish up. And to those who'll never come home." The three clinked glasses and drank. Harris went on, "It's quite a group up there right now. About a dozen Russian boffins, passing on what they learned at Chernobyl and the other disasters they still won't admit happened, picking up the new procedures developed by us; several people from the science cadre of the CCND helping out with the environmental studies. And there are, God bless them every one, the regulars from the Canadian and American services, doing their rotations."

433

Amalie Hebert asked, "How do you feel, Avery, all right? You spent a lot of time right over that missile. Did the Waymer experimental treatment work properly?"

"I had a relatively easy time," Ave said. "It was Morgan over there who really went through the mill with the quacks at Bethesda. It wasn't until I got home and read up on plutonium that I really got scared. You? Any ill effects yet?"

"No, nor Evan either. But, we'll not know until it happens, will we? I'd like to tell my children, if I ever am able to have any, about it." Her voice was wistful. "I wouldn't have missed the adventure for the world, but I am afraid we will all pay a price, sooner or later."

MORGAN AND VINCENT KELLNER walked out onto the small balcony overlooking the river. The late May sun was hot in a sky the color of cornflowers. Morgan relished warmth and light these days, and sought it out whenever he could. It blocked out remembrance of that bone-chilling cold, a cold about which he still dreamed.

"How do you feel, John," Kellner asked, putting his arm over Morgan's shoulders. "I've thought about you so often, wondering. I've felt responsible for the state of your health, since I sent you up there."

Morgan laughed. "Not to worry, Vincent." To be truthful, he was, in fact, feeling far better than he had any right to feel. For one thing, he wasn't still at Bethesda, being poked, prodded, tested, and questioned by every doctor in the place. At least the ones who were stationed at the hospital had pretty much run the course. It was the visitors who were the real bane. Doctors from countries he'd never even heard of marched through at all hours of the day and night, marveling that he was still alive. They discussed his condition in loud voices and bald terms, as if he were not there. Morgan had felt more like a training dummy for medical students than the national hero the media had pronounced him to be.

Doris Waymer had been furious with him for removing a

glove and exposing himself to the toxic water at Soyuz Site. She had alternated between dressing him down for his stupidity and hugging him for proving that the Waymer diving suit was every bit as good as she'd argued it would be. And the experimental ligand treatment Dr. Waymer's laboratory scientists developed had leached the plutonium from his system with astonishing ease.

"I'm getting restless, Vincent. I've had an interesting offer from the nuclear gang at the Department of Energy. In the last few years, they've gone from being the nation's intellectual shield against nuclear war to being considered government surplus, like old army tents. But now they have a real mission. They've invited me to go with them to Belarus, Ukraine and Russia. There are a hell of a lot of warheads over there with the same kind of trigger to be disassembled. They found they can't move them safely." Morgan turned and surveyed Kellner. "Enough about me, though. What about you? I'd say that life in a think tank agrees with you. No regrets? No yearning for Washington?"

"I confess only to putting on weight for the first time in my life," Kellner said, patting his stomach. "I have one of those infernal machines that are supposed to substitute for regular exercise, but I never use it. But you haven't answered my question. Really, how are you?"

Morgan was silent for a moment. In a low voice he said slowly, "I still have nightmares. I can't get to the control panel in time, or I flash back to Marina Suslova with Karmann's hook in her throat. It's not a thing I'll soon forget. They've never found Karmann's body, you know. And I wonder what passed between them before they died."

"That woman was evil, John," Kellner said angrily. "I know that's old-fashioned. *Judgmental.* The late twentieth-century sin. But still, as God is my witness, Marina Suslova was evil."

"Did you ever find out from whom she took her orders?

Someone at the embassy? Or was she Kondratiev's agent?''
Morgan asked.

"Ivan Yulin swears she was a part of the Soyuz plot, but
we may never know the absolute truth. Not from him." He
sipped at his glass of Perrier and looked somberly across the
river.

Morgan said quietly, "And Camilla? I understand her trial
has been put off for several months."

"They're trying, unsuccessfully, I suspect, to get her to tell
them Russian secrets. The lawyers at Justice are fools. Camilla
only wanted the money—she told and they paid, never the
other way. I'm almost able to look at Camilla dispassionately.
Almost."

"Are you going back to La Jolla right away?"

"No, I'm going to New York, to a wedding. Charlotte Conroy and Nathan Abramov are getting married next week. He's
finally out of the hospital. He was tortured in Lefortovo. He
was an enemy of Kondratiev's and that was enough for his
jailers. The plastic surgeons had to reconstruct one of his
hands and do considerable work on the other." Kellner sighed.
"How far we still must go to be civilized, eh?"

They were interrupted by Anna's call from the dining alcove. "Breakfast, everyone."

Kellner stopped Morgan at the door. "What does Anna
think about your job offer? Is she willing to let you go, put
yourself in harm's way like that?"

"Let's just say she wasn't happy," Morgan said. "But then,
who is?"

THE TALK AT THE TABLE was lively, with many reminiscences
about the bad old days at Site X. Evan Harris began a long,
involved story about a problem the Canadians had encountered
with some Inuit hunters when they first arrived at camp.

Anna lost interest almost at once. She had Vincent Kellner
at her side and a chance to find out something about the present situation in Moscow. "Dr. Kellner, I know that Aleksandr

Cherny is still in the Kremlin, at least the titular ruler. He's been called a hero in the West for saving Russia from complete collapse, according to the headline today in the *Washington Post*. He promises that the rebels arrested after dynamiting the mausoleum will be fairly tried. Will he be able to keep his word?"

"Vincent, please, Anna," he said, smiling at her. "Well, you must have read his white paper. It was quite a statement. The Russian military is loyal. That the people want peace and democracy. That Russia is a law-governed state, just as it says in their constitution. But if you remember the constitution of the USSR, you could find all the protections in that, too. Except that no one with any power paid it the slightest mind," Kellner said.

"Morgan once told me that if you quoted any part of it to the authorities, you were immediately put down as a dangerous subversive. Is that true?"

Kellner nodded somberly. "True for years, Anna. Maybe things have changed. Aleksandr Cherny is the best man they have right now. He and his people are trying to govern legally, but there will be a next time, another Kondratiev, or worse."

Anna's face clouded and she started to protest. "After this fiasco, no one would be foolish enough—"

Kellner interrupted her. "My dear, you come from the generation of the counterculture, and it has formed you. Both Plato and Confucius said, 'Let me write the songs the people sing, and you can write the laws.' You and your peers were beguiled by the notion that a country can experience a political and spiritual rebirth under the guidance of the uncorrupted. Every generation has that dream. The trouble is, that most of the uncorrupted don't stay that way, and those who do are devoured by their own revolutions. My generation was as idealistic as yours. And we got fascism and communism for our trouble, two sides of the same coin, and the inevitable war. Then came the cold war. Which we won, by the way, and oddly enough, that is one of the reasons the world is in such a clutter. We've been reluctant to lead the world because it's hard, dangerous work. But if we don't take hold of our victory soon—'' He shrugged and shook his head.

Just then, Amalie Hebert asked Kellner a question, and he turned to answer her. Anna sat quietly, thinking of what he had said. The idea of another upheaval in Russia was horrifying.

"A penny, Anna," Avery Peters, who was seated at her other hand, said. "What's got you so down, today of all days?"

"Oh, I don't know, Avery. Partly the letdown from the high we were carried on during that time, I suppose. Partly the realization that life goes on, and we can't shove decisions under the rug any longer." She looked over at Morgan, talking animatedly to Evan Harris, drawing patterns in the tablecloth with his fork. Which battle was he refighting this time?

"I told you it wouldn't work," Ave said quietly. "You come from opposite ends of the spectrum, girl. Your view is from way up there, chasing those rainbows, with hardly a thought for those whose feet are down on the ground. You've led a privileged life, one of the elite who has always been able to stay in the womb. You're an icon of sorts now. I saw an article about you in the local paper the other day. The lady who wrote it—pardon me, the *woman* who wrote it—said you were 'a shining beacon of environmental feminism, one who didn't need a man to define her as a person.' ''

"That sounds pretty damn pompous to me," Anna said. "Shining beacon, indeed. As for the rainbows, someone has to look for the gold, dream those dreams of peace. And I beg to differ about the womb. I've never had a very happy life. My father blamed me for being a female, not the son he always wanted. And everyone seems to know that Jake Neville and I had a lousy marriage."

"That wasn't the womb I was talking about. Personal relationships can be the pits for the best of us—look at Jesus and his buddies. Hope I'm not offending you by sounding flippant, it's just the way I express myself," Ave said. "Morgan has known what it is to scratch for money, for food. His mom died when he was a kid and his dad was in the service, overseas. He lived from hand to mouth, with relatives who hadn't much to offer themselves except a roof over his head. His appointment to the Naval Academy came as a stroke of luck—the local congressman had seen the stories of how his dad died trying to save little kids and waved his wand. You can see why he feels an obligation to his country. It clothed him and fed him and gave him an education when he could have fallen between the cracks."

"I can see why he feels that way, but surely he's discharged the obligation," Anna said passionately. "Why on earth would any reasonable human being want to go to Russia and relive all that horror? I suppose he's told you about the great offer to go defuse more warheads." Ave nodded, and she rushed on. "We had a terrible fight about it. I was so angry I said all kinds of awful things to him about being a compulsive hero and never able to learn how to live properly." Her eyes were bright with tears.

A burst of laughter from the other end of the table broke the spell. Morgan had wheeled the small television set into the dining room and turned it on. "Here's a treat for you people," he said sardonically.

The screen showed the news set of a local TV station. An announcer was speaking into a handheld microphone. ". . . I have something special for you. You all know April Rogers, hostess of 'April Live'?" A studio audience burst into applause. "Today she is here with a very special guest."

Rogers walked into view, nodding to acknowledge the applause. She tossed her long blond hair back and smiled brightly. "Today is a *very* special day, audience. It's Memorial Day."

"No kidding," Ave muttered.

"After laying a wreath at the Tomb of the Unknowns, President Cole Caidin will host a Rose Garden ceremony to honor

439

the heroes and heroines of last December 7. These are the wonderful people who may have saved us from nuclear winter or worse. And here, to tell you the true story of that great adventure, to describe the dangers and terrors of that dreadful moment, is a distinguished journalist, a man who volunteered to travel north with the Americans who dealt with the crisis. He stayed at ground zero, while the warhead ticked down to the very moment of nuclear explosion. He is here to answer your questions. Our national number is 1-800-WARHEAD. Ladies and gentlemen, say good morning to *JOE RYERSON!*''

"Oh, my God," Anna said.

"He looks different, somehow," Amalie Hebert murmured.

"It's amazing what a toupee can do for a hairline," Kellner said, laughing.

"The little prick," Evan Harris said, "had a nose job!"

"You all can watch," Morgan said, "provided you roll up your pant legs when he gets going. I've seen him twice, and his role in defusing the bomb is truly remarkable. He all but guided my hands. I've got to change into my uniform."

"DO YOU THINK Caidin will be reelected, Vincent?" Ave asked. "I see by the polls he's running scared. Isn't this whole Rose Garden thing part of his campaign, a way to try to con the public that he was in control the whole time?"

"There is no such thing as being in control of everything, all the time, Avery. You of all people should know that. Ten days, that was all we had, to move mountains. The best we could do was to set the right people in motion at the right time, which is always a gigantic gamble."

"Just leave everything as it is," Anna said, when her guests began to get up. "I've got a lovely woman who comes in to clean up for me." She was laughing at something Amalie Hebert said to her and answering in kind when Morgan came back into the room, in his dress whites.

Anna stopped in midsentence, stunned by his appearance. I've never seen him in uniform before, she thought. He's gorgeous, there's no other word for it. She suddenly could hear echoes of brass bands and the sound of marching men, the pageantry of flags flying in the brilliant sunlight. That's the secret weapon *they* use against people like me, she realized, the one that wins out over reasoned thought and civil discourse. The uniform puts a distance between us. Perhaps it's been there all the time, she thought desolately, and I didn't realize it.

"Come on, everyone. They've sent a stretch limo for us from the White House," Morgan said. "It's going to be a long afternoon."

BY FOUR, the ceremonies were over, the band had packed up its instruments, and the guests were trailing out of the Rose Garden.

Avery Peters caught up with Anna, who had strolled ahead of the others. He took Anna's hand in his and patted it. "Caidin looks twenty years older, wouldn't you say? He's lost his baby fat." He looked down at her solicitously. "Don't fret. Life goes on. You're one of the winners, I'd say, certainly not one of the losers."

"I thought you didn't like me," Anna said, blinking to keep back the tears.

"Listen, lady, you're a fox, and I *always* like foxes, except when I think they're going to hurt my friends. You've just got to let go, that's all. Open your hands and let that string to your kite go, let it fly away."

"But it hurts so much. And Morgan, how is he going to feel?"

"For one thing, although you may never have noticed, that good-looking lady doctor who's been treating him has been lying in wait for him to be free. For another, he wants more than anything else for you to be happy. So it's your choice." Ave's face was solemn.

Anna turned to look for Morgan. He was walking toward her. Vincent Kellner was saying something to him, but Morgan

441

was looking at her. Their eyes met and locked. Anna felt an almost physical jolt of pain go through her. It's over, our time together, she thought. It was wonderful and horrible and neither of us will ever know anything quite like it again. He's going off, as warriors have done through the ages. As for me, I have the book to write. And a new life to discover for myself.

The very circumstances that brought us together now conspire to divide us. But tonight, we'll have each other, Morgan and I. Tonight. Tomorrow can take care of itself.

THE PHALANX DRAGON
TIMOTHY RIZZI

"Rizzi's credible scenario and action-filled pace once again carry the day!" —*Publishers Weekly*

After Revolutionary Guard soldiers salvage a U.S. cruise missile that veered off course during the Gulf War, Iran's intelligence bureau assigns a team of experts to decipher the weapon's state-of-the-art computer chips. But fundamentalist leaders in Tehran plan to use the stolen technology to upgrade their defense systems. With improved military forces, they'll have the power to seize the Persian Gulf and cut off worldwide access to Middle-eastern oil fields.

Sent to stop the Iranians, General Duke James has at his command the best pilots in the world and the best aircraft in the skies: A-6 Intruders, F-16s, MH-53J Pave Lows, EF-111As. But he's up against the most advanced antiaircraft machinery known to man—machinery stamped MADE IN THE USA.

_3885-4 $6.99 US/$8.99 CAN

RED TIDE
R. KARL LARGENT

"A writer to watch!" —*Publishers Weekly*

COUNTDOWN: 72 HOURS

Aboard a yacht on the peaceful Caribbean, a secret meeting between the leaders of the U.S. and the former Soviet Union is set to take place. Protected by the most sophisticated technology known to man, they will have nothing to fear— if one of their own isn't a traitor.

OBJECTIVE: DESTROY THE NEW WORLD ORDER

In a tangled battle of nerves and wits, Commander T.C. Bogner has to use his high-tech equipment to defeat a ruthless and cunning foe. If he fails, the ultimate machines of war will plunge the world into nuclear holocaust.

_3366-6 $4.99 US/$5.99 CAN